The Iron Mausoleum

A case of Sherlock Holmes and the Titanic

by

Stephen Lees

This book is the first in a series of five that make up the Pantology

The Iron Mausoleum - A case of Sherlock Holmes and the Titanic,
ISBN No. 978-0-9571629-0-7

The Iron Vault - A case of Sherlock Holmes and Professor Moriarty.
ISBN No. 978-0-9571629-1-4

The Iron Soul - A case of Sherlock Holmes and the Napoleon of Crime.
ISBN No. 978-0-9571629-2-1

The Iron Titan - A case of Sherlock Holmes and the Invisible Presence.
ISBN No. 978-0-9571629-3-8

The Iron Metropolis - A case of Sherlock Holmes and the Titans of Valhalla
ISBN No. 978-0-9571629-4-5

This paperback edition published in 2012

Copyright © Stephen Lees 2012

Edited by Patricia Lamb

Published by SPEL
prodev@globalnet.co.uk

ISBN 978-0-9571629-0-7

A CIP catalogue record of this book is available from the
British Library.

Typeset in Garamond

Printed and bound in England by CPI Group UK, Croydon CR0 4YY

Stephen Lees has asserted his rights under the Copyright Design &
Patents Act 1988 to be identified as the author of this work.

The author acknowledges the kind permission obtained from the
Administrator of the Conan Doyle Copyrights to use some characters by
name, in addition to the permission from the Bloomsbury Publisher
A & C Black to reproduce some images from '*Visions of Architecture*'
ISBN 978-1-4081-2881-7 by the same author.

Contents

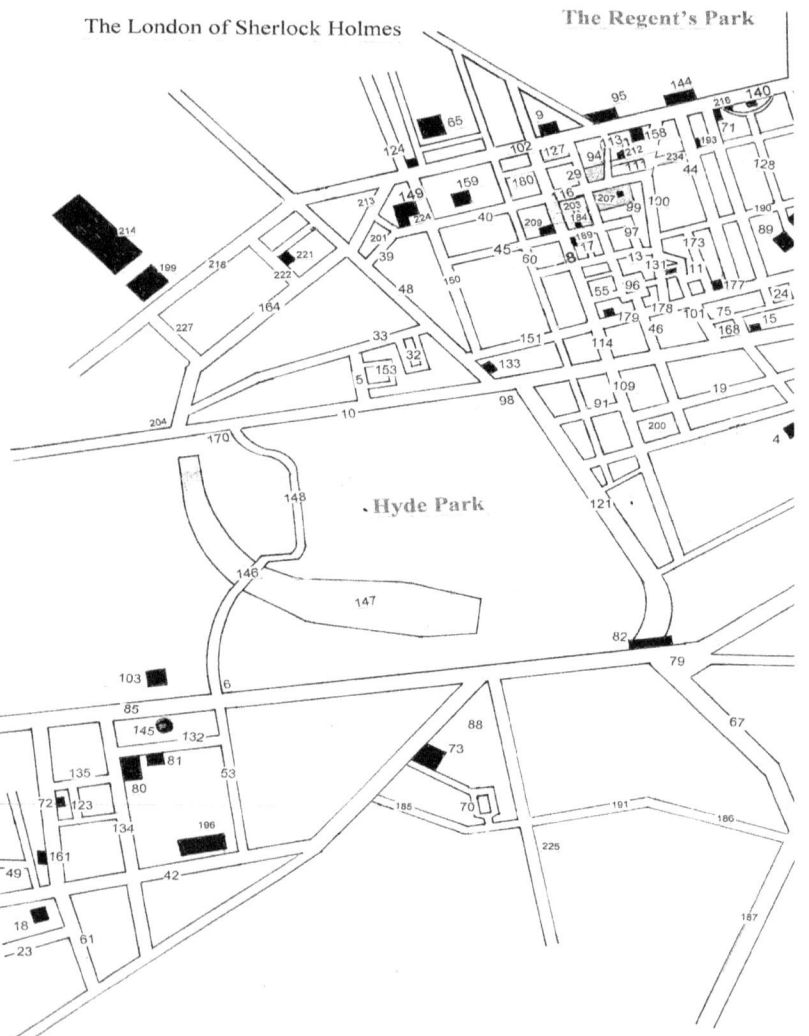

The London of Sherlock Holmes

The Regent's Park

Hyde Park

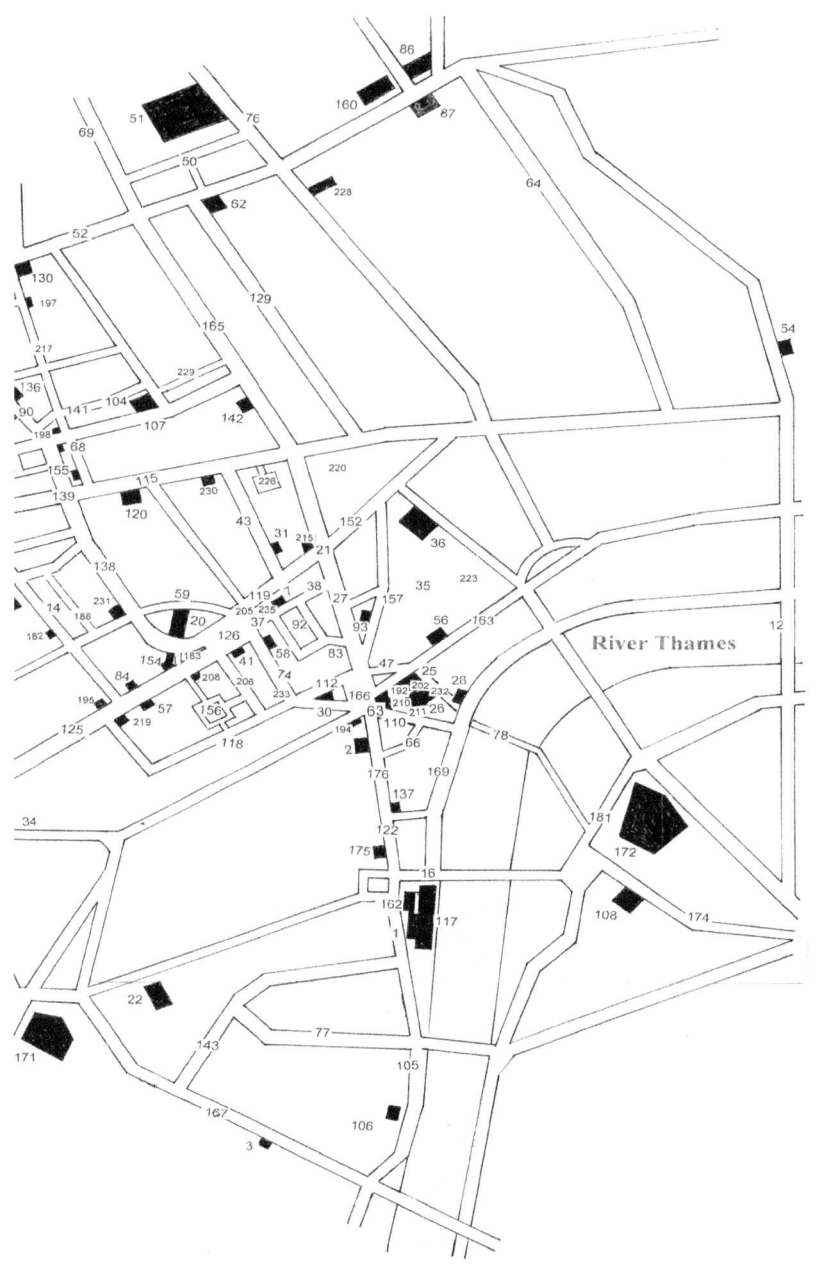

Index of Place Names

156 St. James's Square
157 St. Martin's Lane
158 St. Marylebone Church
159 St. Mary's Church
160 St. Pancras Hotel
161 St. Stephen's Church
162 St. Stephen's Hall
163 Strand
164 Sussex Gardens
165 Tottenham Court Road
166 Trafalgar Square
167 Vauxhall Bridge Road
168 Vere Street
169 Victoria Embankment
170 Victoria Gate
171 Victoria Railway Station
172 Waterloo Railway Station
173 Welbeck Street
174 Westminster Bridge Road
175 Westminster Bridge Road Underground Station
176 Whitehall
177 Wigmore Hall
178 Wigmore Street
179 Wigmore Street Post Office at No.132
180 York Place
181 York Road
182 Agnew's Gallery

Names and places and streets appearing in the Iron Soul
183 Air Street
184 Barley Mow Public House
185 Beauchamp Place
186 Belgrave Place
187 Buckingham Palace Road
188 Burlington Street
189 Camden House
190 Cavendish Street
191 Chesham Place
192 Craven Passage
193 2 Devonshire Place.
194 Drummond's Bank

This book is dedicated to
Eureka Springs in the Ozarks

221. b. Baker Street

Chapter 1

The Visitor in the Night

October was yielding quietly to November now that the equinoctial gales had ceased blowing; and an acrid yellow fog had enveloped most of the Metropolis, including Baker Street. Barely visible through the dense, swirling fog were the Portland stone buildings across the street. Only the Metropolitan Railway was able to operate normally under these conditions. Those brave souls, who had decided to walk, did so by feeling their way along the front of buildings that offered some guidance to their location.

Inside the drawing room of 221. b. Baker Street however, it was a different matter. A cheerful fire radiated a gentle heat. From it, light reflected upon several pieces of highly polished mahogany furniture and glinted on the various brass fittings placed strategically throughout the large, airy, comfortable drawing room. Sparkling in this light were glass bottles, retorts and other items of scientific apparatus arranged on various surfaces. The heavy, dark purple velvet drapes augmented the comfortable atmosphere within the drawing room and kept the inclement weather out.

"What is it this time Holmes?"

"The usual, do you want some?"

I could barely conceal the disgust I felt for my fellow

lodger, with whom I had occupied these rooms for a number of years.

"How dare you! How dare you tempt me with such an abominable concoction as that mind-bending solution; especially considering that I am a doctor."

"Quack," interjected Holmes.

"You may say so," I continued, "I have a respect for my constitution, not yet being fully recovered from the injury to my left shoulder, received whilst serving with the Yorkshire & Lancashire Regiment, during the abortive Egyptian campaign. You ought to consider the consequences. Imagine the damage to your brain, the cost and the elation, only to be followed by despondency and confusion. The rash promises made whilst under its influence, the bravado and your idiotic behaviour. What drives a man to this destructive habit and…."

"You, for one thing Watson, with your continuous berating and moaning, do you want some or not?"

"What strength is it this time, 15%, 20% solution?"

"No, 40% solution!"

"What! 40% solution?"

I staggered back into my armchair with my eyes bulging in disbelief.

"Well?" asked Holmes.

"Oh, all right then," I replied.

"Usual aërated water with your vodka?" inquired Holmes.

"Rather! At that strength I had better have water," I enthused.

"I say Holmes, do you take a pipe or a Trichinopoly cigar?"

" The cigar please," said Holmes, "I can see this is going to be a good long session and, hopefully this fog will ensure that if nothing else, we are not disturbed by visitors ringing our door bell, expecting us to solve their petty domestics problems."

"I hope you are right Holmes. Was it Henry Ward Beecher who said, 'Only unexpected visitors or creditors would ever ring a door bell in quite a Wagnerian manner'?"**

"I do not know, but did I ever tell you about the case of the princess and the baboon?"

"No? Then pass the vodka over and I shall begin."

Holmes had not quite bored me into total submission yet, but I was by now passing in and out of consciousness at too frequent intervals. The expressions upon my face, grimacing with mental anguish, showed clearly I was about to slip away permanently into total oblivion, so Holmes told me later. However, this was not going to be the case on this particular occasion, for at that very moment a sharp knock on the drawing room door heralded, through the *portière* door curtain, the entry of the ubiquitous Mrs. Hudson, the resident housekeeper of 221. b. Baker Street, and bane of Sherlock Holmes' life.

"Mr. Holmes!" she boomed out, and in so doing startled me greatly so that I immediately commenced a series of half mumbled apologies. "Mr. Holmes," she continued, "there is a gentleman downstairs, who wishes to have an audience with you. From the stains upon his left shirt cuff and the mud on his patent leather boots I venture to suggest that he is from Kent, probably Tonbridge. Also, he is engaged with the Southern Eastern Railway Company, in a minor clerical capacity, and is recently widowed because it was evident to me."

"Yes, yes Mrs. Hudson that will be all. Please ask our visitor to come up and, Mrs. Hudson, we need not detain you further; the gentleman may come up by himself."

"That woman!" hissed Holmes at her departure, "that dreadful woman, always ready with her dreary exaggerated opinions based purely on her feminine fancies with absolutely no regard for the systematic analysis of data and a logical deduction of fact. Recently widowed, indeed!"

Presently the gentleman did come up and alone. On entering, he closed the drawing room door behind him in a furtive manner, as if to secure it and prevent any further intrusion into the room. He looked at my recumbent figure, bowed curtly and immediately commenced his narrative.

"Mr. Holmes my name is."

"I am Sherlock Holmes, and this is my friend Doctor Watson in front of whom you may without hesitation speak freely, that is, if he wakes up."

These words startled the visitor who until now was unaware of Holmes' presence.

"What the deu…oh. em. I did not realise, do please forgive me sir."

"Pray do sit down," Holmes said, pointing to an empty cathedral chair, "and tell us why a man from Kent, possibly Tonbridge, who is engaged in a minor clerical capacity with a railway company and recently widowed, should seek my advice on such an inclement evening?"

"Eh?"

Our visitor was very distinguished looking, though the greyness in his haggard face suggested to me, as a doctor, that he had some major concern afflicting him. He wore a frock-coat, silk top hat, striped trousers and grey kid gloves, which he did not remove from his hands.

"My name is Sir James Walter, and I am the head of the Marine Department at the Admiralty, located as you know in Whitehall. A certain Cadogan West, a subordinate *employé* of mine at the Admiralty, was engaged in an inquiry relating to one of the larger shipping companies. We are obliged to monitor, and where necessary investigate, as a mere formality, such companies upon the receipt of information regarding their commercial activities, safety and other such matters. Cadogan West was in the process of doing precisely that when he unravelled some startling aspects about one company's activities in particular. The name of that company I should prefer not to divulge to you, for it involves the economic security of the Empire. I believe further that it cannot possibly have any bearing on your investigation regarding West. I feel confident that when you have heard the facts, you will, I am sure, accept as a matter of a profound sense of patriotic duty to our Sovereign, our country, and deep regard for the Empire."

"Really?" said Holmes, who by now had risen from his armchair and was holding the door open indicating it was time for our visitor to leave.

"Are you a radical perhaps?" demanded the latter.

"Sir James," Holmes continued, disregarding the question, "I deal only in facts and objective data. It follows therefore, that to be robbed, or at any rate denied, crucial data from the outset, is to handicap the performance of my abilities. I will therefore be unable to be of service to you, our Sovereign, patriotic duty to our country, and deep regard for the Empire and so on. I, and only I, shall decide what is relevant and what may be discarded, having regard to all the facts presented to me. Good evening Sir James!"

At this rather unexpected turn of events our visitor looked visibly perturbed and turned to me for support. Clearly, he was not used to being treated in this way and attempted to bluff it out by referring to aspects of national importance and the duty of all to assist.

"Your brother, Mycroft Holmes, advised me to call upon you in the belief that you would lend your support willingly in solving what until now has defeated the greatest brains at Scotland Yard."

"Given my experience of Scotland Yard that is easily done," replied Holmes.

"But Mr. Holmes, it cannot be crucial at this stage to know the name of the shipping company in question. Surely the fact that our Cadogan West was merely investigating it and the subsequent inexplicable events surrounding him, should be sufficient to persuade you to bring your great talents and skills to bear in unravelling this mystery?"

"No," replied Holmes, "it is not sufficient."

"But your brother is a respected member of the Colony Room Club and, accordingly, is held in the highest regard in those exalted circles, and he feels you are the only person now left equal to this task."

"My brother Mycroft and his exalted fellow members of the Colony Room Club are fond of such encomium and making such wild statements about my abilities, given the peculiar lifestyle they lead in that Club devoid, as it is, of any reality. No Sir James you will have to seek advice from another quarter. I am alas, unable to assist you in this respect."

"Alright Mr. Holmes," said our visitor in tones of resignation, "I suppose you are entitled to know that and other facts relating to this dreadful affair. However, I must swear you and your friend Doctor Watson to secrecy."

*No, it was Oscar Wilde.

Chapter 2

The Cryptic Note

Sir James Walters regained his cathedral chair and looked about the drawing room. Clearly, something of great import had compelled this head of the Marine Department at the Admiralty, to seek Holmes' advice and he showed his concern by his facial expressions, which were haggard as if reflecting a deep turmoil within him.

"Before you continue with your narrative, may I press you to a drink?" inquired Holmes.

Sir James looked somewhat bewildered at such an invitation.

"No," he replied, "I do not indulge in the consumption of alcohol, for I believe it is responsible for many evils including damage to the brain, the cost and the elation only to be followed by despondency, the confusion, the rash promises made whilst under its influence, the bravado…"

"Yes, yes, yes," interjected Holmes, impatiently, "another one for you Watson? Watson, wake up! Do you wish that I should pour more vodka for you?"

"Rather!" I gushed.

"To continue then," said Sir James, moving his arm in a broad sweep in front of him, "the matter concerns a certain Cadogan West. He was engaged in examining the records and activities of the shipping company commonly known as the White Star Line. The company is located around the corner from the Admiralty, in offices they occupy in Oceanic House, located at the Trafalgar Square end of Pall Mall in Cockspur Street. From these offices, they operate a fleet of such magnificent ocean liners as the *Olympic*, *Titanic* and soon the *Gigantic*.* These marvels, we are assured, will ensure England's economic viability and place it at the forefront of the highly competitive north Atlantic trade route.

This trade is concerned with carrying, amongst other things, the lucrative immigration traffic from Europe to the New World of the Americas. However, recently as a matter of routine, certain information was submitted to the Admiralty. Consequently, I ordered West to undertake an investigation into the background, as it were, of the White Star Line. You will understand, Mr. Holmes that the British Government is anxious to assist the White Star Line and to coöperate with it in every possible way. I have this instruction from the highest authority, in the person of the First Lord of the Admiralty, this then must be so.

Early yesterday afternoon a message was delivered to Cadogan West, whilst at his desk in Whitehall, which had the most extraordinary effect upon him. Normally a quiet diligent man not given to wild outburst, he turned from being a rational being, into a man possessed, almost as if he were a demoniac. You will appreciate Mr. Holmes, that at the time, I was taking luncheon at my club. I therefore did not witness this spectacle by Cadogan West first hand; but others at the Admiralty, in whom I have absolute confidence, did so. West fell, according to their accounts, into a great panic, muttering over and over again these words, 'the wrong metal, the wrong metal'. After several minutes of his mental torment, he placed the paper, upon which the message was written, into his coat pocket. He then ran out of the Admiralty building and into Whitehall in a state of great agitation. There he was immediately absorbed into the general mass of the crowd which seethes along that thoroughfare.

Peterson, the commissionaire at the main entrance to the Admiralty, immediately gave chase, calling out to West in an effort to restrain and to protect him from harm whilst in his confused and excitable state. Cadogan West by now had gained the Northumberland Avenue and was making his way up the eastern aspect of Trafalgar Square and passing the Grand Hotel. In the meantime, a constable, Harry Murcher, on duty at the top of Whitehall, who also had noticed the commotion and Peterson's shouting at West, joined the commissionaire in his pursuit. Together they followed Cadogan West, who by then had entered Charing Cross Railway Station, but fearing that he may board a train, and thus evade them, they increased their pace in order to intercept him. West, who by now was some distance down a platform, suddenly boarded a moving train. Within a few seconds the train had cleared the platform, thus depriving Peterson and Murcher of apprehending him.

However you may know that the service out of Charing Cross Railway Station is such that a train, though having started and cleared the platform, often will come to an abrupt halt several yards down the railway line. This was so here and accordingly both men seized this opportunity, and running quickly along the permanent way, headed for the carriage into which they had seen West enter. While so doing, the constable shouted at the guard, who had appeared in the brake van at the back of the train, to use his red flag and stop the driver from moving his train down the railway line.

Imagine, Mr. Holmes, the horror that Peterson and the constable experienced when upon opening the train door they looked up and found Cadogan West lying on the floor of the carriage. His arms were flung out and there was a look of terror upon his face, especially with that fixed grin, showing he had endured violent convulsions and a desperate struggle for life during his supreme moment. Only the constable climbed up from the railway lines into the carriage, stating that this was now a police matter and insisting that Peterson remained out of the carriage. Moments later the constable climbed down from the railway carriage and pronounced Cadogan West to be dead!"

"Do you have any notion why West made his way specifically to Charing Cross Railway Station?" asked Holmes.

"I believe he has family out there, a mother, aunt or some such, I think at Woolwich," replied Sir James.

"For how many minutes was West out of sight of Peterson and Murcher?" continued Holmes.

"Possibly two minutes but not more than three, I would venture to offer," said Sir James.

"Do you have any idea by what means he met his death?" asked Holmes.

"None what so ever," replied Sir James, "for alas, there were no marks of violence visible upon his person."

"Was the carriage occupied by any other passengers?"

"No, the carriage is the standard non connecting type, a room effectively with two benches facing each other, and where access is by way of the doors located on the carriage sides," confirmed Sir James.

"Was there anything unusual about the carriage?"

"Nothing unusual, other than it was a South Eastern

Railways carriage that I suppose could not ever be described as usual. However, there was a slip of paper in Cadogan's right hand; the very same paper we believe was delivered to him at the Admiralty, which I have with me. You may wish to examine the paper, for up until now Scotland Yard have been unable to make any sense of the message written upon it."

The visitor reached into his inside coat pocket and produced a metal cylindrical canister from which he pulled out a rolled up foolscap paper, with a flourish that showed his obvious delight in being the bearer of what he considered to be an item of crucial evidence.

"I have preserved this vital piece of evidence for you Mr. Holmes, knowing how fastidious you are!" said Sir James, handing the paper to Holmes.

Holmes laid down his leaded crystal glass of vodka on the table and with a pair of scientific callipers took the paper from Sir James and read out the following cryptic message printed upon it.

'Herculaeneum Docks – Liverpool then 41°46' N, 50° 14' W, at 12-15am. For God's sake be careful!'

Then picking up a powerful convex lens, he examined the paper beneath a table lamp.

"Hmm, expensive cream-laid quarter sheet paper, very heavy with a ribbed texture and an English watermark indicating that it is manufactured in England by Penrice & Company of Highgate. Not much here except a thumb and finger marks possible belonging to West. The paper is warped which indicates that it was saturated at one stage. May I keep it?"

"Yes, by all means Mr. Holmes, but what do you make of message?" persisted the government official.

"At this stage it is foolish to theorise. I need more facts and information in order to synthesise the solution and solve what appears to be an interesting exercise in deductive reasoning."

The effect of this remark by Holmes upon Watson's face was one of an expression of a profound look of incredulity.

Presently Holmes asked the Head of the Marine Department if he could arrange a meeting, at the Admiralty, with commissionaire Peterson and police constable Murcher. Sir James agreed that he would arrange such a meeting.

"Well then let us say noon the day after tomorrow at the Admiralty."

"Does this mean you will accept the challenge?" asked Sir James.

"For the time being I will make some discreet inquiries of my own, and on the basis of those, may look further into this matter for you."

"What about your fees Mr. Holmes?"

"My fees never vary except when I remit them altogether. But in your case I will vary them – upward, since being an official in the government you have access to the Exchequer and to the swollen funds contained in the Treasury," informed Holmes.

"But Holmes this is monstrous, the Treasury cannot be used in such a manner! I appeal to your sense of national patriotism, your duty to your Sovereign and country, the Empire, think of the Empire!"

"Laudable sentiments indeed, but my fee remains as I have indicated."

"Oh very well Holmes," agreed Sir James, "I see it is pointless to appeal to your sense of duty. The Government remains at your disposal in helping you solve this most baffling of problems, which has beset us and thrown the Admiralty into the most frightful state of disarray."

Holmes bowed his assent and opened the door for the visitor.

"Thank you Mr. Holmes. You have the whole of the British Treasury at your disposal!"

"I know," replied Holmes, "I know!"

Sir James raised his eyes upward.

"Oh, by the way," said Holmes, "I see you are from Kent, quite possibly Tonbridge and that you are recently widowed."

The effect of these words upon Sir James Walter made him freeze in his step and look at Holmes with amazement upon his face. Holmes smiled with evident amusement on the accuracy of his remarks to him.

"Mr. Holmes," Sir James said, evidently still somewhat taken aback by Holmes statement, "there is no need to be offensive. I live in Hans Place, Knightsbridge, am a bachelor, have not been to Tonbridge nor have any intention of doing so. Good evening sir!"

And with that *Parthian* shot sailed out of the drawing room. He descended the stairs and climbed into his Barouche carriage drawn by a four-in-hand, waiting in Baker Street, still shrouded in the fog, that in the meantime had become thicker and danker.

"That woman," hissed Holmes, "that dreadful woman, with no regard for the logical deduction of fact. Sir James being recently widowed, indeed!" he continued, cursing our housekeeper.

It was at times like this, that I witnessed a sneering contempt that my fellow lodger exhibited toward women in general and to our long-suffering housekeeper, Mrs. Hudson, in particular. True, she did exhibit all the charm of a repetitive bore and her conversation was limited to those domestic concerns that dominated her life. She evidently delighted in regaling us with her dealings with the barrow boys and stallholders in the street market where she bought her provisions, which finished up on our dining room table as food, so she always claimed.

"Well, what do you make of it Watson, quite interesting eh?"

"I am not so certain," I replied, replenishing each of our cut crystal glasses with more vodka, "it is quite strong."

"What?" exclaimed Holmes, "I am referring to Sir James Walter and his very singular case, not the strength of your drink!"

"Well, since you ask, Holmes, I am of the opinion that your client displays all the pomposity, as is usual, with a sense of propriety normally associated with that class of civil servant, arrogant and totally lacking in any of the social graces. I noticed that when he sat down he did not remove his gloves for fear of soiling his hands in our drawing room! Further, I have never really trusted a man that would decline a drink – especially, since he was about to embark on what I suppose must be a curious series of events – *outré* to say the least. I strongly suspect him of being member of that abominable Blue Ribbon Brigade." **

"And," I continued, "he invokes patriotism as a matter of course, of compulsion even. I forget who said, '.patriotism is the conviction that your country is superior, merely because one was born in it'." Whoever did, *** must have been feeling particularly generous at the time, for it would appear to indicate an aspect very much appropriate to Sir James' character."

"On that point alone," commented Holmes, "I am inclined to agree with you. To continue, what other observations did you discover from Sir James, who at the moment is concerned about his dead *employé?*"

"Apart from the facts that I would put his age at

around three score and two years, is a bachelor and lives on the wrong side of Hyde Park, as he himself described, nothing much beyond that." I offered.

"Well Watson, my fine friend, you have distinguished yourself again in the matter of elementary deduction. For it was clear to me from the outset that this civil servant had much more to offer than the sordid details of Cadogan West's demise in a train carriage, at Charing Cross Railway Station, some yards down the permanent way. As usual Watson, you see but you do not observe!" declared Holmes.

I felt rather offended by this unnecessary put down by Holmes. For I had listened to our visitor's narrative, observed his manner and his attire and thought that I had wrung every bit as much information from him as had Holmes.

"Alright Holmes," I demanded, "pray do share with me your quick incisive observations of Sir James"

"To begin with let us go back to this civil servant Cadogan West. According to Sir James, he is engaged upon an examination of a particular shipping company that is involved with keeping England at the forefront of the highly competitive and lucrative sea trade on the north Atlantic route to the United States. The clerk receives a message whilst at his office in Whitehall and upon reading this message is thrown into a blind panic resulting in his loss of self-control and mumbling something about the wrong metal.

He then abandons his desk for the street, and thus makes his way to Charing Cross Railway Station. Thus far his behaviour might well be described as being perfectly in keeping with that of his fellow clerks engaged in Whitehall. How many clerks suffer continued mental anguish and without reason, simply fall apart? Why, on any working day tens of hundreds of these poor wretches are to be seen streaming out of their various ministries, in varying degree of mental decay, trudging their way back to different London railway stations. This fellow, Cadogan West, from what the facts suggest, merely made his way to Charing Cross Railway Station, rather earlier in the afternoon than he and his colleagues would normally do."

"Quite," I rejoined, "but what of the paper found upon his person in the railway carriage?"

"Cadogan West had that paper about his person as a result of his inquiries. Little did he know that the increasing irritation on his fingers was due to poison, the effects of which, were by now killing him, even before his boarding the train."

"Are you saying Holmes, that there is a greater evil at work here?"

"Precisely Watson, the paper handed to West inside the Admiralty was impregnated with a powerful vegetable alkaloid poison, designed to infiltrate insidiously the body through pores in the skin of the fingers holding the paper. It is a common enough method on the Continent, of poisoning someone surreptitiously."

"Yes, but the note in the railway carriage?"

"Capital Watson! You have touched upon the one fact that remains the key to the mystery so far. For it is obvious to me, that the paper found in the dead clerk's hand, the one that was given to him in his office, should not have been in the railway carriage!"

In the meantime, in order to prove his theory, Holmes had subjected the paper delivered by Sir James to chemical analysis. Finally upon adding a few droplets of rectified spirits and hydrochloric acid, he asked me over to look at the changing colour of the paper.

"What do you make of that?" Holmes asked.

I stooped over the paper with its rapidly changing colour and with a sharp intake of breath recoiled in horror as I realised what was developing.

"Your theory is correct Holmes, the paper has indeed been impregnated with a strong vegetable alkaloid. Possibly a precipitate of strychnine, that is both highly toxic and lethal!"

"You are correct Watson, strychnine is a poison that attacks the nervous system. West was clearly in an initial state of mental degeneration as a result of the effects of the poison. It is probable that he was making his way home instinctively to his mother who, according to Sir James, lives at Woolwich, a part of London served by the Charing Cross Railway Station."

"Interesting," I said.

"Further," said Holmes, more moved than I had ever seen him before, "it would explain why West's body was contorted. It had endured violent convulsions and unimaginable terror alone in the railway carriage as the strychnine took hold, producing tetanus and that feature of *risus sardonicus*, manifested as a fixed grin upon his face."

*   Subsequently renamed RMS *Majestic*
**   A society committed to banning alcohol in drink
***   GB Shaw

Chapter 3

The Dense Fog

I awoke late the next morning with the most appalling headache. Whether it was the vodka and the Beaune that I had consumed the previous evening or merely the excitement generated by Sir James's story I could not be certain. However, on gaining the break-fast room I noticed Holmes looking irritably at an empty table. The fog outside still had not lifted and accordingly my spirits sank, as did I into a chair opposite Holmes.

"As you will see Watson, our dear housekeeper has yet again failed to break our fast, even though the time is only five and twenty past eleven o'clock."

"You have summoned her by ringing the bell in the kitchen with our bell rope, Holmes?"

"Yes, though I remain convinced that the bell rope is attached to no such bell in her kitchen."

Looking through The *Daily Telegraph* newspaper I noted nothing of importance reported, especially now that Parliament was sitting. What could happen during this interminable fog, I thought glancing at the still *opaque* windows to our break-fast room. One article though, did catch my attention. It referred to the Great Central Railway's newly completed railway station located along the Marylebone Road just before the Philological School and not far from our rooms here in Baker Street. The directors had invited the public, so the article informed its readers, to submit a suitable name appropriate for their new railway station. I began to indulge in a fancy of inventing names both preposterous and plausible in order to while away the time until our break-fast arrived. I jotted in the margin of the newspaper the name Blenheim, after all, was not Waterloo station named after a battle somewhere in Europe I reasoned? What of Crimea, I wondered, since the station is located not far from a fashionable residential district of the Metropolis called Maida Vale, that the Church Commissioners have laid out commemorating the victories of the Crimean War? The district of Maida Vale, echoes with the names of the heroes and places of the Crimean War; Balaclava, Elgin, Sutherland or even the name of the hero of the 'Charge of the Light Brigade' – Cardigan."

"What do you think, Holmes, of my suggested names for the new station?" I inquired, handing him the paper.

"Watson," said Holmes, "we really must find an activity for you, to occupy your undoubted intellectual prowess and mental energy, for it is alas, clearly going to waste! Do you imagine for a moment that the directors of the Great Central Railway are going to entertain the notion of naming their new prestigious station after an item of woollen clothing, designed to completely cover the head! – The balaclava, or for that matter, another item made of wool, a woollen jacket no less, the cardigan?"

I looked at the *opaque* windows again with a sense of deep foreboding. Presently a knock was heard at our door. Amidst a cacophony of oaths, mutterings, scrapping and general commotion our housekeeper appeared in the doorway. She held in her mottled arms an elm tray resplendent with gleaming silver dishes with lids, a steaming coffee pot and the morning's post. After what seemed to me to be an inordinately long performance in laying our break-fast table, she stood back. Looking directly at Holmes, and with her hands on her wide hips, as though in a gesture of surly defiance, as if to challenge Holmes with her idea of what might constitute break-fast, and at what time, she opened her mouth to speak.

"There," she said. "I was not sure whether you would prefer luncheon or what, given the time of day it is now. Do you suppose, Mr. Holmes, that we in the kitchen are there to cook for you at all hours?"

"Yes," replied Holmes, absorbed in his morning post.

"Break-fast at luncheon time," she continued, "dinner at break-fast time, when will it cease?"

"I might ask the same of you Mrs. Hudson; when will you cease your infernal berating?"

"Holmes," said I in my attempt to appease both parties, "do try the salted herring and bloater fish."

"Salted what," exploded Holmes, "I deliberately asked for Harrods bacon with egg; what possible use could I have for those…those salted things?"

"When I was a wee slip of a thing," announced Mrs. Hudson, "my mother would make me and my seven brothers and sisters eat at least ten each of these beautiful herring and bloater fish for break-fast. And, let me remind you Mr. Holmes they did me no…"

"May God preserve us!" interjected Holmes, his eyes raised upward in total despair, "must you continue so! Please return to that place you call your kitchen and prepare the bacon and egg I specifically requested some fifty four minutes ago."

With this injunction the housekeeper retired ungracefully to the nether regions of our abode in fog bound Baker Street.

I continued with my rather salty if unappetising

break-fast of fish, hoping that I might derive some nourishment even at the expense of taste. My stint in the Fifth Northumberland Fusiliers during the fateful Jowaki campaign when stationed out in India, had prepared me for such unappealing food. My constitution was therefore more able to deal with it than that of Holmes. Indeed my training as a doctor with the Fusiliers had taught me to recognise quickly the symptoms of a profound attack of food poisoning, such as the one I was undergoing at this very moment.

I began sweating feverishly; my heartbeat increased dramatically. The headache I had awoken with this morning, intensified with such ferocity, the likes of which I had never before in my life experienced. I looked at the portion of uneaten bloater fish on my plate accusingly, felt an acute attack of nausea, and became dizzy, then, all was black.

"You look done in Watson," said Holmes, who was standing over me with his arms folded akimbo, "we had to lay you down on your bed. You simply keeled over at the break-fast table. Whatever ever could have been the matter with you?"

"The bloater fish - poisonous, food poisoning," I mumbled.

"Hardly the case Watson, you had only consumed four. Though I must confess, given the fact our housekeeper buys the fish from that wretched street market, I have never felt the slightest inclination to sample her cooked fish whatever named or however cooked."

"I imagine, as a doctor, that it was a case of inanition."

"Well Watson, you really must eat!"

"The case, are there any developments yet?" I inquired, endeavouring to make up for my poor conduct so far that day.

"No," replied Holmes, "although when I summoned Mrs. Hudson and two of her strong stout girls from downstairs to lift you off the dining-room floor and place you on your bed, I did have a heated discussion with her over some trifling detail regarding evidence. I was somewhat grateful for the fact her arms were occupied carrying your, by now, inert body to your bedroom, so naturally I took advantage of the situation. Now, are you feeling better?"

"Do you come with me to the Charing Cross to look further into this matter regarding Cadogan West - are you equal to the task?"

"Yes, a capital idea." I replied, without much conviction in my voice and regretted my reply the instant I had uttered it.

Whilst putting on my overcoat I remarked to Holmes that he was not wearing his deerstalker cap and Inverness coat. Holmes looked at me imperiously, as he buttoned up his familiar frock-coat and replied,

"The frock-coat Watson, is the suitable garb of choice to wear together with a silk top hat when abroad the Metropolis."

Some minutes later we found ourselves outside in Baker Street, where the fog by now had become denser and if anything, more acrid. The oily brown clouds of swirling fog produced an unpleasant moist and sticky sensation upon one's face, causing an instinctive reaction of wiping it continually with a handkerchief. Baker Street was all but deserted and just a few hardy souls made their way along the silent fog bound canyon that the street had now become.

I had lived for a number of years in Baker Street and felt confident I could match my knowledge of the buildings lining this thoroughfare as any other resident of the locality. However, at that precise instance, my confidence in that knowledge failed me, for I knew nothing about the bland shapes of buildings that came into sight, but as quickly receded from my view. I recognised nothing as we walked along the grease covered York flagstones of the pavement that resounded to our footfall only to be muffled by the all-embracing fog.

Moving shapes of people with shoulders hunched in an appearance of grim deformity came into focus silently and then disappeared into the folds of the dense choking fog. The gabled ends of buildings stuck out in a *grotesque* manner devoid, so it would seem, of any visible means of support. Even the tobacconist, normally a lively place, looked *sombre* and forsaken. The cheap advertisements displayed in the front window now looked like cataracts which had developed spontaneously, giving the shop a minatory and gaunt look about it. The whole effect was to depress my spirits and to create a feeling within me of foreboding vulnerability.

No such feelings however attached themselves to Holmes who appeared oblivious to this oppressive fog. The intellectual challenge of a problem and its solution was the only thing that concerned him. He was indifferent, existing in the centre of the great Metropolis, whether it was in fog or in bright sunlight. I remember his reply to me on first meeting him of why he was attracted to reside specifically in Baker Street. His answer, typical now that I think about it, was because he had worked out with that precise mind of his that Baker Street was the farthest place away from the countryside as is humanly possible to attain on this earth. For all his intolerance of the countryside and his love of buildings and human chaos, I was grateful that he was at my side.

For such persons, by having that detachment, are able to inspire others at a time when their spirits are faltering and giving up to feelings of helplessness.

"Here we go Watson, here is a Hansom carriage approaching. Let us see if we can persuade this fellow to convey us to Charing Cross."

"Where," I inquired, peering with squinted eyes, "I cannot see a Hansom carriage, not even its heralding green tender lamp?"

Looking around me I became aware of Holmes' absence. A slight panic gripped my heart as I found myself alone in the fog with only the faintest of sounds audible.

"Holmes, Holmes, where are you?"

"Watson, over here," came Holmes' injunction.

"Where Holmes, I cannot see you, over where?" I replied.

Then suddenly, through the gloom, I became aware of a tall figure gesticulating to a man high up in a Hansom carriage. A feeling of almost exhilaration swept over me as I focused upon the approaching Hansom's green tender lantern, and its reflection upon the oily wet carriageway. Also, by degrees, I became aware of an argument developing between the Hansom carriage driver and a person whom I took to be Holmes.

"I am simply asking you in a civil manner," I heard Holmes shout, "whether you are able to take us to Charing Cross, not an open invitation to an argument to be conducted in the carriageway. I am, in addition, willing to give you a guinea for your trouble. That fare, I think, represents fourteen shillings over and above the posted rate from Baker Street to Charing Cross."

I noticed that the carriage driver looked impassively at Holmes.

"That may well be the case gov'nor, but this ain't Baker Street, it is in fact Gloucester Place and I am on my way 'ome. And," he continued, despite Holmes' attempt to stem his flow, "I am not going to take my carriage all the way to Charing Cross. My 'orses can barely breathe in this pea souper and I ain't finding it any better myself. Besides the road menders have the carriageway up in the Oxford Street and it is purgatory negotiating around that mess, fog or no fog that is why I am orf 'ome!"

After a few threats and mutterings had been exchanged, Holmes eased himself off the Hansom carriage and down to the ground.

"This rather complicates things Watson, for I must get to the Crown Post Office in Wigmore Street to dispatch a wire. Are you still equal to our continuing to stroll onwards to Charing Cross?"

"A stroll, yes, by all means," I said, pondering his choice of the word 'stroll', "provided we at least head off in the right direction!"

Despite my halfhearted attempt at humour, lost as usual on Holmes, the prospect of trudging down to Wigmore Street, let alone Charing Cross in this fog filled my heart with even more dread and foreboding.

Chapter 4

The Way to Charing Cross

We walked until my leg ached from the wound caused by that murderous savage's jezail bullet tearing into my right thigh, a legacy received when serving with the Third East Kent Regiment during the first Sudanese fiasco. The pain throbbed with a dull persistency. By now, I think, we had gained Crawford Street and then turning back into Baker Street headed, I believe, south towards Blandford Street and into which we wheeled east in the direction of Marylebone Lane.

"It is during such weather conditions that the criminal fraternity are at their busiest," remarked Holmes, "and you can be certain that they use this cover amply afforded by the fog, to perpetrate all manner of atrocities upon an unsuspecting public. They roam the Metropolis with an ease and confidence and then evaporate back into the silent shrouds as quickly as they appeared. We now ought to be approaching the end of Marylebone Lane," continued Holmes, unconvincingly.

"Eventually," I added looking up to try and check on our bearings.

"Good God Holmes, but we are in the Edgware Road and miles from our destination; we have been walking around in circles!"

"Oh!" murmured Holmes.

Crown Post Office, Wigmore Street

A dull thwack of pain seared through my head that made the ache in my thigh enjoyable in comparison. We retraced our steps back along Crawford Street to a junction. Looking up at a large Victorian apartment mansion, I noted we were in Seymour Place and therefore turned right and headed south towards Seymour Street. Making a left turn, led us into Wigmore Street* along which we continued to grope our way east and eventually gained the Crown Post Office located at 132 Wigmore Street. It was gloomy and lit dimly with coal tar gas globe lamps pouring out their weak blue light. Upon entering the deserted place Holmes immediately scribbled off a message. A few moments later he handed the wire to the clerk with instructions that the reply to be delivered to our rooms at Baker Street by return.

With that injunction, we continued our journey on foot through Cavendish Square. However, *en-route* to Regent's Circus, I had an urgent task of my own to perform, which was that of collecting my winnings from a bookmaker's agent on a fancy I had wagered on a horse owned by Sir Robert Norberton called Shoscombe Prince, which had won the handicap at Epsom recently. We then made our way down the Regent's Street through pools of light streaming down from new electrically powered Edison-Swan street lamps. The effects of these lamps were to illuminate the faces of passing pedestrians with a *grotesque* hue that exaggerated their eyes and mouths, making their lips an unnatural purple. Suddenly Holmes grabbed my arm and pulled me over to a doorway.

"I say Watson, you look awful and done in, do you take some refreshment?"

"Well ought not we to get to Charing Cross?"

"Nonsense, there is no desperate hurry. We can continue when you have rested a moment. After all you do have an injury to your left arm received in the Natal campaign with the Duke of York's Regiment."

"Right knee at Khartoum," I reminded him, "when with the Grenadier Guard."

"Whichever it was, I simply cannot bear the thought of you in pain and I know just the place where can we gather our strength before continuing our journey."

"Oh, all right then," I tried to enthuse.

Upon that remark Holmes pulled me off the Regent's Street and led me down a narrower thoroughfare called Glasshouse Street.

Groping our way down the street, avoiding lamp posts at regular intervals, we tried to take a bearing on familiar structures as they loomed into view and as quickly receded back into the swirling banks of yellow fog. That oppressive feeling of claustrophobia returned again to depress my spirits further into near panic at being totally enclosed by the fog. My replies to Holmes' remarks, such as I could utter were of a nervous higher pitch that betrayed my inner tension. Mentally I was struggling with my conscious sanity though this battle paled into insignificance compared with the titanic pain in my right shoulder. This was from an injury, I sustained as a result of the bullet that smashed my right shoulder blade, when attached to the Third Infantry Regiment during the Mesopotamia Emergency. How I ached!

Despite the pain, we felt our way down Glasshouse Street, an infamous street in which Holmes's attackers of previous years made good their escape. Notwithstanding that earlier memory, Holmes pointed into the fog with his ebony cane, vaguely, to where I could just make out faint red lights. Upon approaching them, realised they came from the rear windows of the boisterous Café Royal establishment. This however, was not the bar Holmes had in mind and we continued towards the Regent's Circus at Piccadilly. On entering the Circus at Piccadilly, dominated by Alfred Gilbert's newly commissioned aluminium statue of the Angel of Christian Charity, we found ourselves in front of the Criterion Bar. This famous establishment brought back vivid memories of a happier time and reminded me that we were thankfully at least now near Charing Cross.

The Criterion Bar was large, noisy and illuminated garishly inside with bright red lights. My head swam. I could only think of a Hackney carriage and of its taking me home to Baker Street. Presently we found ourselves inside the *salon* with all its extravagant and exuberant vernacular decoration. It combined Queen Anne and Baroque styles, built of highly polished mahogany woodwork with brass fittings, handrails, marble surfaces and ostentatious acetylene gas-fuelled globe lanterns. Complementing this style was the generous neo-Byzantine opulence of mirrors and mosaics on various walls and surfaces. There were rich velvet drapes of red, framing engraved windows and decorative glazed panel openings in the internal timber partition walls. The ceilings were of painted and gilded moulded plaster looking down on elaborately patterned carpets upon which were positioned several indoor palm trees. The effect was one of an opulent sumptuous, if meretricious establishment, of the 'Gin Palace' variety patronised by the wealthier classes.

Holmes, who clearly knew his way around the place, pushed past a variety of patrons and at length we eventually managed to gain the white *Carrara* marble covered Long Bar. Upon reaching it, Holmes insisted on a pint of heavy and invited me to join him in his questionable choice of beer.

"Certainly not," I retorted, and settled instead for a large, restorative whisky, in order to revive my strength.

As soon as Holmes handed to me my drink, he darted off into the crowd, muttering that he had just recognised someone.

Whilst contemplating my drink and admiring the interior *décor* of the establishment, I became aware that a youth was staring at me intensely and, so it appeared, with intent. There he was standing, complete with all the dumb aloofness of a Greek god. I wished that Holmes would return and alleviate this awkward situation. The youth at length started to walk with determined purpose toward me. I imagined a confrontation and ugly scene; I did not know of what kind, except that I had seen such youths in action in the seedier and rented parts of the Metropolis.

I gripped my cane all the more tightly in readiness to bring down on the approaching youth's head. Then, as the incident developed, it dissolved, for as the youth seemed to approach me, he suddenly veered away. I then realised the reason for this fortuitous turn of fate; it was the presence of Holmes, who by now had re-appeared at my side and in so doing had deflected the youth's advances. However, my elation was short lived as Holmes introduced me to a character whose grubby hand I would have preferred not to have shaken, let alone meet its owner.

"This is Mr. Thomas Wainwright, late of Christie & Manson Auction Rooms in St James' Square," continued Holmes, "and is a fence…eh, one of the Metropolis's accomplished facilitators of works of art! I have asked if we may join him at his club later this evening to discuss a matter of some delicacy. He has agreed that we ought to."

"Sherlock," intimated Wainwright in a familiarity that concerned me, "I am indebted to your help in the past and look forward to meeting you and your esteemed colleague here Doctor Wilson later at the Colony Room Club in Soho."

And with that sneering inaccuracy regarding my surname name, he bowed and took his leave, as indeed we did too, making our way to the street door. Whilst endeavouring to negotiate our way through the crowded Criterion Bar, the youth of previous near encounter was rapidly moving in my direction in his attempt to intercept me.

I was struck with a paroxysm of fear as he came within three feet of my position. Then, thwack! The noise cracked upon my ears as I saw Wainwright deliver an unerringly accurate blow of such force to the youth's head that he immediately collapsed to the gaudy if intricately patterned red silk broadloom carpet. I stepped over youth's now inert body as we made our way into the fog-bound streets again.

Once outside we turned right and continued in that direction for some minutes. By now we had gained the Leicester Square and, despite the intimidating thick fog, we could hear people intent on merry making. Those I did see, I noticed, had been drinking and were drunk. We negotiated our way past the more raucous of them and made our way past the original Panopticon of Science and Art now the Alhambra Music Hall, from which we could hear bawdy verses, which seemed incongruous drifting through the fog. We then left the eastern aspect of the square though Irving Street, I think, or possibly Cranbourn Street and emerged into the Charing Cross Road. Our walk took us into St Martin's Lane and past the large square-topped corner tower of the Lord Salisbury Public House, the interior of which was garishly lit and glowing pink through the dense fog. We then trudged through Duncannon Street and thankfully into the Strand, over which I virtually ran in my eagerness to reach the brightness and fog-less space of the Charing Cross Hotel.

I threw open the main door of the hotel and stepped into a brilliance of incandescent light, emanating from large lanterns of glass and chandeliers suspended from the ceiling which illuminated the plush red silk carpet below. The whole effect was to create in my weary heart, a *crescendo* of light, a euphoric sensation of ecstasy and warmth, all of which I needed so desperately. The light filled my senses as though experiencing the final closing chords of a Wagnerian opera. Despite this sensation, I tried to promise myself that never again would I allow

Holmes to drag me through the fog, no matter how noble the cause.

We ascended the broad, grand staircase on to the *piano-nobile* and made ourselves comfortable on red *damask* covered sofas at the bar, complete with the ubiquitous indoor palm trees ranged around the salon. Armed with a large whisky, I was complimenting myself on having walked to Charing Cross when a fellow came straight up to Holmes and shook his hand. Without so much as acknowledging my presence he then dropped onto the sofa, next to me. In so doing, he caused me to spill part of my drink onto my lap. He clicked his fingers and immediately a waiter materialised in front of him.

"What can I get you Holmes?" he rasped.

"A large whisky with a dash, and only a dash of aërated water, but perhaps you would care to offer a drink to my friend and colleague Doctor John Watson there?"

Upon that suggestion, the newcomer turned around to face me and in so doing managed to knock my glass, causing further spillage onto my sodden lap. I glared into his face, by now just inches away from mine.

"What can I get you Johnny?"

"Well," I replied with a sarcasm that would go unde-tected by this fellow, "I should very much like to try the whisky, thus far unable to drink even though my glass is virtually empty?"

"Right you are Johnny, a small whisky it is!"

I hoped that Holmes' meeting with this functioning sample of crudity would be short. I even contemplated going back into the fog should the meeting prove to drag on. At length I excused myself on the pretence of allowing them to have their conversation unhindered by my presence. I rose from the sofa and went and sat at the bar and had a desultory conversation with the bar tender on the merits of a racehorse called Silver Blaze. It was owned by a Colonel Ross and had been entered in the Wessex Cup race meeting to be held that coming Saturday. Whatever the merits I thought, the odds were appalling, but it would be worth a guinea each way just in case it came in. In any event I was inclined to take Mrs. Hudson's betting certainty tip and bet five guineas on Rasper to win in the same race.

When at length we did step out of the Charing Cross Hotel I insisted we hail a vacant Barouche carriage waiting for a fare. Without hesitation I instructed the liveried coachman, with a promise of a golden guinea, to make all haste to the Colony Room Club in Dean Street, Soho, just west of Cambridge Circus. He obliged and with a flick of his whip turned his horses' heads to face east and we rattled off down the Strand into the fog.

"Who was that bombastic fellow?" I asked of Holmes when we were settled in our carriage.

"John Clay," Holmes informed me, "a man of letters, high born into the aristocracy and a prominent artist, to say nothing of the fact that he is an accomplished faker and forger!"

"Really," I said, "high born eh? That could explain his arrogance and inordinate confidence."

"Believe in it Watson, it is likely that the five-pound note he used to pay for our drinks was printed not in the Royal Mint but rather in his art studios in which I know a secret room exists. There invariably, his forged bank notes are created! You, alas, will never distinguish those notes forged by him and those that are printed at the Royal Mint!

His forgery and fakery activities, in this respect, do not concern me in the least. However, what does concern me is the information he imparted earlier this evening.

He believes that there is some effort, some concerted effort, being applied, where art is being bought up in an attempt to organise an exhibition in America, at the World's Columbian Exposition in Chicago. This, so the promoters claim, will promote to wealthy Americans new works of art not only from England but Europe too.

John Clay feels that this is just a cover for some deeper criminal activity. His years of experience in both the art and criminal worlds tell him something is not right. It is as though, he claims, that there is a silent guiding force behind this scheme. A clever mastermind, an *eminence gris*, that has worked out with a mathematical precision every permutation and contingency. However, he has suggested that I make every effort to find and talk to the elusive Arthur Staunton the noted painter and faker!"

Holmes then lapsed into deep thought as the implications of what John Clay had told him sank in.

"Indeed Watson," he said recovering from his reverie, "I would venture to say we are entering dark times and certainly the facts surrounding the death of Cadogan West begin to acquire a defined clarity of purpose involving unimaginable evil!"

We clattered along the Strand past Fleming's Restaurant and then turned sharply into Covent Garden where, despite the fog, tradesmen were plying their wares and setting up stalls laden with vegetables and fruit. Eventually having traversed a series of back streets illuminated only by the lamps of our Barouche carriage we turned into Dean Street and then arrived at the infamous Colony Room Club embedded in the depths of Soho. As we both entered the street door of the building I overheard the carriage driver hiss something under his breath, and with a look of appalled horror upon his face disappeared into the swirling fog, where I thought, he would prefer to be. What was Holmes up to I wondered?

Though the fog had depressed my spirits, it seemed to have almost the opposite effect on Holmes who thrived upon it. He led me along a dingy corridor with a *terrazzo* stone floor and walls covered in what was at one time a greenish paint, now grimy with age and abuse. At the end of this corridor was a door above which were the words of a motto, I believe quoted from Dante's Il Paradiso.** Holmes opened the door and ascended a rickety staircase. I followed, grasping the banister that nearly came away from the wall when I pulled against it for support.

Presently we entered a small room and the conversation ceased immediately. I then became aware of glowering faces staring at us. Then, as suddenly as the talking had stopped, it continued again after someone in the depths of the room shouted out and addressed Holmes.

"Good God, Sherlock Holmes, where have you been hiding? Marching around on those bleak Devon moors again with that hound of the D'Urbevilles?"

"No," came Holmes' curt reply, "it was with Tess of the Baskervilles."

Notwithstanding this exchange Holmes rushed to meet the ruddy-faced character, of obvious dubious aspect, seated in the recesses of the Colony Room Club. Moments later I was summoned to join them.

"This is Doctor John Watson." commenced Holmes.

"What, the geezer you are living with?" interjected the ruddy-faced seated character.

"Yes," confirmed Holmes, inaudibly.

Suddenly I felt weak at the knees as Holmes' seated friend surveyed me with a piercing look.

"Watson," Holmes intervened, "this Colony Room Club has within its member the greatest collection of

Bohemians and influential persons ever assembled this side of eternity. It is rumoured, and only rumoured, that it contains amongst its august members the accomplished art faker, the incomparable Arthur Staunton. He remains preëminent, if not in this status, then certainly in that of saturating the art market with fakes. Though no person knows what he looks like, nor could identify him, he is able to repeat, in detail, conversations he has over heard within the confines of this very club!"

"That he exists is not in doubt," Holmes continued, "but is often present in this very room! He is part of this club, together with other members, most of who have equipped themselves with prodigious skills in every faculty of the humanities. Were the Colony Room Club not to exist, the Metropolis would indeed be a less interesting place. Some of the members are exponents of what is generally described as Decadent Art. Indeed some members are re-defining, on a daily basis, art as we know it! For myself Watson, I am of the opinion that the Colony Room Club exists, only to keep under one convenient roof, this collection of innovative and versatile geniuses. Were it not to exist, it should have to be invented!

But here comes our friend the noted art connoisseur Thomas Wainwright!" Holmes then informed me.

I was re-introduced to him and again compelled to shake his grubby hand.

"Holmes," said he, after we had acquired our drinks that miraculously appeared from nowhere, "I must ask you to explain what favour you require of me?"

"I shall come straight to the point," insisted Holmes, "it involves the recent attempt to acquire works of art for a supposed American exhibition at the World's Columbian Exposition in Chicago and possibly an ocean liner."

These words had a startling affect on Wainwright, who

did not quite fall back but knew that his reaction had been observed not only by Holmes but also by me. He winked suggestively at my companion but gave me a stern look as if to confirm his lack of faith in my keeping a secret.

"You may say in front of my friend here anything you could say in confidence to me," interposed Holmes, fully aware of Wainwright's misgivings.

I was not convinced, indeed, neither was Wainwright.

"It is like this Holmes, I was engaged to remove... deal with some art work on behalf of a client I cannot name, you understand."

"I certainly do not. I am used to having a mystery at one end of the problem, not at either end. Kindly inform me!" demanded Holmes.

With this stern injunction, Wainwright launched into his narrative, having first sworn us to secrecy and insisting that anything we learned had not come from him. He effectively confirmed John Clay's misgivings and suggested Holmes ought to make contact with the infamous Charles Peace, with whom a meeting would prove to be more illuminating.

After much conversation and drinking heavily with Wainwright, we took our leave of the Colony Room Club. Outside I hailed a passing open Landau carriage from the depths of the merciless and oppressive fog that was still evident. The hooves of the four horses pounded the wet cobblestones as they pulled our carriage through the almost empty and ghostly streets of the Metropolis. Holmes then explained to me during our journey precisely who, in fact, Charles Peace was.

"Charles Peace," explained Holmes, "is not only a notorious art faker, but also a dab hand at playing the violin. Indeed his virtuosic skills have not been impaired,

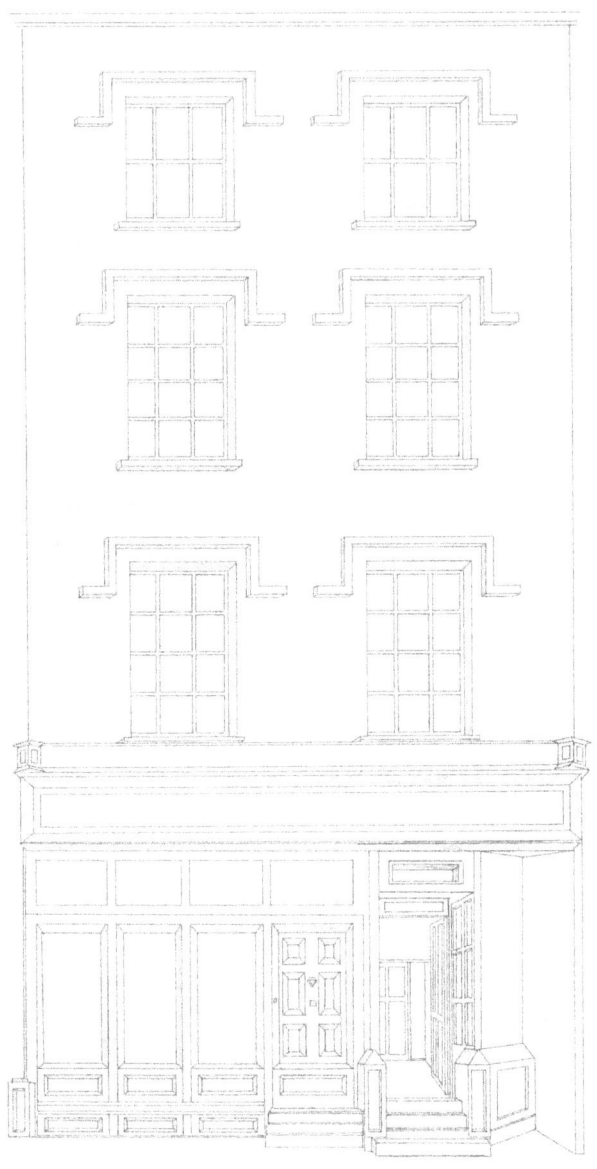

Colony Room Club, Soho

despite being mentally scarred in his youth and physically scarred in his later adolescence. He remains foremost in his chosen profession, that of methodically saturating the art world with his fakes of the works of great painters. However, despite his crippled state he is acknowledged as being preëminent, amongst violin *virtuosi*. His acclaim is well merited, for I too have heard him perform at the Bechstein Hall, and in so doing he dispatches Paganini to oblivion!"

After a dismal and uncomfortable drive and much cursing, for no apparent reason, by the coachman of our open Landau carriage, we eventually pulled up, thankfully outside our rooms at 221. b. Baker Street. Looking up from the pavement, it appeared to me that our rooms were indeed occupied by visitors – probably for Holmes, I imagined. My imagination proved correct, for as we approached our chambers, the commotion from inside increased with intensity with each step we climbed.

*Formerly known as Upper Seymour Street
** No, it was Dante's inscription in Inferno – 'Abandon all hope those who now enter here'.

Chapter 5

The Ascent into the Underworld

The scene on entering our parlour was one of pure pandäemonium. Assembled in our drawing room, summoned by the wire Holmes had sent from the Crown Post Office in Wigmore Street earlier, were several of Holmes' 'clients' though I had not quite realised Holmes had so many friends and acquaintances. They all looked as if they were by way of being revolutionaries in their chosen vocation.

"How do you do?" I inquired of two guests, according them every courtesy and civility, in my attempt to engage their attention in conversation, "and what awful weather we are enduring." Both looked at me askance.

Thinking they were private friends of his, I made my apologies in order to retire to my room, leaving my fellow lodger free to entertain his guests. I was, however, detained by Holmes and in fact introduced one by one to his acquaintances. One person in particular, a certain Neville St. Clair something or other, was wearing a very luxuriant coat with an Astrakhan collar and a gold *pince-nez* on his nose, through which he kept looking at Holmes' collection of friends in a perturbed and agitated manner. He displayed all the symptoms of being ill at ease, at being in such close proximity to Holmes' other guests, which my training as a doctor had taught me to recognise. Nevertheless, we both chatted about the weather and other sundry topics, none of which I realised either of us had the slightest interest in. At that moment Mrs. Hudson came in with a tray of sandwiches, cake and other comestibles with coffee.

"For Mr Holmes' guests since they have been an age waiting for him," she announced.

"Thank you Mrs Hudson," said I, relieving her of the heavily laden tray.

"Might I press you to a cucumber sandwich and what dreadful weather we are having?" I remarked to a baron and to another gentleman nearby. Both appeared to be somewhat perplexed at been accorded such courtesy, let alone cucumber sandwiches and coffee. The sandwiches soon disappeared, as indeed so did the silver coffee pot, as it was nowhere to be found when I offered to get more coffee to re-fill our guests' cups. Indeed one person I think, with the name of James Ryder, was most adamant that he wanted no more coffee and his expression told me he meant it. How considerate I thought!

By degrees however, I became aware that these so called 'clients' of Holmes were in fact nothing more that a loose confederation of Baker Street irregulars. That unofficial police force, as he termed them, comprised a collection of misfits all of dubious and questionable character, somewhat like Wainwright, whom we had met earlier. None appeared to be honest and indeed I witnessed, on two occasions, acts of pilfering of various objects positioned around our drawing room.

Holmes later confided to me that these characters could blend in to any situation on account of their being innocuous. The sight of a uniformed official or Jack, has the immediate effect of terminating conversation. These people are able to get within inches of other persons' talk without being noticed. I found that hard to accept and informed Holmes so. The mere presence of these individuals, would in itself, have the instinctive effect of making me focus my full attention on them, as well as any valuables about my person, especially my wallet and gold Hunter. But at length the assembly thinned out, as people took their leave of Holmes, that is, all but a vulpine looking man called Sherman. After a muffled conversation with Sherman, Holmes dismissed him eventually, leaving only Charles Peace in our drawing room.

"I am pleased, Peace, that you were able to find time from your busy musical tour to accord me a few minutes' discussion. It will be possible for you to appear in this evening's concert featuring your particular interpretation of the Mendelsohn E-minor violin concerto, since I observed your Brougham carriage down in the street, waiting to convey you back to the Queen's Hall, not far away at Langham Place," said Holmes.

"Quite!" responded Peace.

"The reason I wish to talk to you," continued Holmes, "is to discuss not so much your contact between the bow and violin but rather your contact with the criminal underworld, of which you are an esteemed member. In particular, your recent knowledge of a certain exhibition being arranged in Chicago, so I have been informed reliably."

"That Wainwright opening his big mouth again?" said Peace, incisively.

"Come, come Charles you know better than that!"

"You may be more correct than you think Holmes."

"Really?"

"However, what I think is happening could make life difficult for a lot of us living in London for the foreseeable future!"

Holmes looked at Peace intently.

"And that would not suit my plans," continued Charles Peace, "since I neither have the desire to reside at Highgate or Kensal Green in lavender."

"I beg your pardon?" said Holmes.

"Highgate or Kensal Green? They are cemeteries Mr. Holmes, cemeteries!"

"Please do go on with your interesting narrative," encouraged Holmes.

"I believe that a certain long established art gallery in London is organising an exhibition at the World's Columbian Exposition in Chicago. This quiet acquisition of art is supposed to be secret and selective, in that it is not open to all artists. Other credible institutions as the Royal Academy are involved informally, but will deny, if pressed, any formal participation. Their involvement is to lend credence, and verisimilitude, as it were, to the project and to judge some of the works being submitted. Even the artist Lyons agreed with me on this presupposition, when I spoke with him recently in the crush bar during the interval at a concert in the Aëolian Hall in Bond Street," said Peace,

"You will of course know Holmes, that if something is supposed to be secret, people immediately wish to be involved too. They will almost certainly explore and find out how they too can be invited to participate in this opportunity. Very much like the stock market; people buy stock or gilt-edge securities on the basis of inside information and tips, not the commercial probity or performance of a company. So it is with this exhibition, artists are queuing up to be invited to submit work into what they perceive to be an exclusive and lucrative opportunity, and who would not?"

"You are saying in effect," I interposed, "that artists,

on the pretext of assembling artwork for an some international exposition world fair or whatever, to be held in Chicago, will without question submit their art work? Notwithstanding the fact that the artwork submitted is of an inordinately high standard, their endeavour is, to utilise this rare opportunity to achieve accelerated recognition and acclaim?"

"Yes," said Peace, "so far nothing unusual in promoting artwork there. However, I feel there is more to it than a philanthropic exercise in the promotion of artists' works. Believe in it Holmes, there are some of us who remain gifted in the creation of art, especially other peoples! We accept vehemently the adage that the best form of flattery is imitation – well quite literally! Never in my experience though, has there been such a demand for our skills.

It would seem that every 'talented exponent' of our craft has been commissioned to copy works of art almost on a production line basis. The original is delivered and by a certain date, a copy must be returned with the original for a handsome fee! No questions are asked, and in any event, replies would not be given. Everybody involved is sworn to secrecy on pain of retribution, and on that basis, I would not have this conversation with anyone, other than you Holmes!

Now what makes me nervous about this venture is the fact that yes the World's Columbian Exposition in Chicago is without doubt going ahead. However, I believe no English artwork is really planned to be exhibited at the World's Columbian Exposition and nor is it likely to be so. Yes, people are going through the motions of organising one but without the real expectation of conclusion. There is also a feeling, only a feeling, that there is concerted effort here and being applied by a very skilful manipulator, an *eminence gris*, as it were, with influence at the highest levels. By that I mean the ability to make an effect at the Royal Academy and so on. I believe through rumour that there is a professor deep in the background who is influencing events.

That is all I can divulge Holmes," concluded Peace, draining his glass of whisky, and with a shallow bow took his leave of Holmes. I escorted him downstairs to his waiting Brougham in which he departed, immediately absorbed by the all-embracing fog.

On my return to our drawing room, I remarked to Holmes, "I find that Charles Peace refreshingly sarcastic!"

"Do you indeed, Watson. His cynicism is well placed and based upon a profound comprehension of the human psyche with all its greatness or weaknesses."

I noted Holmes' praise of this character, though with surprise.

"Nonetheless Watson, there is villainy in this," Holmes continued, "deep unadulterated villainy. I have always suspected some masterful hand behind certain crimes committed abroad the Metropolis. Some recent crimes perpetrated have the hallmark, not of a typical London petty crook, but the assay mark of ingenuity and considered aforethought!"

Chapter 6

The Expedition to the Admiralty

The next morning after a fitful sleep I came into the dining room for a much-needed break-fast that Mrs. Hudson had prepared for me. Holmes had not appeared yet so I started break-fast alone, on boiled cod. I looked through the morning papers, in particular The *Daily News*, but found nothing absorbing, or of worthwhile interest. Instead I gave some thought to our case. From what I had been able to appreciate, it would appear that there was an art exhibition to be organised in Chicago, but that all was not what it seemed, and that certain knowledgeable persons, such as Charles Peace, suspected an ulterior motive. At this juncture, Mrs. Hudson drew back the *portière* curtain shielding the drawing room from draughts.

Whilst Mrs. Hudson served break-fast, she related her remarkable story to me. Earlier in the morning she has been accosted by roughs in the street whilst collecting provisions from the street market in York Place. Aghast at her news I asked her if she had been hurt.

"Me hurt, what is a little hurt to me? Beside, I got one of them with my linen shopping bag!"

"How could a linen bag ward off an assault upon you?" I asked curiously.

"Very easily doctor, should the linen shopping bag

contain several tin canisters of preserved meat! When I had downed him," she continued, "the others melted back into the fog from whence they came."

I was very impressed with our housekeeper's defiance at her being incommoded. A few moments later Holmes came bursting into the room and before I could inform him of Mrs. Hudson's encounter with the roughs outside, he launched into his tirade.

"I see Mrs. Hudson, our housekeeper, has decided to tax our patience yet again this week. She remains incapable of delivering hot food to our table on time."

"As you say Holmes, our housekeeper is long-suffering with regard to your habits!" I responded, indicating my annoyance with his remarks.

"Typically Watson, you would side with that, that dreadful woman!"

"Well Holmes, you will be shocked to hear that our brave Mrs. Hudson was earlier this morning attacked by roughs in the fog, whilst collecting provisions from the street market in York Place!"

Holmes looked over his newspaper. "Our house keeper was attacked did you say?"

"Yes she has been knocked about and incommoded by the roughs down in the street market!"

"Are you certain Watson, that she did not provoke the roughs? She does alas have the attitude and build to carry out successfully a sustained and vicious attack on even the bravest of souls!"

"Holmes I will not hear of such insensitivity nor tolerate your insulting remarks about Mrs. Hudson! The poor woman has been knocked about and treated shamelessly and deserves our sympathy, not your scorn."

I berated Holmes, as my face flushed with anger, for his sneering tone.

Holmes looked at me impassively and said confidently. "You say that she has *been* knocked about? No Watson surely you meant to say that she has been about!"

"Holmes! How dare you speak about our long-suffering housekeeper in such a way! She has acquitted her self with honour and is all the more to be respected for it. You should do well to remember that Holmes. She is brave and has backbone!" I concluded.

"Brave and has backbone," replied Holmes, "I can see more backbone on that piece of boiled cod you are reluctantly trying to eat!"

"Do tell me Watson, were there any casualties in this encounter, apart from Mrs. Hudson's pride?" asked Holmes.

"Yes," I replied, "one of the footpads received a blow from Mrs Hudson's linen shopping bag that downed him!"

A linen shopping bag downed him?" inquired Holmes.

"Well the bag was full of several tin canisters of preserved meat!" I continued.

Good God Watson, that murderous weapon being wielded in her hands against those defenceless footpads!"

I could not be bothered to engage with Holmes when he was in this facetious or disputatious mood, and so I let the matter drop. However, this exchange had occurred whilst Holmes was filling his pipe with tobacco and was now approaching the break-fast table. He sat down and looked at the collection of letters delivered by the brave Mrs. Hudson earlier. Holmes opened his mail, systematically inspecting carefully each envelope and its contents. I was pouring coffee and looking up. I saw Holmes turning a deathly pallor of grey and staring rigidly in a paroxysm of fear at five orange pips that had dropped out of one of the envelopes and onto the table cloth.

"Holmes," I exclaimed, "are you all right, what ever can the matter be?"

Holmes looked at me with vacant eyes and mumbled the word 'five' over and over. I was somewhat perplexed and perturbed at this singular event. I made my way around the table to attend to Holmes, not only as a concerned friend but also as a physician. However, I was intercepted by the re-appearance of Mrs. Hudson, who terminated my progress to Holmes, with her masterful arm on my shoulder whilst bearing a large tray made of elm with his break-fast upon it on her other arm.

"Good morning Mr. Holmes even though it is still foggy out there! Ah I see you got my mail with the five orange pips in it!"

Holmes looked at her. The features on his face were livid.

"Do not panic, Sherlock," she boomed, "it is only a joke!"

Holmes got up and left the room.

"I have been waiting for ages to do that doctor, ever since he came across those pips in his failed case of his…what did you call it?"

"The Five Orange Pips," I replied.

Holmes re-appeared later in the morning dressed in a frock-coat and top hat.

"Are you ready for our visit to the Admiralty?"

"Yes, just let me finish my whisky and get my coat."

Moments later and suitably attired, we were standing in a fog-bound Baker Street listening for a carriage. Presently, we heard the clattering of horses' hooves, followed by the ghostly apparition, from the shrouds of fog, of a green tender lantern preceding a Clarence carriage.

"Admiralty!" shouted Holmes.

"The what?" came a gruff response from the bowler hatted carriage driver.

Holmes repeated his instruction as we both clambered into the four-wheeler carriage.

Almost at the pace of a funeral *cortège* we traversed the Metropolis, first down Baker Street that leads into Orchard Street and then over the Oxford Street. We then continued down North Audley Street, turning right into Lees Place; this elegant street continues into Park Lane. There we veered left and trundled down this tree-lined road of opulent mansion houses. Most of them were hidden in the fog made denser by the proximity of the Hyde Park that borders the western side of this thorough-fare.

Eventually we drove through the ornate classical architecture of the Ionic screen gateway at Hyde Park Corner that was designed by Decimus Burton. Holmes was too absorbed with his pipe and thoughts to realise that we were in fact heading towards Victoria. At least so I thought and was sure of this, for we had failed to make a left turning into the Constitution Hill and on to Whitehall. Perhaps the carriage driver knew of a better route to our destination especially given the difficult circumstances of finding our way in this fog. I did not wish to alert the driver as to our course, for fear of inviting unpleasantness. These persons are quick to dispense as much at the slightest hint of criticism of their skill in navigating their carriages around the Metropolis.

We continued driving through the gloom and fog along Grosvenor Place. Looking out from the carriage, at the wet pavement outside, punctuated by the blurred halos of solitary street town gas lamps, made for a peculiar experience. At length we appeared to be passing a building, with diffused lights emanating from it, illuminating groups of people wandering around nearby. The building had all the resemblance of a Railway Station, of Victoria Railway Station in fact! My concern was interrupted by the sound of the carriage driver's harsh voice.

"'Ere we are!" he said.

Holmes was the first to alight from the carriage and the first to respond to the driver's remark as to achieving our destination.

"This does not look like the Admiralty my man."

The Clarence carriage driver pointed with his whip to a building just visible through the fog.

"There, what is that building then?"

"What building?"

The driver shrugged his shoulders and said. "It don't matter, that will be fifteen shillings."

"Fifteen shillings to where?" replied Holmes.

"To the Admiralty, that building over there; you wanted the Admiralty Public House and here you are. I have brought you to the Admiralty Public House, in the Vauxhall Bridge Road, Victoria."

With that remarked the bowler hatted carriage driver whipped up his horses and disappeared down the road in the direction of the river Thames uttering all kinds of oaths and recommendations he felt that we both ought to undertake.

"Good God Holmes what are we to do now?"

"Walk!" replied Holmes.

Accordingly, on that injunction we possessed our souls and with grim determination faced east and stumbled off into the swirling, reeking fog made all the more damp and clammy by the presence of the nearby river Thames.

In my association with Holmes I had come to know

of his forays into the meaner less desirable parts of our Metropolis. Indeed his knowledge of the various parts of London was impressive. He could, at a glance of the soil upon a person's boots, predict confidently where the soil had been picked up. I was grateful for this skill of his because now was the time to put his great powers to the test and get us out of the fog and into the Admiralty in Whitehall. We lurched our way down Rochester Row, passing the emerging, partially built Catholic Cathedral of the Precious Blood of Christ. Its Byzantine architecture comprised red and white bands of brick, dominated by the huge two hundred and seventy feet high *campanile* that loomed up as it disappeared into the fog-laden aëther. Holmes remarked that the *campanile*, jerking his head to the direction of the tower, was to be dedicated to St. Edward the Confessor.

"I confess Holmes, that I do not know why!"

Holmes ignored my attempt at my *mot jest* and instead we both turned right into the Horseferry Road and in so doing just missed being hit by a recklessly driven pantechnicon that rushed past our persons, causing a wind upon our faces.

"We are nearing our goal," said Holmes, "for that is the sound of Big Ben striking out the hour, announcing it to be the eleventh."

By a series of quick turns, and my blind faith in Holmes' directional ability in the fog, we gained the thoroughfare next to the Thames called Millbank. I knew this because of the impregnable penitentiary located nearby, partially filled with dubious characters unfortunate enough to have had dealings with Holmes.

I also realized that we were in the vicinity of the Royal Aquarium Building, in nearby in Victoria Street. A place

Royal Aquarium Building, Victoria

renowned for the notorious activities of the Imperial Theatre, located within the confines of the Royal Aquarium Building, which brought the whole establishment into disrepute, having systematically, deteriorated into a raucous and tawdry Music Hall. This infamous theatre, with its reputation, was often in peril of having its licence revoked, because of the dangerous acts performed on stage. This included women being shot out from the mouth of a military cannon, while no less than knives being thrown in an arbitrary manner around the stage, to the accompaniment of fire being played with during an act.

We continued into Abingdon Street, in which the comparatively recently constructed and imposing Palace of Westminster is built and within its confines were located the two houses of Parliament.

"Look Holmes, look at the neo-Gothic architecture of the Houses Parliament. How romantic it looks in the fog! Even in this density, the Palace of Westminster shines out like a beacon to our democracy. No wonder it is referred to as the 'Mother of all Parliaments'!"

Holmes remained lost in thought as we passed beneath the ornate neo-Gothic tracery and architecture of the massive Victoria Tower, but then exploded, as was his custom at times.

"You amaze me Watson," he began, "that building you call the Houses of Parliament represents less democracy, as you call it, than would have existed in that Admiralty Public House, outside which we were standing some time ago. Imagine, if you can Watson, the prospect of supposedly intelligent men, all wearing fancy dress including knickerbockers and powdered wigs, walking backwards, conducting the affairs of the realm."

I attempted to admonish him for his unwarranted sarcasm about our parliamentary democracy.

"The 'Mother of all Parliaments'," continued Holmes, "the mother of all." his voice trailed off into the fog.

After this exchange of views, we walked past the magnificence of St. Stephen's Hall in its original Gothic splendour. Quickening our pace, for no reason, we crossed over Bridge Street into Parliament Street beneath the clock tower from which Big Ben struck out the time of fifteen minutes past the hour. As we gained Whitehall and passed the Westminster Bridge Street Underground Railway Station, I asked Holmes to slow down, as the ache had increased painfully in my left thigh. This was due to a Martine-Henry bullet tearing through it during the second murderous Sudanese campaign, involving the Royal Marine Light Infantry in which I was a surgeon. We did slow our pace as we continued up Whitehall. In so doing, we experienced an ugly encounter with a rough and his women outside the King's Head Public House. *

I noticed both had been drinking heavily; especially so the woman. Who on seeing me purposefully propelled her rickety perambulator, containing an infant of vile and repellent aspect, into my path, causing me to collide with it. Whereupon she grabbed the grubby child, yelling that I had hurt her baby. This incident was staged deliberately in the hope that I might be persuaded, no doubt by her rough male companion, to make compensation to her with money for the supposed harm I had caused. Holmes would have none of it. And before I could marshal my thoughts to deal with this cockney business, Holmes was already squaring up to the rough.

"You are not doing that number on us!" I heard Holmes advise him, and quite audibly.

The face of the rough flushed bright red in colour as he started to raise his hand aloft. However, before he could do so Holmes countered back with the injunction.

"And adopting an obstreperous attitude towards me will avail you nothing, except possibly the freedom of your female accomplice and your own, as you return forthwith to prison from whence you have recently fled!"

This remark had a salutary effect upon the man's attitude for it made him pause to think carefully about continuing with his physical approach to an argument with Holmes.

"And," said Holmes turning to the women, "despite the soiled condition of that child, who clearly does not belong to you, your interest might be better served were you not to consort with violent fugitives."

The women then ceased squawking but now looked intently at Holmes. She was dressed in cheap, tawdry clothes, ill fitting and dirty. Her hair was short and greasy and she wore what looked like the remains of a bonnet that had clearly seen better times. Indeed it was difficult to determine whether it was the lining of a hat, or a hat in its own right. On her thin neck were quite easily observable, bruises she attempted to cover with the aid of a greyish neckerchief. Her dress may have been linen at one stage in its life but was now covered by a matted woollen shawl that she draped upon her shoulders. The scuffed boots she wore on her feet were neither of the same style or colour.

Holmes continued to address the rough. "You should take greater care when in public to conceal the fact that you have recently escaped from goal, no doubt by chiselling your way through its masonry wall."

These words had a magical effect on the man. His sartorial arrangements were even less inviting. He wore a long cord waistcoat with numerous pockets and brass buttons and a pair of baggy, faded velveteen trousers, the kind one throws away after their use. On his feet were dirty heavy boots, but in his case matching. I noticed too, that he wore a silver coloured ring in his ear lobe that looked infected to my medically trained eye. He considered Holmes and with his mind made up, immediately grabbed the woman and her rickety perambulator and barged back inside the public house from whence they had come, to continue drinking, no doubt, with reckless abandon.

"You know my methods Watson! I observed the calluses on his hands that could only have been caused by an intense use of a chisel over a short period of time. Clearly he is not a stonemason and the regulation prison shirt he was careless in not concealing, with those borrowed clothes, led me to conclude he had just escaped from prison. *Voila tout!*"

We walked up Whitehall, past all the great ministries and departments of state set like huge pre-historical monolithic blocks silhouetted in the fog. At length, on reaching Great Scotland Yard we turned left crossing Whitehall and into the Admiralty courtyard. On entering the Admiralty, we presented our credentials to the very man we had come to interview, commissionnaire Peterson.

"Good morning gentlemen. Sir James is expecting you. Please come this way."

We followed Peterson down a lengthy corridor with white painted walls that were punctuated with dark highly polished oak doors. Above us were groin-vaulted ceilings inter-dispersed with acetylene gas-fuelled *chandeliers* and the occasional palm tree, which broke the monotony. Eventually we ascended a wide, ornately carved, timber staircase into what was the higher echelon of the Admiralty. Perhaps Nelson had climbed these very stairs I mused. Peterson showed us into a large, comfortable drawing room and bid us to wait. Looking around the room, I could see that the walls were adorned with the portraits of notable admirals of the fleet in vivid blue uniform complemented with gold braided epaulettes. At the centre of one wall and above the chimneypiece, beneath which a fire blazed, hung a huge painting of Horatio Nelson.

Muffled voices were then heard outside and in walked Sir James.

"Mr. Holmes, Doctor Watson, thank you both for coming; please do come into my office."

A few minutes later, we all were seated in the comfortable office of the head of the Marine Department. Peterson and the off duty constable Murcher, in his ill-fitting civilian clothes, were also present.

Sir James Walter opened the meeting by thanking Holmes and me for making the effort to come to the Admiralty. Clearly Sir James was hoping that Holmes would take on the case and his obsequious manner indicated as much. Holmes asked Peterson to explain the sequence of events leading up to the death of Cadogan West on the stopped train outside Charing Cross Railway Station.

"Omit nothing, however trivial", Holmes had warned Peterson, who then commenced his narrative that Holmes recorded in his green commonplace book.

When Peterson had finished relating his version of events, Sir James dismissed him back to his duties at the front desk in the main reception hall. Then constable Murcher told us, while referring to his notebook, of his singular experience of that afternoon at Charing Cross.

Both stories tallied, except in one detail that Peterson had omitted to mention. It involved the opening of the door of the train carriage. Both men had been present and each experienced the sight of West's body on the floor of the railway carriage.

Murcher said that as a constable he had seen some horrifying sights in his experiences. However, the vision of West's body, made more sinister by that fixed grin on his face, on a railway carriage floor, in a train just out side as busy a terminus as Charing Cross Railway Station, unnerved him momentarily. But, as he climbed up into the carriage, he had noticed that Peterson, standing on the track and looking up into the carriage, had not appeared very much shocked at seeing the death scene in the carriage. It was almost as though he had expected to see West dead on the carriage floor!

"Who was it," interjected Holmes, "that said, 'When

the mind is in torment it seeks refuge in the seemingly insignificant'? ** Clearly the constable's mind was sufficiently alert to notice Peterson's re-action."

Murcher had then pulled himself together and declared the situation to be a police matter and told Peterson to return along the railway track to Charing Cross and there summon and send down other constables, who duly arrived but without Peterson.

Holmes listened intently to Murcher's account. At length he said, "Sir James, are you able to organise a meeting between the White Star Line and myself, preferably in Liverpool and aboard the *Olympic* or *Titanic*, in any event either ship will do?"

"I feel confident that I can arrange such a meeting Mr. Holmes."

Within minutes of the remarkable and singular record being taken from constable Murcher's notebook, we were in a carriage and pair *en-route* back to Baker Street. Whilst in Trafalgar Square, I had mentioned to Holmes that I would like to use this opportunity to visit a particularly good bookmaker's agent nearby in Pall Mall, ironically opposite Oceanic House. The reason was, that I wanted to place a bet on a good tip from Mrs. Hudson on another horse owned by Colonel Ross called Bayard, that would be running the next day at Kempton races. Holmes grudgingly consented to wait in the carriage.

* No. It is called the Red Lion Public House.
** Walter Whitman.

Chapter 7

The Heiress from the Ozarks

Our investigation into the mysterious circumstances surrounding the death of Cadogan West in a railway carriage just outside Charing Cross Railway Station in central London was progressing. The testimonies offered by both Peterson and constable Murcher had thrown up an inconsistency, that had caught Holmes' attention.

"Looking in the London *Times*," I remarked to Holmes, "A new railway concern, the Baker Street & Waterloo Railway Company, in addition to asphyxiating its passengers, now proposes to electrocute them as well. Their scheme involves the conveyance of passengers, those foolhardy enough to allow their being so transported, along an electrified subterranean railway line, in tunnels below the very streets of London!

Imagine Holmes, a system of underground railways where the permanent way is electrified to enormous voltage power. Those volts are then supposed to be able to propel an entire railway train of carriages at speeds approaching the unimaginable. Fantasy in all probability, but I maintain that it cannot be done!"

"Why not?" asked Holmes.

"Well, the rapid evacuation of air, as the train plunges into the tunnel, will ensure that all passengers, including those in 3rd. class and parliamentary carriages* with their dogs, are asphyxiated or at least suffocated by the lack of oxygen in the tunnel. This will certainly cause a dangerous vacuüm to develop, making the train accelerate wildly out of control, especially when the engine driver at the control levers in the front of the train is dead!

It is quite conceivable that the train, with its gruesome cargo of corpses, will emerge at the other end of the tunnel, but at a fantastic and unstoppable velocity of upward of thirty-five miles to the hour! This and other startling, but illuminating facts I have gleaned from no less an authority than that of the eminent scientist the good Doctor Dionysius Lardner. Can you imagine Holmes, the horror of those unsuspecting passengers, waiting on a station platform at the end of the tunnel? Then having to witness the spectacle of the death train, complete with bloated bodies stacked upon each other, emerging from the ground, swaying and rattling by down the permanent way of the railway line out of control and into oblivion?"

"No Watson I cannot! Somehow I perceive your thinking on these matters to be seriously flawed. Ever since we have known each other your immediate re-action to innovative ideas is to condemn them unequivocally as impracticable."

"Well really Holmes! What do you think scientist and engineers today take the public for? Next they will be telling us that it will be possible to send visual images over great distances along electrically charged copper wires just because of the advent of the telephone and telegraph!

I am all in favour of harnessing technology for the benefit of mankind, but let us proceed in a rational and realistic frame of mind devoid of preposterous ideas such as this ridiculous and fantastical notion!" I demanded, throwing down *The Times* onto the sofa.

"Apart from anything else I note the quality of *The Times* is slipping. Next they will be using apostrophes, in order to abbreviate, in written narrative!"

"What?" asked Holmes.

"We do, after all, Holmes," I interrupted, "live in a real and logical world or at least I do. Accordingly, in the meantime, I have been giving some thoughts, to our problem. In my sober, methodical and empirical manner I have the solution at hand!"

Holmes looked up with an expression of repressed surprise.

"What about Great Central Station," I continued, "as an appropriate name for the new railway station along the Marylebone Road that is to be opened by the Sovereign? After all the company that has constructed the station is called the 'Great Central Railway' I say, did you hear me Holmes? Continuing on the theme of railways Holmes," I persevered, "*The Daily Telegraph* has published a letter from someone who claims that he can, by the application of systematic analysis and observation, work out a complete stranger's occupation and habits. What! I should like to see him analyse and use his deductive skills in elucidating the habits and occupations of some of the characters clamped down in the 3rd Class carriage of a parliamentary train. To say nothing of the Metropolitan Railway trains of the Inner Circle or District railway upon which we have so often travelled. The writer exaggerates his skills. I only wish I could have a wager on his inability to do so, and prove it as being pure conjecture!" I concluded.

Holmes was by now standing at our parlour window looking down to the street through the swirling fog.

"You should lose your bet Watson, for it is I who wrote that monograph to which you allude. However, you might wish to wager your monthly army pension, not on your usual horses but on these odds. My contention is that the woman down there in the street is searching for our house number and that she is from the territory of Oklahoma in the United States!"

I glanced over his shoulder and saw in the fog a woman with a vague searching expression upon her face. At length, having sighted our street number of 221. b. she marched over toward our door with a determination somewhat surprising for her demeanour. She then tugged at our bell, the sound of which was barely audible, coming from the depths of the basement, wherein our housekeeper, Mrs. Hudson dwells, patrolling her domain as *Medusa* does hers on the dreaded island of *Seriphos*.

Presently the ubiquitous Mrs. Hudson appeared and ushered in the woman we had observed in the street minutes earlier.

"A visitor for you Mr. Holmes and who, from her accent, I venture is from America and from the stitching in her top coat is probably from the territory of…"

"Thank you Mrs. Hudson, we need not detain you further," interrupted Holmes, before our resident house-keeper could complete her sentence.

"Mr Holmes," she continued undaunted, "you appear stuck for a solution to your case. Well, I was talking to the fishmonger earlier, and we think we have the solution. Therefore let me give you some badly needed advice!"

"How dare you!"

"Let me give you a wee clue then."

"Certainly not!" said Holmes, closing the door firmly on her not inconsiderable bulk.

Holmes then turned to our visitor and offered her a

straight-backed wooden cathedral chair, next to the now roaring fire in the grate that I had just poked back into life.

"This is my friend Doctor Watson, in front of whom you may speak freely."

I offered my hand, which she shook with a strength that took me aback. She then moved across the room and seated herself in Holmes' favourite armchair.

"You must forgive my untidiness, for I have just groped my way along the better part of this Baker Street. I dismissed my Surrey carriage, or as I guess you say here, buckboard carriage, a trifle prematurely not realising this address was way down the track."

"I see you have travelled far, from Oklahoma in fact." Holmes said, in replying to our visitor's opening remarks.

Our visit sprang up in amazement, then regained Holmes' armchair.

"You are correct Mr. Holmes. I am from a wealthy oil family in the Oklahoma Territory, but how did you deduce that fact?"

"By simply observing your clothing and demeanour; I also see, by the state of your *toilette*, that your journey was not a comfortable one and that you left America in some haste!"

"Yes. I have come to England to seek your help."

"That is easily given, but pray do continue," said Holmes.

"Your observation about my journey not being a comfortable one does your reputation justice, in that you are absolutely right! In my haste I got on some boat called the RMS *Olympia*, operated by some outfit called the White Star Line. Apart from the fact that the ship could not even get out of New York harbour without crashing into other ships, I was amazed it got through the Atlantic Ocean during the equinoctial gales without sinking! Throughout the journey things just did not work. The boat appeared to have a pronounced list that never corrected itself throughout the journey. Doors set into the metal internal walls of the ship did not close correctly. I even had to wedge a chair against my cabin door handle before retiring to bed because the door would not shut properly in the doorframe set in the metal cabin wall.

I remember the cause of this. One of my oil engineers, back home, explained to me the phenomenon of a Wagner tension field being present in metal. That is, what happens when sheet metal or metal plate is warped or is subject to unusual tension. This condition is created when the metal is being pulled abnormally. Holmes, what I recognised on that RMS *Olympus* ship, or whatever it is called, was that the basic metal structure of the boat was warped, out of alignment, bent, and the boat creaked like mad. It was literally falling apart, with me in it!

Often the ship would roll where it ought not to. This event would have the crew scuttling around almost as if in a panic. Officers would be seen dashing down the length of the ship only to disappear into a deck hatch or door. These occurrences left me feeling pretty nervous, especially since we were stuck out in the middle of the Atlantic Ocean fifteen hundred miles from any land and during the equinoctial gales that were blowing continuously.

What I did find unnerving was the occasional sharp shudder and deep rumbling noises coming from the depths of the ship, as if it were in its final death struggle. It must have been pure hell for the steerage passengers also located in the bottom of the ship

On numerous occasions, whilst I promenaded on the deck, several curious incidences occurred, which alerted my mind; nothing significant in themselves, but some-how, all adding up. I recall one member of the crew constantly, but furtively, checking and re-checking the lifeboats, as if he felt they were inevitably going to be used on this voyage. During the course of his examina-tion, I think he was loading up the lifeboats up with provisions, such as blankets and tins of biscuits.

Taps failed to deliver hot or even cold water. The ship seemed to be powerless and at times almost drifted in the Atlantic Ocean. The crew acted as if they did not give a damn. I actually overheard a deck hand say that the ship was useful only as an, 'iron mausoleum'! My own feeling was that this metal structure was a wreck and had it been oil field equipment back home we would have junked it in double quick time. I half expected the crew to sink the ship in the middle of the sea and make us climb into those provisioned lifeboats. It was as if we were being fated by death!

Now I have been up and down the Missouri and Mississippi rivers on steam boats and have experienced more elegance and proper functioning on them than ever I got on that RMS *Olympus*. What travelling I have done tells me that function and making some kind of headway in the water are crucial aspects to any journey. Not so on that RMS *Olympus*, or whatever she is called, on which the general consensus amongst us 1st. Class passengers, was that we were riding a wreck on its last voyage and onward to the wrecking yard!

One curious experience remains vividly in my mind. It was late afternoon and the sun was dipping, making for a scarlet sky. I was out of sight behind a bulkhead but I distinctly heard an officer say to a crew-hand, 'we are now in the Labrador Current and that brings the icebergs down from Greenland. Keep your eyes peeled when you get to the crow's nest look out point on the masthead.' We 1st. Class passengers were aware of little white pyramids floating around, but no big bergs to speak of. Well, the crew hand that had gone to the crow's nest not only enjoyed good hearing, he was also given to even better eyesight. Within fifteen minutes, by which time it was getting on for dusk, a loud klaxon bell noise was heard coming from that very same crow's nest, warning of danger ahead. Within less than a minute our boat swerved so abruptly to portside that the suspended lifeboats leaned out to such an extent, that I thought they would depart from their davit brackets.

I raced immediately to the starboard side of the ship to see just what we were supposed to be avoiding. I saw it, but could not believe my eyes. An iceberg towering above us the size of a six storey building and as wide, was bearing down on us at such velocity that I found it hard to believe that something as big as it was, could move so quickly. Either way the helmsman in the wheelhouse steering the boat was having none of it. He got that RMS *Olympic*, right out of there and put as much distance between it and us as was possible, with our engines at full belt. No way was this ship going to be hit by an iceberg, well at least not on that trip.

When we did eventually limp into Liverpool, the ship's butt seemed to be all over the goddamn place. It even hit one of your British navy ships with such force that we 1st. Class passengers thought this is it, forget the wrecking yard, we are going to sink right here in Liverpool, within yards of dry land. The force of the impact was such that it made the steerage passengers frightened and come streaming up from the bowels of the boat and swarm out of the deck hatches. You guys would be wise to stick to Cunard boats for future rides on the oceans!"

"Possibly, but something troubling you very deeply has compelled your undertaking that arduous journey to seek advice from a stranger, since you cannot possible know me."

"True, but I know of your reputation," responded the woman from Oklahoma.

Our visitor looked at Holmes, then at me with the resignation of someone who cannot decide whether they have found a person in whom they can repose trust to help them, or someone who knows too goddamn much about their private life.

"My name is Katherine and I am from a town called Eureka Springs in the Ozark Mountains near the Oklahoma Territory in the Middle Western part of America. You may not know it, but Eureka Springs is an affluent town comprising spas, large houses and exclusive hotels.Many of these cater for a wealthy *clientele* out of New York, Chicago, Philadelphia or Boston who summer at Eureka Springs in order to take the spa waters and enjoy the cool of the mountain air."

Our visitor then re-arranged her attire and produced her cigarettes, one of which she lit by striking a match on the leather sole of her boot. I reached for our geographical encyclopaedia to read about and familiarise myself with Eureka Springs. Holmes would invariably wish to read an account of the place and study any maps of the locality. In this regard he could, as it were, transport his mind to Eureka Springs and gain valuable insight; for he would have little confidence in our female visitor's account or description of the place.

Thumbing through the pages devoted to Eureka Springs, it became clear that our heiress, thus far, did not exaggerate her description. The salient points about the place were described in the opening section and read:

'Eureka Springs, founded in 1879, is a relatively new spa city built in the Ozark Mountains near the Oklahoma Territory and is surrounded by attractive lakes and woods. Because of its geographical layout and mountainous situation it has earned itself the *sobriquet* of 'Little Switzerland'. Indeed the title is an apt one, for the city's reputation is one of providing high-class resort facilities to those wealthier classes from such cities as Chicago, Baltimore, Boston or New York. Because of its location in the mountains, the resort is able to provide several benefits. They include spa baths and well-appointed hotels, chief amongst which is the famous limestone built grand Crescent Hotel. Eureka Springs is much favoured by the rich who wish to escape the stultifying hot air of the big cities in summer and instead enjoy the cool air of the mountains and springs that the city has to offer.

There is in existence an urban railroad on which yellow painted streetcars ply along the beautiful streets, which comprise large stone and timber built residences set back in cultivated gardens behind white painted picket fences. . There are numerous churches catering for all faiths and a library founded by the philanthropist Andrew Carnegie. Other stone buildings in the downtown area include the Federal Building, Post Office, Concert Hall and Assembly Rooms together with an imposing granite built City Hall all of which contribute to this very beautiful and fine city of the Ozarks.'

I handed Holmes the reference book and our visitor continued her story.

"Earlier this year," she went on, "September, in fact, I attended the late Summer Ball at the very grand Crescent Hotel which over looks the town. There I was introduced to a gentleman from New York. It turned

Gustav Mahler

out that he was an *employé* in the merchant banking house of JP Morgan."

"Your friend," I interposed, "had you developed affections for him, as it were, did you dab it up?"

Our visitor blushed modestly.

"Yes, I guess so. We started to walk out together and promenade down the Boardwalk during evenings and attend concerts. We both are passionate about music, especially that composed by Mahler or Wagner and………"

Her words faltered and trailed off and were barely audible.

"And," I encouraged her.

"And that we were to be married next Fall."

At which point Holmes' irritation at my supposed banal line of inquiry got the better of him.

"And I take it madam that your lover has disappeared and deserted you"

"Holmes," I ejaculated, "do show some sensitivity!"

"Yes, do so rather!" enjoined our visitor."

"Well," continued Holmes, "has your lover disappeared?"

"How did you know?" she replied.

"Simply because you would not be here, seeking advice were it not the case. Now if you are serious about consulting me and eliciting my help, then tell me everything. Even if this does mean describing the more lurid of the details surrounding your singular experience amongst the mountains of the Ozark. In this respect madam, spare no detail in recounting your narrative!" said Holmes.

Our visitor flushed at this insinuation but thought better of it and resumed her seat. She clearly considered Holmes to be a confirmed misogynist and the look upon her face conveyed that fact very clearly to him.

"Okay, you want that I should give you details Holmes? Right, you will get them hard and fast served up by me. First of all let me tell you, I am no prim or prissy *'Southern Belle'* from the South."

"That I had realised," interrupted Holmes.

"Where I am from," she expatiated, ignoring his insult, "Oklahoma, is a tough but forgiving land and is oil bearing. Some people struck it rich, others did not. We struck oil and we enjoy a prosperity that goes with our gain. I may be wealthy Holmes, but my feet are firmly on the ground – albeit drenched in oil.

As I stated earlier, I met this banker, my *fiancé*, who works for the JP Morgan Merchant Bank in New York. We started meeting and were getting on fine. On one particular afternoon I was being driven in a Surrey carriage, the one with a fringe on top, around Eureka Springs, as is the custom there for ladies of refinement, like me. Perhaps your women of refinement might even do this in London? Well I was enjoying the ride especially around the fashionable districts of Pine Street, Chestnut Street and the van Buren Avenue, complete with their beautiful Victorian houses. Most of those mansions are adorned with ornate crenellated gable ends, elegant towers, castellated turrets and cute verandas supporting beautiful trestles with vibrantly coloured flowers. There is one particular veranda that links two bay windows I always keep a sharp look out for when passing, because it has the cutest little darling pussycat napping in its cool shade.

Most of these impressive houses are set back in their own extensive gardens and reflect various European styles. A popular design is that of French Second Empire with mansard roofs followed by the Gothic revival as interpreted through the Queen Anne style. Nothing epitomises the Victorian style better than a Queen Anne house, complete with dormer and bay windows, towers or turrets, cross gables and fish scale tiles adorning steeply pitched roofs crowned with metal fencing.

Some of the main buildings in Eureka Springs reflect a neo-Classic or even Greek influence in their architecture. Most of the buildings are of limestone, easily quarried in nearby Missouri, and consequently convey images of strength and permanence that are salient hallmarks of our city. The majority of houses are private and bought, not hired and have the latest in mechanical innovation such as butane gas lighting, indoor plumbing, central heat and electricity, all to promote a comfortable style of living. This approach invariably excludes the existence of shotgun houses."

This lady from Oklahoma was intelligent and it was evident to me that she was deliberately taunting Holmes with her ramblings. I think she was trying to get the measure of him; how far would his patience go and could he be relied upon? She certainly played a skilful game. I considered momentarily that perhaps Holmes had met his match yet again and this might well be his Nemesis. Judging by the look of exasperation upon his face that event may well be imminent. Yet he did not nor dare express his inner conflict verbally or otherwise.

"Anyway, moving on with my story, because my time is important, I saw my *fiancé* in deep discussion with a gentleman. I thought nothing of it until we met that evening on the Boardwalk, where he seemed lost in thought and agitated. Despite the fact we had enjoyed a performance of Schönberg's monumental orchestral and *lieder* epic *'Gurrelieder'*, the evening dragged on and eventually we bade good night and retired to our respective hotels. Before parting, however, we agreed to meet the next evening to attend a concert featuring the music of Gustav Mahler, of which we both are fond.

The next afternoon I was in my carriage leaving the Crescent Hotel on the hill and driving down the driveway past the pretty flowerbeds, resplendent in the subdued light of the early golden fall. Then Holmes, who do you think that I should see but my fiancé! Again he was in heated conversation with the same gentleman. This time, however, all my feminine instincts told me by the manner of the man talking to him, almost talking down at him, that my *fiancé* was in some kind of trouble."

Our visitor put a frilly-edged handkerchief to her moist eyes.

"Might I get you something to drink," I offered, "Tea, coffee, aërated water?"

"No!" she interrupted, "but I sure could do with a large whisky - neat!"

I handed a heavy cut crystal glass of whisky to her and also refilled Holmes' and mine too. I was also horrified to learn that we were precariously low on scotch!

"That evening we met up as arranged," she continued refreshed, "and were drinking at the crush bar prior to our going into the concert hall. My *fiancé* appeared to be easier in his mind and more relaxed than he was the previous evening. We took our seats in the Grand Circle and the music began with the opening chords of Mahler's First Symphony. You know the one, the one in D-major."

"Yes, yes, yes," said Holmes impatiently, "please continue your description"

"Oh very well," she said, "the Symphony originally had five movements, the *andante* - in between the first and third movements, but was removed upon a subsequent revision. The Symphony is now set in the usual four movements, *allegro comodo, scherzo, lento moderato* and finale in the form of *allegro furioso*. The program structure for the Symphony is based freely on that of the literature of Jean Paul Richter's, especially his novel *'The Titan'* from whence the Symphony gets its *sobriquet* name. I believe the Symphony was completed in 1888 at Leipzig in Germany and *premièred* in Budapest the following year. There is however a rumour that Mahler may have been influenced by one of his students * who claims to have created the symphony.

The Symphony is unusual in that the beginning of the first movement is one of the most beautiful openings in the symphonic *repertoire*. The sustained high octave A-major chord gradually unfolds a sequence of descending *Fourths*. The other curious fact about the Symphony is that the whole of the third movement is essentially a funeral march devoted to a dead hunter. His *cortège* is made up of creatures of the forest, which include hares carrying pennons in front of the hearse, followed by deer, cats, foxes, bears and other animals all of whom are playing musical instruments!"

In exasperation, Holmes got up from his chair and went to the window. With his back to both our visitor and me, I could only imagine the seething anger coursing through his veins, as the woman from Oklahoma chatted incessantly about irrelevancies. Though, by now, I was beginning to harbour a sneaking admiration for her tactics.

"Holmes," she continued, "where I am from it is rude to get up and walk away from a person who is talking with you! The reason I mention these details about Mahler's Symphony is because I observe that you too are a musician, if only an amateur one at that!"

That remark compelled Holmes to turn around from the window and face her.

"That Stradivarius violin case proclaims as much," she said, pointing with her cigarette at the battered leather case secreted away in the corner of our drawing room.

Holmes was visibly taken aback by this observational *manoeuvre* by the woman. I also noticed that before she put the cigarette back to her lips, she flicked the excess ash straight onto our carpet!

"However", she continued, "during the concert, when the music was being got up, something singular happened. I turned my head to the right simply to look at my *fiancé* but found him staring at someone who had just entered a box along the Grand Circle. My *fiancé* pretended that he was not looking at this person. But I knew that he was so doing, because the man in the box was the same person who had conversed with my *fiancé* on those previous two occasions!

"Now Holmes, I am not a *devoté* of the new fashion of hysteria, as defined by Sigmund Freud, nor indeed given to exaggeration, but I knew something to be wrong. My *fiancé* from that moment on was highly agitated and restless. Had the ceiling of the concert hall fallen in, it would not have made the slightest impression upon his attention, such was his distraction. Eventually, unable to contain himself any longer, he got up to leave but promised to come back directly. The interval came and I waited in the crush bar for him. I returned to the concert during which he still did not show up. After the concert, I hung around the crush bar in the now dwindling hope that he might re-appear. He did not appear that evening, or indeed the evening after that.

More out of annoyance at being treated in so cavalier a fashion, I went to the Basin Park Hotel, where he had checked in, to square up to and get the goods on him! You cannot imagine Holmes, my surprise on being told by a very straight and considerate manager of the hotel that my *fiancé*, by his name, did not reside there nor had he ever resided in their hotel! He simply did not exist, at least not at that Basin Park Hotel!"

Our visitor dwelt upon what she had said, and though visibly upset, drained her glass of whisky. She then got up and stood in front of the fire into which she threw her cigarette butt and then with a determination of one, who has made up their mind, said directly to my colleague.

"Okay Holmes, you are hired! A hundred bucks in it for you if you just find him, the rest you can leave to me!"

"My fees never vary except."

"Yeah well, still a hundred bucks," she snapped.

Having explained a few more details at Holmes' instigation, our visitor told him that she could be contacted at the St. Pancras Hotel. Gathering up her things

St Pancras Hotel

and checking her crystal glass for any remaining whisky, she shook my hand with even more of a grip than before, no doubt, brought on by her general annoyance with Holmes' attitudes. She then clicked her heels, turned, and vanished out of our room and into the street below, where I distinctly heard her whistle loudly for a cab!

"Well Watson what say you about that woman from Eureka Springs near the Oklahoma Territory?" remarked Holmes, pouring himself another large whisky.

"I thought her quite genteel and that she carried herself

well and her sweet face expressed all the tenderness one has come to expect from our cousins across the Atlantic."

"Watson, what are you saying, have you lost your reason? I am referring to her story not her personality! Really Watson you will have to snap out of this monomania with women. They generally cloud one's judgement and yours in particular."

"Nonsense Holmes, most women are sweet creatures; take my late wife Mary Morstan. What better example was there of sweet perfection than her's, which shone from that angelic face peering out from beneath a floral bonnet?" I said, handing him my silver framed sepia tinted *daguerreotype* of my deceased wife.

Holmes examined the photograph and remarked.

"Perfect? Never in my life have I witnessed such tragic deformity of mind or limb."

"Do you not think that you have had enough whisky this morning?"

"No," came his curt reply.

"Holmes, I fear that since you deal regularly with people of dubious repute, it will invariably lead to a certain degree of cynicism in your view of society, including women."

Clearly Holmes was becoming insufferable and in a bad mood, brought on by his encounter with the Oklahoma woman. Under these circumstances I would normally have gone for a walk, alas though, not in this fog.

"You are beyond redemption Holmes," I replied to his hurtful remarks about my late wife.

"Further," I announced, with as much conviction as I could marshal, "I may write my own autobiography, since I tire of consigning your exploits to the printed word, Holmes."

"I cannot think, Watson, that the public is yet ready to tolerate a tidal wave or onslaught of condensed banality and trivia that would be the foundations of your appalling diatribe you intend to be your autobiography!" he replied.

"My life, for I do have one, has not been entirely without incident," I responded.

"I realise that Watson, and it is for that reason that I contend an unsuspecting world is not yet prepared for such an unrelenting and emotional narrative that would indubitably be the foundation of your work!"

"Holmes, who do you think adds interest and form to your exploits? I do, and I present them to the public in a fascinating and understandable way. Were they to be left to you, they would be boring, dry monstrosities with no feeling and devoid of interest to the public. I have created you, Holmes and you would do well not to forget that fact."

"Indeed Watson, the fact of your saying that really surprises me. Perhaps the title of your proposed biography that springs readily to mind could be *'Failure of the Will!'* And Watson," Holmes continued, "it is fatal to the logical process to make decisions when you are angry, for it clouds your faculty for judgement."

I was flabbergasted at these derogatory insults about my character.

"I will cloud your judgement presently," I retaliated.

"Who was it who said that anger was temporary madness?"** inquired Holmes, in his feeble attempt to deliver his *coup de grâce*.

I have had occasions in the past to remark upon Holmes' hostile attitude to women in general and our landlady Mrs. Hudson in particular, to say nothing of his offensive comments about my deceased wife. Though his client from Oklahoma did not fully appreciate the fact, that Holmes was from the beginning, antagonistic toward her, I did. My only surprise was that he did not dispatch her forthwith rudely and decline to take up her case. Clearly, something in her narrative appealed to his cold, logical mind and it was certainly not her undoubted beauty or demeanour.

Holmes' character was contemptible to say the least and his disdain went deeper where women were concerned. He never quite trusted the sex after his resounding defeat at the hands of *femme fatale* Irene Adler, the protagonist in one of his earlier cases. Although on occasion he could be graceful, it was though, usually with an ulterior motive.

Indeed when I look back at his dealings with female clients, his interest was only, with their problems and the intellectual challenges they afforded him. His interest in their beauty, real or apparent, was in his own words, of superlative indifference to him. And whilst I have had in the past, reasons to remonstrate with him over some of his appalling remarks about the fair sex, I have always felt that to go further in expressing my indignation would be counter-productive. His ascetic character was such that it precluded one from feeling justified in taking anything approaching a liberty with his patience. Or indeed, acting in a confident manner in front of him.

Regarding his views on women I remember one such incident at the Bechstein Hall *** in London. During the interval of a musical concert, it was customary for Holmes and me to drink heavily at the small crush bar, provided by the management of that establishment. The first half of the concert had concluded with a piano recital of the *Abbé* Liszt's monumental Sonata in B-minor and was played to great acclaim by the fabulous German female pianist Clara Hofmannstahl.

We all of us gathered in the crush bar agreed that hers was one of the most accomplished piano recitals yet heard at the Bechstein Hall. Granted, both Holmes and I had been drinking liberally, but, it did not in my opinion justify or indeed excuse his outrageous remarks about Hofmannstahl's performance. Holmes amazed her assembled admirers at the bar, by insisting that had she been born a man, she would have at least possessed the hand structure to play properly those chords and *arpeggios* inherent in any of the piano works by Franz Liszt! Meaning, he explained, that the pianist should have a wide span of hand in order to compress several keys on the piano consecutively to create the *arpeggios*. Women, by their very femininity lack this basic requirement needed to play the piano properly.

On that occasion the management, fearing a hostile re-action to Holmes' remarks, felt it appropriate that we should leave the Bechstein Hall forthwith. Holmes found the event to be one of great hilarity, saying as we walked home in the soaking rain, that it provided the best excuse for quitting such an onslaught upon his sensitive ears.

For myself I was incensed at being ejected from a public hall and of missing the second half of what up until that moment had been an enjoyable evening of fine music, the tickets for which I had purchased. On that occasion I did vent my feelings upon him, but he received them with blank indifference, which only added to my annoyance.

"In the interest of aesthetics and the thorough appreciation of music Watson," he remarked, "I have saved you from that miserable woman masquerading as a pianist and an interpreter of the piano works of Liszt! Indeed Watson, I have saved you from a fate worse than death!"

As a direct consequence of this appalling behaviour of Holmes's I cancelled the tickets I had bought for a symphony concert at the St. James' Hall in Piccadilly**** in a week's time, for fear of a repetition of his insensitive conduct.

*Hans Rott.
**St. Basil.
*** Now the Wigmore Hall.
**** St. James' Hall had been re-located to the Portland Road.

Chapter 8

The Railway to the Necropolis

Our journey to Liverpool was to begin first thing the following day. Holmes had received a wire from Sir James Walter at the Admiralty confirming that a Mr. Arthur Carpenter, a director of the White Star Line, would meet us in Liverpool at the Herculaneum Dock, where the RMS *Olympic* was presently moored. The next morning we break-fasted, but I limited myself simply to strong coffee, as food did not quite appeal to me at four o'clock in the morning.

Apropos of nothing I mentioned to Holmes, "I was thinking about your visitor from Eureka Springs and her interest in music and how remarkable it is that small insignificant details remain in the sub-conscious.

Holmes looked at me in a condescending manner.

I continued.

"We are about to embark on a trip to Liverpool in connection with the *Titanic* boat, and yet I recall that Miss Katherine is fond of the music of Gustav Mahler."

"Well?" inquired Holmes.

"Well, only that I noticed in yesterday's *Times* newspaper that there is to be a concert at the Royal Albert Hall of Arts and Sciences at Kensington. It will be given by the London Symphony Orchestra conducted by Hans Richter where the main work to be performed will be a

Symphony in D-major, by Gustav Mahler, in fact his first Symphony.

"And?" said Holmes.

"And, that ironically, Mahler calls this Symphony the *'Titan'*, as in *'Titanic'*! The reason the article in *The Times* caught my attention was because, as your client said, there is some dispute as to the authenticity of this Symphony by Mahler. It has been claimed, in some quarters in Vienna, that the work is largely based on a symphony in E-major composed by a student named Hans Rott who attended the Vienna Conservatory of Music and was a pupil alongside Mahler."

"In that case Watson we really must avail ourselves of witnessing a performance of this *'Titan'* Symphony which has the distinction of having two creators!"

"Good. I shall purchase tickets for the concert."

By now we had donned our coats and mufflers and I clutching my *portmanteau* and Holmes his gladstone bag, we ventured out into the fog. This time we were *en-route* to Baker Street Metropolitan Station to travel by the underground railway to the Gower Street Metropolitan Station.* After an uneventful ride, we walked through Thomas Hardwick's monumental *Propylaeum*, in the form of a Doric Arch, and into the London & North Western Railway's Euston Square Railway Station. We entered the great terminus from High Seymour Street, located on the eastern side of the station; in order to gain the Liverpool bound express train.

We arrived on time and at the right terminus, thanks to Bradshaw's Railway Guide. Excellent as the guide is, it could not inform us from which platform the express train would leave. In order to ascertain this fact, we approached a railway servant upon the platform, dressed in his velveteen uniform with red piping. The railway

Doric Arch – Propylaeum, Euston

employé listened politely and attentively to our inquiry. He then promptly informed us, in an indifferent manner, that, due to a train accident that had occurred earlier that day, on the London & North Western Railway lines north of London, caused by the fog, all train services had been diverted from this station. He then turned on his heels and walked off smartly down the platform.

The result of this was that we had to make our way to Waterloo Station and thence board a train to Reading, where we would be able to catch a train going north to Liverpool.

Whilst we waited on the deserted platform and in order to while away the time, I surveyed the plethora of advertisements pasted to the station platform walls. Ironically, the American Watch Company assured the reader that precision & accuracy are strengths upon which their time is built! Another poster declaring quite blatantly that 'Every Disease of the Eye Cured by Ede's Eye Liquid' appeared incongruous to my medical mind though testimonials were, I noted, available if so required! My feeling of security did increase somewhat in the knowledge that a Chatwood's Burglar & Fire Resistant Safe was available to me should I care to visit their establishment at 180 Cannon Street, EC4.

Eventually, a train did come into the station and after an inordinately long delay; it began to move slowly along the platform edge, heading west to Charing Cross Underground Station. A few minutes later, we steamed into Mark Lane Underground Station and again waited some time before moving on. Here again I found myself observing advertisement posters affixed to the platform walls. Do the railway companies, I thought, deliberately stop their trains in order to compel their passengers to have to read various and sundry advertisements? I had no option but to read one particularly glaring bill poster immediately in front of our train window extolling the rather dubious claims that Lamplough's Pyretic Saline:

'Is Pleasant & Cures Headaches, Sickness, Bilious & is Skin Affectionate.'

Despite my misgivings about their claims I felt that at the rate things were developing today I might well be in need of their medication and risk the consequences! By contrast though I was rather impressed with the reasonable premium rates offered by the Ocean Railway and General Traveller's Assurance Company in covering my possessions whilst on voyage.

Eventually we gained the Charing Cross Underground Station and emerged onto the Victoria Embankment, near the Obelisk looming up into the fog. We then

The Obelisk

climbed the steps up to the Hungerford railway and pedestrian bridge across the Thames that links Charing Cross to Waterloo. As we walked across the bridge, Holmes pointed through the steel lattice girders of its metal superstructure, to the barely visible platforms and railway tracks running alongside our pedestrian section of the bridge and said;

"That is where Cadogan West met his supreme moment in a railway carriage on those very railway tracks!"

"I recall the words used by Sir James Walter of constable Murcher's description of West's contorted body lying on the railway carriage floor and the look of agony upon his face. At the time it sent a chill through my spine as much as this damp fog off the river Thames below us is doing at this very instant!" I responded.

As we proceeded across the bridge it was as if we were

Charing Cross Railway Bridge

walking in the clouds. Apart from the metal work there was no other visible identifying or distinguishing terrestrial details to relate to.

We descended through the brick ramparts of the bridge, on the Surrey side, down to street level and again groped our way in the fog making our way along dimly lit roads. At last we found an entrance in the Westminster Bridge Road that gave access into Waterloo Station's southern section.

"According to Bradshaw's Railway Guide we need to get onto platform five for our train to Reading. We have only minutes to spare to get on board. Holmes you look is if you are about to have a simple faint, are you alright?"

"I shall come to directly, Watson."

"We really must explore your irrational fear and, dread of the figure, word or symbol representing 'five'- steady

Holmes, steady! Perhaps we ought to consult that eminent Viennese doctor, Sigmund Freud, who has achieved great acclaim and success in what he terms *psycho-analysis*. Here he claims he can identify and treat hysteria! There yet may well be hope even for you Holmes! It may also give us an understanding into your continuing reaction to losing that momentous but failed case, and the saga of the five orange pips that led to the death of your client."

We were by now in the deserted station and we made our way down a platform illuminated only by the dim blue light from coal tar gas globe lamps, above which could be seen a sign proclaiming it indeed to be platform five. Alongside this platform was a train, the coachwork of which was in a dark purple livery. I thought this odd, for I knew, with a betting certainty, that the livery colour of all London & South Western Railways trains operating out of Waterloo was not purple. Despite this uncertainty we climbed aboard the purple painted train shrouded in the swirling fog very early on that November morning - alone.

A sound of a whistle could be heard and with a sharp jolt and clanging, the train began moving along the platform, past coal tar gas globe lamps pouring out their weak blue light. Suddenly the lights ceased and the train cleared the platform. In so doing it plunged both of us into twilight and the dense fog blocked out any prospect of vision through our carriage window. As the train gathered more momentum it began swaying from side to side in a way that was at variance with the syncopated creaking of the train's timber built damp carriages. It continued its rolling and rocking motion and jumped as it clicked over the points on the railway lines below. By now the train's velocity was increasing and it started hurtling through the fog and glooms outside, as if seemingly beyond human control; for we had not seen any servant of the railway upon the platform, or indeed on board the locomotive.

We sat down and on the damp, black *damask* covered buttoned seats and tried to make ourselves comfortable.

"There is something not quite right about this train Watson. Do you realise we are the only passengers on it?"

"That can be explained easily, it is after all quite early in the morning."

"Well I am going to look for a bar where I can get whisky and a cigar."

"Rather," I cried, "I will come with you. I too could do with a large brandy and cigar, since I forwent break-fast."

Together we made our way through the various carriages and corridors, which led to the rear of the train. Both Holmes and I gradually became aware of a pungent smell that I, as a doctor, recognised, as the stench of decaying flesh.

"Do you notice Watson the dull muted colours and peculiar configuration of the carriages we have just walked through? It is as though they were built to carry heavy luggage alongside the passengers," remarked Holmes.

"Perhaps this is a new type of train where passengers are encouraged to keep their own luggage nearby, instead of having them placed in the guard's brake van."

"Plausible Watson, but somewhat I think, highly unlikely. The whole atmosphere on this train is subdued, I might even say that a certain defined solemnity pervades throughout. Look at the upholstery on the seats and curtains - black!"

I had not noticed those details before due to the poor light. Now that Holmes had pointed them out to me the black drapes looked vivid, especially set against the white, *opaque* windows of the carriages looking out into dense swirling mist as the train creaked and swayed its way through the fog's all-embracing white shrouds.

"We must be approaching the end of the train," said Holmes, "so I assume there is life and hopefully a bar beyond this carriage door."

Holmes tugged at the door but it refused to yield.

"Perhaps it is just a bit stiff due to the dampness; here, let me help you," I offered.

Holmes put his shoulder to the door. I was only able to lend partial support with my shoulder, weakened by a bullet striking the sub clavicle bone. This was the price I paid for being at the fateful battle of Maiwand during the second murderous Afghanistan campaign when serving with the Royal Berkshire Regiment. However, our joint effort resulted in our hearing a distinctive crack, as something gave way. In an instant the door flew open and we both fell though into the carriage with the splintered remnants of the timber door latch.

We found ourselves inside a carriage illuminated only by a dim, flickering, blue light emanating from a methane gas globe lamp that augmented the eerie gloom. Immediately a damp musty smell assailed our nostrils. By degrees, as my eyes became accustomed to the gloom, I noticed there was neither seating nor a bar. Instead, though I could hardly believe my eyes, piled high on top of each other, some elaborately polished in glistening varnish, others of a cheaper dull timber finish, were boxes of every shape and size. Amongst this array I became aware of someone staring at me intently from the depths of the gloomy carriage. Believing it to be the guard, I attempted to say something about our bursting into his carriage, but somehow no sound left my mouth as I then realised the boxes were coffins!

The person, with the bleached white distorted face,

continued to stare at me. The skin on his face was pulled tightly around his head, creating a shiny and greasy complexion. His facial muscles were in a state of extreme contraction complete with a fixed grin, reminiscent of *risus sardonicus,* around the mouth exposing his set of protruding rotted teeth of appalling condition. Directly below his face he wore a greyish shirt with a dark blue necktie beneath a dishevelled dark jacket, from which a single flower with yellow petals stuck out of one lapel.

By now my vision was adjusting to the subdued methane gaslight I began to wonder why the person, with a distorted face, that did not move, with whom I had attempted to talk, had not responded to our bursting into the carriage. I stared back at his face expecting a response. Then, suddenly, at that moment I felt as if my heart had stopped. I took a sharp intake of breath when I realised to my horror why no response could ever come from that person. It was not grinning at me, but in fact it was displaying clearly all the symptoms of *rigor mortis*! He was sitting halfway out of a coffin that had jolted from the top of the pile and crashed down on to the floor of the carriage breaking open the lid to reveal its lifeless content!

"Holmes, we are on the Necropolis Express!" I said, in hushed tones realising our predicament.

"I know Watson!"

"Holmes, let us leave this…this hearse carriage now!" I replied, only just able to force the words out of my dry mouth.

Even experience gained over the years serving in various military campaigns around our Empire, where death was all pervasive, could not have prepared me for this encounter on a funeral train, clanking and swaying its way through the shrouds of fog. With a creeping sensation coming over me I realised where this train was journeying towards on this dark November morning. Only one destination lay at the end of this railway. The train was now irreversibly thundering down the railway track at full speed, with its hearse carriages rocking and clanking to the remorseless sound of iron wheels pounding the steel track.

Even with my heart's action frozen, I knew this train's destination could only be the Brookwood Necropolis, that massive *City of the Dead*, where the largest cemetery in the world is constructed. Most people fear to go there; for contained within its high walls is the largest collection of Mausoleums on earth, in which are the interred the dead.

"My God Holmes what are we to do? I do not want to finish up in that place because I know my shattered constitution will not stand up to it."

A greater fear gripped my heart and panic began to envelop my soul.

"Steady Watson, steady, the dead cannot hurt us!"

Perhaps, but I detected the pitch of fear even in his cold voice. We started to retreat as far away as possible from that carriage of death. We made our way back along the train, complete with all its gaudy funereal paraphernalia that now had real meaning for us.

After an interminable time, the swaying motion and loud creaking noises of the carriages began to ease as the train started to slow down. It now glided eerily through the fog. A deeper sense of foreboding swept over me as the carriages started to jolt and career into each other as the train juddered to come to a stop. When it eventually did so, I flung the carriage door open into the fog whilst checking to see if there was a platform on to which we could step.

There was a platform that was illuminated only with the dim light from coal tar gas globe lamps. We made our way to a shape looming up before us in the fog that we took to be the station building. Looking up we realised that we had certainly arrived in the middle of the necropolis at Brookwood and indeed we were standing on the high platform of the station housing the Eastern Funereal Chapel, looking down on the expansive necropolis. From this platform we could only just make out the phäntasmagoric shapes and outlines of the various Mausoleums set in the hanging fog. I wanted very desperately to leave this place.

"I do not suppose there is a bar open here where we can avail ourselves of a drink?" Holmes offered, in an attempt to make light of our situation.

We searched around and on another platform we discovered a building that looked as if it might conceivably have a bar in it. The only door that seemed to lead anywhere was firmly locked, and given our recent experience on the train of forcing a door open, we were reluctant to push too hard against it.

"This is a bit of a mess Watson, thanks to your inability to read and understand Bradshaw's Railway Guide."

"I beg your pardon Holmes, what can you mean, my fault?" I asked.

"How do you propose to get us back on to a main line to Liverpool?"

"I hardly see that it is my fault Holmes," I replied, with some asperity to his criticism, "You may recall we were diverted from Euston to Waterloo as result of a railway accident due to poor visibility caused by the fog on the London & North Western Railway's line to Liverpool."

"Excuses, excuses!" muttered Holmes.

"Now look here Holmes," I began nervously, "they are not excuses and I do not give a damn for your..."

"Sssshh!" intoned Holmes, raising an index finger to his lips, "listen!"

Moments later I could hear, albeit faintly, the increasing noise of an oncoming train.

"We may be in luck with this train," said Holmes.

We both listened attentively to the distant sound. The increasing roar, of the approaching train, however, inferred it was not slowing down. This train may not be stopping after all I thought, abandoning all hope of escaping from the necropolis.

We then saw it. Bursting out of the fog, with a *crescendo* noise made by escaping steam, clanking iron rods, rattling chains and pounding wheels on the steel track, a huge metallic locomotive engine became visible. In so doing it forced out thick, acrid, black smoke from its funnel glistening with condensation. And, from every brass pipe, hissing fiercely with escaping steam, which blended with the fog, making it even denser, the locomotive, rushed by us, making the fog swirl into vortices.

Upon the engine footplate I could see, quite plainly, the gaunt expression on the locomotive engineer's face on whose livid features was reflected the red glare from the locomotive's firebox. The face of the engineer appeared to have a desperate and helpless look as he used his whole body frantically tugging and pulling at the various levers of the engine with a dread-filled manic intensity.

As the creaking carriages of the train swayed and hurtled by us in the fog, we could see what appeared to be the deathly white faces of people, all of whom seem to have the same countenance of fear, dread of an imminent impending doom. They looked as though they were in great torment, as they stared out helplessly from the carriage windows, which framed their grimacing faces. Then, bringing up the rear of the train was the guard's brake van. It roared by us with its wide doors fully opened but with no guard in sight. The train then disappeared, clanking and rocking from side to side as it raced back into the dense fog as quickly as it had appeared. Only that suspended solitary red lantern was seen gradually fading from sight into oblivion.

Both Holmes and I stood upon the platform in silence trying to make sense of our immediate experience. At length we looked at each other. Had we seen what we thought we had? A tingling sensation gripped my nerves as the realisation manifested itself into my mind of a presence directly behind us. We both instinctively turned around to be met by a vision that nearly froze my heart's action. For standing in front of us was the same deathly white face grimacing in torment as we had seen in the railway carriages that had just raced past us!

Holmes broke the silence with his condescending imperious manner when addressing this apparition.

"My good man, we are anxious to get to Reading railway station in order to intercept an express train to Liverpo…..."

The sound of Holmes' voice gradually trailed into silence as I observed the two figures in the fog gesticulating to one another in an effort to make the other understand. Despite Holmes' attempt to be confident I detected that he too was greatly perturbed. As I looked upon the apparition it gradually dawned upon me. He was an *employé*, dressed in a velveteen uniform bearing the insignia of the railway company for whom he worked, and, in fact, he was the stationmaster. But the face, I thought, surely I had seen it elsewhere? I concentrated on his gaunt features and the sudden horror of my predicament became all too obvious. The face of the stationmaster was that of the one reflected in the passing carriage windows of the train. There had been no passengers aboard the train only the reflection of the stationmaster as he stood behind us as the train passed us by in the fog. Holmes, of course had, realised this from the beginning. I had not!

"Pardon," said this stationmaster.

"My colleague here and I are anxious to board a train to Reading station so that we might intercept an express train to Liverpool."

"Really," replied the stationmaster, "might I see your train tickets?"

By this time I had regained all my mental faculties and recovered my courage sufficiently to be slightly put off by this railway servant's attitude to us. I produced our tickets with a great show of reluctance at the inconvenience at my being asked to do so.

After the stationmaster had examined our tickets at great length, he announced in solemn tones; "It is your intention to go to Reading with these tickets? I merely ask because they were issued at Euston Square Station for the express train service direct to Liverpool, in fact to Lime Street Station. I wonder therefore what you are doing at the Eastern Funereal Chapel Station at the Brookwood Necropolis at five minutes past five in the morning."

"Of course we intend to go to Reading with these tickets, what else could we do with them?" I answered pompously.

"Well," delivered the stationmaster, "these tickets were issued at Euston Square Station and are valid only upon the London & *North* Western Railway and not upon this railway line which is operated by the London & *South*

Western Railway. Should you wish to go to Reading you will have to wait for a parliamentary train. That departs from this platform at five minutes past nine this morning."

Holmes again wavered but continued to contain himself. I did not.

"But that is a wait of four hours," I continued, "and those parliamentary trains comprise nothing but 3rd Class carriages and are stocked with a similar class of work person. Where, I ask you, are we supposed to sit?" I demanded, waving our two tickets in the stationmaster's gaunt face.

"On the stout elm benches, provided thoughtfully, by the railway company, or if you so chose, you may wish to stand up," advised the railway flunky.

"How dare you, how dare you be confident with me! Do you know whom you are addressing? Does the name Sherlock Holmes mean nothing to you?"

"No it does not mean anything to me. Should it? However, more importantly, I might ask, why am I addressing two individuals upon the railway's property," interrupted the stationmaster, "both of whom do not have a valid ticket to travel upon the railway and whose presence here is somewhat suspicious. I should also add, you are liable for a fine, for failure to show on demand, valid tickets to travel."

"Well open up the ticket office and we shall prevail upon you to issue the appropriate 1st Class tickets to Reading." I said, thinking this would deliver the *coup de grâce* to this obstreperous and truculent imbecile, dressed in the cheap velveteen uniform with red piping of a railway servant.

The stationmaster's response to my demand was unexpected. He began to move slowly along the platform allowing the fog to enshroud him gradually. As he did so, he announced that no 1st Class trains ever left the Eastern Funereal Chapel Station at this Brookwood Necropolis. And, that the only trains to leave from here were the 3rd Class parliamentary trains. With that *Parthian* shot, his vague form disappeared entirely out of sight into the enveloping folds of the fog.

"Watson, I have been giving some thought to the predicament in which you have caused us to find ourselves."

I did not respond to his thoughtless jibe.

"We entered Waterloo Station from the Westminster Bridge Road and not from the York Road. In so doing we entered the station by the wrong entrance due to the fog, and came into the Necropolis Railway mortuary building! Your misgivings about the livery on the train carriages on that platform were well founded. We were on the necropolis platform away from the main station and we boarded the necropolis train complete with its hearse carriages. You now, of course, know Watson where we are and the reason for our being here at Brookwood necropolis!"

"Yes I have a vague recollection of reading somewhere that London was in urgent need of more cemeteries since Highgate and Kensal Green cemeteries are filled to capacity."

"Yes, Brookwood is built to be the largest necropolis in the world to receive the dead from the largest Metropolis on earth and brought here on the trains of the Necropolis Railway which comprised hearse carriages...!"

Holmes suddenly stopped and pointed with his cane towards the vast expanse of the necropolis including the ghostly shapes of the massive Mausoleums just visible in the fog.

Necropolis Railway Mortuary Building

"Do you see that Watson?"

"What?" I said, peering into the distance, trying to survey the necropolis from the high elevation of the railway platform upon which we were standing. Then imperceptibly I began to make out a flickering red light emanating from one of the larger Mausoleums in the distance.

"There is something singular here!" said Holmes, as he began to walk quickly towards the ramp that led down from the platform to the grounds of the necropolis, with its various funereal structures.

"Holmes! Where are you going, you cannot just enter the necropolis especially at this ungodly hour of the morning?" I asked, with trepidation clearly in my voice betraying the deep sense of foreboding enveloping my being.

By now Holmes had gained the ramp and stopped. I caught up with him and we looked at each other in earnest.

"Well, I suppose we cannot stand around on this platform like lost souls; so let us take a look and see for ourselves, what that red light is all about!" I ventured, with courage of a type unfamiliar to me.

Together we took deep breaths and, possessing our souls, descended down the ramp into the necropolis, to investigate the source of the mysterious red light.

* Now Euston Square Metropolitan Station.

Chapter 9

The Search Amongst the Mausoleums

In our quest to get to the Herculaneum Docks at Liverpool in order to inspect the *Titanic* or *Olympic* boats, we had inadvertently got onto the wrong train at Waterloo Railway Station, due to losing our way in the fog We now found ourselves in the Brookwood Necropolis in the early hours of the morning. Holmes had observed a flickering red light in the depths of the cemetery, and to which we now made our way to investigate.

We made our way down the broad ramp that led to the beginning of several avenues of gravel by which the necropolis was divided. The shallow incline of the ramp showed me that this was where the coffins from the trains entered the necropolis.

The first funereal structure we came across, was an extended columbarium in the form of a colonnade in the ancient Egyptian style complete with columns supporting splayed-out lotus leaf shaped capitals. The stone wall of the colonnade had angled door openings cut into it, creating burial vaults located in the dark recesses of the columbarium's open tombs with their exposed stone sarcophagus. There were several impressive tombs structures located nearby and in one such edifice we saw a faint dull yellow glow emanating from deep with the interior of the Mausoleum, the massive size of which dominated us even though it was partially shrouded in the fog.

Some mortuary temples were covered with elaborate stone symbols of funereal paraphernalia including martial helmets set upon shields or urns. Others symbols were represented in stone including carvings of shoulders and heads of persons, but with their faces hidden from view, by the over-hanging folds falling from a veil. In to these stone walls were carved or fixed, masonry funereal decoration and stone symbols, representing concepts as eternity, and bereavement and its attendant loss. On some of the more elaborate Mausoleums, the symbol of the ancient Egyptian deity, *Nephthys*, with outstretched wings, was emblazoned in the stone fronted vault, guarding the entrance to the Mausoleum.

Walking down one particular avenue of temples, we passed several ornate sealed tombs the size of houses. Some were of Gothic design, most though were of the classical style with colonnades of masculine Doric columns. Interspersed among the columns were monstrously large stone urns set upon pedestals, some of which were draped in black cloth indicating that corpses had been recently interred within them. Nearby fluted columns decorated with Corinthian capitals supported the clerestories of some of the temples. One Mausoleum surrounded by an iron fence resembled nothing more than a series of upright columns and pilasters positioned to receive a roof, but here, no roof had been constructed. For whatever reason, clearly the builders had abandoned this forlorn monument to house the dead. The only beneficiary of this half-built Mausoleum was the pervasive creeping ivy.

Next to this tomb, surmounting seven steps was another structure in the form of an ancient Greek temple complete with four walls creating a square structure. The upper sections of the walls formed a gorge and hollow splayed curved architrave, and immediately above rested a protruding cornice, forming the base of a pitched roof and fronted by a stone-framed triangular pediment. Set into this recessed pediment was a curious emblem, the origin of which appeared to be ancient Egyptian. The motif was in the form of a bronze sculpture, about four feet in height and five feet in width, of an eagle or other bird of prey, with outstretched wings. In this avian sculpture, the bird was holding in its claws the ancient Egyptian symbols of death and eternity. The walls of this Mausoleum were themselves impressed with peculiar design details, some were clearly Greek in style others were ancient Egyptian in origin. Set into the front elevation of the tomb, beneath a prominent architrave, was a massive iron door flanked on either side by ornate metal panels into, which were set detailed sculptural relief. Immediately above these impressive sculptured panels were further recessed apertures with grills in front of them forming ventilation openings!

Another Mausoleum nearby was constructed in the form of an elaborate cruciform structure, comprising four elevations, each having a colonnade of fluted columns. These formed an impressive portico capped by Ionic capitals beneath an undecorated architrave supporting the pediment creating an impressive entablature. At the centre of the edifice was a substantial square plinth that rose up and supported an octagonal rotunda with window reveals surrounded by a colonnade of eight columns. Above this rotunda was yet another octagonal structure complete with architrave that supported a dome. Into the walls of this upper section of the tower, were deep set windows, from one of which a solitary faint blue light was seen to glow.

Continuing down the damp avenue we noticed one

Greek styled temple that comprised nothing more than a stepped crepidoma that led up to a two-foot high plinth. On this platform, surrounded by twelve columns supporting an entablature with pediment roof and corner acroterions, existed nothing! The floor of the temple plinth was empty but showed signs that a sarcophagus had at one time been positioned there. I found the ornate, but empty temple disturbing, to the extent that I leaned against a nearby iron railing to gather my strength. After a few moments I chanced to look behind me and became aware that the iron railings I was leaning against was nothing more than rickety fence at the top of a steep flight of steps leading down into the ground! Not for the first time this day had my heart leapt into my throat.

The ramp made up of about forty stone steps descended straight down into the ground to a depth of twenty feet or so. Peering down into the void, partially obscured by the swirling fog, I became aware that at the end of the steps was a metal grill door, leading into the foundations of rough-hewn stone monumental tomb. This structure continued up to ground level and upon it, had been constructed a massive sarcophagus made of granite. Entry into this granite sarcophagus, I reasoned, was through the metal door at the base of the steps leading into the foundations of the tomb and then by an internal staircase up into the sarcophagus. The detail designs carved into this granite block were harsh as they were clear and meant to indicate impregnability. I noticed other such similar subterranean Mausoleum structures, including one with a huge eight foot in height stone urn, set on top of its limestone roof, still wrapped in ragged black clothe, made more vivid by the surrounding white fog.

Farther down the avenue our attention was arrested by the sight, just visible in the fog, of a Mausoleum of distinct sinister aspect. It was built in style of an ancient Egyptian kiosk, with four solid walls slanting inwards at the top and a colonnade of four columns addressing the avenue, in which Holmes and I were standing. Behind those columns, of which the inner two were broad and tapered to a capital in the style of splayed leaves of a papyrus plant, but in contrast the two adjacent outer columns were square and undecorated. The external walls and columns of the tomb supported a monstrously overhanging curved Egyptian architrave, in the form of a hollow and roll that supported the stone slab roof. On the front *façade* to this vault, forming a portico, immediately behind the columns, was a door architrave in the shape of a metal Masonic winged image above the recessed doorframe cut into the wall of the tomb into which two large burnished copper doors had been positioned. However, apparent even to us, were signs that the copper doors had been forced, because they were both hanging off their hinges!

Immediately opposite that Mausoleum, was another structure that in comparison, appeared modest. It was again in the ancient Egyptian style and built upon two high steps forming the plinth. Four walls slanting inward made up the structure that was capped with a low six foot high pyramid. Each of the walls were built of blue granite slabs upon which were intricate raised patterns repeating the raised door frame outline and symbols that would make sense to the initiated, but neither to Holmes or me. The door opening into the vault was wide at the base and narrowed toward the top as though reflecting the overall pyramid concept behind the design of this blue Mausoleum. I noticed that the door opening had been filled in with *ferro-concrete* and sealed with just visible adamantine chains for added strength, to prevent any person gaining access into this chamber housing the sarcophagus.

Other Mausoleums were of indeterminable architecture with no discernible style. They merely showed that the builder had simply placed large masonry blocks one upon each other in order to create a massive monolithic edifice of stone, no doubt so constructed in order to repel the inquisitive, allowing the interred to repose in undisturbed peace. Or perhaps to contain within the sealed stone structure something that must not be allowed into the necropolis.

The more *sombre* of the sealed Mausoleums were those large foreboding edifices reflecting an ancient Egyptian style of architecture. In so doing their designs, based on those large ancient structures, deployed huge megalithic blocks of limestone to create gigantic monumental mortuary temples, Mausoleums, to house several sarcophagus containing recent corpses. Most of these elaborate mausoleums had only a single entrance to the inner tomb, which was either bricked up for eternity or, was guarded by huge bronze doors. This megalithic monumental style of Mausoleum construction was the most prevalent at the Brookwood Necropolis, containing within its precinct, guarded by high walls, a vast city of the dead. Its long avenues were formed not of buildings wherein the living dwelt but of stone mortuary temples, burial vaults and Mausoleums housing the dead.

Such were the impressive and fantastic temple structures in this massive necropolis that one almost expected to witness a ghostly procession of the gods into Valhalla. We however, did walk down several avenues of Mausoleums including one that was in the process of being constructed. We could see its massive internal stone walls partially built, but now showing clearly the outline of the crypt that would eventually receive the sarcophagus and adjacent mortuary chapels connected by small openings in the walls. The complex designs of these burial vaults for the dead were readily apparent with its various rooms and doors connecting one vault to another chamber.

A singular fact emerged as we walked through this land of the dead. Quite a number of the larger more extravagant of the Mausoleums had the appearance of having been at some stage set on fire! The walls of each temple and burial vault had been scorched and blackened by intense flame. Some structures had partially collapsed as a result of the blaze and in so doing had exposed the interiors of various tombs revealing their sarcophagus. On other Mausoleums a stone bust of a head, an urn or other decorative masonry features had cracked or disintegrated into ruin due to the intense heat of a fire.

Some of the stone ornamentation on several tombs had been struck with heavy objects. On other mortuary temples the columbarium had been compromised and a few of the columns had been toppled, leaving the masonry dangerously unsupported, as though it were floating in mid air.

Why had these monuments to the dead been so attacked, I asked myself? Was it because the persons, in whose memory they had been erected, had behaved badly during their lives to other people?

Other Mausoleums showed that they had been built in haste with little regard for the foundations upon which the edifice had been constructed. Some were in the final throes of chronic subsidence as indicated by the abnormal acute angles their structures leaned at and *grotesquely* out of true. Their fate was now being determined by nature, rather than concerned relatives, who had abandoned their duty to this tomb unable or unwilling to maintain it as a mortuary temple.

On one such Mausoleum, the main load bearing wall had failed catastrophically, due to subsidence and had consequently collapsed taking the stone roof with it into the crypt and onto the sarcophagus, smashing open the granite tomb revealing its shrouded content. The temple was now a pile of jagged stone blocks sticking out in all directions, resembling nothing more than a collapsed ruin partially covered in green ivy now in the process of consuming this abandoned and wrecked temple to the dead.

Another curious feature on some of the more ornate Mausoleums were elaborate *friezes* carved into the masonry walls of the tombs depicting in stone relief a *cortège* as it made its funereal progress to a Mausoleum. The characters depicted in the *friezes* bore a similarity in dress to those of ancient Imperial Roman aristocrats represented on their original mausoleums that lined the Appian Way into ancient Rome.

One isolated, but impressive Mausoleum, was built on a high plinth accessible only by a series of steps. It was raised high into the fog and was constructed of huge masonry block of limestone. It had a gaunt minatory look made more evident by the folds of fog by which it was surrounded allowing only parts of the building to come into view only then to disappear as quickly. I counted fourteen steps leading from the sodden ground that cut into the top of the crepidoma supporting the plinth upon which the mausoleum was built. To each of the four corners of the elevated plinth was erected an obelisk of deep red granite. The architecture of this funereal temple was designed to be impressive. The stone blocks were rough hewn and coarse as if the builder had elected to create size, at the expense of fine detailing and elaborate ornamentation, to express the power of the interred, in whose memory the Mausoleum had been caused to be erected.

The main entrance was framed by two huge blocks of limestone eighteen feet in height that were positioned either side of a single door opening and were inclined at a slant to each other forming a trapezoid entrance. This monumental entrance was constructed in the style of the ancient Egyptians, when erecting the monolithic stone mortuary temple structures, to entomb their dead Pharaohs. The two inclined square stone columns, framed two recessed bronze doors, which were studded with raised bolt heads, conferring on the doors' structure, the impression of massive strength and impregnability, in order to keep the contents intact and to deter the inquisitive.

The central part of the Mausoleum, just visible in the yellow fog, had all the appearance of a fortress. The emphasis was on the formation, in stone blocks that created the *piano-nobile* of the first tier of the edifice. Upon this tier was supported a stone parapet that continued around the mortuary temple. Recessed behind this low parapet wall and forming a central structure to the temple was another fantastic edifice in keeping with the overall general ancient Egyptian design. Rising up into the fog with its apex was an enormous pyramid at least thirty-five feet in height. Into the slanting walls of this giant pyramid structure were small round windows from which a dull white light emanated.

Both Holmes and I felt somewhat disturbed in the presence of this tomb and we therefore continued walking in our quest to locate the building from whence the red light originated. We did not have far to walk. In front of us, dominating the junction of two avenues was a mortuary temple of quite remarkable aspect. From our position but due to the all pervasive fog we could only just discern the lower part of the temple built on what appeared to be a massive plinth of white granite about ten feet in height. To the right of the plinth, were several steps, about seven feet wide, which ascended from the ground giving access into the structure. As we approached the mortuary temple, various building details came into vision, showing it to be a huge monolithic Mausoleum, of indeterminable architecture but resembling, if anything, ancient Egyptian on account of the low pyramid at the very top dominating the building.

The structure built upon the plinth was at least fifty feet in height and was as massive as it was brutal in its visual impact. The temple appeared to have been constructed on a cruciform shape with huge slabs of granite forming vertical piers framing elongated openings into the walls of the tomb. On the front *façade* of the tomb at the top of the steps leading up to it were two massive rusting cast iron doors eighteen feet in height studded with raised bolt heads imparting strength and impregnability. However, it was not the immediate aspect of the temple that caught our attention, nor the low angled pyramid. Rather, it was the solemn minatory looking tower rising from the centre of the building, upon which, the pyramid was constructed. Within the walls of this tower were set deep elongated narrow openings from which a flame light glowed as though the interior of the tomb was on fire! This was the source of the flickering dull red light that we had observed, from the railway platform, of the Eastern Funereal Chapel Station.

Whilst we both stood there transfixed by this strange light I glanced at my gold Hunter to ascertain the time. I did so because it seemed to me that time had stopped in this place, a place of fascination where the pervasive fog was heavy with the sensation of musty dankness intermingled with concepts of death with eternity. As I pondered thus, Holmes caught my elbow and motioning me to be silent pointed with his cane down an avenue of cypress trees in between which were more Mausoleums. Alas we were not alone in this necropolis for we could hear all around us faint footfalls crunching on the damp gravel with which the avenues were covered. Occasionally we saw fleeting figures in the fog crossing the avenues in between the monumental buildings that formed other tomb structures. We also saw other figures making their way amongst the fog-shrouded structures.

Due to the fog we could not see clearly but we could hear the distinctive sound of walking on the damp gravel pathways. Eventually, we did see figures just discernible in the fog. They appeared to be walking in procession. All were shrouded in white cloth some with hoods and others had their heads covered with veils. All had their heads bowed, as in though solemn thought. From a distance a sound began to permeate our ears. It was the sound of their chanting in syncopation to their footfalls on the gravel pathway. By degrees we became aware of the fact that the procession was coordinated. As they gained upon us it became clear that in the midst of the group a long horizontal shape was being carried. On approaching us, their forms became more defined indicating that it was clearly a coffin they were carrying, amongst themselves, at shoulder height to its final resting place. As the mourners came nearer the chanting became louder as did their footfalls crunching on the gravel pathway, and it became apparent this procession was in fact a *cortège*. Eventually when they were only a few feet away from us, I could make out that the group consisted of several mourners, some in veils others in hoods covering their bowed heads. I believe the persons in hoods were monks, but what were they doing in this fog shrouded Brookwood Necropolis so early in the morning?

Suddenly the *cortège* stopped just a few feet beyond us. Two of the hooded mourners left the funeral procession and climbed the steps leading up to the rusting cast iron doors of the Mausoleum surmounted with the low-angled pyramid. Eventually they reached the huge iron doors that guarded the inner sanctum of the tomb. After some time spent in releasing the door locking mechanism they proceeded to push against the heavy doors gradually creating an opening into the interior from which now a deep red glow emanated. It was from this interior that we had observed earlier the light of the flame coming through the narrow openings cut into the walls of the tower. The origin of the flame from what I could see appeared to be in the form of a bed of flames ready to receive an object. I then realised the tomb was in the process of being prepared!

Without a signal being given, the mourners began to ascend the steps of the Mausoleum bearing their coffin. Eventually as the rear of the *cortège* made its way into the Mausoleum, the massive iron doors slammed shut causing a chill to race down my spine.

That act of the doors closing dampened the sound of the chanting. What did however make my blood turn cold, was the very distinctive, if repressed, sounds of muffled screams! Both Holmes and I instinctively began to walk away from this functioning crematorium and active Mausoleum. As we increased our pace along the avenue, I chanced to look back at the tomb and the tower surmounted by its gigantic low pyramid rising up into the fog. This time however, the dull glow of the flame we had noticed before through the narrow openings in the

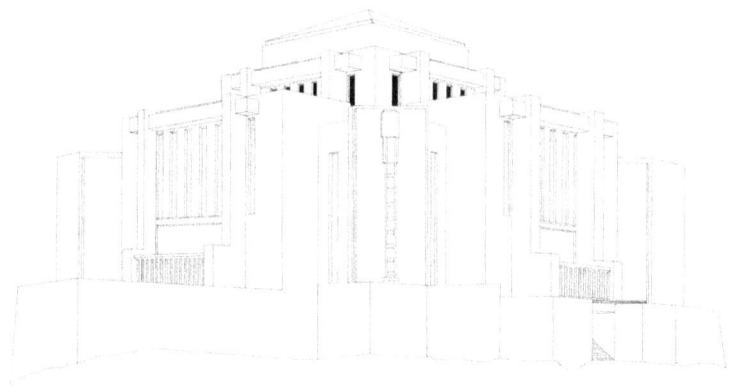

Egyptian Mausoleum

walls of the tower now burned with an intensity of bright red. This fact alone told me the contents of that funereal temple, dead or alive, were now being consumed in an intense conflagration within the very depths of that white granite ancient Egyptian styled Mausoleum. Was this a mass suicide we had witnessed by the mourners unable to continue living after life had ceased in the corpse they had carried to its and their immolation? They were not chanting their grief at losing someone to eternity, but rather their own imminent departure from this world. I then felt dryness in my throat that I never wish to experience again.

However, Holmes's at that moment observed something else and in so doing arrested my attention.

"Have you noticed anything singular about this monumental tomb?"

"Good God Holmes what structure is not odd here? All the tombs in this place are unusual." I said, gazing sideways with my moist eyes at the Egyptian Mausoleum, still moved by the experience.

Holmes pointed with his cane to a particularly lavish

Mausoleum built with massive blocks of polished green granite. I strained to view the tomb partly shrouded in the fog that still lay around the necropolis. As I walked towards the structure it became apparent upon closer examination that an opening in the Mausoleum's bricked up entrance had been forced. Peering inside, I looked uncertain of what to expect, but then suddenly as my eyes became accustomed to the darkness within I recoiled back in shock expelling air from my mouth in the process. Deep in the recesses of the tomb perhaps thirty or more feet away was a distinctive dull blue light glowing adjacent to a crouching veiled figure. I could not control my emotional reaction as a heat sensation went through my brain and more tears filled my eyes in realising, was this the light, the light by which a solitary mourner keeps an eternal vigil? I knew this place would bring out my worst fears and make me confront that which I had no strength left to do so. I felt so weak and vulnerable that I wanted to go home and pray for salvation from my misery.

By now we were becoming distraught due to our experiences in the necropolis that comprised more Mausoleums each one more fantastical and disturbing than the one before it. We both increased our pace in order to leave immediately this place of death.

We took a wrong turning and it became apparent to us that we were now lost in the fog in the largest Necropolis on earth! This is what I feared when we first stepped foot into this place. My worst fears were now about to be released upon my weakened constitution and witnessing that ritual at the Egyptian Mausoleum had removed from my soul any reserves of strength that I may have had.

I did not have long to wait for the inevitable to happen, as our progress was interrupted abruptly. Rising up into

the fog, that for   some reason now felt even danker, was
a structure I could not quite believe capable of being
built. It occupied a raised island site from   which   several avenues radiated out into the necropolis. Immediately
in front of us set in isolation and unreachable, was a huge
Mausoleum   built in the ancient classical style and
constructed of massive limestone blocks set upon each
other to form a sealed tomb. The Mausoleum comprised
four massive walls forming a square structure of at least
twenty feet in height on top of which were a series of
stepped backed terraces culminating in a recessed tower
rising a further fifteen feet. Into this inner tower *façade*,
at the top of a series of steps, was an elongated and dark
recessed door aperture from which no light emanated,
making the Mausoleum as menacing as it was monolithic.

I stood there with Holmes petrified and transfixed by
this monumental edifice and the feeling of stillness it
radiated from the depths of its tomb. As my eyes became
accustomed to the fog surrounding it I also noticed yet
another structure rising even further into the fog but
sufficiently obscured as to make ascertaining its structural
details difficult. Then, my heart nearly failed, as I became
aware of what this tower was supporting. As the fog
swirled around the tower it caused vortices, making the
fog thin out in places, and in so doing created a brief
vision that I observed with my eyes wide open. The vista
came into my sight, and then as quickly, disappeared from
view the enshrouding fog reclaimed the structure, again
making it invisible. I attempted to alert Holmes, but
words failed to leave my dry mouth. Then, again, then
fog receded and coming back into vision, was a gigantic
monumental sculpture, in bronze at least forty-five feet
or so in height, of four interlocking wings, creating a
cross at its base.

What was this Mausoleum, the limestone structure of which had metamorphosized into an upper elaborate and ornate bronze sculpture of wings, were they a symbolic profile of the Wings of Eternity? That the wings were supported on four connected piers creating a cruciform added yet more significance to the whole structure and its sculpture. Consistent with the orthodox concept of a Mausoleum it comprised a *sombre* fortress-like limestone structure to protect the sarcophagus within and a recessed door aperture. The exuberant monument of wings might easily be interpreted as addressing eternity and the symbolic preparation of the journey of flight to the hereinafter. I continued to stare at the upper section to this remarkable structure, focusing on the layout of the limestone blocks, forming the structure thrown high into the fog-laden sky, in the absence of which, it would no doubt dominates the locality. I also realised that we now at the very centre of the necropolis and felt myself begin to panic in despair, made even more so by Holmes' subdued re-action to our vision.

"Watson, come away," said Holmes, "we should not intrude upon the dead. Let us leave them to their existence in whatever state of grace or grief, with eventual splendid release."

I consented willingly and by a series of deductions Holmes worked out that any avenue would inevitably lead us to the perimeter of the Necropolis.

"The question for us here Watson, is which avenue?" he said, pointing with his cane to the beginnings of several avenues ranged around the Mausoleum.

"Good God Holmes! You are not suggesting we climb over that ten foot high perimeter wall to escape this place?"

"No I am not, but merely intimating that we will be at the perimeter and away from the centre of this necropolis.

Wings of Eternity

"Perhaps if we revert to the red light we witnessed on that dreadful Egyptian tomb, it might suggest the way we came and thus our retreat back?" I offered, and regretted the suggestion the moment I uttered it for that would mean retracing our steps past that tomb, which I certainly had no wish to do.

"Watson, we can still see that faint red glow from the functioning Mausoleum and since I remembered we turned left into the avenue in which it is constructed and by deductive reasoning our route back to the Eastern Funereal Chapel Station should be along this avenue."

"I hope to God Holmes, you are correct because I am running out of strength and uncertain whether my nerves can stand any more of these sensations."

The avenue we elected to walk down did not take us anywhere near our objective. Instead, it threaded its way through the necropolis and past even more garish, and in some cases *grotesque,* mortuary temples to the dead. Though not, I was grateful to note, past anything like that Egyptian Mausoleum or the mortuary temple holding up those Wings of Eternity.

Eventually we managed to make our way back to the Eastern Funereal Chapel Station along similar dank avenues of gloomy structures to the dead. What drives men in their vainglory to construct these massive temples to their death? Did they feel at their supreme moment that they had failed in life and needed desperately another opportunity to succeed in the hereinafter? Can it be they believed this is where immortality must now exist? To forever have presence in this huge necropolis in the company of dead souls. Can there be no release, no repose and no rest? As the ancient Egyptians did we too it seems are still eager to build extravagant cities to the dead.

I then remembered reading a learned treatise,* where the author reasons that we as a society today are more overt in our expression of funereal concepts confirmed in the construction of elaborate mausoleum as here in Brookwood. This rationale, he went on to propound, was based partly on the reaction to a perceived weakening of religious authority and its inability to guarantee peaceful repose after death that compels us to seek consolation in fantasy concepts. Complete with crocheted towers, pinnacles, turrets and spires neo-Gothic architecture is now the natural choice in expressing fantasy to fulfil this consoling need and is the preferred style of architecture for important buildings, including the St. Pancras Hotel in London.

The concept that the Mausoleum is a peaceful, isolated sombre stone build edifice complete with crypt housing the dead focusing on the structure where it seems time has ceased to have any effect save only for the weathering of the exterior stonework has become difficult for me to accept. Why do we go to great lengths to construct and embellish our mortuary temples? The structure assumes a significance of the symbols of immortality, powerful, impregnable, indestructible and ideal for perpetuating the memory of the contents therein not their preservation. Or can it be simply the arrogance of man that he should build to immortalise himself by the construction of such gigantic Mausoleums against God? I conjectured, knowing that no answer could, or should come forward.

* A book called 'Visions of Architecture'

Chapter 10

The Parliamentary Train

We arrived back at the Eastern Funereal Chapel Station, but remained subdued and huddled in a doorway waiting for our train to Reading. Our experiences of walking around the Brookwood Necropolis had disturbed us profoundly. Eventually, however we did climb on board a parliamentary train, not at five minutes past nine o'clock but at thirty and seventeen minutes past nine o'clock. From the very beginning I knew boarding this train to be a mistake of monumental proportions. By now the damp had got into the aching wound in my right arm, a legacy of an injury received at the fateful battle of Luxor during the first Egyptian Campaign, when I was attached to the Royal Mallows Regiment. In addition, mental torment and hunger were also taking their toll upon my weakened constitution.

Holmes as ever, seemed impervious to his surroundings, including that of sitting in a parliamentary train. Indeed he appeared to relish the situation of being so close to his fellow travellers from the lower orders. No doubt it gave him inspiration for his various disguises when he would go on his forays into the less fashionable and darker regions of the Metropolis.

Sitting on the wooden bench opposite me, was an individual of such dubious disposition that I feared to close my weary eyes in rest should he in some way take advantage of my sleeping person. I lowered my head but continued to view him through the top of my eyes.

I decided to apply Holmes' scientific methods. By these methods he claims to be able, by deductive analysis, reasoning and careful attention to detail, to discern the occupation and habits of a stranger. The person opposite would make a good candidate and I therefore indulged in some profound deductive analysis of my own.

That he was certainly of working class stock was obvious, because he was travelling in a 3rd Class carriage of a parliamentary train. Such trains, made up of 3rd Class carriages, with cheap fares, were deliberately established by an over-zealous Parliament, eager for votes, to allow the teeming masses, travel around the realm, unescorted; a dangerous adventure. My subject's dress was remarkable in that it resembled a loose collection of worn material in need of urgent repair to avoid being relegated to the status of rag. He wore heavy boots, the kinds of which are prefaced with the word 'pit'. His trousers were baggy and soiled and supported only by a length of twine around his waist, which, I observed, he made no effort to conceal. His jacket, of the Norfolk pea type, was no cleaner and fared even less than his trousers save that it was of a tighter fit. The shirt on his back was of grubby aspect and he wore no completing necktie!

This general assemblage of dirty clothes and ill-fitting attire was surmounted by a head the face of which was pocked-marked and of sallow complexion. The hair on his head though thick was greasy and unkempt. I looked at his hands and found to my surprise not only were they clean, but they showed no signs of rough or manual labour. I wondered what he could be. A 'navigator' perhaps, after all one does see them in ever increasing numbers these days, employed as they are in constructing dams, railways and bridges, but, surely not with those hands? I doubt they had ever handled anything harsher than a bar of soap. Probably an overseer of 'navigators' I conjectured with confidence and a betting certainty.

Looking around me, I noticed that others in the carriage were too of the lower orders. Some were even smoking tobacco. In so doing, their addiction to cheap leaf added to the general unpleasantness of the thick atmosphere and smells that had developed since we had climbed into the carriage. The noise was deafening, and their children squabbled, contributing to the overall disagreeable cacophony that was all pervasive in the parliamentary carriage.

Whilst I was congratulating myself on my incisive ability to probe the inner secrets of my study opposite, I was aghast to watch him reach into his inside jacket pocket and produce a gold-framed *pince-nez*. Having very methodically positioned them on the bridge of his nose, he raised his head and looked straight ahead, into the middle distance, as it were. A few moments later he again reached into his jacket and retrieved a pocket book. At first I assumed it to be a *'Penny Dreadful'**, but on the frontispiece I could read quite clearly the title proclaiming;

THE NEW ANNOTATED
COLLECTED WORKS
et al &c. of
MR. ALFRED TENNYSON - POET'

The book then fell open, revealing a page on the top of which was a poem entitled *'The Deserted House'*. I could scarcely believe my eyes. Why would this fellow have in his possession such a book on a parliamentary train? The fellow opposite me appeared to relish the opportunity to travel and displayed all the appearance of being thoroughly pleased with himself. I settled back and tried to rest from my mental exertion.

A general commotion erupted, which startled me into full consciousness and I realised we were drawing into Reading station. At long last, I thought, we could now catch our express train to Liverpool and quit the unpleasant conditions prevailing on this 3rd Class parliamentary train.

On alighting from the train, I immediately approached a railway servant upon the platform.

"My man," I said, "would you be so kind as to direct us to the correct platform from which the Liverpool express departs?"

"The Liverpool express departs from platform five."

I looked at Homes, who showed symptoms of an imminent faint.

"Are you all right Holmes, you look a little *piqued*?"

"It will pass Watson, it will pass."

"At what time does the express leave?" I continued to the railway servant, dressed in his velveteen uniform with red piping to the edges of his jacket.

"At twelve and thirty-five minutes past the hour," he replied, with great civility.

I looked at my gold Hunter to confirm my suspicions of a wait of one hour and forty minutes!

We stood on the platform exasperated. Holmes broke the silence. "Did you notice who was sitting opposite you on that parliamentary train from which we have just alighted?"

Somewhat astounded by this question I replied. "How could I possibly know a person sitting on a parliamentary train! However, as it happens, clearly whilst not knowing him, I had concluded, applying deductive reasoning, that he was a 'navigator' involved in the construction of major works of engineering!"

"Interesting," remarked Holmes "you did not recognise him as the acclaimed poet Alfred Tennyson!" **

Irritated by this revelation by Holmes I stared out across a series of platforms, and thought that the station buildings and their roofs resembled a part of the Tuilleries Palace*** that I had visited when touring Paris. I remembered at that palace too, fish-scale slate tiles covered the large curved roofs that were also crowned with ornate metal fencing. Both combined to create a decoration in the French chateau style somewhat excessive for a railway station, but nonetheless, making for one of unexpected beauty. I then decided to utilise my waiting time more constructively and responsibly.

"Look here Holmes, I am going for a walk to see what odds I can get for two horses, *Iris*, owned by the Duke of Balmoral, and *Isonomy* which I know are running in a local race today at Ascot. I may be some time but I shall return!"

With only minutes to spare I rejoined Holmes on the

Slough Railway Station

platform. Perhaps it was the wistful smile playing on my lips or that air of smug sensibility showing that my trip to a bookmaker's agent had been successful, very successful indeed, clearly irritated him! A few moments later, an express train of the London & North Western Railway came thundering down the side of the platform pouring out black smoke and steam, creating a sensation of heat upon our faces, as it roared past. We boarded it and made our way to a 1st. Class carriage.

* A cheap book of the popular variety, usually containing literature of a sensational kind, costing one penny.

** Alfred Lord Tennyson, 1809 -1892

*** No it resembles the Richelieu Pavilion at the Louvre and Watson can only be referring to Slough Station not Reading Station.

Chapter 11

The Secrets of the Titanic

Our journey to Liverpool was without incident, as one would expect whilst travelling in a 1st. Class carriage aboard an express train. Another redeeming factor was the fact that the London & North Western Railways use the newly improved patented spring-loaded coupling gear. This ingenious gear assembly removes the dreaded jerks and knocks of carriages as they collide into each other every time the train is started or stopped. These jerks and knocks are familiar features that afflict carriages on other railways including that dreaded parliamentary train we had just abandoned.

Our train eventually clanked into Liverpool's Lime Street Railway Station, underneath the glazed screen braced with iron tracery that checked the weather entering the station. Alighting from the train carriage on to the platform, we found ourselves beneath an extensive iron and glass canopy. From the station roof were suspended enormous town gas light globes. Though not of the *chandelier* type, they illuminated a scene of chaos, as various trade wagons, pantechnicons and delivery carts competed for precedence in the right of way for their horse drawn vehicles amongst the piles of luggage.

Amongst this area of transportation and commerce, children played with their dogs, dodging miraculously the cumbersome wagons. Some were of the street urchin type, others, wearing boots, were clearly passing through the station or waiting for a train. They stood there, wrapped up tightly in their best quality travelling coats, looking out in awe at this novel aspect of society, to which they were clearly unaccustomed. People were also included in this travelling microcosm of the general public. Some, conducting the business of commerce, pointed accusingly to delivery orders or shipping manifests and then in the direction of where none existent goods ought to be; whilst others were appealing in the last resort, to unconvinced servants of the railway. Others merely watched, including nurses pushing their perambulators, oblivious in which direction they did, among the general chaos extant.

The smell of choking smoke from the railway engines was appalling, and for this reason Holmes and I made our way along the platform in a bid to leave the terminal. As we did so, we were unfortunate to be passing at the very instant a locomotive engine evacuated its surplus steam straight into our pathway. This instant fog enveloped us, creating a sticky hot sensation upon our faces and dampness in our clothes. Nonetheless we continued undaunted, by this annoying inconvenience.

What was clearly of greater inconvenience, involved a man at the centre of a commotion just ahead of us. A police constable was intervening between two individuals, one of whom was dressed in checked patterned suit of a pronounced tawdry style. The other was attired in a more sober and restrained manner, and wearing a bowler hat. As we approached the congregation their conversations became audible, in particular the verbal demands being made upon the fellow in the checked suit by the soberly dressed gentleman.

I heard distinctly the words to this effect that 'in the name of the Crown I serve you with this…what!'

"The devil take you!" came the interruption.

Suddenly pandäemonium was let loose. A sheaf of papers and a bowler hat erupted into the air. From beneath this plume of papers and headdress, I noticed that the fellow in the checked suit had crouched down and was removing himself quickly from the *mêlée*. However, in his haste, he collided with a railway pantechnicon with London & North Western Railway Co. Ltd. emblazoned on its side panelling. This, however, did not impede his progress away from what was I think an attempt to serve a writ upon his person. By now of course, the view holloa was in full report as representatives of the law both uniformed and soberly dressed, gave chase. I also observed from the corner of my eye, that a seasoned pickpocket was clearly taking advantage of the commotion.

Surprisingly enough, a woman of quite stout demeanour, wearing a billowing red silk dress of several folds, and an ornate frilly bonnet, intercepted the checked suited fellow. She quite literally fell upon him and very nearly succeeded in frustrating his escape. However, at the last moment, she missed her footing and hit the ground, ornate bonnet and all, with a pronounced force, as the fleeing fellow made good his escape into Lime Street and liberty. We had not yet even left the precincts of Lime Street Station, I thought, before we were compelled to witness behaviour that would be quite simply unacceptable in Baker Street.

On emerging from the station building, we expected to find a line of pony and trap carriages or even dogcarts one sees in the smaller country towns. We were therefore somewhat pleasantly surprised to see, lined up in the carriage rank, several newly improved elegant four wheeler Phäetons and highly varnished Barouche carriages, into one of which, Holmes and I climbed eagerly, to convey us to the Herculaneum Dock. As we clattered down the cobble-stoned streets, flush with my winnings from the Ascot race, I asked the carriage driver to pull up outside a busy looking bookmaker's agent. He did so and I stepped out of the carriage, returning a few minutes later clutching a wad of betting slips for three races to be run at the local racecourse at Aintree. Included in one race was the favourite, a horse called *Desborough,* owned by Lord Backwater, at tolerable odds should the ground remain firm under hoof. We then continued past a series of quays, and from one particular quayside the carriage driver turned his horses east into the Herculaneum Dock.

As we made our way through the dock, we saw in the distance a large building in the process of being constructed.

"What is that building over there?" I asked our carriage driver.

"That is the site on which the new Metropolitan Cathedral of Christ the King is being constructed to the glory of God," he replied, "and is hailed to be, when completed, the largest Cathedral in the world!"

It then occurred to me that I remember reading an article in the *London Times* or was it *The Daily Telegraph*? However, I do recall clearly, it had even at that early stage in its construction then, a few months ago, earned itself the *sobriquet* of '*Ghost Cathedral*' as a result of its incompleteness due to its megalithic and monumental vastness."

That building was not the only monumental structure we saw *en-route* to the Herculaneum Dock. Rising up, almost filling the sky, before us was the terrifying majesty of the Royal Mail Steamer *Olympic* in all her glory and

Ghost Cathedral, Liverpool.

splendour, held securely to her moorings by massive adamantine chains! That she was twin to the newer Royal Mail Steamer *Titanic*, that other engineering marvel, made me look in awe at her superstructure; eight hundred feet long and extending down the full length of the gigantic Herculaneum dock.

The driver of our Barouche carriage deposited us at the office of the White Star Line Shipping Company, owners of the RMS *Titanic* and the RMS *Olympic* ships. We were immediately shown into the offices of the director who introduced himself as one Mr. Arthur Carpenter. After we had gone through formalities, including a reviving drink, Carpenter donned his silk coat complete with Astrakhan collar and a shiny silk top hat. He then escorted us up a gangplank to the deck of the RMS *Olympic*.

"I understand, Mr. Holmes, that the Admiralty has asked you to look into our activities as a shipping company. I am not aware of any shortcomings of my company but will nonetheless attempt to help you in your quest."

"Thank you," responded Holmes, "where is the *Titanic* ship at present?"

"The' *Titanic* 'started out on her maiden voyage to New York five hours ago."

"Steady Holmes!" I said.

Carpenter gave me a perplexed look.

"Gentlemen, shall we commence our inspection of the *Titanic*, sorry I mean the *Olympic*?"

This simple mistake was not lost on Holmes, for I saw him furrow his eyebrows in thought. Something else had also caught his keen eye for detail.

"This *Olympic* ship looks relatively new," said Holmes, "as if it had just come off the slip-way being recently built."

"Oh no," responded Carpenter, "it is our policy to continually paint our ships and keep them in excellent condition. After all we do promote our boats as being of incomparable luxury down to every minute detail of their appointments!"

"Really, that is interesting," said Holmes, "but I expected no less, for this ship looks to be in more than excellent condition, almost as if it were the new *Titanic*!"

I noticed that Carpenter did not respond to Holmes' remark.

Our inspection of the *Olympic* with Carpenter was temporarily postponed, for at that moment a messenger arrived and informed Carpenter that he was needed in the harbourmaster's office farther along the quay. Carpenter gave his apologies and promised to return as soon as he was able.

"Good, Watson whilst we will no doubt need Carpenter's coöperation, we might conduct our own investigation of this magnificent creation wrought by man, without that official getting in the way."

Without doubt the RMS *Olympic* ship was monumental and towered above the not insubstantial Herculaneum dock.

"This ship Holmes, so I have read in *The Daily Telegraph*, is by her enormous and powerful reciprocating steam engines, able to propel herself through the seas at a rate of twenty three knots within an uninterrupted period of one hour. Imagine that! And, not only does she weigh forty-seven thousand tons, which provide for stability on the ocean waves, but is the last word in luxury and appointments. These benefits are available to those passengers wishing to cross the Atlantic in style; for alas, she is a veritable floating palace and symbol of man's final victory over nature and the elements!"

"At this moment Watson she is the object of my examination," said Holmes, whilst clambering up on the metal parapet fencing in order to view the stern of the boat.

"What is it?" I asked, knowing something had attracted his attention.

"Only that the name plate of bronze, has the word, *Olympic* cast into it."

"Nothing unusual in that," I said, "it is standard maritime practice."

By now two officious looking men in uniform were approaching us with some degree of determination.

"What are you two doing aboard this ship at five and thirty-five minutes past, on this dark November evening? asked one of the officials, as they gained our position.

"Do not adopt that confident tone with me my good man," replied Holmes.

"My good man," said the other official looking at his companion.

"We good men are asking for the last time just what you two are doing on this ship."

"We are guests of the White Star Line and here to look over this ship." I interjected, with as much authority in my voice as I was able to muster.

"Really, is that so? Well both of you can just come along with us and look over the cell in our jail. We do not tolerate thieves wandering about on our ships!"

"How dare you! How dare you act in a confident manner in front of me," I declared.

"You do not need to adopt that tone with us," even Holmes was moved to say, "we can explain exactly who we are and what our purpose is on board this ship!"

"Does the name Sherlock Holmes mean nothing to you?" I implored.

"No, the name does not, why, should it?" came an incredulous reply.

These remonstrations had little effect upon the officers and thus for an hour or so we found ourselves incarcerated in a secure room until Carpenter was able to locate us and arrange our release.

I was furious at being maltreated in such a confident fashion by those officers, and made my feelings known to Carpenter, who could only repeat his apology. Holmes, unperturbed by the experience, appeared to have gained an insight into something. I knew not what, except that he had spent our time in the cells in quiet contemplation, whilst I railed passionately at our confinement.

We recommenced our inspection.

"Gentlemen," Carpenter went on to say, "at the White Star Line, our aim is to promote ourselves to the public as the 'White Star Flag' the carrier of excellence in luxury. In order to provide this standard of service to discerning passengers to New York, we use any one of our "Wonder ships" as we call them, of the White Star Line, be it the *Olympic*, *Republic*, *Baltic*, the new *Titanic*, or as will later follow the *Gigantic* now being built."

Holmes, I noticed faltered on hearing the word 'five' and grabbed a nearby railing to steady him self as Carpenter related to him that all five boats are the pride and joy of the White Star Line.

"You will of course know Mr. Holmes, that the names of all the White Star Line ships, that comprise the fleet, bear the suffix 'ic' at the end of their name. This denotes that they are ships of the White Star Line.

Further, we have been able to offer this level of service as a direct consequence of being recently acquired by the great American financier and philanthropist, Mr. John Pierspont Morgan, owner of the International Mercantile & Marine Combine, of which the White Star Line is now an integral and important part."

I noticed that this remark by Carpenter immediately seized Holmes' attention, though I knew not why.

"We conceived the idea," continued Carpenter, "of constructing gigantic ocean liners in order to take on directly the Cunard shipping line, our main competitor in the north Atlantic, who prefer smaller, but faster ships, to complete the voyage to the New World. Cunard can carry a thousand passengers at speed. On any one of our big White Star Line "Wonder ships" of the *"Olympic Class"* type, such as the *Olympic* and *Titanic* weighing forty-seven thousand tons, and soon the *Gigantic*, we are able to convey, at least twenty two hundred persons, in pure abject luxury!"

"You do not promote a particular ship then?" asked Holmes.

"No, because all of our *"Olympic Class"* ships are exactly

the same, save for their name plates fixed to the stern. As I have said, we are anxious to promote the White Star Flag as the preferred provider of luxurious travel to New York, or indeed elsewhere for that matter. It follows therefore, that passengers will be equally at home onboard any of our ships during their journey!"

Carpenter led the way up the very opulent and ornate grand staircase into the first class areas of the ship. We walked through various galleys and state-rooms, including the magnificent ballroom, where no doubt passengers waltzed away the evenings in elegance and sophistication. I became rather envious.

"You have seen, as we have walked through the various galleys and restaurants, that all fittings and furnishings are the same in promoting the 'White Star' emblem, on crockery, tablecloths, cutlery, linen and towels. At no time will you see the name of a particular ship on anything other than the life belts and nameplate on the stern of the boat; everything else is inter-changeable amongst our ships."

"Are the name plates bolted to the stern inter-changeable?" inquired Holmes.

"Well, yes if using a wrench to release the name plate, weighing upwards to half a ton, from the hull of the boat. But, for what reason, the name plate informs one of the name of the ship?" said Carpenter with knitted eyebrows.

Holmes did not reply, but furrowed his brows too, and looked anxiously into the darkening, red, autumnal evening sky over the massive Herculaneum dock.

"Name plates Holmes? This magnificent ship, including the *Titanic,* is about British engineering prowess, which is able to construct awesome vessels of luxury, that even God Almighty himself cannot sink, especially the unsinkable *Titanic*! If you have read the newspapers, you will know that all the *'Olympic Class'* ships have a disposable displacement weight of forty-seven thousand tons. This, and the fact that their reciprocating engines, complete with triple screw propulsion, are able to deliver fifty-four thousand sharp horsepower at the push of a lever. These *Olympic Class'* ships draw thirty-five feet in the water and can maintain a surface speed of twenty-three knots to the hour!" I enthused.

Having uttered these remarks, I paused, pleased with myself, to witness a reaction to my patriotic remarks. For some unfathomable reason, both Holmes and Carpenter stared at me, incredulously. Eventually, Holmes looked down at a flat piece of metal about the size of a dinner plate lying on the deck.

"Is this fragment of metal plate the same type of metal plate used to construct the *Titanic*?" inquired Holmes of Carpenter.

"Yes," replied the White Star Line official, "as you can see, we are still in the process of re-fitting the *Olympic*. All the ships of this class, including the *Titanic* and *Olympic*, are built to the same specification and design. They are for all practical purposes identical in every detail and their parts interchangeable. Only a few days ago, we were compelled to exchange part of the propeller shaft from the *Titanic* in order to complete urgent repairs to the propeller shaft of the *Olympic*. As I say, both ships are identical in every respect."

Holmes leaned back on the ship's railings and asked if he could take that piece of plate metal with him, to which Arthur Carpenter agreed readily, albeit with a rather perplexed look upon his face. A smile crossed Holmes' face as if he had just reached the solution to a problem. We both moved away from Carpenter, whose attention was now focused on looking at some inadequate repairs to a timber frame window reveal.

"There is something devilish in this, Watson," said Holmes, more moved than I had ever seen him before.

A few moments later having examined the metal plate he was holding said, "What do you make of this?"

I looked at the object and thought long and hard before I exclaimed with decisiveness, "It is a piece of metal; what pray, Holmes, do you expect me to say?"

Carpenter rejoined us and said, "Now gentlemen I have a Coach & Four waiting to take you to the Adelphi Hotel, where I have reserved rooms in your name. Before then, I would be honoured if you will join me for dinner at the Philharmonic Bar & Grill in Hope Street."

We arrived at the resplendent Philharmonic Bar & Grill dining rooms, adjacent to the Philharmonic Hall, home of the Royal Liverpool Philharmonic Orchestra. Indeed as we drove past, the very distinctive closings syncopated bars of Tschaikowsky's F-minor Symphony assailed our ears. Once inside the building, we made our way through various bars, the likes of which I have never encountered before. I recall the Brahms & Liszt Bar and later the huge Richard Wagner Bar, that we elected to patronise. Eventually we made our way into a grill-room not dissimilar to the main dining room aboard the *Olympic* ship, that we had previously explored.

Our waiter obviously knew who Carpenter was, and showed us to a table in a quiet alcove away from the general clatter of silverware striking Crown Derby porcelain. Having glanced at the menu, I elected to have the potted shrimp and prawns with tartaric cream. The roast pork looked appetizing, especially with apple sauce and also red-current port jelly. To complete, I chose the almond cheesecake with compote of fruit and grape jelly. Holmes went for the celery soup & croutons, much to my surprise and the carpet-bag steaks with mushroom and parsley sauce. He concluded with maraschino wine jelly with brandied peaches. Carpenter, who looked generally as if he could do with a substantial meals on a regular basis, to counteract the effects of obvious inanition, restricted himself to simply having the eggs *a la* St James's followed by the hot tongue with cherry sauce. He ordered no dessert. However, he did order two bottles of Beaune red burgundy wine and two bottles of Veuve Clicquot champagne.

"To welcome and celebrate the renowned and incomparable Mr Holmes, at our dinner table!"

Holmes gave a shallow, if cautious bow.

The next morning after break-fast, we checked out of the Adelphi Hotel and boarded our non stop express train leaving Liverpool for the journey back to London. We found ourselves comfortable seats in an empty 1st. Class compartment and settled down for the return trip. The train pulled away without the customary sharp jolts and glided down the platform and burst out from beneath the iron and glass canopy over the platforms into an overcast dark November morning. Still, we were cosseted in our quiet 1st. Class carriage. I was staring out from the window watching the countryside passing by rapidly when the guard appeared in the doorway.

"Tickets please gentlemen!"

I reached into my inside pocket, and produced with a flourish, a leather wallet containing our 1st. Class tickets, purchased for us by the White Star Line, for our journey from Liverpool back to London. Without a second thought or concern, but with confidence, I handed them to the guard. I continued to survey, through the carriage window, the countryside fleeting by. Whilst enjoying the view I became aware of Holmes' kicking at my ankle.

"Ah-hem Watson! I think this gentleman needs your attention!"

"Thank you." I said, expecting the return of our tickets, duly perforated by the railway servant and assuming he would busy himself elsewhere on the express.

"Just a remark," said the guard, in a distinctive Liverpool accent, "but are you enjoying yourselves in this 1st. Class carriage?"

I was somewhat taken aback by the fellow's impudence.

"How dare you...!"

"The reason I ask," interjected the guard, "is because these tickets are for 3rd. Class accommodation, not 1st. Class. I am afraid these tickets do not entitle you to occupy this carriage. I must therefore ask you to vacate, and remove yourself to the parliamentary carriage located at the end of this train. There you shall be accommodated in the style and dignity befitting the class of ticket you hold!"

At this juncture Holmes intervened.

"Does the name Sherlock Holmes mean nothing to you?"

"No, it does not," answered the guard.

"There has clearly been a misunderstanding…"

"Not as far as I am concerned," interrupted the guard, "I hear gents such as you bemoaning the advent of the parliamentary train; yet when persons as yourselves occupy a 1st. Class carriage with a 3rd. Class ticket, I am somewhat compelled to force your immediate vacation from the carriage, in all fairness to other passengers."

"I appreciate fully your concerns," he continued, stifling our protest, "and the lack of a cotton *antimacassar* covered headrest on your un-upholstered seats, but the timber benches are of English elm and will suffice for your needs. In addition, for your comfort, the London & North Western Railway now covers, with a rain proof membrane, our parliamentary carriages!"

"This is outrageous." I protested.

"It may well be," said the guard, "but it does not require much systematic reasoning, deductive or otherwise, to conclude that you are both occupying a carriage that you ought not to be doing. Or, I might add, in having a basic understanding of the information contained in that most excellent of pocket books – Bradshaw's Railway Guide, which I highly recommend you purchase, read and apply its uplifting and useful information! Availing yourselves of that useful book might help you appreciate the class of ticket you hold and your correct location on a train and thus avoid being in embarrassing situations, such as this one!"

And with that *Parthian* shot, directed, I hoped, at Holmes, he invited us to follow him down to the parliamentary carriage for the completion of our journey on this non-stop express train to London. Needless to say, the embarrassment and ignominy of our being escorted by this velveteen uniformed supercilious *employé* of the railway, through twelve packed carriages to the rear parliamentary carriage was too much for me to bear. All of a sudden the pain in my right leg, a momento of the Candahar battle fiasco with the Duke of Cornwall's Own Regiment, manifested itself with a vengeance. So did my feelings for the parsimonious White Star Line in giving us 3rd. Class tickets, valid only in a parliamentary carriage.

I noted in my diary that I could not bring myself to make a written record of our experiences that we were compelled to endure in that train, save for the injunction that would to God I should ever enter such a carriage again.

As we approached London, the fog that had still not dispersed enveloped us gradually. Eventually we arrived, several hours late, at the St. Pancras Railway Station, having been diverted, yet again, due to the previous accident on the railway line of two days earlier.

Stepping out into the Euston Road, we flagged down a Brougham carriage to take us home. I noticed the phäntasmagoric and cliff-like *façade* of the imposing magnificence of the London Midland Railway's St. Pancras Hotel looming up out of the fog, which seemed powerless to shroud it. The six storey grand hotel, dressed in red brick neo-Gothic splendour, now with a pink hue, due to the fog, dominated the Euston Road, not only that, but indeed all other buildings in the vicinity, including the smaller, neighbouring King's Cross Railway Station operated by the London & North Eastern Railway. The St. Pancras Hotel's tower, housing an illuminated clock face, told me with its brilliant light penetrating the fog, even at that height, that the time was two and thirty five minutes past. We were back in London, albeit in a fog-bound London.

The next day I rose early, having slept badly and had already break-fasted when Holmes came into our dining room. I put down wearily the stop press edition of *The Times* in which a particular article had caught my attention.

"Let us hope that our dear house-keeper, Mrs. Hudson, has not forgotten me!" said Holmes, pulling vigorously on the bell rope that alerts the kitchen to his need for break-fast.

"That would be unlikely," I countered.

"I discern that you have been break-fasting, Watson,

on the ubiquitous bloater and herring, for the smell of them is still present. During that time, I have been smoking in my room, and giving a great deal of thought to our problem regarding our journey to Liverpool and the *Titanic* and, *voila*! I have the solution to hand!"

"I am indeed intrigued Holmes, do explain."

"Aha! Watson you know my methods. It is my intention that I shall board the *Titanic* on her return from New York to these shores, to confirm some theories I have, and to tie up some loose ends!"

"Can you be certain Holmes, really certain?" I inquired, in earnest.

"Never have I been more certain in my life, depend upon it Watson, you shall see me in my crowning glory, my apotheosis! I shall resolve the mysteries not only of Cadogan West's death, the White Star Line's commercial activities, but also that of the one surrounding the *Titanic,* that I recognised whilst on board the deck of the *Olympic!*"

On occasions as this Holmes could be unbearable, and feeling not too energetic as a result of our exertions of day before, and somewhat low in spirit, I therefore wished to retire to my own chamber. However, for the time being, I continued to listen patiently and nodded my head at suitable intervals to claims and other sundry boasts Holmes felt confident to expound upon. Eventually, on the pretext of a headache, I got up to leave the room in silence, but before doing so tossed *The Times* newspaper over to Holmes, who picked it up as I closed our diing room door behind me. I knew Holmes would read the banner headline in *The Times*:

'Titanic Sunk! − Great Loss of Life!'

Chapter 12

The Titanic is Sunk!

Later in the day, I came into our parlour. Holmes showed no outward sign of having barely recovered from the sensational turn of events, of great moment, and clearly had been in a *reverie* for at last three hours or so.

"Good God Holmes!" I remarked on re-reading *The Times* headline yet again in disbelief, "the enormity of this dreadful event is shocking news! The loss of life; hundreds of souls are perished in the depths of the Atlantic Ocean."

Holmes looked drained, demonstrated by the greyish pallor of his complexion and the purple hue around his eyes. The news had profoundly disturbed him, not least because he thought his intervention would avert the tragedy. Clearly the evil that had been let loose upon the world, was happening now, today, this instant. It was a plan not for the future, but had been planned for the previous day and had caught Holmes, and everybody else for that matter, off guard.

I tried to console Holmes.

"Was it Henry Ward Beecher," I said, "who propounded the maxim, that we reach the stage where life stops giving us things and starts taking them away?"*

We spent the morning sending out for, and receiving, special editions of all the newspapers, in our quest to obtain as much information about the sinking of the forty-seven thousand ton ill-fated RMS *Titanic* ship.

"'Man's symbol of progress, and eventual triumphant domination, over nature!' Who ever uttered those infamous words must now have ample reason to regret them," I said to Holmes, whilst reviewing headlines from various newspapers, brought in for us by Billy, our button pageboy.

We managed to assemble, from the latest reports in the newspapers, facts being received from a truly remarkable electrical device, called a 'Marconi apparatus. The advent of this innovative piece of equipment, now carried on board most ships, means that messages, in the form of electrically coded signals, known as 'Morse' could be sent, through the aëther to another receiving apparatus, hundreds of miles away, using Marconi wire-less telegraphy. From these 'Morse' coded signals, other ships in the vicinity of the sunken *Titanic*, looking for survivors, had been able to supply an anxious Fleet Street, with fresh information about the tragedy.

Of the reports in the special editions, the one contained in *The Daily Telegraph* was probably the more illuminating. It read:

'Sunday 14 inst. at approximately ten and thirty minutes past the hour of eleven at night, the steam ship ocean liner RMS *Titanic*, owned and operated by the White Star Line, collided head-on with an iceberg. The damage, so it is reported, was restricted to her prow that received the brunt of the collision. Those survivors who witnessed the collision spoke of a crunching sound that reverberated throughout the ship, causing anxiety amongst the passengers. Many were awakened from their slumbers and some even decided to go up to the deck to discover the reason for the commotion. Minutes later, it is reported, the ship was listing heavily and the crew were rushing about advising people to put on their cork filled life jackets. One deck officer is reported to have distinctly replied when a survivor asked why? 'Just in case, because there is a bit of damage to the prow of the ship but there is no danger, nothing to fear, as only the front is leaking water which will find its way to the stern and right the boat level again. That is why God himself cannot sink this boat!'

'By now,' *The Daily Telegraph* continued, having received more recent reports of the collision; 'the scene was becoming one of chaos. The beginnings of hysteria were clearly visible in some passengers as a scramble for the all too few lifeboats gathered pace. This fact alone caused passengers to panic as the dreadful realisation swept amongst those assembled on deck, that the *Titanic* was fatally wounded and sinking! We are also reliably informed by a Marconi apparatus signalling Morse coded reports from the scene of the sinking, that no other vessels were on hand, to lend assistance to the stricken liner. Though, as we go to press, we learn that there was a stationary ship, some five miles off the port side of the mortally afflicted *Titanic*. Survivors have recounted how they witnessed some of the crew of the *Titanic,* firing off frantically, distress rockets, in a desperate bid to alert the stationary ship five miles away, to their terrifying predicament.'

The Daily Telegraph became more virulent in its reporting as the enormity of their analysis of the disaster unfolded.

"'An unsinkable ship that God himself could not sink" - so we were reliably informed by the creator of ill-fated *Titanic*! What then has gone wrong to reduce this marvel of British marine engineering to an iron necropolis on the floor of the Atlantic Ocean, where hundreds of British people have been consigned? Further, we were told that the ship was in the capable hands of Captain Edward Smith, an experienced captain and commodore, no less, of the White Star Line. The new Marconi wireless telegraphy apparatus, signalling Morse coded messages, was also an advertised feature aboard the RMS *Titanic*. Why then, was this facility not deployed to greater use, in an attempt to alert the ill-fated *Titanic*, to the presence of icebergs in the area, and avert this dreadful catastrophe?'

"The futility of it all," I sighed, as I handed the paper to Holmes, "how is it a ship so big can collide with an iceberg?"

"Quite simply," remarked Holmes, "do not for a moment imagine that the captain of this ocean liner the ill-fated *Titanic*, and previously captain of her sister ship the *Olympic,* was a careful operator of those marvels of the sea. For the *Olympic* only a few months' ago hit some thing even bigger and harder than an iceberg."

"What?" I demanded.

"England!" replied Holmes.

As the *sombre* news in the special editions became more refined, the full enormity of the cataclysm began to unfold. The sober *Daily Chronicle* reported briefly in the latest of its special editions:

'We learn from Reuters Telegraph Agency, that the damage to the *Titanic* is more serious than originally supposed. The *Titanic* hit an iceberg sideways, creating on her starboard side, a jagged gash one-third the length of the boat's eight hundred feet, with grave flooding consequences. Believe great loss of life to sound of hymn 'Nearer my God to Thee' being sung over the waters of the Atlantic.'

And the *Sporting Life* merely reported in its side margin:

'It is a betting certainty that the predicted number of survivors will be reduced as facts about this ruinous calamity become apparent. There are odds on, even now, that there is more to this event than have been posted regarding the fate of the Royal Mail Steamer *Titanic*.'

Then Billy, our new pageboy knocked on our drawing room door and entered, bearing the latest edition of the *London Times*. In it a small 'Stop Press' notice reporting the following:

'We now understand that the loss of life was under estimated. Passengers assumed safe and accounted for have in fact perished in the ocean. Reports are now coming in of a catastrophic calamity involving a great loss of life, with whole swathes of the Atlantic Ocean brimming with corpses, from the ill-fated *Titanic*. We believe from these reports, that the stricken *Titanic* eventually sank at five and twenty past two o'clock in the morning of the 15 inst. We can confirm that eight hundred and three survivors are accounted for, which leaves us with the terrible knowledge in the certainty that over fifteen hundred souls have perished.'

* Anon

Chapter 13

The Curious Incident of the Irregular Professional

The enormity of the dreadful sinking of the ill-fated *Titanic*, in the middle of the Atlantic Ocean in the early hours of Monday morning, had clearly sent a shudder through out not only Holmes and myself; but of course England and the Empire. It is still difficult to comprehend that a capital ship of the line, weighing forty two thousand tons, could sink within three hours of hitting an iceberg. That the *Titanic* represented British marine engineering at its best is a major blow to our worldwide prestige and competence. However, there was now the question of precisely what did go wrong and from whom did one exact responsibility? Holmes had been working on some theories; it was to be hoped they were relevant and could now be used in resolving clearly, certain unanswered questions.

"Come Watson, there is work to be done," said Holmes, all of a sudden, "if we could not avert those deaths, then let us at least avenge their lives, being so cruelly taken!"

We stepped out smartly into Baker Street and immediately approached a Carriage & Pair, pulled by a couple of chestnut horses, waiting by the kerb.

"Whitechapel," bellowed Holmes, to the liveried carriage driver, as we both climbed in and sat down on the buttoned leather seat.

"This carriage is taken sir," said the driver, "I am waiting for my fare, who is inside that tobacconist's shop."

"Ten guineas now, for you, if you take us to Whitechapel," bargained Holmes, "I am sure the gentleman in the tobacconist will not object."

"My fare is a lady," replied the liveried carriage driver.

"The offer still stands," negotiated Holmes!

"Holmes," I exclaimed.

After some oaths had been exchanged freely, the dense fog muffled most of which, we were still compelled to alight from the carriage.

We found ourselves outside still, and in the fog, standing on the junction of Dorset Street and Baker Street, immediately next to Broadstone Place, in which Camden House is located. It was from this infamous building, that the murderous colonel Moran, with an air rifle, tried to shoot Holmes, as he sat in our drawing room, on the north-western side of the junction. Our rooms, adjacent to the distinct red-brick and Portland stone dressing, that is the National Provincial Bank next to number 221. b. Baker Street.

"It is ironic you know Watson, that visitors to our rooms think that 221. b. Baker Street is farther up Baker Street, almost opposite the Regent's Park!" said Holmes.

"I agree, everybody makes that basic mistake. Why there is even a shop that claims the address and sells notions based on dishonesty, because its rationale can only be fictitious, but designed to fleece the gullible in search of answers!" I replied.

"It is only the very observant who recognise our residential chambers at 221. b. are in fact next door to this bank. However, Watson, we have better things to do than hang around in this fog. I suggest we start walking towards Oxford Street and may be we can intercept a carriage going east along that busy thoroughfare."

I fell in eagerly with his suggestion, and we started to walk south down the fog-shrouded canyon Baker Street had become. First having crossed over Dorset Street, we continued down past the Baker Street *Bazaar* and the Sub Telegraph Office on our right, until we turned left into Blandford Street, I expected then to wheel into Manchester Street. Instead Holmes grabbed my weak left arm, made so by a stray bullet striking the collarbone during the Pashwar campaign when attached to the Coldstream Guards, and pulled me into Kendal Place.

We emerged from Kendal Place into George Street that we used to cross over Manchester Street and continuing past the rear of Hertford House and so onward into Marylebone High Street, as a short conduit to the narrow winding Marylebone Lane. I knew this to be so because we were directly in front of the Prince Alfred Public House, inside which bright lights and talk of the ill-fated *Titanic* could be witnessed and where both seemed undiminished despite the damp, foggy weather we were enduring outside.

We continued at a pace in the direction of Bentinck Street, the end of which took us to the notorious junction with Welbeck Street. Here some years ago, Holmes was nearly run down and seriously injured by a pantechnicon, being driven furiously, in yet another murderous attack upon his person. Reminiscing on this life-threatening episode, we crossed over Wigmore Street and Henrietta Place into Vere Street past the Aërated Bread Company's premises and thence into the Oxford Street. There we availed ourselves of *Trichinopoly* cigars and a variety of leaf from Bradley's excellent tobacco emporium that dominates the junction.

"Holmes, you never cease to amaze me. I did not even know of the existence of this network of small lanes and mews. It is as if you have a map in your brain!"

"It is as well to know how to follow, without being noticed, as it is to traverse the Metropolis without being followed by one's adversary!" came his response, as he ordered several ounces of his favourite tobacco leaf.

"Such dreadful news Mr. Holmes," announced Bradley, "the whole of England is talking about the sinking of that ill-fated *Titanic*. How the crew fired rounds at the passengers to stop mutiny breaking out. And, how some of the passengers tried to lynch the captain from a yardarm, but were prevented from doing so by the fact the *Titanic* then broke in two. With the captain on one side and the frustrated lynchers, ropes in hand, on the other side; all to the background hymn of, 'Nearer my God to Thee' being played by the band! How pandäemonium erupted on the forecastle, just before she sank. Dreadful news Mr. Holmes dreadful! There you are Sir, sixteen ounces of your Grosvenor Blend and Doctor Watson, do you take your usual half pound of Schipper's Tabak Special and eight of Arcadia Mixture?"

"Rather!" I replied keenly, "both Holmes and I much prefer to avail ourselves of your fine tobaccos, than from that other place!"

"Oh, you mean Fribourg & Treyer's establishment in the Haymarket, with their fancy double bow windows." replied Bradley, with an ill concealed smirk upon his lips.

Loaded down with our wares, we hailed a passing Hackney carriage, lumbering out of the fog toward us.

"Whitechapel," instructed Holmes.

"Whereabouts in the Whitechapel?" came a surly reply, laced with contempt.

"Swan Lane," advised Holmes.

"Oh, behind the St. George's Brewery in the Commercial Road, near Aldgate, linking the Whitechapel Road; why did you not say that at first?" asked the driver.

"Because I do not give carriage drivers directions, to my destination, based on the location of various and sundry breweries ranged around the Metropolis," said Holmes.

"Oh very well, get in."

And with that gracious invitation, we clambered aboard and cantered off into the fog, along the Oxford Street heading east. In so doing we drove past several horse-drawn omnibuses forming a continuous traffic. Despite the weather, the street was a hive of activity, with various street traders, costermongers and other sundry vendors, selling their wares to anybody who would stoop to such misplaced trust.

The street has never been a favourite of mine. I detested being part of the pressure of humanity that seethed along its crowded and busy thoroughfare, preferring instead the relative calm of the parallel Wigmore Street on its north side or the elegance of Brook Street on the Mayfair side. Holmes, by contrast, was always in his element among the prevalent vendors of tawdry goods and services, existing in Oxford Street. He liked especially those persons of dubious repute, who ought to be confined to living out their lives in parliamentary trains.

Our Hackney carriage came to an abrupt halt as some altercation erupted in front of us, involving a pantechnicon with the 'Fortnum & Mason' cipher emblazoned on its side, and a wagonette carriage under the control of a loquacious individual. To avoid this unpleasantness I looked to my right and could just make out the Princess Theatre looking forlorn but promising, so a prominent advertisement poster declared, an entertaining evening of Bellini's operetta '*The Sonnambulist*'* followed by a *burlesque* called 'The Yellow Dwarf'. Entertaining, I thought, if you are amused by the *grotesque*.

We continued our progress as the Hackney carriage negotiated its way through the street with the Regent's Circus behind us. Here I remarked to Holmes how the street deteriorates as one travels east. His response was that the street reflected every aspect of life from the rich and fortunate to the desperate and poor. I dwelt on his word poor as we rattled down what was becoming a seedier and grubbier street almost by the yard. Occasionally a fine looking building came into view such as the Pantheon with its massive dome sheltering those in need of entertainment.

An age seemed to go by before the carriage driver announced, "This is far as I go Guv."

"What," said Holmes, "but this is not Swan Lane?"

"Correct," replied the driver holding out his hand for his fare, "Swan Lane is through that alley, toward St George's Street and the Thames and I ain't taking my horse and carriage in there. And, do not bother to ask, no cab driver would take his carriage in there!"

"Come Watson ," Holmes decreed and we both alighted and started to walk. I noticed that the driver did not whip up his horse to leave, but sat there motionless with hunched shoulders, watching us disappear down into the fog bound alley, only dimly lit with coal tar gas globe lamps.

We found ourselves walking along side a large brick building I took to be the St. George's Brewery and judging by the strong smell of fermenting hops felt confident that it was. Swan Lane was a miserable place with the dregs of society clinging to lamp posts or huddled in doorways.

Mingling with the dense fog, was the odour of rotted vegetation that assailed our nostrils, made all the more unbearable by the stench coming off the nearby river Thames. The lane comprised the usual gin shops and dens where all kinds of abuses took place. Just in front of us, though invisible, we could hear a commotion of some kind. We slowed our pace and proceeded cautiously.

"Look out Watson!"

I heard Holmes shout as he pushed me to the ground. Then one sharp thwack was heard, as Holmes brought his cane down onto the head of our attacker, who immediately fell down on to the wet pavement and, in an instant it was all over! By now I had recovered and was standing behind Holmes, about to deliver a blow of my own to the attacker's inert body when Holmes intervened grabbing my raised arm.

"Watson, no; I think our pickpocket has learned his lesson today," said Holmes.

We did not care to linger in the vicinity, to field questions from angry neighbours, who were gathering around us indignant that one of their own had met with such injurious results at our hands.

We continued through the swirling fog, and I felt grateful that for once it made us invisible to the mob that had assembled and were shouting insults at us. By dodging a ceaseless onslaught of drunks, and stepping over various inert bodies on the footpath, we made our way through a *labyrinth* of streets and alleys. This situation was brought about by the fact that the Hackney carriage driver had deposited us quite some distance from our destination and we were therefore compelled to walk further than anticipated. In so doing, a singular event unfolded upon us, where we could not quite believe what happened.

Harnessed to a carriage, with ornate glazed panels to

its sides, were two black horses stamping their hooves on the carriageway and snorting, as though impatient. Through the fog, I became aware of a person sitting on some steps leading up to the front door of a large, but forlorn and run-down looking house. The person's face was of a deathly white pallor, matching the white gloves he wore, but the remainder of his attire was black, including a stovepipe top hat, wrapped in black crinkled *crepe* material. His manner was one of extreme agitation, alerting me as a doctor that he may be in the process of suffering from apoplexy or indeed a heart attack at this very instant! As I approached, he kept clutching at his throat, as though gasping for air. His face stretched upward, in agonising desperation to the fog whilst his eyes rolled aimlessly around inside their deep sockets, seemingly oblivious to vision.

I assumed that he was in the act trying to summon help from within the household, but had collapsed on the steps. Therefore, abandoning all concerns, including that of safety, in order to carry out my duty as a doctor, compelled as I am, under that Hippocratic oath, I rushed to the poor unfortunate wretch's assistance.

As I grabbed his wrist in order to ascertain the strength of his pulse, he appeared surprised. In his confused state, he began to struggle with me, and indeed resisted my every effort to deal with his symptoms. At length he mumbled gibberish, which told me, as a doctor, that his condition was deteriorating rapidly, and was now becoming critical. This required that I lay him down, flat on his back, to relieve his symptoms.

At the very moment of my trying to do precisely that, the front door to the house opened, and out stepped a maidservant, wearing a blue linen dress with a white cotton pinafore and black laced-up boots. In her arms, she carried a mahogany tray, upon which was a flagon jug of porter.

"Here you are sir," she said, handing me the draught and a pair of black gloves.

Somewhat surprised but nonetheless grateful, I attempted to administer the drink to the victim. As I did so, he took a turn for the worse, and his arms began to flay out, as the agony gripped his heart. Consequently, in trying to pour the liquid into his mouth, I succeeded only in emptying the entire contents of the jug over his face and chest due to his struggling arms. At that very instant, his face assumed a more natural colour, and the white seemed to dissipate. Encouraged by this good indication, I handed the empty jug back to the maid, whose facial expression, was as if in awe at my prompt action upon the victim.

However, I knew from experience that one ought to complete the medical process, and accordingly began with my clenched fists to pound the man's chest to assist the heart maintain its rhythm. It worked, for no sooner had I commenced this procedure, than the victim hauled himself up onto his feet!

I stood back, pleased with myself for having administered my life-saving action. I then picked up the victim's stovepipe top hat that had fallen off his head, onto the steps, and handed it to him. His reaction took me by surprise, for he launched into a tirade of abuse aimed solely at me. Thinking he was in shock, I attempted to remonstrate with him, but his verbal violence intensified.

"Now look here my good man..." I said.

"I am not your good man; and look what has become of me? See what you have done to my frock-coat and attire?" he interrupted, whilst wiping the porter from his livid face and coat, with a black-edged handkerchief.

At which stage the maid, with a look of total bewilderment upon her face, interjected.

"Sir, he is but the dumb mute, we have employed, to re-live the agonies of dying for the benefit of those members of the family and friends who were unfortunate to miss the actual death of the master of this house, who died but these two days past!"

"The dumb what?"

The maid went on to explain to me.

"It is customary in this part of London, as an optional extra to any funereal proceedings, to hire the services of a professional dumb mute at six pennies an hour. His sole function," she said, pointing to the dumb mute, who by now was anything but, "is to locate himself outside on the doorstep of the house, where death had occurred, and imitate the death scene, including painting his face white. This is so, for the benefit of those who were unfortunate to miss the actual death. I thought you had come to pay your last respects, hence the flagon of porter, and the pair of black gloves I handed to you, with which to hold the jug, and drink to the deceased!"

I stood there dumbfounded, trying to absorb the enormity of the situation and ludicrous state of affairs that had enveloped me. A more shocking and *grotesque* an experience I had never endured in all my life, and one that certainly transcended even the pathos of a Greek melodrama.

I rejoined Holmes who had witnessed my performance in stunned disbelief.

"You must bear in mind Watson, the reason for this morbid requirement, based as it is on a growing disillusionment with religion. We know that the teachings of scripture are being discredited with irrefutable advances being made in science, not least those in evolution. It makes one question what people can believe in. The attractiveness of the supernatural, including ghosts and fairies, is all too apparent in funereal ritual and paraphernalia."

"But Holmes, you cannot be serious, think of the Christ," I replied.

"I do Watson, believe me, I do. And, in so doing, derive strength in my private conviction!

"Really."

"It may be easy," continued Holmes, "to comprehend why the cult of mourning is seen as the last remnant of a religious age. No longer certain of what may lie beyond the grave, they hold on to life for as long as possible in delaying the inevitable. When that inevitability happens, it is dreadful for some. You have just witnessed how this dread is given elaborate expression in the funereal ritual of the dumb-mute that will no doubt culminate at the some monumental tomb, and thereafter nothingness. But, as the ancient Egyptians did, so we too, are compelled to construct extravagant mortuary temples to our dead. Often, it might be said, in more superior buildings than those they inhabited when alive, certainly judging at the state of that forlorn looking house, outside which we are standing."

*The Sleepwalker

Chapter 14

The Vault of Darkness

Despite our *bizarre* experience with the dumb mute, we at last arrived at our destination. We achieved this feat by focusing on a flickering green lantern above a door that led into the infamous Diogenes Club. As we entered, my eyesight became blurred, not with the light, for there was very little, but due to the dense acrid smoke from every type of impregnated combustible leaf and alkaloid substance. I recognised immediately, as a doctor, the distinctive aroma of paregoric, a tincture of opium, often used in the relief of pain, or abuse.

Through the haze and dimness, a vision of bodies presented themselves to us. Some were reclining in a strange and unnatural manner. Others were almost interlocked in a mass of humanity huddled together for mutual support and comfort. The damp atmosphere was punctuated with dark lack-lustre eyes that were trying to focus on us, as interlopers, in their den. From these dark shadows glimmered little red circles of flame as laudanum addicts coughed and inhaled their burning, insidiously additive poison. Some addicts muttered to themselves, but most were silent. A few attempted to communicate with each other, in monotonous and strange low voices. Sometimes their conversation was vivid and nervous, as each addict mumbled out thoughts of his own, but with little attention to the words mumbled by his neighbour. Then, silence reigned as they descended again into melancholic stupor. As we moved through the club, people looked up and stared at us. At the farther end however, next to a fireplace, was seated a person who looked at us with a greater intensity than that of his fellow laudanum addicts.

Presently, a dubious, sallow looking attendant came up and asked whether he could do anything for us.

"Nothing," replied Holmes, darting off into the gloom, into which I followed him, to the man seated at the fireplace. Holmes accepted a pipe, containing some laudanum-drenched tobacco leaf from the man, who was introduced to me as Mr. Elias Whitney, Principal of the Theological College of St. George.

Looking at him I noticed, even in the dim light, that one of his eyes had ceased to function, due to a morbid deterioration of the living tissue of which the eye is made. Drawing on his pipe, Whitney commenced his convoluted, if singular, narrative to Holmes and me. I took no active part in the proceedings; merely sitting there and listening.

"I got the telegram Holmes about your wishing to meet me and indeed I can impart some information, that might be of interest to you.

Some time ago I dismissed a teacher, a mathematics professor from the College. I released him, not because he was academically wanting, rather he was the opposite, very gifted, bordering on genius, one might say. However, the man displayed worrying signs of an inner turmoil, which intensified as the months went by. His intensity increased to such a level, as to induce monomania in him. His psychotic condition continued to manifest itself, in a very serious and disturbing form, for he developed a manic, insatiable addiction for newspapers! Newspapers of every kind, from London or Liverpool, and even such far off places as New York, Chicago and St. Louis on the Mississippi River in Missouri.

His craze for collecting newspapers continued unbounded, reaching critical psychotic levels, to the extent that I considered calling in the eminent psycho-analyst and commentator on hysteria, Sigmund Freud. The teacher would not hear of it, rejecting vehemently my suggestion as inordinately extravagant, and then promptly, denounced me!

Clearly his position at the College was now untenable, and I was, consequently, compelled to dismiss him. But Holmes I have yet to divulge to you the strange and singular aspect of this occurrence. The teacher never read any of the newspapers!

From what I can gather, he now gives private tuition to the children of wealthy families. You may know Holmes, but your doctor friend here does not, but St. George's College is the proud owner of a picture collection, including some notable and valuable oil paintings. The pictures have been acquired over the decades, as a result of bequests and legacies from munificent benefactors. The gallery is not open for display, and certainly not open to the public, on the basis that we are a Jesuit establishment, and do not encourage the heathen public onto our consecrated grounds."

I started at this ridiculous remark by Whitney, and showed my intolerance of it, by pushing out my chest, and rubbing the palms of my hands on my knees. Ignoring my reaction, he continued to narrate his story.

"The gallery is a self contained room, a vault you might say, with just four small windows and is kept dark in order to protect the paintings from the effects of direct sunlight. Whilst the existence of the gallery is generally known, including by the teacher whose employment I terminated, few have access through its locked doors.

I was therefore rather perplexed Mr. Holmes, when a few months ago, the very teacher I had discharged, appeared in my outer offices, demanding that my secretary obtain for him an immediate audience with me. My secretary so advised and I consented. An interview between the teacher and myself was granted.

He walked into my office; we shook hands and I waved him in to a chair opposite my desk. Yes, he was giving private tuition, but what had brought him to see here to the College, was a proposition he wished to put to me. A proposal, he felt confident, that would not only meet with my enthusiasm and approval, but would benefit the College financially. He outlined the scheme, in which he went on to explain that the father of a pupil of his, in his capacity as director of one of the nation's great art institutions, was organising an exhibition of English paintings, to be shown at the forthcoming World's Columbian Exposition in Chicago."

The principal went on to explain the relevance of the World's Columbian Exposition and the opportunities it afforded.

"The World's Columbian Exposition at Chicago has been organised to nominally celebrate Columbus' discovery, four hundred years ago, of the New World of Americas, and to particularly give recognition to the achievements of the American people. This Exposition, we are told, will accelerate the growth of civilisation in the United States. The promoters of the World's Columbian Exposition in Chicago are especially eager to establish the fact that there are numerous wealthy Americans, who consider themselves a significant force in the art world, and are willing to purchase artwork, especially from England and Europe.

There will be ten thousand items of art on display, from the eighteenth and nineteenth centuries, and from private and public collections around the world, making it the largest exhibition of art ever held in the United States. The exhibition is expected to attract upwards of twenty-seven millions of visitors, half of the total population of the United States. Even the composer Antonín Dvořák, to celebrate and mark the occasion of the Chicago World's Columbian Exposition, has written a symphony, his ninth in E-minor and he calls it, '*From the New World*' in celebration of the Exposition.

You can imagine Holmes, the importance that the World's Columbian Exposition, is generating. Not only in terms of art, but other related disciplines, as engineering, architecture and manufacturing. Indeed the whole site comprises over six hundred acres, and is a fantastic collection of Neo Classical-inspired buildings, based on designs emanating from what they call *Beaux-Arts* style. The eminent American architect, D H Burnham, a great exponent of the *Beaux-Arts* architectural style, is leading the architectural designs, including reproducing huge buildings, based on European palaces.

The hundred and fifty feet high Gothic Water Tower dominates the entrance into the area, in which the Columbian Exposition buildings are located. The tower was designed, more as a practical solution, to the problem of equalising the piped water pressure in central Chicago. Despite the highly romantic design of the tower, built of Illinois limestone blocks, complete with turret, pinnacles and crenellation, it survived the Great Fire, which engulfed and destroyed the city of Chicago in 1871. As a result of that calamity, all buildings in Metropolitan

Gothic Water Tower, Chicago

Chicago have to be constructed using fire retardant materials, including stone and iron in order to prevent a repeat of the disaster. The construction of the tower, using iron and stone, is in a class of structures, which includes the Fuller Building * in New York and the St. Pancras Hotel in London, and are pioneering the way for the evolution of the iron framed fire-proof buildings for the safety of all.

Located around a vast lake, are many of the structures with such names as, the Palace of Fine Arts, and Federal Government Building. Other buildings are dedicated to Transportation, Manufacturing & Liberal Arts, Agriculture and Horticulture, the last three of which are modelled on the Petit Palace in Paris. Added to this collection is a huge structure they call the Court of Honor. An enormous grand dome dominates the building that is illuminated at night by the exciting innovation they call electricity, powering Edison-Swan lamps. This vast collection of over two hundred buildings, covered in white painted *staff*, ** has earned itself the *sobriquet* of, 'City of Dreams', and is more reminiscent of the Forum in ancient Rome. The buildings are of course, much larger, and are erected clearly as symbols of America's intellectual succession to European Classical architecture. In this respect, it is an auxiliary requirement that the World's Columbian Exposition, will effectively civilise the world, and complete the work started elsewhere. This goal will be achieved by combining art, especially paintings, with the untold wealth in America, which is available to commission new works of art and purchase old and recent paintings.

Some paintings would, where appropriate, would be sold others, not so, but will be returned to their owners. The paintings, including those at the College that are to be lent to the exhibition, would attract a fee of several thousands of pounds. The promoters feel justified in being able to pay this fee. It will be paid on the basis of the more fine paintings and old masters exhibited, the greater the interest generated with consequential financial gain and commissions for new paintings obtained. With regard to the College's collection, the insurance, packaging and transportation, would be entirely paid for by the promoters.

He then went on to list the august organisations, including the great royal academic establishments in England, which were participating. Who was he, with his comparatively insignificant collection, to reject this offer that could secure the College's financial future? As a sign of the promoters' sincere intention, they had authorised him to offer the College a cheque drawn on the Capital & Counties Bank in Oxford Street. *Laus Deo*, I thought.

We spoke at length and he explained further the arrangements of the exhibition. I in turn put pertinent questions to him, which he answered immediately and without difficulty or hesitation; indeed, he had a reasoned reply for every conceivable situation. At length, we agreed to consider his proposition, and arranged to meet in a week's time to finalise the arrangements. We did so and legal documents were duly drafted and exchanged. Thereafter the paintings were witnessed, catalogued and crated with the lids sealed and loaded upon a pantechnicon, belonging to the Royal Academy of Arts. I felt certain that I was doing the right thing, and the sight of the pantechnicon and the august cipher emblazoned on its side, confirmed in my mind, this was so.

You can imagine my surprise Mr. Holmes. After only six weeks he visited me at the College, and said that while the World's Columbian Exposition in Chicago was going ahead, their involvement in the exhibition of paintings had been delayed indefinitely. Therefore the promoters were returning all the paintings to their owners! He was deeply sorry for not being able to endow the College, with the promised fees, but that the promoters had again authorised him to offer me a cheque, drawn on the same Capital & Counties Bank, as compensation for the inconvenience they felt they had caused the College. In truth there was little inconvenience, and the College was marginally financially richer for the exercise. The paintings, he said, would be returned within the next few days. This duly took place on a particularly dark and rainy day and the original seals were opened and the pictures removed from their crates and re-hung on the gallery walls.

Sometime later I received the news from one of our regular benefactors, that it was his intention, to bestow a further bequest upon the College, in the form of an oil painting by a young artist called Atkinson Grimshaw entitled *'The Deserted House'*. At the appointed time, the benefactor arrived, and after a short ceremony in the gallery, handed the painting over to me. Two members of staff were on hand to physically lift and position the new painting into its place upon the gallery wall.

As I have previously pointed out Holmes, light in the gallery, is provided through four small windows, and therefore is subdued. Possibly as a result of the poor light, one of the men offering the painting to the wall stumbled. In so doing, he caused the frame of the new painting, to rub against a painting, positioned on the wall immediately below. Not wishing to make a fuss in front of our benefactor, not least in emphasising our ineptitude and clumsiness in handling paintings entrusted to us, I instructed the men to continue with their endeavours.

They eventually did so and we all left the gallery, locking the doors on our way out.

Later that evening I returned to the gallery, with a powerful lamp, fuelled by acetylene gas and examined the damaged painting. It was not the damage that had caught my attention earlier in the day, but something else, and to my horror my suspicion was confirmed. That particular painting is at least thirty-five years old. Yet when I put my fingers into the damaged area on the canvass, I expected the paint finish to be dry and brittle, instead the paint was still damp and as I ran my finger along the short gash, wet paint was deposited on it. The painting was wet, Holmes, wet! I went to the next painting and discovered that by pushing gently onto area of thick daubs of paint, it gave way forming a little round indentation. The paint should be dry and hard as adamantine chain, not spongy and soft.

Needless to say Mr. Holmes, I spent the entire evening examining those paintings within my reach, and each one of them was a fake! Our paintings represent no more than a collection of canvass and oil paint, fit only for the furnaces that heat the College, than they are for display. Furthermore, the paintings were not insured. What is now a matter of desperation is the fact that in the past, the paintings have been used to provide collateral, to secure bank loans, when funds were needed. The College is potentially bankrupt and I am powerless to prevent this calamity, since I can neither conceal the fraud nor expose it!"

"One question, what is the name of the dismissed teacher?" asked Holmes.

"Moriarty, James Moriarty," replied the principal of the Theological College of St. George.

Had the principal lost his mind? I found the juxtaposition between this fantastic story, the principal narrating it, and our presence in an opium den incongruous to say the least. In addition, the principal relating the story, appeared delirious and to have only the slightest interest in what he was saying. He seemed more interested in what was going on over my shoulders, in the recesses of the Diogenes Club, keeping his one good eye, as it were, on the main chance.

More for reasons of health than sanity, I persuaded Holmes to leave this den of addicts, for I knew that when he started, the habit would stay and engulf him for days, let alone hours. At length and after much persuasion, we found ourselves back in that vile Swan Lane. Whilst Holmes gathered his wits, I wondered whether those angry neighbours and friends of the pickpocket that Holmes had crowned earlier, were still there, and congregating, lying in wait for us. I noticed too, that the professional dumb mute had, apparently abandoned his prime position outside the derelict-looking house of death.

We did negotiate our way back to the Whitechapel Road, where I just managed to get a bet on a horse owned, by colonel Wardlaw, called *Pugilist* running at Newmarket the next morning. Whilst waiting in the Whitechapel Road, for a carriage back to the West End, I observed the crowds of hurrying people, engaged in commercial activity, which prevailed along this thoroughfare of Empire that links the City to the mercantile areas and docks into which the wealth and produce of our Empire are delivered.

Children were in evidence everywhere; and some had that look of being undernourished and in a perpetual state of inanition, but they did, however, look contented and cheerful. Especially so did the girls, wearing their cotton dresses and their tiny boots, as they played and danced amongst the horses pulling dray carts and other lumbering wagons transporting goods of every description from the nearby docks. Costermongers abounded, and pestered every passing pedestrian. Suddenly, as if by magic they melted back into the fog, as did the children. The reason was the arrival of two police constables on horseback, trotting down the middle of the Whitechapel Road. Their appearance caused pantechnicons and other carriages to slow down and swerve to avoid them. Some drivers actually turned the horses completely around and clattered off quickly in the opposite direction.

Having waited a short time, Holmes hailed a passing Brougham carriage and we headed west along a series of badly cobbled streets alongside the river. To our right and just visible, was St. Paul's Cathedral, looking like a domed Mausoleum looming up into the shrouds of fog. Finally we emerged beneath the Blackfriars Railway Bridge into the broad thoroughfare of the new Victoria Embankment.

Holmes broke the silence, save for the noise of the horses' hooves upon the road surface. "You realise what has happened Watson?" he said

"Not really," I mumbled, somewhat lost in my own thoughts.

"Moriarty planned this substitution on his former College employer; motivated not only by revenge at being dismissed, but more importantly, to test his scheme to fake works of art on a grand scale. His plan is to organise fakers and forgers, in order to substitute original works of art, and to identify and eradicate flaws in preparation for his *magnum opus,* which he has now achieved!

Think Watson. Moriarty knew that the collection of valuable paintings at the College was rarely seen and even less displayed in public. They existed only as an investment to provide funding for the College. They were stored in a room with poor lighting, ostensibly to protect the paintings from the effects of harsh sunlight. When they were returned to St. George's Theological College, it was during a 'particularly dark and rainy day.'

Instructive, do you not think, Watson?" inquired Holmes.

"Moriarty did not want the paintings examined too closely in daylight on their way into the gallery because of the real possibility of their being found to be fakes," I confirmed.

"What concerns me here, is the fact of concerted effort, going back some months, and arranged by a perverted genius. So we know it to be a long-standing plan, with the possibility of permutations and consequences, which have yet to manifest themselves, including, the extent of Moriarty's influence in high places, and the size of his criminal organisation spread throughout the Metropolis."

"Is this Moriarty capable of engineering such an exploit?" I asked.

"I am afraid to say that it would appear so. Nevertheless we have, I think, made some progress, if we but knew it," remarked Holmes, looking very concerned.

"I am relieved to hear you say that," I responded nervously.

"The principal's remarkable narrative has more meaning than at first we supposed. For it impinges on a consultation I had with an artist by the name of Lyons who sought my advice some months ago," continued Holmes.

We both sat in our Brougham carriage, clattering along the road trying to absorb the enormity of what the principal had told us. Clearly, the information had more meaning for Holmes, but I could from my position of ignorance, detect something that was of concern to Holmes; and it was that very fact that made me concerned too.

"On our way back through Covent Garden shall we chance our luck and see if we cannot get seats for Richard Wagner's apotheosis of all the operatic works, no less than his music drama, '*Götterdämmerung*'?" ***

"Capital idea! Yes, let us do so," enthused Holmes.

"I prefer the German opera rather than French or Italian!" remarked Holmes, for no apparent reason, but with which I agreed.

"But first we must dine at Fleming's excellent restaurant here in the Strand, for sustenance before we cope with the trauma to be unleashed in '*Götterdämmerung*' at Covent Garden.

"Rather!" I said.

"Driver, pull up here please," came Holmes's decisive injunction.

We made our way into Fleming's establishment, and I was glad to get some food into me, after enduring that poisonous atmosphere in the Diogenes Club. Having found a table, we sat down and perused the menu. There was not a great deal of time to ponder since we knew that curtain up would be in eighty minutes. I instructed the waiter accordingly.

"Roast sirloin beef olives in mushroom sauce for me and I will have the baked custard with stewed fruits and chilled glass of rosewater."

Holmes followed with the stuffed roast veal with anchovy sauce and for dessert he chose the Boodle's Orange Fool trifle. He also ordered a bottle of Bordeaux and one of Chablis, followed by port and a selection of cigars from the proprietor's collection. I reëxamined the menu. I had not noticed the alcoholic-laced Boodle's Orange Fool trifle, for if I had it would have been my preference too. Now I was stuck with baked custard with stewed fruits!

I had dined at this restaurant in the past, and the whole establishment was quite remarkable for its interior *décor*. It was often patronised by the editorial staff of *The Observer* newspaper, whose offices were next door. The restaurant was quite long but not necessarily narrow. The bar was about thirty feet in length and the front fabricated with highly varnished carved mahogany panels. The surface of the bar was completed in a lavish style, with slabs of marble; deep yellow in colour, but warm in appearance that only *Giallo Siena* exudes, and upon which were various *gasogenes* and *carafes* filled with liquid. Despite its plush opulence and general air of ostentatious extravagance, I was always amused when looking down at several spittoons placed strategically on the floor against the front of the bar! Behind the bar, in bottles on shelves fixed to the wall, was a wide range of spirits and wines from around the world. The restaurant was also renowned for the amount of daylight that was able to penetrate its deepest recesses. This daylight was afforded by the fact that the ceiling of the restaurant comprised a glazed apex roof, running the full length of the room.

We had no sooner finished our brandy and cigars than it was time to leave and step as quickly as we could in the fog to make curtain up at Covent Garden. We arrived just in time, though with some degree of inconvenience, as we took our seats in the crowded Dress Circle.

I enjoyed '*Götterdämmerung*'. It seemed appropriate for these dark times, especially given the dread-filled news about the ill-fated *Titanic* we were being bombarded with, together with the actions of the murderous professor, creating fakes and organising college bankruptcies. Was the whole world, descending into *'Twilight of the Gods'*, as Richard Wagner has portrayed in his opera? On returning home, I was glad to be able to enjoy an extra large whisky, and without aërated water, since Holmes, by his own volition, had staggered off to his bedroom delirious, as a result of his ingesting laudanum in the Diogenes Club!

* Flatiron Building, Broadway and Times Square.
** Cement stucco.
***'Twilight of the Gods'.

Chapter 15

The Visitation to Well House

Our investigation, thus far, had not turned up anything tangible that might, in itself, lead to a full explanation of Cadogan West's mysterious death in a railway carriage just beyond Charing Cross Railway Station. This was our prime investigation; but what was becoming evident, even to me, was the existence of a guiding force, a mastermind, an *eminence gris*, as it were, motivating, controlling all for an ulterior purpose. Holmes had for some time suspected the existence of such an individual, lurking at the centre of an extensive criminal web. Petty villains, previously content with small crimes in their locality, were now willing to go abroad the Metropolis, into unfamiliar districts, in order to perpetrate some villainy, as if carrying out a planned and well-coördinated instruction, from which they would benefit financially, and without question.

The next morning Holmes and I discussed the singular narrative that the principal had related to us. He then broke off from our conversation and simply looked into the fireplace, deep in thought.

"It is probable, Watson, that there is concerted effort here, and it is being controlled by a determined and intelligent brain. The story related to us by the principal, confirms this fact, if nothing else. What did the he say regarding the intelligence of the *employé* he dismissed?"

I referred to my green commonplace book, and looked through the notes that I had taken down, during Holmes' and the principal's discourse.

"Here we are," I replied: ..."Some time ago I dismissed a teacher, a mathematics professor from the College. I released him, not because he was academically wanting, rather he was the opposite, very gifted, bordering on genius, one might say...'"

"Bordering on genius," murmured Holmes.

"Watson, I have been going over some details in my mind and there is only one course of action open to us. We must make a visit to this Professor Moriarty, albeit of opprobrious infamy, at our earliest convenience – in fact today."

"Is that wise Holmes?" I asked, "He appears to be a dangerous individual as I can determine, and exhibits all the symptoms of being a psychopath."

"Possibly, but we must confront him," countered Holmes.

"Where do you suggest that we meet him, somewhere in public?" I cautioned.

"No, we shall go to his house at Hampstead, and there have an encounter with him. Our arriving unannounced or unexpectedly might just throw him off guard!"

"True Holmes, but our arriving uninvited might well result in his over reacting to our being there, on his premises," I warned.

"In the meantime Watson, I believe we have tickets for the Queen's Hall concert today. It is there that our immediate destiny lies, and where we shall experience perfection in harmony, before confronting the imperfective Moriarty!"

We left the Queen's Hall near the Regent's Circus,

having revived our spirits with a performance by the Queen's Hall Orchestra conducted by Henry Wood, of the mighty Third Symphony by Bruckner, in the dark key of D-minor, following Sibelius' Violin Concerto, in the same key, and performed by the incomparable, Néruda. Opposite the Queen's Hall, on the other side of Langham Place was the barely visible Langham Hotel, and it was to this well-appointed establishment that we now headed for much needed refreshment.

"I will show you something that will make your eyes boggle, Watson! There is a rather interesting bar located in the basement of this hotel," declared Holmes, "that is dedicated to the provision of every type of vodka known to man!"

"I feel we may well need some fortification," I said, "if we are to deal effectively with the odious Professor Moriarty later today, when we call upon him at his residence in Hampstead."

We walked under the magnificent and huge elaborately sculptured stone vestibule, gathered our wits, and stepped up smartly into the Langham Hotel, in the knowledge that within the Hotel, inside in his own state apartment, was the exiled French Emperor, Napoleon III, chaffing at his confinement. Holmes, who clearly knew his way, propelled me towards the grand staircase, whereupon, we immediately descended into the depths of the building, and onwards to the subterranean vodka bar. Making our way along a rather less grand corridor, we came to a red leather covered door upon which, Holmes knocked gently. A few moments later the door flew open, and standing there in the doorway, was a person attired in what I took to be the red silk garb of a Cossack.

"Mr. Holmes, a pleasant surprise, as always, to see

you!" the Cossack said, whilst pulling at my friend and me in his eagerness to usher us both into a large chamber, the appointment and *décor* of which, I have never experienced before.

The general effect of the room was crimson and gaudy with gold relief here and there. We walked upon a deep red carpet among items of furniture ranging from red *damask* covered *chaise-longue* to burgundy coloured buttoned leather Chesterfields. Tall, gilt-framed mirrors hung upon the walls and some were affixed to the ceiling, precariously, so I thought.

We were not the only patrons present, for throughout the large, dimly lit room I could make out other persons sitting at tables in deep conversation with each other. No one looked at either Holmes or me as we entered and our presence had no appreciable effect of the proceedings taking place prior to our arrival.

"This is what will make your eyes bulge Watson," said Holmes, as he indicated, with a sweep of his hand the back wall of the bar.

There before my very eyes, in full sight of God and man, was the largest collection of bottles containing various kinds of vodka that I had ever seen. The wall of glass bottles, in which the spirits were imprisoned, must have measured at least twenty feet in length by eight feet in height. Indeed, Holmes had not exaggerated his claim, as I realised through my bulging eyes!

I was then introduced to Alexis, the proprietor of the bar, dressed in his Cossack garb. He immediately began to ply us with a range of exotic vodkas, made from, so it seemed, every vegetable or fruit, and some even containing gold leaf. The drinks went down well enough, in conjunction with freely exchanged experiences and anecdotes. It was, therefore, with great reluctance that we eventually agreed to leave, and had even more difficulty in getting off the bar stools, and attempting to make our way into the fog-bound world upstairs,

"Carriage sir?" asked the liveried doorman, on our eventually reaching the ornate stone porch in the front of the hotel.

"No," I responded, "not before I have placed a bet on a certainty on a race at Epsom."

And with that vow, I lurched off into the fog with only a vague notion of where my bookmaker's agent was located; though I knew him to be around the corner, somewhere in the vicinity of Cavendish Square. At length, I did find him and eventually returned to the hotel vestibule only to find Holmes standing there motionless, as though a statue. The doorman stepped out of the hotel, and with a short shrill whistle, summoned a Landau four-wheeler carriage, that presently materialised from out of the fog.

"Well House in Well Road, junction of East Heath Road, Hampstead," instructed Holmes.

And with that injunction, our carriage driver shook his reins, flicked his whip and turned the horses' heads east into Riding House Street. He then turned the carriage left, into the Portland Road, driving north, and upon reaching the Portland Road Metropolitan Station,* reined his horses east along the Euston Road. We traversed this busy thoroughfare until we reached the St. Pancras Church, complete with its replication of the Temple of Erechtheion, at the Acropolis in Athens. Here he turned the horses left into Upper Seymour Street and north-wards on our journey to Holmes' antagonist, Professor Moriarty. The hooves of our two horses clattered on the cobbled stone road as they negotiated their way through the fog.

Temple of Erechtheion

"Had that ill-fated *Titanic* boat been built on the Clyde shipyards in Scotland, it would have gone straight through that iceberg and sunk it without trace!" boomed a voice in the fog directly ahead of us.

Holmes and I looked at each other.

"Quite!" responded Holmes, in a manner deliberately intoned to discourage the carriage driver from any thoughts of engaging in any banal conversation with us, during the course of our journey.

"It must have been quite a performance on that *Titanic* boat," continued the carriage driver, undeterred by Holmes' verbal dismissal, "what with the mutiny and the fire that broke out, into which the crew tossed recalcitrant passengers who refused to pay them a fee in order to gain access into the all but too few life boats. And, what about that band of musicians, what! Floating around on a raft, in the waters of the Atlantic Ocean, and playing popular tunes, including '*Abide With Me*' and even requests from those struggling in the water, cor, what a performance!"

"Indeed," said Holmes.

"Cor, what a palaver; it would not happen on a Cunard boat."

"No doubt..." continued Holmes.

"You take that Lusitania boat," butted in the carriage

driver, "safe as 'ouses. It has got none of your *triple screw reciprocating engines* powering forty-seven thousand tons of boat, into what, straight into an iceberg? That captain Smith - a bit of a lad, what, and almost certainly must have been seriously at the bottle too; that *Titanic* boat was not the only wreck, plying the waters of the Atlantic during that fateful night. How can you not miss an iceberg the size of St. Paul's Cathedral, I ask you?"

"I really do not know," said Holmes, impatiently, but to no avail, as the carriage driver continued, remorselessly.

"My old lady is from Liverpool, and when up there, I have seen those big boats coming round the headland, and they are all over the place; do they have rudders, I kept asking myself then? The chances are if they have, then they do not know how to use them, banging around and crashing into other boats and hitting harbour walls and the like. One even managed to ram a ship of His Majesty's Navy. Cor guv, if I drove my carriage around London like that, I would have to go up to the Hackney Carriage Office and give a good account of myself or I could find myself in Queer Street. *Reciprocating engines*, what!"

The Landau carriage driver continued to offload his diatribe irrespective of the lack of encouragement from either Holmes or myself.

"It is wise to use the a Landau when travelling to Hampstead by way of Camden Town," remarked Holmes, "if only to frustrate the intentions of footpads that line the route and remain always ready with their *ambuscade* of the unwary traveller. You can imagine Watson, especially in this fog, such individuals can operate under its concealment and invariably have the advantage in any incident, staged or otherwise," he continued.

I had, in the mean time, given some thought to the continuing challenge, fuelled no doubt by the vodka.

"Perhaps we could call the recently built station, *'Marylebone Road Station'* in keeping with other railway stations as *'Liverpool Street'*, *'Broad Street'* or *'Cannon Street'* since they reflect the name of the streets in which they are constructed?"

"I say Holmes, did you hear what I have said?"

The driver of our carriage delivered us to Moriarty's house, located on the junction of Well Road and East Heath Road opposite Hampstead Heath. We alighted from the carriage, and in an instant it went clattering off into the fog, with only its ghostly red lantern visible and swinging eerily, as it eventually disappeared into the folds of white shrouds of fog. Holmes pulled at the cast iron doorbell plunger that operated a bell, the faint sound from which was just audible. The sound came from within the depths of the house, that stood in its own grounds, behind a high stone wall, topped with broken glass.

Whilst waiting for a response to our summons, I surveyed the door immediately in front of us. It was centred in a massive Gothic archway which surrounded the heavy iron-clamped oak door, that formed an entrance through the wall, into the garden and thus to the house. The impression given by this entrance into the grounds of the house was one of decay, emphasised by the damp fog. It also appeared something like a fortress, showing clearly that Moriarty, not only guarded his privacy jealously, but that no casual visitor would ever breach his domain. In short the surrounding masonry and brickwork framing the door, had all the appearance of an entrance to a Gothic ruin, rather than the residence of a wealthy, if criminally per-verted, individual.

The sound of a retaining iron bar behind the wooden

door being scraped back, told us that our summons was being answered. At length, we heard a clanking and jarring of keys, and the door began to open very slowly, creating an opening in which stood a servant of the household, Brunton the butler, so we learned later. He bowed and waved his arm in the direction of the house at the end of a rising pathway of wet flagstones. We entered the premises through the arched portal and waited there in desolated grounds, most of which had been dug up, forming craters, as if the occupiers had been busy burying objects. Meanwhile Brunton spent what I thought to be an inordinate amount of time re-locking the door and thus securing the premises from unwarranted intrusion.

From what I could discern, in the gloom, the house that rose up before us in the mist, appeared to be a tall Gothic mansion complete with ancient Egyptian stone symbols and detailing. Just visible in the fog, amidst the protruding crenellated gable-ends, was a massive and foreboding looking tower, rising ominously from the centre of the mansion. The tower appeared all the more sinister, by the fact that on top of it was a truncated pyramid, surrounded by four massive carved stone pinnacles, placed at each corner. The vast mansion, in its deathly, fog-shrouded silence, was evidently some way back from the road, and well secluded. This fact alone caused me great anxiety, in case we should we find ourselves in the clutches of the venal Moriarty and at his mercy. With this trepidation occupying my mind, Brunton beckoned us to follow him up to the house.

We walked along the damp, slippery York flagstones, which formed a path to the mansion. The pathway led us through the lifeless vegetation of a desolate garden, speckled with dead autumnal leaves amongst the mon-

Well House, Hampstead

strously overgrown laurel bushes, set in clumps and partially obscured by the fog. Several large deformed-looking trees dominated the garden, with their extended glistening branches, some of which were arching down, as though bearing the oppressive weight of the pervasive fog and dampness lingering in the garden within the precincts of the high wall that surrounded the house.

By degrees aspects of the mansion came into view, revealing even more detail of this sinister looking building. Many of the walls of the house were covered with dark green ivy that was creeping its way around, as if in the process of actually consuming the building's bricks and stonework. Some of the ivy had fallen away, leaving gaps in its conquest, and lay upon the ground forlorn and rotting. Occasionally, within the matted mass of this creepy greenery, a solitary window could be seen, though by now already in the process of being swallowed up and covered completely, by the relentless plant; its tentacles ever searching for new surfaces upon which to colonise its grasp.

As we approached the front door, framed by a stone porch, that comprised wide columns which supported its heavy stone canopy and castellated parapet, we could discern to our right, a large curved stone wall, with window openings cut into its surface, forming window reveals. The mansion was built of stone, with areas of brickwork to its *façade*. The overall effect was one not of beauty, but of a pervasive and heavy ugliness, as if the builder had wanted to repel visitors to his creation.

Some of the windows of the house were either boarded up or covered by heavy drapes within, permanently drawn, to exclude the outside world from intruding into this structure. Those windows that were visible were smeared with years of grime and neglect, giving them a gaunt minatory look, as though openings not on to light, but on to a dead soul. The general impression of the mansion was one of neglect and decay, as though the building, were crumbling slowly apart. There was an overbearing sensation of dampness and desolation, such as that often captured and conveyed in the paintings of abandoned mansions, by the currently fashionable artist, Atkinson Grimshaw and others, including members of that innovative school of art known as the *'Pre-Raphaelite Brotherhood'*.

Having gained the interior of the house, our eyes became accustomed to a gloomy hall, into which Brunton had shown us before departing to collect his master. The hallway was large and illuminated only with the blue flame from coal tar gas jets, in the form of wall-mounted brass *appliqués* shaped as angels, holding forth their firebrand of gas flame. Every surface was covered in a thick layer of dust that had accumulated over the years, which made breathing difficult, in this still and suffocating atmosphere.

I was on the verge of choking, but stopped only by the shock of the vision that confronted us, for it was one causing utter astonishment. Piled high almost to the ceiling of the hall and on every step of a grand staircase in front of us, were stacks of newspapers going back over the decades. I had never witnessed such extreme degrees of monomania before. The collection of old newspapers was not made up of papers such as *The Times, The Daily Telegraph* or even the *Daily Chronicle,* which one might expect a person such as Moriarty to read. But rather the hoard comprised newspapers from America, such as *The Chicago Tribune*, the *New York Times* and even the Missouri based, *St. Louis Post-Dispatch* and the *Joplin Globe.* Clearly, Moriarty's monomania, as described by the principal in the laudanum den, had not abated over the months, but in fact, had become chronically worse.

I could see in Holmes' features that this revelation too, had surprised him; and despite his keen examination of the newspapers nearby, a look of anxiety swept across his face, giving me further cause for concern.

"Look Watson, look at this banner headline in the *St. Louis Post-Dispatch.*"

I did so and asked, "Why would Moriarty wish to read, on a daily basis, newspapers from America?"

"Quite simply Watson, if you wished to be fully informed of developments taking place in the United States, but in a way that would not attract attention, what would you do? Clearly to be kept informed by telegraph would alert the authorities and leave a trail of evidence as to the subject matter of the telegraph messages. No Watson, you would have newspaper delivered daily to you, from a variety of newsagents, nothing unusual in that. And see for yourself; look at the different types of handwriting used to write the address labels fixed to each newspaper. The newsagent's handwriting on *The New York Times* is different from that on *The Chicago Tribune*."

"So is the script on this *St. Louis Post-Dispatch*," I added.

"This means Watson, that Moriarty wished to keep secret his need to monitor various American newspapers, by at least having each paper delivered by a separate newsagent!"

A further examination of the hall in which we were still waiting, revealed other idiosyncrasies of this deranged Professor Moriarty. For looking down onto the bare floorboards of the hallway, I noticed that some had been recently pulled up, and nailed back into place in a rushed and haphazard manner. On some of the floorboards, the nails had not been hammered home, and were protruding. What had happened to this flawed genius, that had caused him to step out of the light, and instead, to dwell in darkness? I thought to myself.

"This is a singular set of circumstances, Watson," I heard Holmes proclaim.

I did not respond, but instead, continued to gaze around the hall. In so doing, I noticed, that at the far end of the hall, a huge tarpaulin had been draped over part of a wall from where the plaster had been hacked away, revealing bare brickwork. Upon looking carefully, the brickwork seemed to be fairly recent, as though a large hole in the wall had been bricked up to conceal something or someone. What was Moriarty up to, I wondered, whilst coming to the conclusion that this mansion was assuming quickly all the attributes of a functioning Mausoleum! I shuddered at the thoughts of what Moriarty may have done behind that recently bricked up wall, or buried beneath the floorboards upon which I was standing. Were these the outward signs of his attempt to cover up some atrocity that he had perpetrated on a hapless individual, held prisoner in this mansion?

Both Holmes and I were so absorbed in examining Moriarty's hallway that we failed to notice a singular sound that was becoming louder. It was the distinct tinkling of musical notes, made by a piano, which were drifting down the grand staircase from the upper floors of this rambling mansion. I stood there, momentarily transfixed, listening to the music and realised that no accomplished pianist was actually playing a piano. Instead, I reasoned that the music was either being created by one of the new fangled mechanical sound preserving devices, involving a wax cylinder and called a *phonograph*, or, more likely, from one of those novel contraptions, I believe, called an Aëolian Pianola. In any event, I recognised something else. The music being played was Franz Liszt's piano transcription of Bellini's opera, '*Reminiscences de Norma*'. This ethereal combination of sensual musical *arpeggio* technique and the sinister atmosphere, in which we found ourselves, was too incongruous for me to take in, and I felt myself beginning to panic.

"Steady, Watson, steady," I heard Holmes' reassuring voice.

The music had in, fact, heralded the return of Brunton, who had now descended the creaking staircase, glided straight past us, and then flung open a set of large, green baize-covered double doors. He pointed with his hand, and motioned us to enter and wait in the room, whilst advising us that the professor would be joining us presently.

As we entered the room Brunton closed the doors silently behind us. The air inside became still again, but was marginally more breathable than the air in the hallway. Here at least, I thought, an attempt had been made to make what was a drawing room, habitable, though by no means to the level one might describe as being voluptuary. The windows were covered with long, heavy, faded, purple velvet drapes of the kind that block out all daylight. The room was sparsely furnished; and the items of furniture present were of a heavy varnished type, the origins of which resembled more Queen Anne in style than Victorian. The walls may have been painted white at one time, but now gave off a greyish hue, adding to the general gloominess of the room.

In a corner of the drawing room, occupying an inordinate amount of space, stood a grand piano that was covered in faded red velvet, folded partly back, to reveal the keyboard. On the music rest, to my great surprise, was the score of Richard Wagner's opera *'Das Rheingold'* in the piano transcription version, by the *Abbé* Liszt. I also observed the music was that of the opera's closing section to the *finale*, known as the *'Entry of the Gods into Valhalla.'* Wagner was also represented, in the form of a *Carrara* marble bust, which rested on top of the piano. Clearly Moriarty cannot be all that bad, I theorised, and was possibly a *devoté* of the piano works of the *Abbé* Franz Liszt.

On the wall, next to the piano, was a painting of *surreal* aspect. Upon closer examination of the brass nameplate fixed to the gilt frame, I read that it was entitled *Astarte Syriaca*** and painted by a fellow called Dante Gabriel Rosetti. On the opposite wall, above a large ornate and lavishly carved green *Verde Patrizia* marble chimneypiece, was another sizeable painting, which I recognised as being *'The Island of the Dead'* by the Swiss artist Arnold Böcklin.

On another wall, and built of timber, were shelves that had perhaps at one time contained an enormous and extensive library; though most of the shelves now only contained layers of dust, in place of books. Those that I glanced at showed me that the original creator of the library was of a mathematical leaning. Other books were devoted to marine engineering and the science of hydraulics. Scattered about the library shelves were several booklets, with the title '*Binomial Theorem*' imprinted on their front covers. A few books were concerned with the classification and indexing of art works, both ancient and recent. I looked at again at the Böcklin above the fireplace and the Rosetti next to the piano, and concluded Moriarty to be an art collector.

Curiously, what did catch my attention, as Holmes busied himself examining the room minutely, was a boiler hidden in the darker recesses afforded by one of the corners in the room. The boiler looked as if it were being fitted to receive the lengths of lead pipes that were placed around it on the floor. I picked up one of the pipes and examined it. Possibly central heat is being laid on, or so I thought. This drawing room, though uninviting, cold and musty, had an eclectic, incongruous collection of items scattered about, adding to the general atmosphere of foreboding.

Presently we heard a muffled sound outside in the hallway. A few minutes went by before the double doors to the drawing room, in which we were waiting, suddenly burst open, and in stepped Professor Moriarty, late of the Theological College of St. George. He was wearing a frock-coat beneath a coat of deep red velvet with an Astrakhan collar. The trousers he wore were striped and his ensemble completed with black-varnished patent leather boots. His smile of conde-scending welcome, greeted us as he held out his hand to me. I took it out of convention. Holmes rejected, ungallantly this offer of courtesy. Unperturbed by Holmes' rudeness, Moriarty opened the conversation.

"Mr. Sherlock Holmes and the good Doctor Watson, I am honoured that you both grace my house with your august presence."

"Moriarty," Holmes interjected, "let us dispense with the pleasantries. I am here to ask you about your involvement in a major art exhibition to be held at the World's Columbian Exposition in Chicago."

This line of questioning totally threw me, as I had expected Holmes, to launch straight into the sinking of the ill-fated *Titanic*. However, nothing, it appeared then, could be further from Holmes' intention, as he continued with his line of inquiry.

"I have it on good authority Moriarty that you are involved deeply with this exhibition, are you not?"

A silence fell on the room as Holmes and Moriarty sized one another up. Neither spoke, but looked rather intently at each other, as if acknowledging mutual thoughts, racing across their minds. Eventually, after several seconds, Holmes broke the silence.

"What can you hope to gain from the perpetration of such a monstrous crime?" asked Holmes.

"Notoriety and wealth, for they are of course, as cheap as life itself!" responded Moriarty.

"You have the capacity to achieve intellectual recog-nition and celebration without the need to resort to the depths of callous criminality. Or," reminded Holmes, "to dominate the world of crime and…"

"Ah!" interjected Moriarty, "before one can seriously contemplate confidently world domination, one has to deal with a little matter of the Vatican and the Catholic Church!"

To which I responded. "Yes, but as a force for good not evil."

Moriarty gave very little consideration to my outburst and turning back to Holmes resumed his conversation.

"We are both men of the world," he continued, "you have chosen your profession and path; I too have done so."

"My path," countered Holmes, "is to serve society, not perpetrate crimes against it."

"Such misplaced concern is of supreme indifference to me," stated Moriarty.

"Really?" responded Holmes, "such concern may become of importance to you and sooner than expected."

Moriarty did not reply immediately, but rather seemed lost in thought for several moments. Then, with the determination of a person who has resolved a problem, said to Holmes:

"I expected your cranium to be larger. Instead, I find that I am dealing with an intellectual inferior, and a common thief, who in this instance, I have disturbed burgling my house, aided and abetted by your confederate in crime the bad Doctor Watson."

"What!" I exploded, "how dare you act in a confident manner in front of us; do you really know whom you are addressing?" I demanded.

"Yes I most certainly do," replied Moriarty, "I am addressing two thieves who are going to regret the fact that they have broken into my house, my isolated house!"

Holmes looked at Moriarty impassively, and then picked up his cane and hat and beckoned me to do the same.

"Thank you professor, we shall not detain you any

longer," said Holmes, while we made our way to the drawing room's double doors leading to the hallway.

Moriarty stepped out of our way, but said:

"Detain me Mr. Holmes? I think not; rather it is I who shall detain you. It is you and the Doctor who are trespassing and have gained access into my property. You may have concealed your breaking into my home successfully enough that no one saw you enter my house. Therefore why would anybody know you are here or indeed expect you to leave?"

Moriarty pronounced these final words, slowly and deliberately, and in so doing, made clear his calculated intentions toward us, now that he had us at his mercy. Accordingly, our attempt to gain the front door was checked by the bald headed Brunton, and two of Moriarty's henchmen.

"Good day gentlemen," said Moriarty, as he disappeared into the recesses of his rambling mansion.

"This rather complicates things Watson, do you have a weapon to hand?"

"No, but I have secreted about my person, a two-foot length of the heavy gauge lead piping, that I picked up from the drawing room floor near the stove!"

One of the henchmen however, waited for no such formal introduction and seized Holmes, who repelled him with a left hook to his jaw, and uttering an oath, followed by a dull thud, the thug fell to the floor. All was momentarily quiet; but then Brunton started towards me. With his bulk, and weight, he bowled into my left knee, made weak by a lance, when serving with the King's Own Hussars at the battle of Sherpur near Kabul, during the second Afghan war. His attack had the effect of making me fall against a wall, but in so doing, I deflected most of his efforts, as he sailed by down the hallway. I regained my composure and upon realising that Holmes was being set upon by another of Moriarty's thugs, rushed towards them. Abandoning all regard for the medical or legal consequences, I produced my length of lead piping, from inside my coat, and gripping it firmly, brought it down on to the head of Holmes' attacker. I confess to being quite horrified, at seeing the lead-pipe wrap around and adopt the same shape and outline as the assailant's head!

Next, Brunton, the butler, reappeared, this time brandishing a poker, and shouting that, 'we were not to be allowed to leave the house, save in coffins!' I immediately took steps to protect my person again from his onslaught, and attempted to disengage the lead piping from around my unconscious assailant's head. The force I had used, in bringing down the pipe, however, made releasing it impossible. Retracing my steps back into the drawing room, I picked up another piece of lead piping, even longer in length. I reëmerged into the hall wielding the lead pipe and instantly made for Brunton

Neither Brunton, nor myself for that matter, expected to witness the sequence of events that unfolded. For whilst I was in full flight to deliver a blow with my lead pipe on to his bald head, I tripped on one of the protruding floorboard nails, as it caught my shoe. In my fall, I released my grip on the lead piping, which continued in flight over Brunton's head. It made contact with a purple *Rosso Lepanto* marble bust, of some worthy general, Lord Kitchener I think, positioned on a shelf on the wall above Brunton's head. On making contact with it, the heavy lead pipe had the effect of dislodging the bust, whereupon it came crashing down on to Brunton's head. Still lying on the floor, but looking up in disbelief, I saw Brunton give a sickening grimace; clasp his head with blood pouring through his fingers, and reel backwards onto the floor. As he did so, he careered into a nearby ceiling-high stack of newspapers, which immediately collapsed, engulfing him in an *avalanche* of printed matter and a cloud of choking dust.

By now, Holmes had bounded up the staircase and having gained upon another of one of Moriarty's unfortunate henchmen, was practising his self-defence art of *Baritsu*. I remember thinking at the time that Holmes seemed to be practising not so much the art of self-defence but rather gratuitous offence against his adversary, whose head he was now holding firmly in an arm grip. The livid features on the face of Holmes' opponent, now rapidly turning purple, together with his ranine eyes bulging out of their sockets, told me, as a physician, that he had clearly ceased to be a threat to Holmes' person. I therefore resisted the urge to rain down, with my re-acquired lead piping, a blow to his swollen head.

No doubt Moriarty had gone in search of more odious henchmen, to abet him in his designs to incommode us. The fact that we could now hear the sound of voices, and a general view-holloa being raised from within the very depths of the mansion, confirmed this. The voices were becoming louder and mingled with the still undisrupted music of Liszt's final paraphrase of the piano transcription of Bellini's opera, *Reminiscences de Norma'* however mechanically contrived or created, that continued to tinkle down the grand staircase having accompanied the *mêlée* in the hallway.

We both collected our wits and made for the front door. With some difficulty we managed to release a series of catches and locks, more appropriate to a bank vault than a house, and having gained the outside, we slid down the grimy and wet pathway to the road door entrance. We were only feet away from making good our escape, when a blood curdling chill went through my spine, as I heard the unmistakable barking of hounds, let loose upon us in the fog. We both jerked frantically at the cast iron door beam, until finally it slid out from its tight bracket. And, whilst Holmes released other locks and catches on the door, I immediately held this iron bar aloft above my head, ready to bring down upon the head of the first hound, to present itself to us from out of the fog.

Eventually, we fell out through the road door into Well Road; and as we did so, Holmes thoughtfully pulled the door shut behind us, whereupon we heard various automatic deadlocks whirring and clicking back into a locked position and thus preventing Moriarty's murderous henchmen and the hounds from pursuing us over the heath. For the first time, I was grateful for Moriarty's sense of insecurity and mused on the fact that his own paranoid need for security in keeping people out, had in fact saved us!

Having left the stifling atmosphere of Moriarty's residence for the infinitely preferable, albeit choking, envelopment of the fog, we trod quickly along the East Heath Road, adjacent to the great expanse that is Hampstead Heath. Suddenly, Holmes darted forward and intercepted a passing drag carriage drawn by a four-in-hand that loomed out of the swirling mist like a ghostly apparition.

"221.b. Baker Street!" came the injunction from Holmes.

* Now called Great Portland Street Metropolitan Station
** Phoenician goddess of love

Chapter 16

The Science of Deduction

Our visit to Well House to interview Professor Moriarty had met with little success, save only to indicate that he is involved somehow with the sinking of the ill-fated *Titanic*. Holmes had changed his tactic when we first encountered Moriarty, by astutely avoided any reference to the sinking of the Titanic. Instead he restricted his questions to the major art exhibition, to be held at the World's Columbian Exposition in Chicago, to which several promising artists hoped to have their work submitted.

I was relieved to be back in our rooms in Baker Street and out of that stultifying air that pervaded Well House; accordingly, I headed straight for the drinks cabinet next to our mahogany sideboard.

"Make mine an extra large neat whisky!" yelled Holmes as he disappeared into his bedroom.

"A bit of a problem Holmes," I replied, "we are running out of whisky."

"Well, get that Hudson woman to buy some then," came a command from the depths of his room.

He later emerged with a book containing a monograph on art, which he placed on the table next to his chair. I handed him his whisky.

At that moment a knock at our door heralded not the

ubiquitous Mrs. Hudson, but rather Billy our new pageboy, who handed a telegram to Holmes, in quite a theatrical and convoluted manner. Holmes tore open the buff coloured envelope, and looked at Billy, who then commenced a series of exaggerated bows and, moving his hand in an arch in front of him, retreated from our room.

"You must be thinking Watson," Holmes said, while opening the telegram, "why I inquired about missing artwork rather than the ill-fated *Titanic* when addressing Moriarty earlier this evening?"

"I confess to being surprised Holmes," I said, "since I thought that was the very reason for our having to visit that odious individual."

"Well, when we were in the hallway waiting on the professor, did you notice anything in the American newspapers stacked about the hall?" asked Holmes.

"No." I responded.

"I did," continued Holmes, "and one can be certain that Moriarty is up to his neck in some concentrated evil he has perpetrated only recently. I may also add, that the *Titanic* is only a part of his grand scheme of things. The mystery grows deeper Watson, but I think that we have the evidence, as the various threads come together. However, what seems to me to be incredible is the sheer scale of the crime, so that I can scarcely believe it myself. If I am correct, this Moriarty has surpassed himself in the annals of crime."

"What is it?" I pleaded with him to tell me.

"You know my methods, Watson, all in good time, all in good time," was his reply to me, as he raised his crystal glass, filled to the brim with whisky, and drank deeply and liberally.

"Holmes we are going to the Royal Albert Hall of Arts

and Sciences, this evening to witness a performance of Mahler's First Symphony, *The Titan,* you may remember."

"I know, a capital idea, Watson!"

We dressed, and had a light supper of cold meats from a tray upon the sideboard and descending our staircase went out to a waiting Hansom carriage in the street, that Billy, our pageboy had somehow secured for us. The oppressive fog was still with us, but our spirits were raised, partly because we were looking forward to the concert and evening of fine music, but more probably due to the amount of alcohol we had consumed. Given the quest upon which we were currently engaged, we were in need of an aesthetic experience to rejuvenate our souls.

We set off along Baker Street and then turned left into Crawford Street and clattered over Gloucester Place. In so doing, we nearly collided with a Phäeton carriage, being driven furiously in the fog, by a man who looked possessed. After our horse had settled down, we continued along Crawford Street, now devoid of pedestrians. At length we passed Robert Smirke's prototype, for his masterpiece in creating the British Museum - St Mary's Church, complete with its classical limestone portico of columns capped with *Ionic* capitals surrounding a *rotunda* supporting an impressive tall *campanile*. As we approached Seymour Place, we entered the junction cautiously, given our recent near collision, and even the horse seemed to sense this precaution too. A Victoria carriage went clattering by, but at no great velocity to speak of.

Looking up from the junction, I noticed the same Victorian apartment building we had seen the other day when both of us had lost our bearings in the fog. This time, as our Hansom carriage approached the building,

I could see a large notice proclaiming it to be called Seymour Buildings. Despite the fog, I could recognise clearly ornate architectural details to building's ornate *façade*. These included several elaborate *terra-cotta* mouldings of the bearded heads of the pre-ancient Greek gods called *Titans* complete with drain pipes protruding from their mouths. What a curious architectural detail, I pondered, designed to remove rainwater from the flat fenced roof of this Victorian apartment building. Nor was the connection lost on me between these *Titan* heads and our destination to witnessed Mahler's First Symphony that he calls *The Titan* to say nothing of a sunken boat, called the *Titanic!*

Our Hansom carriage progressed along Crawford Street and into Crawford Place and then turned left into the Edgware Road, at the Junction Road end.* This road is yet another major thoroughfare of the Metropolis and along it seethes almost every mode of transportation known to man. Our journey south down the road was slow due simply to the sheer volume of traffic made up of the various types of vehicle all lumbering to their respective destinations. The commerce and trade being conducted in the road was not in any way diminished by the presence of the damp fog. Coal tar gas flames blazed from large brass lanterns hanging in front of the shops and establishments lining the pavement.

I began to fear that the traffic might incommode us and make us arrive late at the Royal Albert Hall of Arts and Sciences. At this point I remembered an article in *The Daily Telegraph* informing the reader that just down the road in front of us at Marble Arch, was a proposed new railway station to be called '*West End*' and to be operated by the Edgware Road & Victoria Railway Company. This railway would traverse south, beneath

Hyde Park, from the Marble Arch end of Oxford Street to Hyde Park Corner. There, according to the newspaper report, it would be possible to connect to the trains operated by the Great Northern - Piccadilly & Brompton Railway Company to destinations as South Kensington Underground Station and Brompton Road Underground Station. ** From either of those stations, I knew, it would be possible to walk to the Royal Albert Hall of Arts and Sciences and accordingly arrive on time.

"Driver, has that new West End station, down the road at Marble Arch, actually opened yet?" I asked.

"No!" came his curt reply, and promptly reined his horse right, swerving across the carriageway giving both Holmes and myself a sharp jolt as he did so.

Peering from the carriage, I observed that we were entering Connaught Street in the direction of Connaught Square. Having emerged from Connaught Square we re-joined Connaught Street along which we then wheeled left into Albion Street passing St. George's Fields in the process. Hyde Park was nearby and not surprisingly the fog became denser; still we were making progress, to the extent that I hoped we might not after all arrive late. I checked my gold Hunter to confirm this hope.

At last, turning right and facing west, we travelled along the Bayswater Road that defines the northern boundary of the park. Eventually the Hansom cab driver reined his horse left off this road and entered Hyde Park through the Victoria Gate, adjacent to the canine cemetery. We continued into the park, down the Serpentine Road, accompanied only by the sound of our horse's hooves on the roadway, and the passing of ghostly shapes, set in the fog, of the large forest trees of which the park is made up. One could almost believe that we were in the depths of the countryside rather than in the middle of the largest Metropolis on earth, I mused, to Holmes! At length, we clattered over the ornately decorated stone Serpentine Bridge. From our Hansom cab, I could just make out, by leaning on the carriage door window apron, the black stilled waters of the Serpentine Lake below us. As we continued our way through the park, past the impressive Magazine Armoury, we could just discern to our right the tall ornate Gothic canopied memorial to the Prince Albert, located in Kinsington Gardens, which indicated we were approaching the Kensington side.

A few moments later, we left Hyde Park through the Alexandra Gate and joined the throng of traffic moving in a purposeful manner west along Kensington Gore. At the same time we passed a building located on the junction of the Gore and what I took to be the Exhibition Road. In the forecourt of this red brick, vernacular styled building, were several men dressed in balaclavas and wearing heavy weatherproof clothing and boots, as though preparing to go on an expedition.

Despite our drive being slow, due to the fog, we approached the Royal Albert Hall of Arts and Sciences to our right and on time. There were several carriages of every type, Broughams, Clarences, Victorias and improved Phäetons all delivering guests. Having alighted from our humble Hansom carriage, we immediately joined this large gathering on their way into the massive hall where at length we took our seats in a box and settled down for the concert.

"I have always preferred the profound Teutonic music over the frivolous Latin," Holmes confided in me, as he sat back in his seat, fingers together and his eyes closed to the world.

A hush descended upon the hall and with one sweep

of his baton, the acclaimed conductor, Hans Richter, launched into the sublime opening section of Gustav Mahler's First Symphony, introducing the sustained high octave A-major chord gradually unfolding a sequence of descending *Fourths*. My mind drifted, with the music, into the heavens. Occasionally, I observed the architecture of this magnificent building, especially the columns supporting the arches of which the upper perimeter of the hall is comprised, and where people were walking round slowly, as if on a promenade. Towards the *finale* of the Symphony, I could not help but think that the architecture of the hall with its towering columns and extensive arches reflected the soaring chords and the marshalled massive orchestral forces of this *Titan* Symphony. Both, I concluded, were architectural masterpieces. The Symphony concluded with its rapturous hammer chords reverberating throughout the hall and in doing, brought the music to triumphant conclusion and to ecstatic applause, which I think awakened Holmes.

We made our way out of the Royal Albert Hall of Arts and Sciences along with other patrons, at an agonisingly slow pace. Eventually, on emerging into the Kensington Gore, we were confronted by a chaotic scene, as the stampede for the too few available carriages, was as discourteous as it was tremendous. So much so that we decided to walk to Goldini's restaurant in the Gloucester Road, only a short walk away, rather than involve ourselves in an undignified struggle to gain a carriage.

We battled our way through the crowds mingling around the outside of the hall until both Holmes and I had reached the steps leading down to the Prince Consort Road. Making our way along this road we passed the Imperial College on our right and then to our left the grand and imposing Imperial Institute, with its tall Gothic tower rising into the fog. Turning left into Queen's Gate we crossed the road into Queen's Gate Terrace that brought us into the Gloucester Road. However, just before we entered the Gloucester Road, made evident in the fog by the increasing din and activity emanating from it, Holmes grabbed my coat sleeve and pulled me into a back street called Petersham Lane. Somewhat dumbfounded I asked him why he had done so.

"Watson, my friend, I thought we might avail ourselves of a drink; the music of Gustav Mahler has given me, and I am sure you too, quite a thirst."

"A drink, in this fog-bound back street – are you serious?"

"Faith, dear doctor, have faith!" he implored.

Then, he led the way down a narrow lane. I had my reservations, but nonetheless, followed him farther down the lane, groping our way as we did so. I then began to detect a faint sound of revellers and a general commotion coming from somewhere in front of us. And then I saw, just above my head, several windows from which warm red light radiated, glowing pink in the dank fog. This was the rear entrance to the Harrington Arms Public House, Holmes announced, as we climbed the steps leading into the vault and tap room bars.

We made our way through a series of bars and groups of persons until we had reached what I think was designated the saloon bar. It was bright and illuminated with a plethora of *chandeliers*, the existence of which one would not expect in such an establishment. It was a very well appointed and comfortable looking interior, with polished elm surfaces and hinged etched glazed screens providing privacy to those who required it for their conversation. The walls were covered with dark purple-flocked wallpaper that lent an air of restrained dignity to the place. On the walls were large mirrors, which augmented the feeling of space. The rich, luxuriant carpet, upon which I was standing, was of such an ornate and intricate auburn pattern, that it defied one finding any object, inadvertently dropped onto it, such was the complexity of its design.

"This is my friend and colleague, Doctor John Watson."

Holmes said, introducing me to a person who sported a handlebar moustache, below a gold framed *pince-nez* through which he surveyed us and who wore a white apron on top of his checked trousers. I assumed him to be the landlord, and expected the usual inquiry as to my being a physician and Holmes being a valetudinarian.

"Pleased to meet you doctor. What can I get you two gentlemen - on the house?"

"That is uncommonly decent of you. I will have a large whisky and aërated water."

"And for the good doctor," inquired the landlord.

"A large cognac please, neat." I replied.

We had those drinks and in fact several more, such was our conversation with our genial landlord.

"I understand doctor, that you have just been to the Royal Albert Hall of Arts and Sciences to listen to a concert. What was the name of the orchestra playing this evening?"

"The London Symphony Orchestra conducted by the renowned Hans Richter, the orchestra that broke away from the Queen's Hall Orchestra," I ventured.

The landlord raised his eyes to the heavens and said:

"So we can expect that lot to come storming in, demanding beer and comfort as they always do. I thought this accursed fog might keep them at bay, but if you and Mr. Holmes could find your way here, they will certainly follow their noses to any establishment that serves beer and spirits!"

I attempted to commiserate.

"You probably do not know doctor, but we have had trouble with that orchestra in the past. Nothing serious but they do like to unwind after a day's rehearsal and an evening's concert. Though we are not the nearest public house to the Royal Albert Hall of Arts and Science, we remain the favoured resort with all of the orchestras that play there. Not least when they do turn up, they will insist on getting out their instruments and playing an *impromptu* medley of tunes, much to the delight of my customers. Alas though not to my neighbours, who complain bitterly to the police inspector, who then comes down hard on me for failing to keep an orderly public house. One day I shall lose my licence, you will see," said the landlord, in tones of despair.

At that moment, a commotion of music erupted from the back of the bar. Indeed it seemed to come from that very back door Holmes and I had entered through earlier. The landlord moved swiftly to intercept the crowd but was too late. All of a sudden his saloon bar was full of brass instruments, stringed instruments and wind instruments as the cacophony of sound gathered apace.

"Are you still playing that viola Holmes?"

"Violin actually and a Stradivarius at that, I will have you know!" said Holmes turning around to face his accuser.

"Why, if it is not my old friend Victor Trevor," Holmes continued.

The person to whom Holmes addressed his comments, was dressed in black trousers and tailcoat with extremely well polished shoes. He was clearly a member of the orchestra that had just invaded this Public House in search of drink. In his right hand he held a violin, in his other a glass of wine.

"Forgive me Watson, this is Victor, Victor Trevor; we were at college together," said Holmes.

Introductions were exchanged and I held out my right hand to him. Whereupon he tucked the violin under his right arm and shook my hand with strength unexpected from a person who played such a delicate and fragile instrument as the violin. The landlord gave up trying to stop this informal concert by members of the London Symphony Orchestra. At one stage, as my attention was distracted whilst talking to a violoncello player, I became aware of syncopated clapping and words of encouragement being freely bandied about.

I looked around the corner of a highly polished mahogany glazed screen to see what the commotion was about. It became all too readily apparent to me, when I found myself observing Holmes standing on a bar stool, having acquired a violin from someone or somewhere. To my horror, his eyes looked as though in a manic trance, as he manipulated the fragile instrument with a surprising dexterity. He played furiously, a quick succession of *virtuoso* themes and melodies for violin, in an abandoned manner, but to general acclaim, including that of the landlord's! Aghast, I removed myself from this *impromptu* recital to enjoy my cognac and cigar with dignity and solitude, reinforced in my belief that there was something of the gypsy in Holmes. And, this outrageous and overt eruption of exhibitionism, and without shame, I noted, confirmed my worst suspicions.

Later, as we both staggered out into the Gloucester Road from the front door of the Harrington Arms Public House, we did so to a *crescendo* of a chorus of farewells from sundry patrons, including the entire brass section of the London Symphony Orchestra. Pulling our wits together, we headed south down this road with its shops creating a hive of activity, even this late into the night. Located above the shops I could just discern the fronts of respectable and expensive looking mansion buildings, containing apartments that are a distinctive architectural feature in the South Kensington area of London. Approaching St. Stephen's Church on our right I knew we were in the vicinity of Caulfield Gardens*** near the Emperor's Gate, where the houses are those with flat fronted *façades* of white stucco punctuated with pilasters and square porticoes of four *Ionic* columns framing the front door porch. I recalled that Holmes and I visited one such particular house in Caulfield Gardens some time ago, during a previous case, but the events of which I think are best left un-chronicled.

At last we came to another major artery of the Metropolis, the Cromwell Road. However, something was amiss because my knowledge of this road suggested that it should as busy as the Marylebone Road. It was not, and instead constables were seen rushing around with their bull-eye lanterns trying to keep some semblance of order. Just ahead of us in the road was a commotion indicated by the fact that the lights from several lamps seemed to dance in the yellow fog.

As we started to cross the road a constable held out his hand in a gesture to us to stop and said. "You cannot cross the road for a moment because there has been an accident."

"Can I help? I am a physician; oh and this is my colleague Sherlock Holmes," I replied.

The constable gave Holmes a searching glance and then waved us through without hesitation. I had the distinct impression it was Holmes's name and not the fact of my being a doctor that got us through.

"Not a pleasant sight doctor, apparently there has been

a collision between an omnibus and dray-wagon, that has shed its load of caskets of beer. You can imagine that the moment the word was out people came streaming in from everywhere to help themselves to free beer. Now, it is not my concern if folks want to act the fool on a busy fog-bound highway, such as the Cromwell Road, and risk being run over, but the police inspector has given orders to us to clear the road of all looters."

The constable had not exaggerated because gradually taking form in front of us was a scene of carnage, made worse by the stench of beer. It looked as if the heavier omnibus had careered into the dray-wagon, causing it to roll over onto its side, and thus discharge its load of caskets of beer. The dray wagon may have finished up on its side, but in so doing, had somehow managed to remove and deposit on the road the highly varnished timber side panelling of the omnibus. Apart from a few dazed and shaken omnibus passengers, miraculously no one had been badly injured. The only injury sustained appeared to be to the pride of a very loud and loquacious drayman who informed anyone that would listen to him, that his guts would be had for garters, when he returned to the Fuller, Smith & Turner's Griffin Brewery at Chiswick. A near by constable told him to shut up. I attended one lady who appeared to have just superficial scratches and wrapped my handkerchief around the only visible evidence of a wound that was on her hand.

Suddenly at that moment, a military wagon went thundering by within inches of the woman I was attending. His reckless progression was made more dangerous by the blinding fog, and the slippery road surface wet with beer, gave ample credence to what the constable had said about the road conditions and looters. There was nothing much more I could do, so I fell in eagerly with Holmes's suggestion that we quit this place of danger, for the infinitely more preferable comfort and safety of Goldini's restaurant.

We crossed the Cromwell Road intact and continued down the Gloucester Road past the Stanhope Public House, and at last marched into Goldini's. The proprietor immediately broke off from dealing with some customers seated at a table and rushed over to us, greeting Holmes as a much valued and revered friend. He escorted us to a large table with an excellent view of the restaurant and of the considerable activity going on. He clicked his fingers and a waiter came up and gave the proprietor two menus, which he then handed to Holmes and me.

"You have heard no doubt about the incident in the Cromwell Road?" Holmes asked, whilst accepting the menu.

"Of course, these things happen. I knew something to be wrong the moment two characters came in trying to sell to me, for cash, three caskets of beer. Every time the fog descends upon us that Cromwell Road seems to have more accidents than any other thoroughfare in London. Now then gentlemen, what would you like me to serve you?" he inquired.

"Yes, *hors-d'oeuvre* of jellied eels with a selection of whelks, mussels and oyster creams followed by the Baron of Beef with Wow-Wow sauce of walnut made with the usual port and mushrooms," instructed Holmes.

"And to complete your order, Mr. Holmes?" asked Goldini.

"What do you recommend?" asked Holmes.

"Mr Holmes, for you, I suggest our speciality of the day being the *Eugènies* and Royal Creams made with *curaçao* that I know you are fond of.

"Very well," said Holmes, evidently satisfied with his choice.

"The devilled whitebait," I began, "topped and tailed, with cayenne pepper and *Souchet* clear fish soup. The baked ham *a la Café Royal* with Cumberland sauce sounds attractive. And to finish, I fancy the Whipped London Syllabub of Madeira and Cream. For wine," I suggested, looking at Holmes for approval, "we shall have a bottle of your finest Beaune and a bottle of chilled Tokay."

"Are they between you or each?" asked the proprietor.

"Each," I replied.

Later when we were taking our Santiago *noir* coffee, brandy and large cigars from the proprietor's collection, we discussed Mahler's *Titan* Symphony.

By now, the time had flown by and even the proprietor's patience showed signs of waning. He and a few waiters stood amongst a forest of chairs staked high upon tables throughout the restaurant. I cannot believe for a moment that the proprietor of Goldini's was sad that we were leaving when we did. Still, we headed into the nearby Brompton Road Underground Station to take the train of the District Railway to Baker Street Metropolitan Station. Thankfully we did not have long to wait for a train. However, any benefit we derived from that fact, was immediately offset by the company of other railway passengers we were compelled to tolerate. Some of them appeared drunk, whilst others broke into loud songs, mostly of a lewd nature. I felt quite upset, especially having experienced earlier in the evening, the divine sonority of Mahler's First Symphony.

We got back to our chambers at Baker Street thoroughly exhausted but content with our evening. Holmes and I spent the rest of the evening in quiet thought, contemplating the remarkable events we had witnessed the last day or so, not least that incident of the Irregular Professional during our recent visit to the East End. Eventually, I retired for the night, leaving Holmes with his whisky reviewing the entries he had made in his commonplace book and scrapbooks, into which he consigned all kinds of information both trivial and sensational.

The next morning I break-fasted early and alone, there being no sign of Holmes, who I suspected, had gone out before me. I drained my coffee and completed my break-fast, for I too had visits to make that morning. I donned my extra thick army great coat, a relic, from my days with the Royal Munster Fusiliers, that kept me warm through those freezing nights in the Khyber Pass, during the savage fighting of the North West Frontier campaigns. I stepped out into Baker Street still shrouded in the suffocating yellow and acrid fog.

I groped my way along the eastern aspect of the street until I came to the Marylebone Road. Here I thought one takes one's life in one's hands in endeavouring to cross one of the busiest thoroughfares of the Metropolis. Standing on the kerb, I saw to the left of me, a ghostly procession of moving shapes, that I knew to be various four-wheeler carriages, all bearing green light lanterns as they approached and displaying their red lamp as they passed and receded back into the fog. I possessed myself and started to walk briskly into the fog in my attempt to cross the busy road. Dodging various lumbering military wagons, furniture pantechnicons and ubiquitous Hackney carriages clattering along the roadway with reckless abandon, I managed to gain the other side of the road intact. I then descended into the Baker Street Metropolitan Station.

This large Victorian underground railway station was

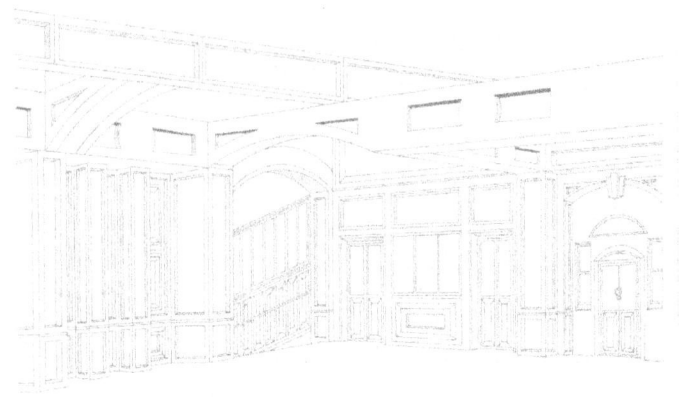

Baker Street Metropolitan Station Hall

a hive of activity and refuge from the fog outside. Even children, especially little girls in their cotton smocks and wearing boots, played and danced with each other in the cavernous ticket hall. The ubiquitous costermonger was in evidence, as were other tradesmen, all plying their wares to unsuspecting railway passengers compelled to use the station. I made my way cautiously through this mass of seething humanity from every country, including our imperial colonies, which made up the known world. Eventually, having rejected numerous offers of goods, services and demands for outright charity, I gained the actual ticket counter. After, in my opinion, an inordinate amount of time spent waiting, I managed to avail myself of a ticket. With it, I could traverse along the Inner Circle Railway, in a train of the Metropolitan Railway, to Aldgate Metropolitan Station. There change to a train operated by the District Railway to St. Mary's Underground Station at Whitechapel in the East End of London.

Whilst waiting on the eastbound platform, I was surprised to see a large number of other travellers using the railway. I supposed that the fog made travelling in a carriage on a railway line more certain than walking or resorting to a road carriage.

Rather than make eye contact with my fellow travellers on the platform, I instead concentrated my attention on an adjacent advertisement, on the station wall proclaiming that 'John Brinsmead & Sons of 18 Wigmore Street could provide you with their Gold Medal Winning Pianos.

The *pathos* of life never distant enough to escapes its repercussion; the following advertisement plastered to the platform wall, in this respect, spoke volumes:

Alcock & Rayment Co. Ltd
41 Dean Street, Soho, London

Established Suppliers of Improved Wooden or refined Aluminium Artificial Legs & Arm

with

RUBBER FEET & HANDS !

Approved by HM Government and the most eminent of Surgeons.

Over 8,000 persons wearing them throughout the Empire!

The **Rubber Foot & Hand** possess the most natural appearance, with the greatest durability and comfort of all Artificial Prosthetic Limbs & Protuberances

Large illustrated pamphlet and instructions for taking measurements sent free

* * *

I did not need an advertisement poster to enlighten me of this fact, for I have often admired the pianos displayed in their extensive studio not far from this very station. However, I was rather aghast to read on yet another poster that Crossby's '*Improved Balsamic Cough Elixir*' was now available, due to their '*Patented Reducing Process*', in the form of '*Hardened Lozenges*'. My medical experience of that '*Improved Elixir*' is that it was anything but, and in my opinion, did more to exacerbate the coughing discomfort rather than relieve the symptoms and ...then, suddenly, a report from a loud bang was heard. It seemed to emanate from the entrance to the railway tunnel at the end of the platform. People leaned forward to look from whence the report had originated. Equally startling was the sharp click that sounded next to my ear and instantly it was all over!

I turned to see a person on the ground beneath a burly looking fellow, wearing a fawn-checked coat and who had just handcuffed a seasoned pick-pocket! Those who saw him arrested, decided promptly that the pick-pockets, and they were numerous, had staged the incident in the tunnel of the Metropolitan Railway, in order to divert their victims' attention during the commotion.

Suddenly, an engine came bursting out of the tunnel and roared along the side of the platform pulling a train and billowing out black smoke and steam as it passed by, depositing quite visible black smuts onto my coat. Using my handkerchief I wiped my face clean. The train had originated at Marlborough Road Metropolitan Station. After some pushing and discourtesy by others I boarded the train and found a vacant seat.

Looking around the carriage at my fellow passengers, I remembered a conversation I had held with Holmes recently. In it Holmes claimed he could, by simply looking at a person's general demeanour, discern their occupation and habits. Brag and bounce! I thought. But, since I was now sitting in a carriage of the Metropolitan Railway, this might be a good opportunity to indulge in this exercise. I had done *en-route* to Liverpool, clapped down on that parliamentary train, and, if only, I reasoned, to while away the time to my destination and hopefully, prove Holmes wrong.

The collection of persons in my carriage, and in my immediate vicinity was not in any way distinguishable. I focused on one particular fellow to my right who I could observe without openly staring at him. He was a corpulent person of about six and fifty years with receding greyish hair. He appeared well to do, for he was examining intensely the financial pages of *The Times* through a gold-framed *Pince-nez*. He was dressed soberly in a sensible Inverness coat to keep out this inclement weather. Under his open coat he wore a dark jacket with silver waistcoat complete with a heavy gold Albert chain in front, that was attached to a bulge in his pocket, which usually indicates the presence of a gold Hunter watch. He wore striped trousers, hinting at membership of a learned profession, probably law, I postulated.

Possibly he was a country lawyer up from the county to settle some legal business in town. In addition, he carried a rough-hewn walking stick used by country gentlemen known as a *'Penang Lawyer'*, though he exhibited no sign of infirmity. His black shiny patent leather boots showed signs of mud splashes one might expect to receive walking down a muddy country lane to a railway station, from which he had caught his train to bring him up to town. I reasoned this lawyer would alight at the King's Cross station since this station is located at the top of the Gray's Inn Road, the home of the legal fraternity of which this gentleman, I concluded, was a member.

Confidence swept over me as I began to unravel this stranger's intimate personal details. What Holmes had postulated was nothing more than sheer common sense! I was quite congratulating myself on my newly found ability to detect secrets from the appearance of a stranger. Suddenly the object of my analysis folded away his copy of *The Times* and reached into his inner coat pocket and produced the edition of *Investors' Chronicle*. He then proceeded to tick off indexes of various stock and gilt-edged securities indicating most probably, that his profession was almost certainly that of a stockbroker. We both continued to ride the Metropolitan Railway, in order to traverse our way through the King's Cross Metropolitan Station and onward to the city. Feeling slightly deflated, but by no means deflected in my quest, I cast around the carriage looking for another alternative and suitable subject.

I found one in the form of a woman of quite tawdry aspect. She wore a large fur boa around her neck, clasped with an imitation *lapis lazuli* stone and a large blue feather in her broad brimmed hat, worn tilted to one side over her ear. Her short hair was auburn and matched the colour of her eyes, which were set in a round face of overwhelming anonymity and a vague searching expression. A blank face as it were, ready to be filled with experience. She looked nervous and agitated as the fingers of one hand caressed the fringes of the dove coloured carriage jacket she wore, whilst her other hand held a *'Penny Dreadful'*. Her jacket complemented her deep blue dress, underneath which she wore a pair of brown dulled and scuffed leather high-heeled boots, tied up tightly with black cotton laces. Her gloves were made of fine linen, the fingertips of which appeared stained with blue ink.

I reasoned that she was probably in regular contact with one of those new-fangled finger operated mechanical contraptions, one reads about called the 'Improved Patented Typewriting Apparatus', an invention by an American from New York whose name I remembered was Charles Babbage. **** I therefore concluded with a betting certainty and confidence that my subject under scrutiny was one of those women who are prepared to operate such a type-writing device, used in the rapid production of documents containing the written word without recourse to the pen.

Whilst I was concluding my analysis, a gentleman sat down next to her. Within seconds they seemed to be conversing with a familiarity that led me to conclude they knew each other rather well. I could not avoid overhearing their conversation that within seconds of commencing degenerated into the most outrageous language and series of appalling suggestions. I then realised to my horror she was definitely not an operator of a typewriting device, patented or not. Her vocation became apparent to me as I distinctly heard her, with no shame, proposition the gentleman, who to my disgust accepted her lewd suggestions and, without hesitation. I was appalled to realise that such encounters and behaviour could take place in an underground railway carriage and more disturbingly, so soon after break-fast! Both alighted to my relief having gained the Farringdon Street Metropolitan Station. ***** I was grateful to see them disappear down the platform to conclude their business. As they went, they passed a large advertisement poster about C. Ward & Sons of Curzon Street and their Mayfair Sherry being a bargain at 36/-. That poster seemed somewhat at variance with its neighbour, another poster informing me that Feltoe & Sons in Conduit Street, near Curzon Street, Sole Importers *Specialité* Sherry at 30/-. I wondered if these two companies were locked into an unremitting death struggle over the price of sherry, since both had establishments in Mayfair around the corner from each other in fact.

I realised suddenly, that in my coat was Holmes's pocket edition of the works of the poet Petrarch that I had borrowed and placed there some time earlier. I reached eagerly into my pocket to retrieve it in order to content myself in reading its uplifting and improving verses. Eventually I arrived at my destination in Whitechapel. A surly *commissionaire* in the reception hall then informed me of a cancellation. The gentlemen with whom the meeting was arranged had wired through earlier to say he would be unable to keep our appointment due to the detrimental effects of the fog. The *commissionaire*, I thought, appeared to take great delight in informing me of this set back to my personal plans. I returned to Baker Street Metropolitan Station, but rather than going straight home, I stepped into a nearby bookmaker's agent to collect some winnings I knew were due to me and to erase from my mind a thoroughly wasted train journey.

* Now called Sussex Gardens
** Now called Gloucester Road Underground Station
*** Now called Courtfield Road
**** No, it was Philo Remington.
***** Now called Farringdon Road Metropolitan Station

Chapter 17

The Revelation of the Arts

My journey to the East End may have been futile, but I was curious to see if Holmes had met with success in his continuing quest to solve the mystery of the sinking of the ill-fated *Titanic*. In addition, to making progress in unravelling the circumstances regarding the death of the Admiralty clerk, Cadogan West, in a railway carriage, along the permanent way just outside Charing Cross Railway Station

"I see you have been to the East End of London, in particular Whitechapel." Holmes remarked to me as I entered our parlour.

"Well life goes on even after the disaster that attended the ill-fated *Titanic*; but good, God Holmes, how did you deduce that fact, by the mud on my boots?"

"No," replied Holmes, "by the careful and systematic analysis of fact, and in the recognition of important details. Remember, Watson, you doubted my ability to deduce a person's general demeanour, and discern their occupation and habits by merely looking at them? Therefore, applying this systematic analysis of fact, I concluded that you have been to Whitechapel!"

"I am impressed because that is exactly where I have been this morning, though without success. What cryptic clues enabled you to elucidate my destination abroad the

Metropolis? Tell me what minor detail or incisive fact enabled you to conclude so and correctly?"

"The fact that you are displaying in your coat breast pocket, a Metropolitan Railway return ticket issued at Whitechapel!

Our excitement over the Moriarty affair is not yet over yet Watson," said Holmes, realizing my slight irritation with him, "I need to visit the mysterious and elusive Arthur Staunton, for I have finally detected his identity! He is by way of being a revolutionary and innovator in the creation of artwork and is, I believe, at this moment in his art gallery in the Tottenham Court Road, in which is contained a secret room!

Do you come with me to visit Staunton?" asked Holmes.

"Have I time to finish this whisky?" I replied.

"Of course and another if you so wish!"

Still feeling slightly put out, by Holmes' being light with me about my return ticket from Whitechapel, I said with deliberately facetious asperity:

"Holmes, perhaps even you could bring your undoubted gifts of analysis and observation to bear on this article I have just read in *The Daily Telegraph*."

Holmes took the paper I handed to him, and he read allowed the article about a machine called an '*Aëro-plane*'.

'An intrepid and resourceful American *aëronaut,* or 'aviator', as he has styled himself, proposes to elevate his body by no visible or physical means of support into the very aëther. He will achieve this feat by constructing a wooden apparatus he calls an '*aëro-plane*'. This invention, so he propounds, is a milestone in an unstoppable technological progress and domination over nature, and a symbol of man's innovative and relentless ability to harness the power of science and engineering.'

"Where have we heard those very words before eh?"
I asked of Holmes.

Holmes continued.

'This contraption will enable man to circumnavigate
the globe in a matter of days rather than months. His
'aëro-plane', so he predicts, is constructed in such a fashion
as to enable the apparatus supporting him to be conveyed
through the aëther by means of a 'propulsion mechanism', utilising a revolving propeller fixed to the front of
his contraption. By this ingenious and innovative
method, this intrepid aviator expects, with confidence,
to be able to gain in flight a staggering distance of twelve
nautical miles during a continuous period of one hour!'

I think our intrepid *'aviator'* Wilbur, or whatever his
name is, must have sun stroke, though I cannot for the
life of me imagine from where, certainly not in fog bound
London. Notwithstanding that, he must be insane, for
it simply cannot be done! Does he not realise that the
aëther alone will his wreck his contraption and that the
pressure of the atmosphere will cause it disintegrate? He
must be oblivious to the fact that the aëther, battering
his exposed body at the frightening velocity of twelve
nautical miles to the hour will disrupt his internal organs,
crushing the very life out of him. He will certainly
suffocate, for the aëther passing over him will cause a
terrifying vacuüm to envelop his very person, depriving
him of that life-giving oxygen we know to be present in
aëther. He must have lost his reason altogether for he is
tampering with the laws of nature, to say nothing of those
inviolate Newtonian laws of gravity. I declare Holmes,
how can an object heavier than air, stay floating without
physical support?" I demanded.

"Perhaps, Watson," said Holmes, "though I remain
uncertain those American inventors are quite without

regard for historical precedent, in that they do not feel constrained by scientific convention. Rather they possess their confidence, and pioneer ahead with the zeal of innovation and an inquiring mind. Look at how they have opened up the territories and regions of the North American continent with railroads, commerce and industry"

"You amaze me Holmes. I thought you to be a man of science, an observer of the logical process and a dealer in fact. How can you then endorse such an irresponsible presupposition of this unsubstantiated proposal of flying through the aëther?"

"It is precisely because of those qualities that you ascribe to me so admirably, that I believe more in the American's claim than I doubt it. After all, his brother, Orville, has demonstrated that a flat plane surface can initiate upon itself an upward tendency when subjected to wind. He equates this wind, acting on that surface, as the equivalent of the surface moving through static aëther, creating the same lift phenomenon," Holmes informed me.

"Ridiculous," I said, "from what you have stated Holmes, that would be the equivalent of leaping off the top of a cliff with the kitchen door and hoping to achieve a landing intact!"

"The Wright brothers would give you no argument!"

"I beg to differ," I erupted "it will end in disaster, which is the price one invariably pays when tampering with the inviolate laws of nature.

Sometimes Holmes I despair at your unconditional belief in scientists and in their apparent progress. As a doctor, I learned from observing and applying reliable and proven facts; one fact leading on to another fact, which either propounds or establishes an unassailable theory. Accordingly, Holmes you will never hear me talk nonsense about medicine. Such idiotic notions that an organ, such as a kidney, can be taken from a person who has recently died, and given to person in need of one, simply cannot hold water; it remains an impossibility and medical science dictates as much."

"May be Watson, but this discussion will have to be held over for another time, for alas, we have a mission to undertake."

Not for the first time that day, I left the comfortable warmth of our drawing room with its blazing fire, for the damp cold fog into which we now ventured.

"Where exactly are we going?" I asked of Holmes.

"I have the address on this wire," he replied looking at the slip of paper in his hand, "35 Tottenham Court Road. Come, Watson the game is afoot!"

"Oh I thought it was in hand!"

"Our quest then, takes us to a fashionable part of the Metropolis!" I remarked to Holmes, as we started walking down Baker Street in the direction of Oxford Street.

Presently we came to Fitzhardinge Street and turned right, following the kerb into Manchester Square dimly lit with gas globe lamps and past the magnificent large mansion that is Hertford House, just discernible in the fog. Leaving the square we swung into Duke Street and then into Wigmore Street, where we hailed a passing Clarence carriage into which climbed and headed east. Our journey brought us into Cavendish Square, deserted and silent in the fog. It seemed that we were the only souls abroad in the Metropolis that afternoon.

"The fog, like snow, has the effect of muffling sound," said Holmes, peering out from our open carriage, "and made the more sinister by the blindness that its shrouds produce. Imagine Watson, how many persons are at this moment fending off an attack? How many cries go unheard? How many lives will be lost under this dense blanket of fog?"

I was not to answer those questions, for in that instant we felt a shudder and a jarring, immediately followed by a crunching sound, as we moved in a sideways motion. I then realised that we had just collided with a Barouche carriage. Inside it, sitting upright, totally unperturbed, was a gentleman of aristocratic bearing, wearing striped trousers, a black frock-coat and top hat and smoking a cigar. He looked at us in such a way, as though we had been personally responsible for the accident. The two carriage drivers had, in the meantime, begun a heated argument, in their typical manner of trying to apportion blame.

"You two, yes, you two in the carriage," came an imperious command from the gentleman sitting in the Barouche, "try and make yourselves useful, and see if you can disengage your carriage from mine, taking the utmost care not to scratch the varnish on my Barouche!"

I did not hear quite what Holmes' reply was to this gentleman, due to the increasing shouting of the carriage drivers next to me. However, we both alighted from our Clarence and walked off into the fog, leaving a rather perplexed aristocrat to fend for himself, in the midst of an ever increasingly ferocious argument between the two carriage drivers.

At length we reach the Regent's Street and continued over it into Mortimer Street. We passed Guivier's, the violin restorers patronised by Holmes, and over the Portland Road onwards to Goodge Street. Here we passed the huge heavy neo-Grecian *façade* of the Middlesex Hospital with its protruding, decorated, triangular pediment and tympanum, just barely visible in the fog, as though suspended in mid air. We paused to gather our wits before entering the great thoroughfare, and one of the main life arteries of the Metropolis, the Tottenham Court Road. All the varieties of humanity seemed to be groping their way along its thoroughfare, and carriages of every type trundled by, along with omnibuses carrying people and carts conveying produce.

Again, street urchins, including cotton dressed and booted girls, and Cockney boys of precocious disposition, were everywhere to be seen. Some clearly engaged in street business, others, one instinctively knew, were keeping a look out for the law, or even better still, opportunities for theft. It was along this very highway at the junction of Goodge Street, I recalled, that Holmes had investigated the curious case of a bowler hat, a goose and a precious stone. They, in turn, led to the singular case of the jilted *fiancée*, a broken shop window and the disappearance of a bridegroom as he stepped out of his Hackney carriage into oblivion, when arriving at the St Pancras Hotel to attend his own wedding break-fast!

"Number thirty-five should be here," said Holmes, looking into a recessed doorway. It was, and with a tug of a wire, a peel of bells was heard within the building. Presently the door swung open, and a short fellow in an artist's smock stood in the doorway, peering at us from the brightly illuminated interior of his establishment.

"Mr Holmes," he inquired, "Mr Sherlock Holmes?"

"Yes," replied Holmes, "and this is my colleague, Doctor Watson"

"Oh, are you ill?" inquired the fellow still standing in the doorway "perhaps you are a valetudinarian? But gentlemen please do come in. May I offer you refreshment? Jackson's of Piccadilly do a particularly fine refreshing tea. Some compressed orange juice perhaps, or may I press you to enjoy a soured-lemon drink with a little aërated hydrogen dioxide?"

"Whisky," snapped Holmes, "whisky with aërated water for me and a large whisky without for Dr. Watson."

Arthur Staunton proved to be an amiable person, given to jokes and witticisms, most of which were lost on Holmes. He was an excellent host, but not wishing to impose my presence on their discussion, I excused myself from their company. I knew that my continuing presence would perforce inhibit their conversation and the frank exchange of information that was crucial to Holmes' investigation.

"Feel free to look around the gallery doctor and let me know if any of the paintings tickle your fancy!

Now then, Holmes about this Moriarty…" I heard Staunton say.

I did look around the gallery. It was filled with impressive paintings by artists some of whom were familiar to me. There was William Etty's *Nude,* Frith's *The Railway Station,* and works by the New Olympians, including Albert Moore's *A Summer Night.* The gallery was teeming with works by some contemporary artists who termed themselves the *'Pre-Raphaelite Brotherhood.* In their ranks, they counted such unheard of artists as Burne-Jones, Leighton and Holman Hunt. They preferred, so it seemed, to paint subjects taken from literature or poetry dealing with love and death, including scenes of chivalry and romance, and paintings based on the mythical legend.

Some of the *'Pre-Raphaelite'* paintings, though well executed and beautiful, were disturbing. Two in particular caught my attention, including one by an unknown artist called John Everett Millais. In his painting called, *'Speak, Speak!'* he quite clearly depicted a dead wife, in

Visions of Architecture

her bridal gown, at the foot of the bed exhorting her very much-alive husband who was lying on it, to join her! Can this be art I thought? Other members of this new *'Pre-Raphaelite Brotherhood'* included a fellow called Dante Gabriel Rosetti, probably Italian* I thought. His art, in my medical opinion, displayed symptoms of incipient mental instability and imminent collapse. These facts were clearly shown in the painting he called *Astarte Syriaca*. The painting haunted me with a familiarity I could not immediately explain.

Then my eyes beheld the most sublime drawing of a collection of classical buildings I have ever witnessed. It was a drawing, a very beautiful and detailed drawing, entitled, 'Visions of Architecture'. The drawing combined an exquisite elegance with serenity interpreted as a perspective, but ethereal vision of buildings from antiquity. Alas, it was unsigned lending even more of an air of mystery as to its skilful creator.

Other painters were more openly Romantic their in

subject matter, as Danby's *Wood Nymph,* and Scott's *The Enchanted Island.* Several paintings by Atkinson Grimshaw, were on display including, *The Deserted House,* which I liked immensely. There were paintings too, by European artists including Böcklin's *The Island of the Dead,* Casper Friedrich's *The Ship Among the Icebergs* and huge paintings of classical architectural scenes by Moreau and Claude Lorrain. One painting I thought Holmes might appreciate was by an unknown French painter called Manet. He had captured, on a massive canvass, a typical Parisian bar scene at the *Folies-Bergere.* The painting was dominated by the figure of a rather surly looking female bar tender standing in front of a huge wall mirror that reflected the busy *salon.* It was reminiscent of the Café Royal or the Criterion Bar here in London I thought.

I went back again to look at Grimshaw's *The Deserted House.* So absorbed was I in this brilliantly atmospheric painting of a mysterious house, set in an large overgrown autumnal garden, that I failed to notice Holmes and Staunton who by now were standing next to me.

"I see you are interested in the Grimshaw; a very popular painting," remarked Staunton, "very popular indeed."

"How much is that original?" I asked, out of polite curiosity, pointing to the canvass on the wall.

"Eight hundred guineas; would you like it doctor?" he asked, giving me a searching glance.

"I should love to own…"

"Come back next week and bring two hundred guineas," interrupted Staunton, "by then I shall have one finished for you."

I was astounded at the fellow's impudence and his confident behaviour in front of me.

"Next week," I replied, "as long as that?"

Holmes then took me by the arm and all three of us made our way to the farthest reaches of the deserted gallery. Here Staunton pulled at a secreted lever, and instantly a little narrow door sprang open, creating a small aperture in the wall, through which we all entered. Presently we found ourselves in a small studio, illuminated dimly with gas globe lamps, but in which I could see numerous paintings in various stages of completion.

"This is where original paintings and old masters come in and are copied," remarked Staunton to Holmes, in such a casual off hand manner, as if they were oranges on display on a street market stall!

"Good God, it is!" I exclaimed, on recognising, in all its glory, the infamous missing portrait by Thomas Gainsborough.

The painting I stared at in utter disbelief was the famous portrait of Georgiana Cavendish, Duchess of Devonshire. It had become infamous after it was stolen in an outrageous raid on the Bond Street picture gallery of Agnew & Sons some years before. The raid was made all the more daring as a result of the *outré* features attending the removal of the picture by the accomplished and notorious jewel thief, Adam Worth, sometimes known, rather fancifully, as the '*Napoleon of Crime*'. The picture was eventually recovered in Chicago by Pinkerton agents and sold to none other than John Pierpont Morgan, owner of the *Titanic* ship! But, what was it doing in this room? I asked myself. Did Morgan possess the original or a fake? Given the events unfolding around me, I would be willing to bet with certainty, that it was a fake.

Having bade our farewells to Staunton and thanked him repeatedly for his time, information and drinks, we found ourselves in the fog-bound Tottenham Court

Road. Holmes however, assured me that nearby was a huge quality wet Public House called the Rising Sun. I remember that Rising Sun Public House for good reason. I seem to recall it had highly decorated intricate *Gothick* raised tracery designs to its exterior *façade*. That exterior decorative detail always reminds me of the fact that despite our early Victorians' industrial might and brave innovative spirit, they still retained in their hearts, a deep and affectionate fondness for the *Gothick* style.

We headed for the Rising Sun Public House in a hurry, barging through the fog with absolutely no regard or concern. Inside it was warm and bright. I went up to the bar and ordered two large whiskies.

"To keep out the chill no doubt," said a friendly bar tender.

"No" I replied, and rejoined Holmes with our drinks.

Holmes tried to explain to me the significance of what Staunton had told him.

"His information is first class, and he is to be trusted in whatever he imparts. He has confirmed that original artwork has being assembled for the exhibition to be held at the World's Columbian Exposition in Chicago. And, more importantly, as each original was accepted for the exhibition, a copy was made of it!"

"How can that be done?" I inquired.

"The originals," replied Holmes, "were accepted into a trusted and reputable art gallery or auction house, such as the Christie & Manson Auction Rooms, where Thomas Wainwright works, but where Moriarty had gained influence. The originals were then spirited away to be copied at one of several art studios, as Staunton's or John Clay's. The fakes were then returned to the holding gallery or auction house where they were crated for shipment to Chicago on the *Titanic*."

"But surely it cannot be just an insurance fraud, because the forgeries would eventually be revealed as not being the authentic paintings? What could there have been to gain?"

"The fraudulent acquisition of original artwork, amongst other things," replied Holmes.

A few hours, later as we were leaving the Rising Sun Public House, I remarked to Holmes.

"I have it; I have the solution to hand! We could name the new railway station Regent's Station, for the Regent's Park is nearby, is it not?"

Holmes looked at me.

"Or," I continued, "'Britannia Station?' Surely there is merit in the name, 'Trafalgar'?" I expostulated.

Holmes walked straight in front of an oncoming Hackney carriage in his attempt to bring it to an abrupt halt, which he succeeded in doing and promptly jumped in, causing me to run after it!

* No. he was born in London.

Chapter 18

The Reëncounter

Despite the fog we were making progress. Clearly Holmes felt that having spoken with Arthur Staunton, the way ahead lay reasonably open. However, I knew from previous experience that it is fatal to theorise in the absence of all the relevant facts. To me the facts as I understood them appeared to be so confused and far ranging, with no viable link, as to make them meaningless. I suspected Holmes could weave a link through them all to present a plausible explanation and theory that might suggest even a solution to our investigation.

"Watson, I have been giving our problem some thought, no, not about a suitable name for your railway station; but more particularly regarding the circumstances of that woman from Eureka Springs, near the Oklahoma territory."

"Oh?" I inquired.

"The more I ponder the problem, the more convinced I become, of the existence of one insuperable fact; that of her *fiancé* being done away with. It has to be the case, when all else fails, what remains must be the truth. His was a life that simply could not be allowed to continue, because of its being a flaw in Moriarty's strategy, and therefore impossible to ignore," said Holmes, thoughtfully.

"Are you sure, Holmes, can you be so certain?" I said.

Holmes did not reply but reached into a drawer and produced a card that he looked at intently for some time. At length and almost with a sigh he handed it to me and said:

"Well Watson, I was going to send a wire to that woman at the St. Pancras Hotel. However, I suppose she is entitled somewhat to our sympathy in being informed as to the fate that has befallen her *fiancé* and an end put to her searching for him. Perhaps you might undertake that chore, for I do not feel quite equal to the task?"

"Should you feel that I can be of service then I shall convey willingly your thoughts to her in person," I responded.

"You might also Watson, in your communication with the lady, advise in your own emotional way, that in all probability the *fiancé* was an honourable man, and had not deserted her but rather, was murdered."

And with that parting remark, Holmes retired to his room. I could well believe his reluctance to encounter yet again the woman from Eureka Springs, given his recent painful and resounding defeat at her hands. His reference to her as an inanimate object, as opposed to availing himself of the proper noun of Katherine, indicated his innate derision. For Holmes to undertake a mission to the St. Pancras Hotel in which she resided would be unthinkable, though by now I had detected in him what might be called cautiously, a concern for her feelings. For myself, I had nothing but admiration for her stance against Holmes, who at times could be ascetic, if not decidedly cold. She had a character I found passionate, yet gentle but with the intelligence, wit and resourcefulness native to her American ancestry. I was relieved though, that I was neither the object nor target of her contempt, as she clearly felt for Holmes, however expressed as witticism!

I looked at the card Holmes had given to me and pondered her name beneath which were printed the words:

Crescent Hotel
Eureka Springs
Oklahoma Territory
United States of America

Who was this woman, this Katherine that we had encountered previously in our rooms in Baker Street? What had driven her to cross the Atlantic Ocean to seek an answer to her quest, beyond that of searching for her missing *fiancé*? I knew from my experience of previously meeting her, that she was a clever, resourceful and a determined woman, but beyond those characteristics nothing else about her personality was evident to me.

I changed my clothes and put on my back a white shirt and attached a starched wing collar and studs to it, completing the ensemble with a pearl grey necktie and diamond pin. I then climbed into my striped trousers and attached braces, tied up my polished, black, patent leather boots and finished off my attire by donning my best frock-coat. It then struck me that I had not worn this combination of clothes for some months past. With my top hat and cane I ventured out into Baker Street still in the grip of the yellow clammy fog, and began to walk toward the Marylebone Road.

Suddenly, a Rudge-Whitworth velocipede two-wheeler came upon me out of the blinding fog like a ghostly apparition and at such a velocity that it gave me a start as it glided past my face. The shock was made all the more intense by the fact that the two wheeler's appearance was silent due to the new improved Dunlop pneumatic, rubber tires fitted to its metal wheel rims.

The rider was sitting upright and high on his saddle as he pedalled his bi-cycle furiously. Indeed his eyes set in his glistening face appeared to be in some sort of manic trance and he was totally oblivious to the fact he had just driven his dangerous contraption into my person. By the time I had gathered my wits and recovered to react, he had disappeared back into the *opaque* folds of fog and out of sight.

Outrageous, I thought. Outrageous, that a person, by using a mechanical device as a velocipede, is able to propel himself in such a reckless manner, abandoning all sense of propriety and public regard. And, more alarmingly, that the driver of such a dangerous locomotion contraption, was often able to achieve a velocity of more than six statute miles within a continuous period of one hour, which is allowed on the on the roads in the midst of the Metropolis.

Not withstanding this incident, I continued along Baker Street, for I had more pressing matters to attend to, not least how to break the dreadful news to Katherine from Eureka Springs. She was a lady, who from my last encounter, suggested that her intelligent, if *Protean* and volatile sensibilities would be difficult to control, were she to react in a less than dignified manner.

I then realised that the velocipede had driven over my right foot and in so doing had deposited a tire imprint onto my polished boot that would not rub away.

On reaching the Marylebone Road, the other side of which is located the Baker Street Metropolitan Station, I paused to consider the heavy traffic, lumbering along its thoroughfare. Along this road, veiled in the swirling fog, moved a ghostly procession of faint green and red lights from the tender lanterns fixed to the various carriages. Still somewhat shaken by my experience with the reckless rider on the velocipede not seeing me in the fog, I concluded that it would not be safe to cross the road and risk being knocked down by a carriage, especially since I was wearing my best clothes. Accordingly, I decided to stay on the same side of the road and gain the Portland Road Metropolitan Station, as a more viable and safe, though inconvenient, option.

The distance to the station, despite the prohibiting and pungent fog, was not far, so I decided to walk and in so doing immediately passed Madame Tussaud's museum of novel, if *grotesque*, wax effigies of famous or indeed infamous characters. I continued to walk carefully and arrived at the neo-Grecian styled St Marylebone Church, with its massive colonnaded portico of columns supporting the distinctive, architrave framed, triangular pediment projecting out from the banks of fog. It is from the church that the name of that part of the Metropolis, in which Holmes and I resided, is derived. It was built by Thomas Hardwick, the creator of that another marvel of classical architecture, in the form of the *Propyleum*, Doric Arch entrance, to Euston Station, that we had walked under recently on our way to catch the express train to Liverpool.

Continuing along the road, I could hear the students of the Royal Academy of Music developing skills with which to manipulate their fragile instruments, their chords resounding through the fog. At length I gained the upper reaches of the doctors' quarter in and around Harley Street. I then remembered that an artist called Lyons, who had consulted Holmes on, I think, a matter of no great import some months previously, lived hard by in a building dominating the junction of the Marylebone Road and Harley Street. I paused to look at this four square Portland stone clad building and in particular its recessed window frames, which created an image of power and strength, and not in my opinion, the natural choice of the abode for such a *Bohemian* as an artist.

Still, I was congratulating myself on making reasonable headway along the Marylebone Road, despite the fog, when to my utter dismay I became aware that the footpath and adjacent carriageway had been dug up. This made traversing the pavement difficult. I was thus compelled to resort to the carriageway amongst the numbers of pantechnicons and other road wagons lumbering along, with the probable risk of being struck down by one. This inconvenience somewhat defeated the object of my walking to the Portland Road Metropolitan Station in the first place and avoiding resorting to the road carriageway for reasons of safety.

In addition to this obstacle to my progress, I had to make my way through lumps of clay and mounds of spoil dug up from the depths of the earth. This excavation in the street was, so a wooded signboard bearing a notice proclaimed, necessary in creating the Regent's Park Underground Railway Station. I also noticed that some enterprising individual had plastered an advertisement poster over crucial details of the printed notice, in order to enlighten anyone who cared to be so, that Mr. Streeter of 18 New Bond Street, was still a 'Manufacturer of 18 Carat Gold and General Jewellery'. Perhaps our housekeeper, Mrs. Hudson, might wish, at some stage in the future, to pursue this information, and bedeck herself in glory, I thought to myself.

At length, having just walked under the apple tree,

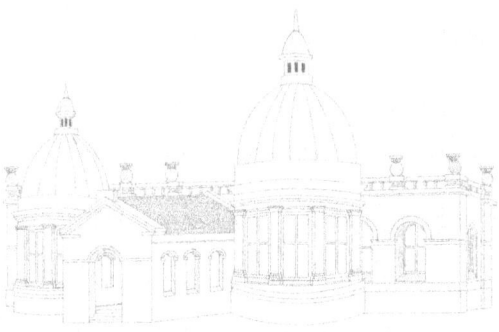

Portland Road Metropolitan Station

bearing late over-ripe apples, that shelters the bronze bust of a dead president, I reached the Portland Road Metropolitan Station with its distinctive twin circular domes. It was as quiet as it was deserted, save for a solitary railway servant behind his glass window, at which I purchased a ticket to King's Cross Metropolitan Station. Descending to the eastbound platform, I noticed that the fog had penetrated this subterranean station pulled in by the passage of trains along the rails of the permanent way. I could scarcely see the other platform, even though it was only yards away. A feeling of claustrophobia began to grip my heart as the realisation came upon me that I was quite, quite alone and could scarcely see ahead.

What I did see were the gaudy advertisements pasted on to the station platform wall immediately next to me. I began to search the posters, more to occupy my nervous mind, rather than of wishing to be informed of various and sundry boasts; one of which extolled the virtues of an improved and Extra-Refined Pear's Amber Soap – Matchless for the Complexion. Another promoted the rather implausible health benefits of Bovril Meat Extract. Wedged in between them, was a poster proclaiming the advisability of taking Scott's Emulsion of Pure Cod Liver Oil Further down the wall were other advertisements, one of which introduced a dark beverage called *Coca-Cola*, unknown to me. However, the poster assured me; it was as 'Refreshing as it is Delicious!' and I could quite believe in this claim, as the beverage was laced with a generous amount of cocaine. Adjacent was a bill informatively advising the public that Allsopp's Pale Ale was now available in bottles. About that information I did make a mental note. An exaggerated claim that Sanitas Disinfectant Fluid Destroys Disease seemed rather over optimistic to me but in comparison did lend credence, at least, to the claim emanating from an advertisement that Paterson's Camp Coffee 'Is The Best as it is Incomparable!'

After what seemed an age, a train did come roaring into the station pushing the dense fog before it as it progressed along the platform edge. I climbed aboard and sat down on the wooden cross benches. It was then that I noticed that the lower part of my trousers and polished boots were covered in clay and mud picked up earlier from the excavation in the road. After a short ride, I arrived at the King's Cross Metropolitan Station and then made my way along the front of the huge St. Pancras Hotel, with its phäntasmagoric *façade*. It was with trepidation that I ascended the broad steps leading up in to this magnificent red brick High Victorian Gothic decorated edifice to ostentatious monumentalism. I entered the Hotel through the *Porte Cochere* to the west wing leading to the Entrance Hall through the honey coloured Ancaster stone framed doorway, flanked by columns of polished green and pink limestone.

Nothing could have prepared me for the sheer feeling of beauty emanating from its lavish decoration and

St. Pancras Hotel

opulence, including murals that decorated the main hall beneath several bright and glittering *chandeliers*. An impressive cantilevered grand staircase progressed dramatically into the vaulted ceiling of the fifth floor. The walls were covered with maroon coloured flock wallpaper punctuated with golden *fleurs de lys*.

I approached the *concièrge* who was dressed in a red tail-coat and black top hat, and informed him of the nature of my visit. He immediately looked at my soiled trousers and boots.

"Who did you say you were?" he asked, accusingly and without averting his gaze from my boots.

"Watson, Doctor John Watson come to see this lady," I said handing him Katherine's card.

"Very good sir, if you would care to wait I shall make inquiries to ascertain whether the lady in question is available to grant you an audience," said the *concierge* in a lugubrious voice.

I stood there for quite some time, in awe of the sumptuous beauty of this Hotel. The wealthy heiress from Eureka Springs had been wise in her choice of this Hotel. The St. Pancras Hotel was built onto the new and innovative iron frame, which allowed the creator of the building to form large rooms and span spacious openings within the structure. The Hotel included new hydraulically operated elevator cars, a pneumatically powered postal system, clean acetylene gas-fuelled *chandeliers* and electrically operated bells.

The Hotel also provided bedrooms with an anti chamber in which a whole bathtub was located, and a considerable army of servants and chambermaids to wait on every need and fad of guests. One particular innovative piece of equipment, I observed, was an electro-phone that linked hotel guests by wire to music being played at various London concert halls, including the Queen's Hall in Portland Place and the Aëolian Hall in Bond Street. In the main reception were several elaborate murals, including one by Thomas Wallis Hay, impressed into the plaster with which the walls are lined. The ubiquitous indoor palm tree was, as usual, much in evidence.

Eventually the red tail-coated *concierge* re-appeared and informed me that I would be received in a few minutes. But first. did I care to use the facilities located in the washroom he intoned whilst handing back card to me, but still looking at my boots I nd followed a bellboy through a *labyrinth* of deep piled Axminster carpets laid out along the floors of the cream painted walls of corridors with vaulted ceilings from which were suspended glittering acetylene gas-fuelled *chandeliers*. There, in the washroom, I set about trying to remove the mud from my trousers and endeavouring to put a shine back on my patent leather boots. Having washed my hands with Vinolia Otto Toilet Soap, I returned to the main reception to await the heiress from Eureka Springs.

Katherine appeared at last and descended the wide staircase with an elegance that took me quite by surprise, given my previous recollection of her. She was dressed in a black and white dress, the style beloved of artists when portraying the Greek goddess Diana. From her right shoulder was draped an electric blue sash fastened by a brooch of *lapis lazuli*. Her dark, rich, luxuriant hair was secured back with a black velvet Alice band, in place of the more familiar diamond tiara. Beneath her radiant face, and secured around her neck, was a magnificent brilliant faceted ruby stone that complemented her elbow-length red silk gloves. She approached me and held out her hand with such dignity that I felt obliged to kiss it with a bow, if not a flourish.

After I had re-introduced myself as the colleague of Holmes, whom she had recently consulted, she suggested that we repair to the Grand Drawing Room situated on the *piano-nobile*. We both walked through the main *salon* to what looked like ornate bronze door set flush into the wall. She pulled at a bell rope and a few seconds later the bronze doors slid apart, revealing a small room panelled in mahogany.

"*Piano-nobile*," Katherine instructed the bellboy as we both stepped in. Moments later the door closed and with a pull of a lever the bellboy set in motion the room ir which we were standing and instantly I felt as if my stomach had dropped.

"Do tell me doctor, is this the first time you have ever ridden in a hydraulically powered elevator car?"

"It is indeed my first experience of being so propelled through the floors of a building in such a contraption," I responded.

"Yeah well, it sure saves time running up and down the steep stairs in this Hotel! And, I believe there is a gent by the name of Seeberger out of Yonkers, New York, who is building a moving stairway he calls an escalator that takes passengers from one floor to another and is powered by electricity. Can you beat that?" she enthused.

With a hissing noise accompanied by a grinding feeling, the elevator carriage in which we stood came to an abrupt stop. The bellboy opened the doors and out we stepped into a red-carpeted corridor at the end of which were two large highly polished walnut panelled doors and through this imposing portal we entered the Grand Drawing Room.

A waiter glided into our vicinity and offered to escort us to a table surrounded by red *damask* covered sofas, complemented with *antimacassars* of white lace on their fronts.

"May I get you something to drink?" inquired the waiter.

Katherine gestured towards me to answer the question.

"Yes," I replied, "hock and seltzer," thinking this choice would show my responsible attitude and moderation in drink.

"And for Madame," continued the waiter.

"Me, a large whisky – neat!" replied Katherine.

After the waiter had brought our drinks and an ashtray for Katherine, he departed but remained nearby. I think he felt our demands for drink would increase exponentially as time went on.

I am not certain quite how she achieved it, but all of a sudden I noticed that a small cigar was in between her lips whilst she drew air through it to get the tip aflame. Contented, she sat back, glass in one hand and cigar in the other.

"Thank you for receiving me," I began, "but my report to you is, I am afraid, one of sadness. Mr. Sherlock Holmes has charged me with the delicate task of explaining to you what he believes has happened to your *fiancé.*"

"Doctor Watson, my *fiancé* is dead, is he not?"

"What makes you say that?" I asked.

"Because you would not have come to this Hotel dressed as you are unless you were the bearer of bad news," she answered incisively.

"Your instincts and feminine intuition are correct and they serve you faithfully," was all I could splutter out.

"Alas, they usually are," she said, averting her gaze and looking into her glass.

"What I knew of my poor *fiancé's* character," she continued, "would indicate to me that his was one of *naïveté* but honour, though he was a fine man. It therefore did not make any kind of sense for him to take flight without getting a message to me to explain his behaviour. I knew when the man spoke down to him in the Crescent Hotel garden on that fateful September day that somehow things just did not seem right. Again when he left the concert hall, never to return, confirmed my worst fears; if only because I knew him to be very fond of the music of Mahler and nothing would have prevented him from experiencing it, especially with me."

Whilst I listened to her, my thoughts began to drift and I found myself admiring the ornate plaster and gilded details of the ceiling with an intricate architrave around the walls of the immense Grand Drawing Room. It was clear to me this Hotel was built using an iron frame that supports the building. Indeed one could just make out the presence of the metal frame albeit *camouflaged* by elaborate plaster mouldings and timber encasement.

"Waiter," I heard her say, as my thoughts came down to earth, "another large whisky and would you like a drink too, doctor?"

"Rather!" I responded, whilst noticing, in order to cover her ankles, she wore tall polished red patent leather boots of the type that are closed by means of the newly patented Singer brass zip fastener.

I talked about Holmes' conclusions regarding her *fiancé's* fate, as a result of his being an *employé* with the JP Morgan Bank and of the possibility of Professor Moriarty's involvement. Also, I talked about the probable *rôle* of the manager of the Basin Park Hotel, and that almost certainly, he was bribed by Moriarty to deny the fact of her *fiancé's* stay there. Of course, I concluded with the devastating news of the sinking of the ill-fated *Titanic*.

"The sinking of the what," she interrupted, "you mean that boat, that wreck I miraculously crossed the Atlantic in, it actually sank?" she inquired, with an expression of questioning surprise upon her features.

I had neither the information nor the desire to reply to her question but in any event did not wish to pursue what was by any account a dreadful and distressing matter for her. She had already suffered a loss due to the machinations of the demented Professor Moriarty, who had dispatched forthwith, her *fiancé* to the hereafter. It seemed a futile exercise to pursue what could only result in perpetuating her distress. In my attempt to divert the conversation to a more acceptable topic I asked rather inanely:

"Will you be staying in London for long, in this fog bound London, I should say?"

"It kind of depends, doctor. You have been considerate and I really do appreciate your making the effort to come here and at least convey information that confirms what I have always suspected in my heart. Now that I know what has became of my *fiancé* there is very little to keep me in London, in this fog bound London, as you say," she said, with her voice quivering whilst expressing an air of resignation, but smiling with her pale lips.

"Might you not go on an ocean voyage to take the sea air?" I inquired.

"My experience of riding that White Star boat, what was it called – the *Olympus* or whatever, across the Atlantic has kind of put me off floating around on the oceans," Katherine replied.

My training as a doctor alerted me to her condition and internal emotional turmoil expressed clearly by her moist eyes. I felt my continued presence would impinge on her desire for solitude, to enable her to take in the enormity of what I had said regarding her *fiancé*. Accordingly, I got up to indicate my imminent departure,

"Do you know doctor," she offered, "I have not actually seen anything of London because of this fog that we are enduring. When I get back to Eureka Springs, and I do so want to, if only to escape this oppressive and insidious fog, I shall not be able to describe to the folks back home, one single street scene or view in London!"

Eventually she rose from the sofa and in a gesture of farewell held out her gloved hand to me that I instinctively kissed. She smiled again, then turned around and took her leave. As she glided out of the Grand Drawing

Room with considerable poise and elegance, I could not help but admire her *stoic* character. At the same time I felt tinges of regret for her loss, or was it indeed, for mine, I could not then determine which? But the strength of character she possessed would, I knew, not fail her. While pondering these thoughts, the waiter coughed quietly and presented the bill to me with the implication that since I was not staying at the Hotel and that my guest had retired, I too might consider vacating the Grand Drawing Room!

A few minutes later, whilst stepping out into the omnipresent fog the words Katherine had uttered came back to me in a flash, particularly those about the wreck she had crossed the Atlantic in and of its actually sinking. Not just those words, but also of the look of pained surprise upon her face, which haunted me for reasons I could quite fathom but which instilled in my soul a deep sense of foreboding. Possibly I knew in my heart that she had worked out in that intelligent mind of hers, something very true about the *Titanic* and its fate.

I stood outside the Hotel trying to decide which form of transport I should use to go home. It was with a vague intention that I waited for any available Hackney cab to take me back to Baker Street. The Metropolitan Railway was an attractive option, but then I remembered that resorting to it would mean crossing that dangerous Marylebone Road. However, at that instant, a loud coughing behind my head interrupted my thoughts. I turned around to find myself facing the supercilious red tail-coated *concièrge* of earlier encounter on my arrival at the Hotel.

"Doctor Watson, Doctor John Watson?"

"Yes," I replied, thinking there was a problem with my tariff drinks bill that I had just settled, such was his evident delight in his detaining me.

"I have a message for you," he continued, "the lady with whom you had just a meeting, has asked me to invite you back into the Hotel and awaits your presence in the Ladies' Smoking Room. If you would care to step this way, I shall escort you there."

I consented and followed him thinking that Katherine must have tipped him generously to effect a marked change in his previously condescending attitude towards me. Nonetheless, I was curious as to why I should be summoned in this manner. Perhaps she wanted further information about her *fiancé's* fate that I had not supplied or had overlooked or had I said something that demanded further explanation? I was soon to find out. The *concièrge* flung open the large highly polished mahogany doors that led into the airy and spacious Ladies' Smoking Room. Dividing up this chamber were columns of polished granite and limestone supporting intricately decorated arches that held up an even more ornate plaster ceiling with a richly detailed deep gilded cornice around the walls.

The *concièrge* negotiated us both through a *labyrinth* of green silk covered sofas and armchairs, until we reached Katherine who, upon my arrival, stood up to greet me. In so doing she nearly ascended into yet another indoor palm tree placed next to the sofa. As I approached a smile seemed to play upon her lips, and she appeared relieved that I had consented to join her.

"Doctor Watson, I am so pleased you could spare the time to accept my invitation. It occurred to me that my manners are a little wanting and, as my guest, I should have offered you dinner. That is the custom in England, is it not?"

"It can be madam, but at any rate I should be delighted to join you for dinner!"

"Good. Then you shall escort me to the Grand Dining Room on the *piano-nobile*, and by the way, my name is Katherine."

"Mine is John."

We approached the same ornate bronze door set into the wall and waited for the doors to open.

"Well John, I guess this is the second time that you have ridden an elevator car in as many hours eh?"

"It is becoming a habit, a very enjoyable habit, especially in such charming company," I said, as we stepped into the small mahogany panelled room again.

As we did so, I noticed in a mirror mounted on the elevator car wall that she blushed at my remark. Having arrived on the *piano-nobile,* we glided down the corridor and made our entrance into a Grand Dining Room. Before I could utter a word of amazement as to the sumptuous *décor* of the room, a rather obsequious waiter appeared from nowhere and asked that we follow him. He guided us to a table located in a deep bay windowed alcove framed with purple drapes partially open to reveal a large window overlooking the Euston Road, which was obscured by the folds of fog. My attention though was on my guest not the fog, and I attempted to engage her in conversation. Suddenly, a portly person, with a distinctive black moustache and dressed as a chef, in his blue checked trousers, came into sight and with no regard for other diners, spoke loudly whilst rushing across the room in our direction.

"Ah ha! Miss Katerina, my favourite lady from the New World, how are we today? Do you want that I should cook for you my delicious recipe that you so appreciate and so adore?" he said with a flourish and much arm waving.

"No François, I am dining with Doctor Watson here," replied Katherine.

"Are you not feeling well? Are you poorly my dear

lady?" he inquired, ignoring me almost with a total disregard for my presence.

"Yes, yes, yes!" I said, and waiter, may we have the menu," I said clearly and loudly.

This well-designed remark had the desired effect upon François who immediately acknowledged my presence, albeit with a vengeful look in his eyes. His charm too, appeared to have evaporated, along with his superficial manners. Eventually, a more courteous waiter, with appropriate servile attitude, appeared and took our orders.

"I do not really know my way around your English food," she said, whilst pondering what I thought was a rather inordinately over-sized menu card measuring at least twenty inches in height and with a red tassel. At length though, she made up her mind instructed the waiter accordingly.

"Turtle soup flavoured with Madeira port followed by the boiled chicken with artichoke and cucumber sauce impressed with vermouth. To complete I guess I will have the Lord Mayor's trifle laced with sherry – it sounds cute!"

"And for you, Sir?," came the inquiry from the waiter.

For myself, I restricted my choice to food where alcohol was not an integral part of the cooking process. Angels on Horseback I elected made with oysters wrapped in bacon rashers, which were complemented by the Devils on Horseback, comprising prunes wrapped in rashers of bacon. I followed with braised duck with oranges and peas with gravy, and then by warmed *Éclair* Cream Bun and custard made with Madeira port - my only concession to alcohol in food, at least on this occasion.

"And waiter, a bottle of your finest Chablis and a bottle of Beaune," said Katherine, "they will wash the food down real well!"

As dinner progressed, we spoke of several topics; and at one stage I even managed to elicit a laugh from Katherine, which showed me that she was capable of seeing things in perspective and with a positive frame of mind.

"Will you stay in London?" I ventured.

"I do not know," said Katherine, "what I do know is this London fog is oppressive to my spirit and I must escape, perhaps to Paris. I have heard there is a new palace there built of glass called the *Hall of Machines*, and am reliably informed is as big as your English Palace of Westminster, whatever that is. Perhaps I shall ride the *Express d'Orient* to the Gare de l'Est, in Paris, and check out that glass *Hall of Machines?*"

"The fog will not last forever," I said.

"The *concièrge* has stated that he has known fog to last for several days going on into weeks. Then all of a sudden it disappears as quickly as it came and no one is able to foretell how long it will last or when it might disperse," informed Katherine.

We enjoyed our dinner and talked of various matters of mutual interest. At length we decided, at the waiter's instigation, to repair to the Coffee *Salon* on the ground floor in order to take our coffee.

"Only if we get to ride the elevator car to that floor," said Katherine.

"Absolutely," I enjoined.

We did ride the elevator down to the ground floor and made our way again down the corridors of this magnificent structure to Gothic beauty. We entered the Coffee *Salon* and I, immediately thought the name to be a misnomer. The Grand Coffee *Salon* would have been more appropriate for it was a room of such proportions as to subjugate any person standing within its precinct.

Hall of Machines

The room was quite impressive, the proportions of which were based not on a regular rectilinear shape, but on a curved style. One curved wall that overlooked the front of the Hotel comprised a series of Gothic pointed *trefoil* arches of stone and into it was set large windows at least twenty feet in height. However, due to the fog no clear vision through them was possible and the windows merely took on the appearance of white *opaqueness* with only a hint of the movement of shadows scuttling by.

The room was magnificent, if metallic and its construction easily recognised as being based on the innovative iron frame for which the Hotel is renowned. The curved room, measuring at least one hundred and fifty feet in length and thirty-five feet in width, is divided into bays by the formation of a web of iron girders reflected both on the walls and in the ceiling. Set within the walls were iron beams encased by limestone piers fronted by columns of red marble. From the top of these piers of stone rested another iron beam spanning the entire thirty-five foot width of the room. Again the iron beam was encased by elaborate gilded plaster designs which complimented the general intricately moulded plaster ceilings throughout and other raised detailed designs of *filigree* on other surfaces. The whole effect was one of a provision of a generous and uninhibited large space, in order to physically create an airy and sumptuous environment. The designer had, in my opinion, surpassed himself.

"I did ask earlier, what you might intend doing now; might you go back to Eureka Springs immediately?" I said, while we both sat back, in the palatial splendour of the Coffee *Salon*, to enjoy our brandy, and in her case, cigars too.

"Well John, given my experience on that boat whilst crossing the Atlantic and the dreadful news about the *Titanic* I do not much feel like gambling my life with the White Star Line again. I appreciate how lucky I am to be alive today and not resting on the bottom of the Atlantic."

"Have you travelled much around the United States?" I inquired.

"Yes mainly around the Middle West of the States. Up as far as Chicago and steamed along the Missouri and Mississippi Rivers. I even travelled by railroad, from the new magnificent railroad station in Joplin, Missouri, not far from Eureka Springs, and caught railroad trains all the way to San Francisco City! Have you been to America?"

"No, but it is a place I should like to visit. I have been elsewhere, mainly around our Empire ranging from Egypt to India, whilst serving as doctor in the British army," I answered.

"Well whatever holds for me now I have to get back

Joplin Railroad Station, Missouri

to the United States soon to attend the greatest show on earth to be held in Chicago..." she responded.

"Would that be the World's Columbian Exposition in Chicago?" I interrupted triumphantly, of knowing something without being prompted.

She looked at me with an air of surprise that I should know this fact.

"You are absolutely right John," she said.

I gave a shallow bow, in appreciation of her acknowledging my current information on this Columbian Exposition.

"The idea of the Exposition is to restore confidence in Metropolitan Chicago and the state of Illinois," informed Katherine.

"Why, what happened," I asked.

"Chicago suffered from a devastating fire in 1871 that damn near wiped out the city. A few buildings survived including the hundred and fifty-foot high stone clad Gothic Water Tower that dominates the area in which the Chicago World Fair Columbian Exposition is being built. The phoenix represents the re-birth of Chicago and the Exposition to mark Chicago's place in the world scheme of things.

The whole Exposition is given over to celebrating various aspects of American life; and not just in the humanities, but also rather in industry, science, agriculture and engineering. There are buildings being constructed now, as we speak, that are based on European palaces, but four times the size of the original buildings! There is, according to a brochure I have read, one building, the stone-colonnaded *Peristyle*, that is embellished with statues, and punctuated at the centre with a huge dominating arch, four times the size of the that *Propylaeum* Arch you have at Euston Station, here in London. But this arch is supporting a huge equestrian sculptural group!

What catches my attention John, is the enormous expanse of the Manufactures and Liberal Arts Building. That remarkable structure is said to cover over eleven acres, and will exhibit objects ranging from the University of Chicago's Charles Yerkes' telescope, all seventy tons of it, to one of Johann Sebastian Bach's fully-functioning clavichords!

I cannot wait to get there and breathe the clean cool air coming off Lake Michigan," said Katherine.

"It seems a place one really ought to visit," I said, knowing my army pension could never stretch to such reckless dreams.

"Well, you should come out and see it for yourself!" Katherine said, smiling, as if she could read my concerns, "I even have my ticket with me now to remind me of what lies in store when I get to Chicago," she said whilst looking in her purse and handing to me a certificate that allowed her access, as honoured guest, into the Exposition on Chicago Day.

Upon closer examination, it proclaimed to be for herself only, and was adorned with decoration and ciphers all surrounding a phoenix bird rising from ashes. I handed the ticket back to her, relieved of any responsibility for its value, which was immense.

"What is the significance of the phoenix on the certificate number 2355?" I asked, surprised at my memory in retaining the number of the certificate, but thinking Holmes would be impressed.

"The phoenix just represents re-birth of the city of Chicago after the great fire," she replied.

We talked farther into the evening but by now my spirits were waning and an ache, a legacy from the Egyptian Campaign that had been gnawing in my right thigh, due to my sitting down for too long, was becoming unbearable. Eventually, probably driven by the amount of alcohol we had consumed, we parted company. She accompanied me to the well-appointed main Entrance Hall where I thanked her for an enjoyable evening, but said good-bye.

"Good-bye John, though I never like saying good-bye to friends," she replied, still smiling.

I turned to leave the Hotel but before doing so glanced back at where she was standing only to see her running

World's Columbian Exposition, Ticket

up the grand staircase up to the *piano-nobile* with the energy and enthusiasm of a young girl!

Later, I fell into our rooms at Baker Street and collapsed into an armchair. I had just poured myself some whisky and had settled down to enjoy it, and a cigarette, when Holmes appeared in his mouse coloured dressing gown, clutching a his pipe and immediately launched into a tirade that took me aback somewhat.

"I asked you to go there, did I not, as my emissary, not as a potential suitor?" he said.

Flabbergasted I replied: "Holmes, I recall you asked me to undertake a task you did not feel quite equal to. I relieved you of a burden that, you of all people, could never assume. Besides, I have nevertheless carried out your wishes – very successfully as it happens – so what concerns you now?"

"You Watson, and your obsession with that, that woman from Eureka Springs," replied Holmes.

"Holmes, Holmes! You really must take control of yourself and attempt to regain your composure." I said reaching for the ashtray but succeeding only in dropping my burning cigarette on to the carpet, where it immediately began to make the rug smoulder. Holmes picked up the cigarette and handed it to me.

"Whilst you were gallivanting around with that, that woman, events have developed regarding my quest that required our presence elsewhere today. I waited for you in the insane hope that you would deliver our message and then return here *post haste*. After three hours I knew this expectation to be futile. About an hour after you left I received a telegram from Charles Peace, you know, the eminent violinist, informing me that an artist by the name of Lyons was found dead earlier this afternoon! Ironically, you were in the vicinity of the crime since you must have walked passed his house at the top of Harley Street?"

"Holmes, how dare you!" I exploded, my head now swimming, "how could you know I was anywhere near Lyons's house?" I stammered out, just barely concealing my disgust at Holmes' insinuation based on his facetiousness.

"Quite simply Watson, by observing, as I am sure your female companion of today also did, your feeble attempt to remove the mud from your boots and trousers. Earth picked up whilst clambering over the piles of spoil deposited on the pavement out side the new underground station along the Marylebone Road along which you travelled on foot to your *rendezvous* with that, that woman," responded Holmes.

"Look here Holmes, I will not sit..."

"When you have finished your drunken behaviour," interrupted Holmes, "and found your way to bed and sobered up by the morning, we have work to do. Good night, or rather good morning Watson!"

I sat there reviewing the events of the day or more accurately the day before, and the enormity of the infamous artist, Lyons being done away with. Could Holmes be the next victim I wondered, indeed could I be in line to be removed or more frighteningly the prospect of Katherine being done in too, given her *fiancé* had been made away with? A panic gripped my chest as I realised in my stupor this was a real possibility. I must get word to Katherine, or better still go myself and warn her of these developments and the dark forces around us. I attempted to get up to act but then was struck down with a most violent stomach ache. For minutes I felt my life was in danger and when I did come to, it was all I could do to stagger to my own bedchamber wherein I fell into a fitful sleep.

Chapter 19

The House in Harley Street

The following morning I arose from my slumbers feeling remarkably fit and energetic. However, I knew from bitter experience this euphoria could be short lived and replaced by *Rhadamanthus's* judgement and its revenge descending upon me as the day wore on. Nevertheless, I entered our break-fast room to find Holmes progressing through a plate of ham and eggs. I poured coffee for us both, before tugging at the bell rope to summon Mrs Hudson to deliver break-fast to me too.

"Are you recovered from your indulgences of yesterday Watson or is it just a vague memory?"

I ignored his jibe, and instead simply asked in a crisp manner:

"What precisely happened in my absence, what went wrong whilst I was away for but a short time? You mumbled something on my return but it was incoherent. Perhaps you would care to try again now that you are refreshed and explain to me why Lyons was done away with in his house?"

I pronounced these words in such a manner as to impute failure in Holmes in not being able to deal with the situation as a result of my short absence.

Without looking up from his break-fast Holmes replied:

"Charles Peace has communicated with me, only by wire, to advise that the artist Lyons was dead. The housekeeper had called in the local police inspector, who determined Lyons died of natural causes. Peace concludes that I should be watchful. Clearly, he thought Moriarty to be behind the crime, and indicated that this vindictive professor is still in the business of revenge killings of those persons who fail or cross him. Peace, as we talk, has cancelled all his concert engagements and is now *en-route* to a safer destination away from London. He has left word with Lyons' household that nothing is to be touched, including the body, until we arrive to investigate the scene of the crime. That was yesterday, it is now today. When you have break-fasted, I suggest we visit the scene of the crime before events beyond our control compromise any clues that may have been evident and useful."

My break-fast arrived, as did fresh, steaming hot coffee.

"Mrs Hudson has surpassed herself with break-fast today," I announced, whilst cutting into thick rashers of Harrod's prime smoked bacon. The eggs, I noticed, were of goose.

After break-fast we discussed further the implications of Lyons' death and the possible motives for it.

"Does this killing make sense in the scheme of things, or was it an isolated incident of murder?" I asked Holmes.

"I cannot be certain at this stage, but the chances are it was organised by Moriarty, and therefore in this respect it was not an isolated incident," came his reply, "but now we ought to make our way to Harley Street, in order to try and ascertain a motive."

For reasons that were valid for my walking to the Portland Road Metropolitan Station yesterday; prevailed for our walking to Harley Street today. For an explanation known only to Holmes, we turned from Baker Street into Porter Street and right into Chiltern Street. That took

Marylebone Mausoleum

us into Paddington Street. On either side of this street
are located the Marylebone burial grounds, complete with
funereal structures and a modestly sized Mausoleum
looking *sombre* and melancholic. In these grounds, I
noticed, the fog ceased swirling and had become still. A
Drag and Four went clattering arrogantly by, and I was
minded to intercept it, but since we were only minutes
away from our destination I resisted the urge. Instead
we wheeled hard left into Northumberland Street * and
then right into Nottingham Street.

Suddenly Holmes tugged at my coat sleeve and pulled
me into a narrow lane called Oldbury Place. A more
desolate and quiet a lane I have yet to experience; it was
as if we had just stepped out of the world. No sound
could be heard, save those of our footfalls. The fog
appeared more virulent and concentrated, as if being
compelled into a confined space and in so doing created

that feeling of imminent panic, I so closely associated with dense fog and claustrophobia. Had I not walked in this same fog yesterday without mishap or panic? Why then did I, within seconds of coping, find myself in the grip of an irrational fear? The mere presence of fog by itself need not necessarily have been a cause of my anxiety, especially when it was affected by signs of human activity, represented by noise, moving carriages or the flicker of dull lights.

Fog, of course, is an attendant feature of cold and damp low-lying areas, especially in the proximity of water. London is laid out in the flat alluvial valley of the River Thames, and is subject to intermittent periods of fog, light or dense. What makes London fogs unbearable and capable of killing people, is the fact that it mixes with the soot and smoke, from countless chimneys, ranged across England's huge Metropolis, the largest on earth. And, accordingly, it is this combination that makes it unpleasant at best and deadly at worst. It can irritate the eyes mercilessly and infect the lungs with dreadful effect.

Most people in London remember the very bad fog that lasted from November 1879 to March 1880, during which several hundreds of persons lost their lives, as did cattle at Smithfield market, near St Paul's Cathedral.

I forget which witty commentator penned a romanticised description of the fog, but I do try to remember the words from it, when feeling the claustrophobic effects of the fog:

'At present people see fogs, not because there are fogs, but because poets and painters have taught them the mysterious loveliness of such effects. There may have been fogs for centuries in London; I dare say there were, but no one saw them, so we did not know anything about them. They did not exist until art invented them! Now it must be admitted, fogs are carried to excess. They have become the mere mannerism of a *clique* and the exaggerated realism of their method, gives people bronchitis.' **

Despite these uplifting sentiments, what can initiate alarm in the heart is the isolation that the fog can instil in a person within seconds. Oldbury Place was such a place where the ability of the fog to isolate the person was at its most effective. The concoction of silence and the *opaqueness* of the fog together with the melancholic nature of our visit, destined to finish at a *sombre* scene of death, combined to depress my spirits still further. The lane seemed to go nowhere, accept along a blank wall and I began to wish that I had intercepted that passing Drag and Four carriage, pulled by four white horses, only partially visible in the fog. We groped along for several more minutes, seemingly making little progress in our quest.

"Watson," Holmes said, pointing with his cane to a flight of steps leading from an opening in a wall. He climbed the steps that led into what seemed a void, into which I followed him, "do you know where we are?"

"No" I responded.

"Look ahead of you, strain your eyes, look!"

"Holmes, I am trying," I replied.

"Can you not see the ghostly march of carriage lights?" he asked.

"What, have we arrived at the Marylebone Road, but Holmes how could...?"

"Do you not recognise this building we are approaching and can now see – the *portico*, the *colonnade* and its columns?"

"It is the St. Marylebone Church!" I said, with delighted enthusiasm.

"I should have difficulty in bright daylight, navigating

a route through these *labyrinths* of back streets and mews, let alone doing so in the midst of this fog, as you Holmes, are able to do, and with the ease of *Thesius*!"

We made our way along the side of the church and emerged into the *colonnade* of tall columns capped with *Corinthian* capitals of ornate foliage design. We progressed into the *portico* and along the *stylobate*, in front of the church, upon which the columns are constructed. We then descended the steps of the *crepidoma*, down to the gates, which open onto the Marylebone Road. Upon stepping on to this wide thoroughfare, we turned east and continued walking towards Harley Street.

"Who is this fellow Lyons anyway?" I asked now that my confidence had returned and my claustrophobia partially abated.

"Lyons was an artist of no great repute, but was involved in a case I settled some time ago, involving the Baskerville inheritance on Dartmoor. He married the daughter of one of the protagonists in the case, but deserted her and came to live in London, at the house in which we are about to conduct our investigation.

His death, though regrettable, is not in itself of great moment, but may provide clues to enable me to tie up some loose ends. Moriarty almost certainly orchestrated his demise, no doubt for some likely disloyalty. We have experienced recently evidence of Moriarty's manic vengefulness. His is a character that knows no bounds in its desire to expand evil. To Moriarty, life is as cheap as life itself," Holmes informed me.

"I cannot believe," I remarked, "that this murderous, this poisonous maniac is allowed to go abroad the Metropolis. Why do the police not arrest him?"

"Because Watson, be careful as we cross this Marylebone High Street, the more I learn about Moriarty, by talking to people such as Charles Peace and Staunton, the more I have come to understand this Professor's character. He is, Watson, quite simply, the apotheosis of criminality, and occupies the apex of a pyramid of crime. He is the great organiser, he facilitates, he develops strategies, he plans, but never will he execute those criminal schemes. He is above such concerns, and instead leaves such matters to an army of slavish criminals, who owe their loyalty and indeed their lives to him," said Holmes.

"But the man is steeped in crime, not least he is responsible for the death of Katherine's *fiancé,* the premature demise of Cadogan West and this fellow Lyons, also being done away with! And, this is excluding that horrendous crime he has perpetrated on the poor souls that exist in the permanent *'Iron Mausoleum',* that the *Titanic* has now become, at the bottom of the Atlantic Ocean," I stated.

"'*Iron Mausoleum',* Watson?"

"Yes, the newspapers have resorted to calling the ill-fated *Titanic* the *'Iron Mausoleum'* for that is precisely what it has become," I replied.

"You remain a mine of information, Watson," said Holmes.

"Never the less Holmes, I still remember with horror being in Moriarty's mansion in Well Road, Hampstead and the feeling of concentrated evil seeping out of every crevice and opening, not least from Moriarty himself. How the flesh creeps! However, the possibility remains, if Professor Moriarty is seeking revenge might he not turn his attention to you, to me or indeed, to Katherine at the St. Pancras Hotel?" I said, and in so doing realised the implication of my statement and the safety of all three of us.

"I do not know…" Holmes replied.

"Well I do!" I interrupted, "if that vicious maniac Moriarty incommodes or causes an inconvenience to Katherine's well-being, then I shall go for him. He may well be evading Scotland Yard at the moment, but by God, when I am finished with him he will be seeking Scotland Yard's protection from me!"

"Watson!" said Holmes, as we both hurried across Devonshire Place.

"So help me, I shall rid the Metropolis of his evil influence at what ever price to my own liberty. Perhaps Holmes you ought to consider applying those undoubted talents you possess, and do society a favour, rather than theorising from your armchair!" I exploded, my face flushed with anger, at the very thought of the criminal and murderous Moriarty being free to roam the Metropolis, unchallenged by either Holmes or Scotland Yard.

"We have arrived Watson," said Holmes.

Whilst Holmes tugged at the doorbell, I surveyed what could be seen of the fog-bound house from Harley Street.

It was a substantial four-storey house built of Portland stone and occupied a site on the junction of Harley Street and the Marylebone Road and set in a clump of large road trees partially concealing it. Running the length of the front and side *façades* of the building, were *pilasters* capped with flattened *Ionic* capitals that divided the deep set window reveals of stone into which glazed panels had been inserted. Stone panelled spandrels, rich in Roman foliage relief decoration, were set in between the windows on the *piano-nobile* and the second floor. The *façades* to the building were dominated by a substantial and richly ornate overhanging deep architrave, supported by pronounced and ornate recessed alternate deep consoles. Here they were used for corbelling which supported a

The House in Harley Street

detailed stepped cornice, above which was a stone balustrade fronting the *attic* at the top of the building.

The ground floor had two door entrances, and each comprised tall oak double doors, set in frames of stone, with intricately decorated corbels, supporting the entablatures, of ancient Greek design, above both sets of doors. The door frames built of stone, displayed peculiar design details upon them; especially on their upper sections above each door, the relief panels were of a later fashion and not consistent with the overall deign of the building. In between these doors, was a large stone-framed arched window reveal, that comprised wedge-shaped *voussoirs* blocks forming a shallow arch on top of which was inserted, for decoration only, a prominent outset keystone. Into this shallow elliptical arched reveal was inserted a glazed panel at least twelve feet in height and seven feet in width immediately above a basement area opening, in the foot path, surrounded by a simple cross-braced patterned metal fence.

The building was of indeterminate architectural design, but reflected a combination of pseudo classical Greek and Roman motifs and renaissance styles. It was designed clearly to reflect the success of a wealthy patron, who had caused the structure to be created, and resembled very much a prosperous merchant's house.

Something, however, was not quite right; so in order to gain a better view of the building, I stepped back into the carriageway in Harley Street. I did this at considerable risk to my person, for traffic was still busy and lumbering along only feet away.

On reëxamining the building's *façades* I gradually realised what it was that had caught my attention. Immediately above the ground floor window frame arches, where the keystones were fitted, was a protuberance of stone resembling a balcony three feet in height and jutting out by about twenty inches. This regular undecorated projection girdled the building, creating an overhanging plinth upon which, so it appeared, the rest of the upper section of the building had been constructed.

I gazed at this protruding architectural detail, uncertain as to its function. I was however certain that its presence there was at variance with the general architectural design of the building.

"Watson, I think we have managed at long last to raise a soul inside this house. I think someone is approaching the door," Holmes informed me.

After much scraping and releasing of locks and latches, the door swung back to reveal a diminutive woman with white hair tied up in the shape of a bun behind her head. In her shaking hand, she held a substantial brass *candelabrum*, the size of which dominated her small frame.

"Are you that detective we were expecting yesterday?" she launched into Holmes, without any introduction or hesitation. Before Holmes could answer she continued:

"Mr Lyons' body has been up there, unattended now for these two days past, and I want it out of the building and treated with respect, for I do not want an outbreak of cholera here. Well, have you come to collect it?" she inquired.

"We have not come to collect the body. However, my name is Sherlock Holmes and this is my colleague, Doctor Watson," replied Holmes.

"Doctor, it is a bit late for a doctor is it not? The man has been dead these two days past!" she said.

"Well that may be so, but may we come in and examine the body and his possessions?" Holmes said, while moving to enter through the door.

"No, no not this door, that door there," she said, pointing to the other front door of the building on the other side of the large arched window.

"That door there, it leads up to his rooms on the first floor. He was the only person with access to that floor through that door. All the other tenants use this door entrance, in which we are standing, in order for them to gain access to their rooms," she said.

This fact momentarily threw Holmes off balance, but he regained his composure and asked:

"From my previous dealings with Mr Lyons, he informed me that he was the owner of this building. Is he in fact the owner of this building?"

"Yes, yes of course he is the owner, or was, who do you suppose owns it, me?" she replied, "I am just the housekeeper."

"Why then did Mr Lyons let rooms out to tenants?" asked Holmes.

"Because Mr Lyons is, was," she corrected herself, "of a sociable turn, and preferred the company of people, rather than being alone."

"But none of the tenants had access to his first floor rooms or indeed to him," inquired Holmes.

"That may well be the case, but he liked the fact of people occupying those parts of the house he had no call for. He often said to me, whilst cleaning his rooms that he wished only for a simple life with a roof over his head. I will have you know that he was a very religious man and liked his tenants or, family, as he called them," said the housekeeper.

And with that abstract piece of information, she slammed the front door closed behind her, and hobbled to the other front door that led to the *piano-nobile* of the deceased. We followed her and the lighted brass *candelabrum* provided an eerie illumination, through the fog. Moments later we entered through the other front door she had now unlocked.

"Gentlemen, you will understand that I have no wish to trespass on the dead, and certainly not on Mr Lyons. You will, I feel certain, understand if I leave you to conduct your searches by yourselves, as you see fit and without me. At the top of the stairs there is, as you will find, a lighted coal tar gas jet next to the door leading into Mr Lyons' chambers. It will enable you to take flame from that gas mantel to light other gas-jets ranged throughout his rooms to provide lighting for you."

At this stage the housekeeper was beginning to show signs of becoming upset over what had happened recently. Her whole world had been shaken to its foundations; so I put my hand gently on her arm and said:

"We can take it from here. Actually, we do not know your name."

"Bernstone sir, Mrs. Bernstone," she replied.

"Well, as I say, we can take it from here, for there is no need to upset yourself further over this affair. My colleague Mr Holmes will, I am sure, sort everything out, and you might like to call the mortuary, and arrange for the removal of the corpse".

"Oh thank you sir, you are so kind!" she said, handing me the brass *candelabrum,* the weight of which took me by surprise, as my arm dipped when accepting it.

She then dropped a curtsey and left us in the hallway. Holmes took the *candelabrum* from me and waved it about in front of him. There was nothing unusual there except that the ceiling appeared low. I followed Holmes and the brass *candelabrum* down the hallway corridor that cut straight into the building. On reaching the end, the corridor turned left on to a noticeably steep flight of stairs leading up to the *piano-nobile*. I found this configuration to be a peculiar way in constructing access to the first floor, especially since we had not seen evidence of the ground floor ceiling. Why not have the stairs rising straight up from the front door, rather than have the wasted space of a corridor leading to those stairs. The staircase leading up to the *piano-nobile*, seemed to me to be inordinately steep and of a considerable height.

Mrs Bernstone was correct, in that we did find a coal

tar gas jet flickering outside the main door to Lyons' apartment. Holmes availed himself of a wax taper from a sheath below the burning gas mantel and took a light from it. Then pushing open the door, he led us both into the gloomy chambers. It was dingy and subdued of course but the poor light did not stop Holmes finding and lighting two large town gas-jets *appliqués* in the form of angels holding forth firebrands in front of them. They provided enough light to see clearly the extent of Lyons' large drawing room.

It was sparsely furnished, but what items of furniture that I could immediately see, indicated that they were of the highest quality, including furniture by *Salon Français, Beau-Arts* and *Biedermeier*, which I think, enjoyed a European vogue for a while. There was no real systematic coördination, but somehow the eclectic mix of furniture styles co-existed successfully in creating an interesting collection to look at. Notwithstanding this and even in the dim light, I could discern quality, though not in the loose carpets, which covered the timber floorboards. Certainly the paintings on the walls were not what I would have expected of someone like Lyons. They were of a middle range quality, not at all appropriate for a man whose taste ran to acquiring items of exquisite furniture. More suited, I thought, to adorn the walls of our housekeeper Mrs Hudson's quarters in Baker Street.

In one corner I saw a tall elegant chest of drawers, with a fold down writing shelf, that was made of a honey coloured wood inlaid with intricately shaped marble and red veneers impressed into its various surfaces. Ranged around the room were *Biedermeier* sofas covered in fine striped silks and plain *moiré* watermarked silk covered chairs with armrests. Very particular about his comfort this Lyons, I thought.

Holmes looked neither at the furniture or the paintings on the walls, but busied himself examining the floor. Placed against a wall but near a front window was a fairly substantial item of French Second Empire furniture in the form of a *Salon Français* ornate sideboard. As I approached it I saw that it too, was made of golden coloured wood but with distinctive fluted Corinthian columns made of black ebony and gilded ornate Capitals attached to its four corners. How did they, I wondered, get this large item of furniture from the street up those stairs we had just climbed, and into this room? I then noticed that the heavy sideboard was on polished brass casters shaped as lion paws, which would help moving it about. I looked out of the adjacent window to check the height from the street level still discernible in the fog. I could not believe what I saw. It seemed that we were much higher in the building than one would have expected from the street level. This realisation left me puzzled, so that I felt disorientated.

I looked around for Holmes to share my experience only to discover he had moved on. I vacated the drawing room in favour of the hall and immediately realised where Holmes was, by the flickering light due to his moving the brass *candelabrum* that he had not relinquished. I walked towards the room, from which the flickering lights emanated and moved towards the door. In so doing a nameless foreboding overtook me, which I always experience when in the presence of death. I continued and pushed my head around the corner only to see the *candelabrum,* suspended in the air, and below it, a dark shape. As I peered at this shadow, Holmes raised himself up to the level of the *candelabrum* and in so doing revealed a vision of Lyons' fixed grinning vivid features, staring at me!

"We have seen this method before, have we not?"

Still recovering from my shock of seeing suddenly the dead Lyons, I mumbled some incoherent reply.

"You might recall Watson, our friend Cadogan West met his supreme moment in a similar manner; that of holding, with his fingers, paper soaked with strychnine poison, the effects of which killed him."

"I do so now recall." I said, moving over toward the corpse, "*Rigor Mortis,* has of course set in, with a vengeance and would indicate the time of death to be approximately forty odd hours ago."

"Be careful with his fingers Watson, because there are likely to have traces of a vegetable alkaloid poison still on them!" cautioned Holmes.

I dropped his hand immediately, and looked around for the incriminating paper, as evidence. I found on his bedside table. The paper, though lethal to touch, did not look so. It was light grey and of foolscap size. The message written upon it was clear and unambiguous, but designed to make Lyons consider the message, and its implication in terms of his own treachery. It read: '*Can I trust you with valuable information?*'

I imagined Lyons sitting on this *moiré* silk covered *Biedermeier* chair in this bedchamber, secure in the belief that he was safe whilst in the depths of his apartment, holding that paper with his fingers trying to determine whether Moriarty knew of his plans or was this message co-incidence? Did Moriarty want him to carry out an assignment involving valuable information, or was the game up? Whatever, Lyons was now dead, because the strychnine-impregnated paper had done what it was designed to do, at Moriarty's instigation.

"Look here Holmes why is Lyons so important; is he not yet another henchman, albeit one who has fallen out with Moriarty?" I said, whilst carefully folding the poisoned paper and replacing it into the envelope on the bedside table to stop any further contamination. I then handed the envelope to Holmes.

"There is more to it than that, Watson, because Lyons' death is meant to be a signal mark to anyone who feels like resigning as an *employé* from Moriarty's service. It also means that Moriarty may not feel so secure, as we have supposed, especially if he has to resort to this vicious method of re-action or retaliation to perceived disloyalty. You and I, and now possibly that Oklahoma woman, may, in Moriarty's opinion, know of his involvement in the sinking of the *Titanic* and other sundry crimes. No Watson, something is not right and that bothers me deeply," said Holmes, more moved than I had ever seen him before.

He continued his searches throughout Lyons' chambers, moving around with the *candelabrum* and creating *grotesque* shadows upon the walls. At length he announced there was nothing else to be gained from his examination and extinguished the *candelabrum,* leaving me momentarily in the dark recesses of Lyons' bedchamber. The imminent prospect of my falling onto Lyons' corpse, that I knew was nearby, momentarily filled with me with dread and anxiety.

At length though, we both descended the stairs and regained the slightly more breathable air outside in Harley Street. Again I looked at the *façade* of the building, trying in my mind to work out why I was surprised by the height of the drawing room floor on the *piano-nobile*. Holmes, having raised Mrs Bernstone, handed back the *candelabrum* to her.

"And Mr Holmes, what is to become of me now that my master is dead; am I to be abandoned to my fate?" she implored.

Holmes did not reply but patted her gently on her shoulder. She responded by dropping a curtsey. I was still absorbed in my study of the building and unaware that Holmes had moved on and by now had crossed Harley Street and was walking westward along the Marylebone Road. He was in deep thought, so we walked in silence for a few minutes. My attention was concentrated on where I was stepping until my eyes had became used to the *opaqueness* of the yellow fog that had become in the meantime, slightly denser and acidic.

"Well my dear doctor, what do you think about our visit?" asked Holmes.

"About which one in particular," I asked, "Mrs Bernstone, Lyons' death, the house or the melancholy business that we have found ourselves in?"

"My knowledge of Lyons," Holmes continued, "was such that his artistic skills were not, what one might say, good or accomplished. No, there is something unsettling about that house and I do not refer to Lyons' death therein. It is the location of the house and its prominence on such a busy thoroughfare, albeit concealed by several large road trees, which lends an innocuous aspect to the house. You realise of course that Lyons acquired that house through monies derived from Moriarty. He must have been in league with Moriarty from the first, and though not a talented artist, he was a venal, if a very confident individual, but easily bent to Moriarty's will and it is this link that concerns me Watson," said Holmes.

"Given the fact then, that he was an artist, good or bad, why would he cause to have built for himself, such a striking and ostentatious house as the one we have just left? And, I might add, a building that resembles more a house of a prosperous merchant, than a home for a *Bohemian* artist?" I remarked.

"I agree Watson; probably vanity, but what is the point of having the trappings of wealth, if one cannot enjoy it?"

"I remembered your saying this was the house of an artist who had consulted you some months previously," I prattled away, as we walked home, even though Holmes showed little sign of attentiveness to my words.

"You yourself have described that house," Holmes responded to my surprise, "as resembling a prosperous merchant's house not the house of a *Bohemian* artist."

"True Holmes, because, it is precisely that, but I..."

"I have Watson," Holmes interrupted, "I have always maintained that there is more horror perpetrated in the midst of the Metropolis than in some lonely cottage isolated in the depths of the countryside. How many times have you or I walked past a seemingly innocent and respectable looking house in the West End, oblivious to the fact that feet away on the other side of a wall or a window with drawn drapes, is being perpetrated murder, an imprisonment or torture?"

"There is nothing secretive about that house behind windows with drawn drapes or anything of the kind, for he has tenants living in the house, including that house-keeper Mrs Bernstone, hardly a place to conduct clandestine activities," I postulated.

Holmes stopped and thought for a few seconds.

"True Watson, but nevertheless a foil I suspect, given the fact that his tenants did not actually have access to his rooms, had they? Are there not two doors allowing access, one to Lyon's chambers on the *piano-nobile* and the other to the upper floors of the building?"

"Yes Holmes but we examined Lyon's chambers and found nothing incriminating. Besides are we not forgetting one vital fact; it was he who was murdered?" I offered.

"I know Watson, but it is why he was murdered that concerns me!" conjectured Holmes.

"While you were conducting your searches, I looked about the drawing room and noticed several large pieces of furniture on caster wheels, to allow their ease in being re-positioned or moved. On approaching that substantial *Salon Français* sideboard with the fluted columns, the elegance and beauty of which took my fancy, I peered through the windowpane to the street below. And, let me tell you Holmes, I got quite a shock when it became clear to me to realise, just how high the room was above the street level. It was as though a *mezzanine* floor had been built into in the building, especially when one thinks of that stone protuberance, three feet in height and jutting out from between the ground floor ceiling and the timber floor on the first floor *piano-nobile* on which Lyons' chambers are located."

Holmes clapped his hand to his forehead.

"What a fool I have been, what a fool!" he admitted, "that is it Watson! As usual, you are a conduit through which the flash of inspiration burns!"

"Why? I inquired, somewhat flabbergasted by this unexpected praise." And, would you be prepared to put your recognition of my flash of inspirational abilities in writing?"

"Later Watson later," he said, as he grabbed my sleeve and turned me around to face east and back to Harley Street. We walked at a pace now much increased, since we were on a mission to solve one distinct problem Holmes had obviously worked out in the cold mathematical and logical mind of his. Though I had been the inspiration I knew not how, no doubt all will be revealed.

On regaining the front door, Holmes knocked loudly

upon it. Whilst we were waiting for Mrs. Bernstone, the housekeeper, I took the opportunity of studying the house again, and still found its construction to be peculiar. A few moments' later a rather surprised Mrs Bernstone opened her front door. I could detect from the red rings around her eyes that she had been crying, but nonetheless, looked more pleased to see us than annoyed.

"Mrs Bernstone, we need access to Lyons' rooms again," said Holmes.

Her demeanour changed upon hearing Holmes' demand.

"Why, have you left something behind, perhaps even your manners? Mr Holmes," she continued, "I do not have time for this tomfoolery of opening and locking doors. This is a house of death and not the Alhambra Music Hall! I would be grateful if you were to appreciate this fact."

My intervention was called for, and I informed the housekeeper that we had need to re-visit Lyons' chambers in order to conclude our investigation, but sincerely regretted deeply having to disturb her, yet again, in order to do so.

"Oh very well then, wait there and I shall get that brass *candelabrum* as illumination for you," she said.

Whilst she scuttled off down her hallway, I noticed that it was Holmes, who now looked intently at the outside details of the building.

Again, we ascended the staircase to the first floor, Holmes leading the way with the *candelabrum*. Once inside the drawing room, we lit as many candles and town gas-jets mantels as were available to us. I pulled back the heavy drapes against the windows in order to get what light there was from the fog-bound street. Holmes looked about and started to examine the large *Salon Français* sideboard and in particular, the immediate area of the wooden floor upon which it stood. He then began to unlock some of the doors on the front of the sideboard. For some reason a creeping sensation came over me as Holmes slowly and methodically prepared the large sideboard to reveal its contents.

"Just as I thought Watson, nothing, but wait, what is this?" exclaimed Holmes.

"What, what is it, what have you found?" I inquired, while approaching him.

Holmes by now was on his knees intently feeling the floor with his fingers in particular grooves, quite deep grooves in the timber battens from which the floor was made.

"These grooves have been made by a heavy object and made on a regular basis judging by the dirt and dust which have been impressed into the floor. Shifting this heavy *Salon Français* sideboard no doubt made the scratches and dents in the wooden floor. But, why would one regularly move an item of furniture back and forth from its position against the wall?"

My attention was drawn to the wall, on hearing those words. I looked at the flock wallpaper covered wall with apprehension. I thought of Moriarty's walls at Well House and the possibility of persons being walled up in them. Was Lyons of such an evil inclination, I asked myself? By now Holmes was in full flight and pulling hard at the sideboard trying to shift it from the wall. I lent my weight to the task, despite my weak left arm, made so by a stray bullet received during the third Egyptian Expedition when temporarily attached to the Middlesex Hussars Regiment of the Imperial Yeomanry.

Together we succeeded in moving the *Salon Français*

sideboard a few feet away from the wall and in so doing, propelled it into an adjacent *Biedermeier* style item of furniture and, a *Beau-Arts* designed *moiré* covered sofa. Holmes then reached down and removed a small rug on the floor that the sideboard had been covering. We then saw it, cut fine finely into the timber floor, an outline of a regular groove. Holmes went to the front of the sideboard and rummaged through a couple of drawers and returned with a flat knife shaped implement and immediately set about inserting it into the grooves on the floor. After a few moments, to the accompanying sounds of creaking and cracking, the clear outline in the floor was revealed to us. It was a hatch, a door, a trap door which Holmes flung back revealing a void, a hidden vault!

"Come on Watson!" Holmes said, grabbing a lighted candle from the *candelabrum*. I did the same, and without any concern for our danger leap into the dark void behind him.

The secret chamber was about four feet in height and from the light of our candles appeared to extend throughout the dimensions of the whole building. Where internal walls ought to have been, were instead, iron columns, allowing the whole space to be opened up. However, it was not this hidden chamber with its forest of iron columns but what was on the floor that had Holmes and me transfixed. Ranged around the vault propped up against the walls or iron columns, were oil paintings of every description some of them were immediately recognisable even to my untutored eye. Holmes too was visibly moved by the sight of this hidden *caché* of art work.

Holmes and I spent the next few minutes searching and examining the hoard of art treasures acquired by some nefarious means. Most of the great schools of art were represented, both old and modern. Indeed my elbow brushed against a painting by Aubrey Beardsley, not a favourite artist of mine, but his painting *The Rheingold* was executed with *finesse* and astonishing detail and even by the light of my candle I could appreciate its beauty. Immediately adjacent was a painting by Delville entitled *The End of a Reign*. Then my eyes caught something of great import.

"Holmes, Holmes, just look at that will you!" I said, pointing with my candle to a canvass some several feet away.

Holmes and I made our way to the painting, abandoned against the wall, as if placed there without regard or consideration.

"Do you see Holmes; I recognised that painting to be *The Island of the Dead* by that Swiss artist Böcklin. And, there, is another painting called, *Astarte Syriaca,* that I recognise to be painted by that Rossetti fellow. Do you know where I remembered seeing these paintings Holmes?" I said.

"Yes," replied Holmes, "it was at Moriarty's house in Hampstead, but wait, quiet!" said Holmes, putting his index finger to his lips.

From where we were crouching on the *mezzanine* floor in that secret chamber, we could hear voices, and they sounded official.

"Quick Watson out, we must cover our find, at least for the time being," ordered Holmes.

And with that instruction we both scrambled out of the secret vault. We carefully replaced the trap door, taking care to remove any traces of its being opened recently, and, having put the carpet back, heaved the sideboard back into its customary position against the wall and in doing added to the grooves on the timber floor. I then went to the window to see what was happening. Down in the street I could see two horses harnessed to a long, black varnished, windowless wagon with a cipher impressed on its side panel, proclaiming it to be a carriage from the Middlesex Hospital, located but a few streets away, in Goodge Street.

"The *morticians* have arrived Holmes, to collect Lyons' remains."

Replacing our candles into the brass *candelabrum* and extinguishing the gas jets, plunging the apartment into darkness, we descended the stairs towards the street. As we approached the front door, it opened and in stepped Mrs Bernstone, followed by persons wearing uniform.

"Ah Mrs. Bernstone," said Holmes, handing her the *candelabrum*," we have finished our searches and inquiries. And gentlemen, you will find the body in the bed chamber; and we have left the town gas jets on in that bed chamber for your convenience."

At length, we entered our rooms in Baker Street and I pulled hard on the bell rope to alert our housekeeper Mrs. Hudson of our arrival and desire for luncheon. Holmes was already pouring what I considered to be over generous measures of whisky.

"Well Holmes, this is a sensational turn of events, and I still remain uncertain as to the significance of our find, but significance there must be," I said, whilst accepting a cut crystal full of whisky from Holmes' shaking hand.

"You are correct Watson, our find is significant!" he intimated.

"Lyons got the money from Moriarty to build his house and created a false vault when constructing it, in order to perpetrate his real intentions against Moriarty. Now Lyons may have had that chamber constructed for any number of reasons, but since he was a close confederate of Moriarty, he would have known about the art forgeries. At one stage the thought must have entered his mind that he too could enrich himself at Moriarty's expense," postulated Holmes.

"Are you saying that Lyons fooled Moriarty, and in so doing, tricked Moriarty into thinking that his stolen artwork comprises originals, but in fact is nothing but a collection of fakes? That surely would be a lethal exercise for Lyons to involve himself against Moriarty?" I questioned.

"Well yes, as we have seen in Harley Street. But Lyons had a reptilian kind of intelligence, as became apparent to me when I met him some months ago. The real purpose of the consultation was to sound me out me and to see how much I knew. I also believe that he made sure Moriarty knew of our meeting, so as to obliquely inform Moriarty that I would be acting for Lyons, should anything untoward happen to him," confided Holmes.

"But Holmes, this is monstrous!" I replied.

"This is a true portrayal of the character of Lyons, even to the extent of his hiding his loot from Moriarty by secreting it in his own house! No one would expect this, certainly not even his housekeeper, who thought him religious. The tenants of course knew nothing. Their *rôle* was simply to add verisimilitude, as it were, to his public image, if truth can be so lent to one of venal aspect. Imagine Watson, would you ever consider that he had diverted Moriarty's claim on the stolen artwork to his own house? His thinking was that because his house was occupied it would be the last place he would hide the artwork." Holmes said.

"Do not forget Watson," Holmes continued, "on the one hand Lyons had to acquire and hide the artwork, but in a place where he could keep an eye on it. He would be able to bring in to his house, rolled up canvasses of original artwork with ease, even if he were being watched. It is likely that Moriarty trusts no one, and will have all his henchmen followed. It is by such methods of distrust, that he maintains a rigid *regime* of forced loyalty. It goes without saying that an alternative site elsewhere to hide the artwork would be impossible, especially if Lyons was being watched," stated Holmes.

"I find what you are saying incredible Holmes. Imagine those tenants and the housekeeper in Harley Street making their way through a secret vault in the building without their knowing it. What a cover, what confidence Lyons had, and only feet away from the public walking in the street!" I said, incredulously.

"I am pleased you now see this fact," replied Holmes.

"One can imagine constructing a false chamber in the *attic* away from people, but in between the ground and first floor!" I continued, "you are right Holmes, there is more horror or mystery perpetrated in the midst of the Metropolis, than in some lonely cottage isolated in the depths of the countryside!"

"Absolutely Watson, however, with regard to the artwork we have discovered, I am only charged with the task of determining why Cadogan West was done away with and latterly why the same fate befell the *fiancé* of that, that Oklahoma woman. The collection of stolen artwork and that of its existence is best left undisturbed for the present. For the moment we now have more pressing matters to deal with, not least how to do justice to this breaded York ham Mrs. Hudson has left on our sideboard in preparation for our luncheon!"

After we had eaten Holmes retired to his room. I felt that the strands of this case, this complex case, were being drawn together. I knew from my many years with

Holmes that the end of the case was in sight, because it was at such times that he would discuss any subject, rather than the mystery in hand, as if he knew there was little else to discuss to add to his findings. Before retiring, he had delivered a discourse on the motets of Lassus, together with the bowing technique of Sarasate when applied to his violin, to create an astounding *chromatic* progression of scales. It was at such times that I drifted off into slumber.

However, armed with a heavy lead crystal of whisky, I too retired to my room to distil the sensational events of the day and indeed of the last few days. However, I still retained only a vague idea of the full extent of the mystery to which a full solution seamed impossible. Had I not been exposed to the same information as Holmes, and heard first-hand the testimonies offered by those intimately involved in the case?

I read into the evening to occupy my mind with higher thoughts of humanity.

Exhausted from my exertions, especially of the day before, I fell into a fitful sleep. It was dominated by the spectre of Moriarty roaming the Metropolis. He was making his way through a stone *Porte Cochere* that led to a honey coloured Ancaster stone framed doorway to a grand Entrance Hall flanked by columns of polished green and pink limestone, which in turn led into the St. Pancras Hotel!

*Now Luxborough Street.
** Quoted by Oscar Wilde, from his '*Decay of Lying*'.

Chapter 20

The Mystery of the Ill-fated Titanic

I awoke the following morning feeling tired, and with a sense of foreboding. Having pulled at the bell-rope to inform Mrs Hudson of my wish for break-fast, I occupied my wait by searching through *The Daily Telegraph* and the *Daily Chronicle* in the expectation of reading an article about Lyons, but to no avail. Holmes came bursting in to the break-fast room full of energy.

"Well Watson, did you sleep well last night?" he asked, whilst clapping his hands together loudly, causing me to start momentarily.

"Why do you ask?" I inquired, tartly.

"Because you look dreadful, that is why!" he replied.

"Possibly Holmes, because I have neither availed myself of black Santiago coffee, a stimulant you know I need first thing in morning, or break-fasted. And, unlike you, I do not resort to narcotics, as you clearly have, before break-fast!" I stated.

The fog, if paler, was still with us and I wondered whether it would ever dissipate or become a permanent feature of life in the Metropolis. It had the effect of making Katherine from Eureka Springs, wish to leave London immediately, for cleaner air. I envied her wish and financial ability to do so. I, with my small army pension, was stuck in London fog or no fog. I knew one thing though, as the years went by the fog bothered me more and more. It was the feeling of being trapped, unable to see or know what lay ahead. It was all pervasive, clammy, acrid and injurious to breathing. More importantly, as I realised yet again whilst in Oldbury Place, it could subjugate me in an irrational embrace, leaving me feeling vulnerable and uncertain. I was pondering these thoughts when Mrs Hudson appeared in our doorway holding our break-fast tray.

"Good morning Mr Holmes and morning to the good doctor! I trust your wee challenge, Holmes, is progressing as well as can be reasonably expected, given you have a formidable adversary in the person of Professor Moriarty to contend with! And, I might say, next time you go gallivanting abroad the Metropolis on whatever quest takes your fancy, you might have the courtesy to let me know. As it happens yesterday, I would have asked you to pick up for me some wet fish from the fish stall in York Place. As you may know, I feel a wee bit nervous now, since I had that unpleasant experience with street toughs in the fog these two days past!" said Mrs. Hudson.

"The street toughs you downed," remarked Holmes.

I knew from bitter experience to keep my face buried in the *Daily Chronicle* and compelled myself to appreciate one particular advertisement informing me of the benefits, and there were several, all contained in a remarkable preparation called, Sutton's Compound Cream of Ammonia'. Using this preparation on or near one's body would in my medical opinion, cause chronic illness to those who did. However, despite the advertisement's lethal invitation, reading it kept me from being drawn into the tense atmosphere that had ignited spontaneously between Holmes and Mrs. Hudson.

"Here you are, doctor," said our housekeeper, as she pushed a plate of eggs and rashers of smoked bacon

Sutton's Compound Cream of Ammonia

Cleans and restores colours to carpets

Acts as a disinfectant in the sick room or hospital

Has no equal for removing grease spots from clothes

Invaluable to engineers for removing oil and grease

Makes linen white and woollen goods soft

Cleans culinary utensils and plate

For laundry purposes softens hard water

In your morning bath removes that tired feeling!

under my newspaper. I continued to read it rather than put it down at the moment because I knew Holmes to be seething with anger. It was just as well for in that instant my eyes were arrested by a small headline in the Stop-press section on the left hand side. It was the *Daily Chronicle* that broke the story and it read:

'We learned yesterday via Reuter's News Agency, that a senior director of the White Star Line, one

Mr. Arthur Carpenter, was arrested and charged with gross negligence involving the sinking of the RMS *Titanic* with a subsequent loss of life amounting to over fifteen hundred souls who perished in the waters of the Atlantic.'

"Holmes! Let me read this stop-press to you!" I interrupted.

I read the article out aloud to Holmes and Mrs. Hudson, but it was Mrs Hudson's re-action that I waited for, not that of Holmes'.

Holmes laid down his knife and fork and sat there looking into space. It was Mrs Hudson who broke the silence.

"Well Doctor Watson, what can you expect? The authorities are hardly going to sit back, and let such a traumatic event as the deliberate scuttling, in the middle of the Atlantic Ocean, of a boat such as the RMS *Titanic*, go by without consequences. Carpenter, being the director in charge of her before she set out from Liverpool, is going to be the first they will haul in; and, quite right too," she concluded.

At length Holmes responded:

"Watson, I suggest we finish our break-fast quickly, for we have work to do. I think it is time that we brought this case to a conclusion. Do you come with me to the Crown Post Office in Wigmore Street in the first instance?"

"Of course Holmes," I mumbled, whist pushing more rashers of the smoked bacon into my mouth, determined that whatever the outcome of today, I should not go hungry, and therefore have the strength to deal with whatever fortune brings.

A few minutes later, we emerged into swirling fog that

still held Baker Street in its grip. Immediately we hailed and secured a Brougham carriage and pair that, within moments of giving the driver our destination, was clattering down the street in the direction of the Wigmore Street Post Office. We arrived, and once there, Holmes scribbled off three telegrams with instructions that replies were not necessary.

Whilst in the vicinity of Wigmore Street, both Holmes and I repaired to Bradley's Tobacconist in Oxford Street, to avail ourselves of fresh supplies of tobacco and *trichinopoly* cigars. I also had a small task to perform involving a horse running at Newmarket the next day, and thought it prudent to get the odds on now, whilst in my favour. On our way back home, whilst walking up Baker Street, I remarked to Holmes that the fog seemed to be swirling about in a more pronounced manner, though still a hindrance to our vision.

At two o'clock pm precisely, gathered in our parlour at 221. b. Baker Street, were Sir James Walter, head of the Marine Department at the Admiralty and Paterson, his door commissionnaire whom Holmes considered should be in at the end.

Also present was an intense looking fellow whom Holmes had asked along as an observer, and he was introduced to us simply as Mr. Stanley Hopkins. I supplied drinks liberally to our guests, who had seated themselves around our drawing room.

"Let us now examine the facts surrounding this case," said Holmes, as he drew upon his *trichinopoly* cigar.

"The north Atlantic immigration trade route between Europe and America is becoming a lucrative business and accordingly, attracts capital for profitable investment. One of the shipping companies operating on this route is the English White Star Line. That line was acquired by the International Mercantile & Marine Combine, a corporation owned by John Pierpont Morgan, the wealthy American merchant banker who has on two occasions bailed out the United States Federal Government!" stated Holmes.

"Bailed out the what?" I asked.

"Bailed out the United States Government," continued Holmes, "with loans to support the Federal Treasury during a short fall in taxes. As you can imagine, to be able to bail out the United States Government indicates unimaginable wealth, a wealth, I venture to say, accumulated by hardheaded business practices and deals.

The White Star Line now has access to investment capital through its new owners, the International Mercantile & Marine Combine of New York, owned by JP Morgan.

In order to get ahead of the competition, White Star Line commissions the construction of three massive ocean liners, each weighing a staggering forty-seven thousand tons. They are the *Olympic*, *Titanic* and *Majestic*.

The rationale behind this concerted effort against the competition is that while the Cunard Line and other European shipping companies as the German Hapag-Lloyd Line and the French Line, rely upon speed of the voyage to America, White Star Line's approach is to convey their passengers in style, in abject luxury in fact.

What they lack in speed they more than make up in great luxury and comfort on the crossing that is only slower by a day or so. The size of a White Star Line boat, forty-seven thousand tons, facilitates greater numbers of passengers and staff, up to twenty two hundred, that can be conveyed in a single crossing.

The first of the three ships, the *Olympic* was launched as the proto-type vessel. However, from the beginning the boat was a failure, progressing from one collision to another, primarily because of the difficulty in manoeu-vring and steering it, due to her size and draft."

What do you mean uncontrollable due to its size and draft?" I interposed.

Because the *Olympic* was the largest boat in the world to be constructed to date; and therefore had problems when being manoeuvred in congested ports, as Liverpool or New York. In addition, the *Olympic* was fitted with new gigantic engines and propellers, which were needed to propel its forty-seven thousand tons through the waters, at twenty-three knots. Typically, as the boat moved through the water, its massive size and powerful draft, produced dynamic forces that could create suction. This in turn, might have drawn stationary or moored boats into its path, subsequently causing a collision of truly monumental proportions. Remember, it collided recently with a ship of the Royal Navy.

To say the *Olympic* was prone to accident would be a gross understatement. As we read in the paper some months ago, the misfortunes of the *Olympic* continued unabated, when she famously hit a very large object we all know is called England!

You may also remember Watson, the relevant parts of the narrative from the lady from Eureka Springs, near the Oklahoma Territory, when she visited us here. Oklahoma is in the Middle Western part of America and is as far away from the oceans as is humanly possible to be within the United States. Yet, even she realised that something was wrong with the RMS *Olympic* that con-veyed her to England. What did she say?" said Holmes, referring to his green covered commonplace book, wherein he recorded all his clients' relevant statements.

'Apart from the fact the ship could not even get out of New York harbour without crashing into other ships,

I was amazed it got through the Atlantic Ocean equinoctial gales without sinking! The ship had a pronounced list and its basic metal structure was warped, out of alignment, bent and the boat creaked like mad. It was literally falling apart, with me in it! Throughout the journey things did not work. Taps failed to deliver water. The ship seemed to be powerless at times, almost drifting in the water. The crew acted as if they did not give a damn, and it was common talk that the ship was useful only as an, 'Iron Mausoleum'. On that *Olympus* boat the overriding status was of riding a wreck on its last voyage to the scrap yard.'

It may answer a question in your mind Watson why I tolerated that woman from Oklahoma. The reason was, that whilst she did not know it, her narration was in fact describing precisely the *Olympic* ship's real condition and the compelling reasons for its imminent removal from the face of the earth. Her testimony was literally, a first hand critical description of the state of the *Olympic* boat. The ship was a wreck, as indicated by the Wagner tension fields evident in the boat's metal superstructure. When she expressed her surprise that the ship did not sink during the equinoctial gales in the Atlantic, she was nearer to the truth than she could ever have supposed."

"So the lady from Eureka Springs, near the Oklahoma Territory, did impart vital clues and relevant information to you Holmes, in helping you solve this mystery," I declared.

"Well yes Watson, but only in terms of describing the *Olympic* boat's structurally wrecked state from a first hand witness's experience – as it were,"

That was as nearer an admission from Holmes as one was ever likely to elicit, in acknowledging a debt to a woman.

"However, moving on, these collisions necessitated the withdrawal of the *Olympic* from service. Often the *Olympic* would have to be repaired in the Thomson Graving Dock, where she was fitted out, with a resultant loss of revenue to Morgan's International Mercantile & Marine Combine. The loss of this revenue and expected profits from potential passengers on the lucrative north Atlantic trade route could not have been welcome news for a man of Morgan's ambitious temperament. And, far making profit, the *Olympic* was costing the White Star Line vast amounts in lost revenue and in the cost of repairs.

How John Pierpont Morgan must have wished he could just lose the irreparably damaged and compromised *Olympic*. At that moment the boat was more capable of sinking his precious International Mercantile & Marine Combine than making a profit for it. 'Sink it in the middle of the Atlantic!' He was over heard saying to one of his directors. This remark must have filtered back to both to Cadogan West at the Admiralty and, more alarmingly, to Professor Moriarty. West, on investigating, began to assemble an array of facts that suggested a planned sinking of a White Star Line ship, and probably the imminent sinking of the *Olympic*. Do not forget gentlemen, ships have been sunk deliberately at sea since time immemorial.

Enter Professor Moriarty into the scheme. I believe he was approached by one of Morgan's henchmen, and a plan concocted between them. No doubt for an exorbitant fee Moriarty would 'arrange' to have carried out Morgan's wishes regarding the *Olympic* boat.

It is also to be remembered these men, are in their own right, powerful with influence in high places, either bought with money or through instilling fear. They hold themselves above the law, and when you have the ability to bail out the United States Federal Government, the chances favour that you are just that! Nor for that matter was Moriarty ever beneath the law, in the whole of his career. Therefore, to remove a ship of the line, to him, would present no great challenge.

For the benefit of our guests Watson, you might recall our visitor from Eureka Springs and the fact her *fiancé* worked for the JP Morgan Bank in New York. No doubt he discovered something untoward in that organisation. It is probable that the gentleman in the garden of the Crescent Hotel in Eureka Springs, was trying to determine just how much the *fiancé* knew or thought he might know. Clearly his knowledge, however much or however gained, ensured his death somewhere in Eureka Springs or in the surrounding Ozarks Mountains."

"The heiress from the Ozarks was in that respect then, correct in her assumption about the danger facing her *fiancé*," I offered, in my attempt to give due credit to the Katherine, despite Holmes' dismissal of her.

"We now come to the Admiralty and involvement with Moriarty. It must be assumed that somehow information reached Moriarty that an investigation was being conducted by the Admiralty, and in particular by young Cadogan West. Clearly there had been a breach of a death-pledged silence in his organisation and he reacted swiftly and mercilessly to correct this failure in keeping secret his plan.

He immediately arranged to have Cadogan West killed by the delivery of a document impregnated with a strong alkaloid poison that would seep into West's body through his fingers whilst holding the paper. The paper had information on it in the form of a short sentence that referred to the White Star Line's Herculaeneum Dock at Liverpool and north Atlantic coördinates.

'Herculaneum Docks - Liverpool then 41°46' N, 50° 14' W, at 12-30am. For God's sake be careful',

The message revealed nothing, but would have made West think and certainly hold the paper that was beginning to poison him. That we now know these were the coördinates at which the *Titanic* sank, shows that West had clearly uncovered a conspiracy. A plan to at least, sink a boat of the White Star Line, in or around those coördinates.

To ensure that West held the paper long enough for the poison to take effect, there would have to be a message on it. West could understand the cryptic message as being pertinent to his investigation but meaningless to the casual reader. He would continue to hold the paper in his fingers for a considerable time, whilst rereading. It would of course eventually kill him without leaving any physical means of violence visited upon his body.

Remember the note and his muttering over and over again, 'the wrong metal, the wrong metal!' Clearly he had stumbled upon the existence of the flawed metal of which the Royal Mail Steamer *Olympic* was constructed. This metal would make sinking her a viable proposition should the *Olympic* be rammed by one of the several icebergs, which are prevalent in the north Atlantic at that time of the year. West's apparent incoherent rambling was due to the strychnine beginning to attack his nervous system. The poison, affecting his mind and body, was now in the process of killing him."

"But this is incredible not to say outrageous Holmes," exclaimed Sir James, "I cannot possibly go back to the Admiralty or to the Government and report this information as the solution. How do you suppose the First

Lord of the Treasury* or the President of the Board of Trade or indeed my own First Lord of the Admiralty, will react to these sensational events? They will think me mad, Mr. Holmes, mad even to suggest that the White Star Line be involved in this criminal conspiracy to sink an ocean liner and commit mass murder! Can it be that you have constructed a confabulation to fit your hypothesis devoid of real facts?"

Holmes terminated abruptly Sir James's line of questioning and proceeded to continue his narrative.

"The second of these wonder ships, if we may so call them, the *Titanic*, though launched in May of 1911 was nearing completion and her sea trials, and had been moved to the Thompson Graving Dock for the final fitting-out to her superstructure. Note Watson, the *Titanic* was created in the same month in which Gustav Mahler died; that composer so beloved of your heiress from Eureka Springs. At that very same time, the damaged *Olympic* also had, not surprisingly, a rendezvous with the same Thompson Graving Dock, as a result of a collision with a ship of the Royal Navy. For the first time both ships would be in the same dock side by side!

It must have been irresistible to take advantage of this situation. Professor Moriarty and his intellectual prowess together with the colossal wealth of Morgan, the lethal combination of which could only create an unimaginable evil of monumental proportions with imminent and frightening consequences!

Both ships were identical in construction and shape and were often mistaken for each other even by their owners! Remember, Watson, Arthur Carpenter, the senior director of the White Star Line in Liverpool, was confused by the names of the two ships. This meant at that stage an evil plan was unfolding and already in progress toward its ultimate conclusion!

One should also remember that the White Star Line presented itself to the public as the 'White Star Flag'; a carrier of excellence and luxury using any one of its identical ships, be it the *Olympic*, *Titanic* or later the *Majestic* now being built, to convey its passengers to New York. You may recall too, Watson how Arthur Carpenter enthused about the 'inter-changeability' of items in the boats. He mentioned especially their fittings, including all removable items, crockery, cutlery and linen that carried the name 'White Star Line' and the white star flag emblem, but never the name of a particular ship. The only unique item was the removable bronze name-plate bolted onto the stern of a ship."

"Therefore it would be reasonable to suppose, that having removed or exchanged the bronze name-plates, plus a few other minor details, including the transfer to other ships of certain members of the crew, one could effectively replace one ship with another?" I interposed.

"Quite correct Watson, you excel yourself! In addition, we have to remember that Morgan was not going to sanction the deliberate sinking of a perfectly sound and brand new profit making *Titanic* ship. What he intended was, to sink the defective *Olympic*, and put it down to an incident of the perils on the sea with minimum loss of life. Moriarty's involvement would ensure that the loss of life would be the maximum in any maritime disaster to date. Especially in this case the new *Titanic* was exchanged for the impaired *Olympic* whilst adjacent to each other in the Thompson Graving Dock. A few loyal workers aptly rewarded and sworn to secrecy, especially under Moriarty's power, could change a few details under the cover of the darkness of night!

What sailed from Liverpool into the bleak Atlantic

Ocean on that fateful day in April was without doubt a ship of the White Star Line. The question becomes, gentlemen, precisely which ship sailed out to make that ill-fated voyage! The ship was the *Olympic* disguised as the *Titanic*! From now on the ship that sank is the '*Olympic*', for that is what she was!"

"Good God Holmes, this is preposterous! I simply cannot accept your version of events," declared Sir James, with a look of total disbelief upon his face.

I too interrupted. "Yet again Holmes, your client, Miss Katherine from Eureka Springs in the Oklahoma Territory seemed to have realised, with her feminine intuition, that something was wrong. Her description of the *Olympic* would in my opinion suffice to establish the reality of life aboard that stricken ship. Even she was compelled to feel that it was like riding a wreck to the scrap yard. Of all the narratives I have heard expressed by persons in this dreadful affair, hers is the more compelling, for establishing a *raison d'etre* to sink the boat and have done with it."

"As usual Watson you are driven by emotional attachment to that woman because of her pretty…"

At this point Holmes' asperity was interrupted abruptly, as Mrs. Hudson came bursting into the room bearing a tray containing steaming coffee, cucumber sandwiches and some delicacies of her own devising, based on the ubiquitous bloater fish.

"You cannot sit around here all day gentlemen smoking and drinking heavily," she declared, "it is unhealthy and like a fog in here, unlike outside. You must take in nourishment; otherwise you will succumb to inanition! Here try one of my *Bloater Paté Delights*," she said, proffering one to Sir James, in much an intimidating manner, that he quickly accepted her offer.

Our housekeeper then busied herself dispensing sandwiches and coffee to others in our drawing room.

"Oh, and Sherlock, do not forget to mention the brittleness of iron plate when in freezing water, a bit like my finger nails becoming brittle and breaking off when I am scrubbing the doors steps with near freezing water in cold weather!"

And leaving us all with our mouths open, but in the case of Sir James, with a *Bloater Paté Delight* in his, she departed in the tornado like manner in which she had arrived. Holmes stepped smartly to the parlour door and locking it, placed the key in his pocket, thus preventing Mrs. Hudson reëmerging and disrupting our meeting.

"That woman," he hissed, "that woman. Gentlemen," continued Holmes, "hopefully we will not be disturbed by her again."

He then continued with his narration.

"Where were we? Ah yes, the captain of the boat, Edward Smith, a commodore of the White Star Line, no less, has thirty years' experience of crossing the north Atlantic and this was to be his last command before retiring. In other words his working life and involvement with the White Star Line was effectively at an end. He took the *Titanic* into the North Atlantic Ocean on its so-called maiden voyage. He avowed not to attempt to wrest away the coveted Blue Ribbon Trophy from Cunard Line for the fastest crossing of the Atlantic to America. Were he to do so, the White Star Line would gain the lucrative Royal Mail contract and accordingly, Smith endeavoured to do precisely that. In so doing, he without doubt, was steaming recklessly into a visible ice field in which giant icebergs were known to exist. He did this under the guise of trying to reclaim the lucrative Blue Ribbon for the White Star Line."

"Blue Ribbon?" I asked, incredulously.

"Yes," said Sir James, "the Blue Ribbon means that its holder, a shipping company, is awarded by the British Post Office the financially lucrative contract to deliver the Royal Mail from England to the United States and other countries and vice versa."

"Smith ignored repeated warnings of icebergs," continued Holmes, "drifting down on the Labrador Current immediately ahead and in the direct path of the Royal Mail Steamer '*Titanic*'. Despite these warnings Smith took his ship, weighing forty-seven thousand tons with its triple screw propulsion powered by enormous reciprocating engines, roaring at full revolutions. This would propel the boat at an unprecedented speed of twenty-three knots - straight into an ice field dead ahead of the ship. One could not fail to hit something and that would be most likely an iceberg.

The lookouts abandoned at the crow's nest only sighted the monolithic iceberg dead ahead, too late to raise a cry and give the alarum in a desperate attempt to avert the dread-filled calamity that ensued. On that fateful night the ocean was unusually 'flat calm' - as a millpond, making the sighting of icebergs difficult, because no wakes or frontal tidal wave, that might indicate their presence, was created that could be observed by the look-outs high up in the crow's nest.

The *Titanic*, almost on cue, struck the iceberg at the right speed, the right angle and at the right temperature. All three combined to seal her fate and from that instant the *Titanic* was doomed and would eventually founder and sink".

At that point Holmes produced the flat piece of metal he had collected from the deck of the *Olympic* when moored at the Herculaeneum dock in Liverpool.

"This is the same metal that the *Titanic* is constructed of and it has been immersed in freezing water for several hours."

He lifted the metal and placed it on the floor rug. And then with a two pound in weight lump hammer, he struck the metal with a powerful blow whereupon it cracked in several place in front of our very eyes!

"That is a force delivered by a two pound weight. Imagine forty-seven thousand tons hitting a huge iceberg! This is exactly what happened to the hull of the *Titanic* when she struck the iceberg!"

"Holmes what is the significance of this?" I asked.

"It means concentrated evil Watson, including cold and deliberate mass murder by act of an *eminence gris*," replied Holmes

On hearing these words Peterson nearly fainted. I offered to pour more brandy into his glass, which he held out to me with his shaking hands, visibly disturbed by what he had heard. Even the faces of Sir James and Stanley Hopkins had turned ashen, such was the enormity of Holmes' report to the assembled guests in our rooms on the piano-nobile, at 221. b. Baker Street.

*British Prime Minister.

Chapter 21

The Futility of It All

The information which Holmes imparted to us, was as astounding as it was incredible. It was becoming evident that there was much more to this case than we had originally supposed. It was not only a mere death of a clerk in a railway carriage outside Charing Cross Railway-Station, or the removal of a *fiancé* in the Ozark Mountains near the Oklahoma territory, nor indeed that of a minor villain being done away with. Nor was it the dread-filled news attending the sinking of the ill-fated *Titanic*, or whatever it was called; it was something profoundly sinister, and manifest in the form of an *eminence gris*. Peterson and the rest of us could scarcely believe what we had heard. We tried to take in the magnitude of what Holmes had said and sat there in silence, with only the sound of the wind outside, which had now got up, and was rattling the windowpanes of our parlour.

Holmes broke the silence.

"You may recall Watson, the books that Moriarty had on the library shelf in his house at Hampstead? One was entitled 'Marine Engineering,' together with other book-lets with the title 'Binomial Theorem.' That theorem allowed Moriarty to work out mathematically, that certain types of low grade steel, when subjected to freezing temperature, as you would expect in the icy north Atlantic, becomes brittle and consequently useless in resisting impact forces. You have just witnessed what damage a two-pound lump hammer can inflict on the same metal that the *Olympic* is built of. As part of my inquiries, I consulted the eminent engineer and metallurgist, Victor Hatherley, on the *rôle* of metal in the Binomial Theorem. He told me that ice, unlike metal, does not give; rather, it absorbs energy when in compression against another surface. Effectively, compacted ice can rip through steel plates, especially when the steel or iron is immersed in the freezing water, typical of the freezing temperatures of the North Atlantic in April.

The position of another ship, the *Californian* is instructive. At that time the ship was stationary in order to avoid entering the ice field contaminated with icebergs. However, as we have read in the newspapers, the ship was less than five miles away and could have come to the rescue of the stricken *Titanic*. She failed to do so, despite numerous distress signals being fired continually by rockets into the clear night sky. Distress flares are designed deliberately, to attract attention, especially on a clear night. Her captain was bribed by Moriarty, and ordered to stay put!"

"Holmes," intervened Sir James, "your monstrous assertion about the *rôle* of the White Star Line in sinking one of their own ships with such a massive loss of life, is unthinkable and with respect, frankly, I have great difficulty accepting your findings!"

"I do not say the White Star Line intended to sink the *Titanic* quite so quickly," countered Holmes, "Moriarty, however, certainly intended to do precisely that. He had to do so, in order to remove all traces of his own criminal activities, which were even then unfolding on board the doomed *Titanic*, in her death throes as she began to sink after hitting the iceberg," said Holmes decisively.

"Both men had essentially an interest in sinking the *Titanic;* Morgan to be rid of the irreparably damaged wreck that the *Olympic* boat had become, and Moriarty to remove permanently the forged artwork and their artists. It is possible Morgan would have been content with 'gradually' sinking the *Titanic,* in order to allow a carefully coördinated evacuation and rescue of passengers. Moriarty clearly wanted no such rescue of passengers, and set about with his henchmen, ensuring precisely that.

I also remain convinced, that Moriarty not only saw this opportunity, but also realised in his calculating mind other means of enriching himself further by combining five events in the same act! One was the accumulation of artwork, via untraceable substitution. Two was the damage to the White Star Line's safety reputation, in operating ocean liners with the consequent financial gratitude from White Star's competitors. Three was the calculated death of Cadogan West from the Admiralty, in order to actually sink the *Titanic.* Four, reward from a grateful, if sceptical, Morgan. And five, as an act of pure revenge; the probable destruction of the College of St. George, where he was previously an *employé.*"

At this last remark, Sir James rose from his chair and looked Holmes straight in the face.

"Holmes, are you suggesting that the Admiralty was in some way involved in this dreadful affair?"

"West was poisoned in the Admiralty, was he not?" replied Holmes.

"Ah," countered Sir James, "by a letter sent to him there!"

"No. Sir James, the document was delivered to him from *inside* the Admiralty!" answered Holmes.

"Who at the Admiralty would resort to such a callous act?" pondered Sir James Walter, as he resumed his seat.

Holmes continued to expand Sir James' thoughts.

"It would have to be someone who had access to the Admiralty building and able to move throughout its corridors and rooms without question. Reasonably enough this person would be entrusted with delivering messages brought to the main reception hall at the Admiralty for delivery. We have to bear in mind Moriarty's wealth and ability to bribe people into his service," said Holmes.

"Think Sir James, having delivered a poisoned document to the Admiralty, the next thing to do would be to remove that incriminating evidence. This opportunity was afforded when West removed himself from the Admiralty in a great state of agitation and who offered to run after him? Quite naturally *commissionaire* Peterson, who upon intercepting West, could then retrieve the poisoned document and dispose of the evidence.

However, Peterson was prevented from retrieving that poisoned document from West's person by a constable joining the pursuit and who refused him access to West's body in the railway carriage. This intervention of the constable was unplanned and an unforeseen flaw in Moriarty's stratagem," concluded Holmes.

At this revelation, a startled Peterson jumped out of his seat and rushed to the drawing room door! Holmes stood watching him impassively with the door key in his hand. Peterson tried again and again to open the locked door but on realising the futility of his action looked around for another means of escape. Then suddenly a sharp click was heard as Hopkins snapped a pair of spring-loaded shiny chromium plated handcuffs on him and instantly it was all over!

"Who are you that you make free with me and handle

my person in such a rough manner?" demanded a very emotional Peterson.

"I am Stanley Hopkins of Scotland Yard and, how dare you display your emotions in front of me Peterson!"

On hearing these words Peterson collapsed to the floor. Sir James still standing, stared with astonishment at him and said very slowly:

"I recall constable Murcher's remarking on your reaction to finding Cadogan West's body in the railway carriage. What did he say, something along the lines of …as though you were expecting to see West dead on the floor."

Holmes intervened:

"I might also add Sir James; you too were nearly a victim, because you came into contact with the poisoned paper. Only by the fact of your wearing kid gloves, did you unwittingly prevent that virulent poison from seeping into your body!"

Remember Watson, on first meeting Sir James, you remarked, as a doctor, upon the greyness in his haggard face and the fact that he removed his kid gloves from his hands? The greyness in your face, Sir James, showed that your body had been only partially exposed to the strychnine, but due to your habit of wearing gloves, the effects were insufficient to kill you.

Finally, in your zeal to preserve the document, as important evidence, you took the precaution of keeping the paper in a metal cylindrical canister. In so doing, you again unwittingly prevented exposure to the poison, and thus avoided further contamination by the strychnine."

Sir James, who by now had risen from his seat, was glaring down at Peterson. From the agitated look upon his face it was clear to see that his mind was in inner turmoil from the truth Holmes had just revealed. His expression turned quickly into one of anger as his face flushed to a bright red hue, and only by the swift intervention of Stanley Hopkins, was he prevented from bringing his heavy gold capped ebony walking stick down upon Peterson's head!

"Sit there on the floor," instructed Hopkins to a now cowering Peterson, "until we have finished here; then it is Scotland Yard for you. There you will explain your treachery and involvement in this business."

Having exposed Peterson's real intention, Holmes continued his narration to its conclusion.

"Moriarty then went through the motions of arranging an exhibition of English paintings to be exhibited at the World's Columbian Exposition in Chicago, under the guise of promoting this art to wealthy Americans. He had no intention of sending the original paintings to America, but instead gathered around him forgers who made copies of the original paintings. The faked paintings were then returned to their 'owners', as in the case of St. George's College. Or they were witnessed for insurance purposes by inexperienced shipping clerks, immediately before being placed onboard the *Titanic*.

The faked paintings were to go to America accompanied by the artist who created the genuine paintings, who upon arrival in Chicago, would promote and sell their works. Imagine gentlemen, what artist would resist this opportunity to sell their work in America and possibly achieve instant fame and wealth?

The original paintings were spirited away to Moriarty's secret horde and the fakes packed in sealed crates in readiness to be loaded onto the *Titanic* for transhipment to Chicago via New York. Before being loaded aboard ship the faked paintings were seen only by a *naïve* insurance clerk to verify their actual existence and for insurance claim purposes. It is unlikely that the clerk would be able to recognise the forgeries from the genuine.

It was also imperative that these paintings did not reach the exhibition at the World's Columbian Exposition where the fact they were fakes would be discovered and revealed by experts, or by the very artists responsible for the original paintings. Therefore the *Titanic* must be sunk without trace!

Indeed Moriarty went as far to have some of his trusted henchmen on board the stricken *Titanic*. They were there to ensure that the artists on board accompanying their paintings did not make it into the lifeboats, thus ensuring their inevitable deaths in the freezing waters of the north Atlantic."

"Are you saying Holmes that Moriarty went to these inordinate lengths to kill the artists in order that his secret would be preserved?" Sir James asked.

"Yes, just think of it, this is where Moriarty's undoubted, if perverted genius, came into its own. He had, at the behest of Morgan, achieved the sinking of the damaged ship *Olympic*, we know to have been *masquerading* as the *Titanic*. At the same time, he sank a vast collection of faked artwork, which now lies at the bottom of the Atlantic Ocean, beyond any possibility of examination. And, by the same stroke, he drowned the very artists who had created the original paintings now in Moriarty's collection, which now has increased vastly in value!

Do you recall Watson the paintings in Moriarty's mansion at Hampstead, the Böcklin and the Rossetti? They were almost certainly the original paintings. Though we both now know it is possible they too were forgeries carried out by the double-crossing Lyons, but that is another matter.

Moriarty, whatever else he may be, clearly predicted the rise in popularity and acceptance of the Pre-Raphaelite painters' idiom and expression of art. Subsequently, they became the first of his victims. It is this kind of thinking and foresight that is the hallmark of Moriarty and makes him therefore extremely dangerous. That he can think has never been in doubt. Witness the Principal of St. George's College extolling him as, 'very gifted, bordering on genius one might say'. That Moriarty can strategize is something we are now alas, evidently witnessing!"

"Will there be an end to this Professor's evil machinations?" asked a very concerned Sir James.

"Sir James, I am unable to offer an iron-clad guarantee about the unpredictable actions of this individual for the reasons, I have just alluded to. However, it is possible that his evil will abate, in that he may have achieved finally his *coup de grâce*.

"What?" I demanded.

"The collection of original paintings," said Holmes, "of now doubtful authenticity, thanks to Lyons, which Moriarty amassed, has increased dramatically in value because of the death of those artists! However, as collateral to that, he has also brought about the disintegration of the Colony Room Club in Soho. For now its members are dispersed to the four *zephyrs*, including those souls that ride the gales which blast their way to Heaven!"

† † †

"By Jove!" exploded Stanley Hopkins, in a spirit one would not have expected of him, "this diseased Moriarty and his gang will hang for their crimes. I will have their life's blood should it be the last thing I do on this earth.

I shall go to that house at Hampstead with warrants for anyone on the premises including a warrant for this psychopath Moriarty!"

"Your journey would be a wasted one, for precisely those reasons I have just alluded," intoned Holmes, "be certain, Hopkins, Moriarty will by now have abandoned his house, and left these shores and is almost certainly living in the depths of Europe, most probably in Meiringen near the Reichenbach Falls, a favourite vacation resort of his. Let us be realistic gentlemen, the loss of the *Olympic* and resultant damage to White Star's reputation and safety is not going to weigh heavily on the minds of Europeans who operate rival shipping lines to the White Star Line. It is to be remembered that it was they who were the commercial target of White Star's bid for a monopolised supremacy of the lucrative North Atlantic trade. It is probable that Moriarty has done these European shipping companies a favour that will no doubt gain him a very generous emolument.

"No gentlemen, this was his *magnum opus,* if I may so put it; he knew that in executing his avowed desire to perpetrate this horrendous and evil plan, would ensure his never being able to live in England or America as a free man. His reputation of infamy is made, as is his wealth and suspect collection of stolen art. No Hopkins, he is beyond our laws for the present, only the *Furies* can make a visitation upon him now!"

"That may be so Mr. Holmes, and we may not be able to arrest him and his gang today, but Scotland Yard does not forget. It could be that, with our American cousins at the Pinkerton Agency, we may be able to exact justice on this Moriarty yet!" Thus spoke Stanley Hopkins, delivering his determination and intention upon the subject.

Holmes smiled at him.

These were the lengths to which Moriarty would go to ensure his success, including having the *Titanic* scrape along the iceberg which punctured and smashed open the brittle steel walls of her hull. From that moment onward the ill-fated *Titanic* was doomed and her fate sealed. I could barely believe my ears and the explanations Holmes had offered to us in our drawing room.

"Remember Watson," said Holmes, "when we were in the Landau being driven to Moriarty's house, the driver said something very perceptive?"

"Yes I recall. Something about the mutiny and the fire that broke out, into which the crew tossed recalcitrant passengers who refused to pay them a fee to get into the life boats," I replied, pleased with my instant memory.

"No Watson," replied Holmes.

"Ah, the indestructibility of the Cunard boat '*Lusitania*'?"

"Really Watson, come, think," demanded Holmes.

"Yes, the carriage driver remarked, how can you not miss an iceberg the size of St. Paul's Cathedral?" I offered.

"Reciprocating engines, no?" I ventured.

"No Watson, it was, had that *Titanic* been built on the Clyde shipyards in Scotland rather than elsewhere, it would have gone straight through that iceberg and sunk it without trace!" Holmes reminded me.

"It was therefore crucial that the *Titanic* hit the iceberg, with a glancing blow, at just the right angle, to cause fatal damage to the side of the ship. Moriarty knew, via his Binomial Theorem, that the freezing brittle steel would shatter," Holmes went on.

"But this solution sounds too fantastic Holmes!" I pleaded.

"You know my methods, Watson," said Holmes, "this series of events has culminated with a great loss of life, a wealthy psychotic monomaniac on the loose and untold damage to the art world. When all other possibilities have been exhausted, then what ever remains, however improbable, must be the truth, whatever the futility of it all!" said Holmes, in tones of resignation.

He sat down next to the fire and stared intently into it. I motioned the others to leave quietly, to which they assented, each taking their leave of a preoccupied Holmes. Closing our drawing room door behind them, they descended the stairs into Baker Street where I saw through the window, Sir James climb into his waiting Barouche, drawn by a four-in-hand. By contrast Hopkins escorted Peterson into a much sturdier, if less comfortable, box wagon that had bars across its only window. Both carriages clattered off down the street, blending into the traffic.

I then realised that the fog had cleared with the wind, revealing bright sunlight over the Metropolis! My spirits soared as never before at the release of the fog's grip upon my being these last few days. Holmes, in comparison, looked vacant and drawn. I knew, from my many years with him, that now the case was solved, a brown study would come over him. With nothing to absorb his unique talents an inevitable and deep reaction would overwhelm him. It did so. A few minutes later, he reached into his desk, and retrieved a deep red leather case and from it produced an Everett syringe. A further search brought him into contact with a glass phial of a 7% solution. I left him alone and went down into Baker Street to embrace the sunlight streaming down from the heavens.

With my eyes blinking in the bright light, I focused on a news billboard in the street. The billboard informed me, in large distinct graphic letters, that a new railway station, operated by the Great Central Railway, was to be opened that day by the Sovereign, and to be called the Marylebone Railway Station, in honour of the district in which it was constructed!